I Always Did

Trust & Tequila Book Two

Evangeline Williams

Copyright © 2023 by Evangeline Williams

Published by Evangeline Williams

All rights reserved.

This book or any portion thereof may not reproduced or used in any manner whatsoever without the express written permission of the publisher except for the use of brief quotations in a book review. No portion of this book may be reproduced in any form without written permission from the publisher or author, except as permitted by U.S. copyright law. This is a work of fiction and any resemblance to actual persons, living or dead, is solely coincidental. Names, businesses, characters, places, locales, and events are either used in a fictitious manner or the sole product of the author's imagination. They are intended solely for the purpose of entertainment and are in no way based on real events.

Edited by Kristin Scearce, Kim Deister, and Keeley Catarineau of Hot Tree Editing

Cover by Getcovers

COPYRIGHT

Content Notes

Spoilers

Your mental health is important. Please be aware this work of fiction contains adult themes and language that may be disturbing to some readers. They are as follows:

*Swearing *On-page consensual sexual intimacy using graphic language *Stalking *Manipulation *Alcohol consumption and intoxication *Emesis * Maternal death *Premature infant *Adoption *Military combat and death of side characters in combat *Grief/mourning *Survivor guilt *Reference to past emotional abuse by a narcissistic parent *PTSD, codependence, and mental health issues *Abandonment Issues *Unwanted sexual advances/attempted SA (does not occur between main characters) *Depiction of violence, blood, and injury *Medical Emergency including a contagious illness/quarantine (not COVID-related) *On-page gun violence *Vigilante justice

According to www.cdc.gov, the United States currently has the highest pregnancy-related death rate among developed nations. In 2021 the rate was 32.9 deaths per 100,000 live births. The maternal death in this novel is not a fluke. It's a tragedy.

Playlist

Dear Reader,

Did you guess the chapter titles for this novel came directly from my playlist? Then you're absolutely right. Every chapter title is also a song title.

Music has always helped me connect to characters and emotion, and I'm really excited about the songs I've included in this playlist. They provided the soundtrack to Bronwyn and Dean's story as I wrote it.

Listening to the playlist is not a requirement to enjoy the novel. However, if you're like me and enjoy music as an additional emotional connection, you can access an expanded playlist directly by logging into your Spotify account and entering "I Always Did" into the search feature. Or you can enter each song title/artist individually into whatever music streaming service you prefer. You can listen to the playlist songs at any time: before, during, or after reading.

Lyrics should not be taken literally. Instead, they're about emotion. The playlist is a vibe. Enjoy.

Playlist

Mastermind | Taylor Swift
F**kn' Perfect | P!nk
Natural | Imagine Dragons
Somebody | Dagny

We're Not Friends | Ingrid Andress
Emperor's New Clothes | Panic! At The Disco
I Guess I'm in Love | Clinton Kane
Till Forever Falls Apart | Ashe, FINNEAS
Ceilings | Lizzy McAlpine
Going Under | Evanescence
Stick Season | Noah Kahan
Could Have Been Me | The Struts
In A Perfect World | Dean Lewis, Julia Michaels
I See You | Priscilla Ahn
You Don't Know | Katelyn Tarver
Come Back, Be Here | Taylor Swift
What A Time | Julia Michaels, Niall Horan
Rock You Like A Hurricane | Scorpions
All Too Well | Taylor Swift
Breathe Me | Sia
Quarter Life Crisis | Taylor Bickett
Not Gonna Die | Skillet
Please Stay | Francois Klark
If You Love Her | Forest Blakk
Long Way to Go | P!nk, The Lumineers
Dancing Queen | Abba
The Last Time | Taylor Swift, Gary Lightbody
Liability | Lorde
Just Us | James Arthur
Outsider | Rachel Grae
Mr. Loverman | Ricky Montgomery
Chosen Family | Rina Sawayama
This Love | Taylor Swift
So Easy | Phillip Phillips
Darkside | Neoni
Kryptonite | 3 Doors Down
Work Song | Hozier
Skinny Love | Birdy

PLAYLIST

Enemy | Tommee Profitt, Beacon Light, Sam Tinnesz
You & Me | James TW
Secrets | Imagine Dragons
In The Air Tonight | State of Mine
Something Real | Post Malone
Please Keep Loving Me | James TW
Dance with Me Tonight | Olly Murs

This book is dedicated to
Westin Adam
In Loving Memory
February 22, 2007 —June 11, 2023

"Grief, I say, come in. Sit down.

I have tea. There is honey. This

will take as long as it takes."

www.thishallowedwilderness.com

Contents

1. Mastermind — 1
2. F**kn' Perfect — 9
3. Natural — 18
4. Somebody — 21
5. We're Not Friends — 29
6. Emperor's New Clothes — 35
7. Come and Get Your Love — 40
8. Till Forever Falls Apart — 48
9. Ceilings — 60
10. Going Under — 66
11. Stick Season — 71
12. Could Have Been Me — 75
13. In A Perfect World — 80
14. I See You — 90
15. You Don't Know — 98
16. Come Back, Be Here — 101
17. What A Time — 111
18. Rock You Like A Hurricane — 118

19.	All Too Well	128
20.	Breathe Me	133
21.	Quarter Life Crisis	137
22.	Not Gonna Die	141
23.	Please Stay	149
24.	If You Love Her	157
25.	Long Way to Go	163
26.	Dancing Queen	167
27.	The Last Time	170
28.	Liability	175
29.	Just Us	177
30.	Outsider	182
31.	Mr. Loverman	187
32.	Chosen Family	197
33.	This Love	200
34.	So Easy	204
35.	Darkside	214
36.	Kryptonite	222
37.	Work Song	231
38.	Skinny Love	239
39.	Enemy	245
40.	You & Me	247
41.	Secrets	253
42.	In The Air Tonight	258
43.	Something Real	264
44.	Please Keep Loving Me	268
Epilogue		279
What's Next?		283

Sneak Peek	284
Afterword	286
Acknowledgements	287

1
Mastermind

DEAN

The Beer Barrel Bar and Grill is a small wooden building that stands well back from the road in the middle of nowhere, Pennsylvania. The parking lot is gravel, and, at a guess, I'd say the only thing that's been updated here since the early nineties are the TV screens.

It sits just outside Blackwater, the college town that houses Blackwater State University. And absolutely nobody calls it The Beer Barrel Bar and Grill.

It's Jack's Place, no matter what the faded sign over the door says.

The beer is cold, people generally stay out of my way, and if I sit here long enough, my current addiction is going to walk through that door in a pair of tight jeans and a black bar logo T-shirt.

I'll pretend not to notice her. I always do. And when she isn't looking, I'll drink her in like the sight of her is what keeps my heart beating.

It's stupid. I know it, but it doesn't stop me. It never has.

Jack stops by my table and gives me a jerk of his red-bearded chin. The guy is built like a bear. His own black T-shirt strains across shoulders regularly used for hauling around kegs of beer and cases of liquor. He looks more like a lumberjack than a bar owner.

My chair scrapes as I rise, and without a word, we both head through the kitchen and out to the small back lot.

I already know what I'll find. I checked it out more than a month ago when Bronwyn started picking up shifts here.

Jack's employees are bringing the trash out to the dumpster alone late at night. They park back here and leave at closing. He has no security cameras, no fence, and no alarm. The lot is completely isolated from view and backs up to a wooded area with nothing but a single light over the back door for illumination.

I've been here to keep an eye on Bronwyn every single night since.

I also installed a couple of small cameras that Jack has no idea about. If Bronwyn disappears from the front of the bar, I open the camera app on my phone and watch. Just in case.

Jack rubs the back of his neck with a calloused hand. "You got a point," he says, as if I've been giving him a lecture instead of a flat stare.

His lips twist to the side. "My dad owned this place before me. It's always been like this from the day it opened in 1981. I never really thought about it."

My eyebrows lift a little.

"Yeah. It's not good," he admits. "Especially on those nights when I can't be here."

He looks a little defensive. "I usually am here. If not me, then Neppy is."

Neppy is more likely to hide behind the women than put himself in the line of fire. He'd rather flirt with them than fight for them.

Jack puffs out his cheeks and blows out a rough blast of air. "But me or Neppy don't mean shit if we're at the front of the house when the women come out here."

I finally open my mouth. "I know you don't want to hear this, but it's not just about the women. Size and strength mean nothing when you're caught unaware."

Jack crosses his arms over that barrel chest, expression surly. Finally, he drops his arms and says, "What do I need to keep my *employees* safe, and how much is it going to set me back?"

I don't give even a flicker of a reaction. I just tell him what he needs to know and start making plans.

Inside, though? There's an unwinding of tension. Because Bronwyn can't be working here for Jack and putting herself in that kind of danger night after night. I see the way men watch her. Flirt with her. Constantly try to put their hands on her.

Most of the time, her shifts are completely uneventful. But weekends get rowdy. And more than once, I've escorted asshole men off the premises without her even realizing I've done it.

I don't understand why she's here. And when I don't understand something, it drives me crazy until I work it out.

But there's nothing new in my fascination with the woman. I've been trying to figure her out for a while now. I'm starting to think it's never going to happen.

She's a rich girl who grew up in a mansion on Long Island. And, in addition to all the real estate her father owns and some of his less-savory connections, he's some high-priced lawyer for the elite of New York City.

Still, night after night, she's here pouring drinks at her cousin's dingy bar and then attending classes at BSU during the day.

I took on the job of driving Clarissa Harcourt for her father a year and a half ago. It was supposed to be easy—something short and sweet to transition me back to civilian life. And it's a cakewalk.

Except for the addition of one sassy little blonde in the form of Clarissa's best friend, who seems to be hell-bent on distracting me from my duties.

I'm not a chauffeur. I'm a bodyguard. But most of the time, this job is boring. Day after day, I'm protecting a young woman who keeps her head down, does as she's told regarding her safety, and is, in most ways, a dream client.

This job has been preventive maintenance more than anything. I've never even had to draw my sidearm. But it does require me to remain alert at all times. I can't be flirting with my client's friend or distracted from potential threats.

I can't afford to give Bronwyn my time or attention while I'm still employed by Clarissa.

Yet here I am. I've organized my nights off so I'm always available when Bronwyn is working. Hell, I accepted the transfer to Blackwater in the first place because I knew Bronwyn was going to school here and would be my client's roommate.

It's unprofessional as hell.

I met Bronwyn McRae a year and a half ago on the same day Marcus Harcourt introduced me to his daughter.

I'll never forget Marcus's wry warning about Bronwyn. "She's a sweet girl, but she's a handful. Just... keep those girls out of trouble. On her own, my daughter won't give you any issues. But Bronwyn will test you. If you give an inch, she'll take a football stadium."

I'd almost cracked a smile at that. The idea of some nineteen-year-old heiress posing any kind of challenge struck me as funny. I couldn't wait to meet the young woman who

Marcus Harcourt described as a combination of a human grenade, a honey badger, and a golden retriever.

My reaction should have been a warning in itself. The woman both intrigued me and amused me before I'd even laid eyes on her.

"Ms. McRae will not be an issue, Mr. Harcourt," I'd assured him.

That, as it turns out, was a lie.

Bronwyn McRae is an issue I enjoy way more than I should.

She's a study in contrasts, by turns loud and introspective. She's fiercely protective of the people she loves but rarely defends herself. She's the kind of person who will walk out of a restaurant with her phone forgotten on the table, then turn around and organize a million-dollar charity fundraiser, seemingly in her sleep.

She's class and sass. And damn, it's a combination I can't resist.

My phone buzzes with an incoming text, and I pull it from my pocket.

I raise my hand to Jack as he heads back inside, and then I take a short walk across the back lot toward the trees and press the FaceTime button.

I keep an eye out for Bronwyn's car as my sister's face shows up on-screen.

When I glance down at my phone, I grimace. The circles under her eyes look like someone painted them on with watercolors. Her light brown hair is a greasy mess thrown into a sloppy ponytail, and her face is puffy. "Maddie, you look like hell."

She snorts. "Thanks. I feel like it too. It's good to know I'm consistent." The mildest hint of a Virginia accent tints her words, as it does mine. She moved to New York a year ago, straight out of high school, and is chasing her dreams of acting professionally. She's had some minor roles, but mostly she's made ends meet as a waitress.

Her arm moves as she rubs her swollen belly. "This kid isn't letting me sleep much."

When she was looking for a place to call home, I'd offered to move her into my small house with me. Now, of course, I'm glad I know she has somewhere safe to stay, even if I'm not able to be there with her.

"Why are you lying about Peanut? My niece would never do that to her mama."

She rolls her eyes at me but smiles a little. "I chose her name. Ophelia Belle."

"Very theatrical of you," I tease.

She squints at me. "It's pretty, you big jerk."

I fight a smile but acknowledge the truth. "It is very pretty. I think I'll call her Fifi."

Her look is pure horrified amusement. "If you nickname my child after a poodle, I will murder you. You will call her Phee or Ophelia."

Her smile drops away, and she leans back against my brown leather sofa, closing her eyes.

"You're more than tired. What can I do?"

Maddie's eyes water before she swipes an angry palm across them. "I'm sorry. I didn't call you to bitch. I just needed to see your face. I knew it was going to be difficult doing this alone, but this is brutal."

"I'm not trying to be a jackass, but does your doctor think you should still be working?"

"Lots of women work right up until they deliver."

I scowl at her. "Maybe you're right. But does she know how tired and sick you are?"

Her shoulders slump. "I have an appointment next week, and I'll talk to her about it. But I really hate the idea of you completely supporting us. You saved that money to start your business."

"And there's plenty of it. Jacob is getting out of the service next year, and we're pooling our resources. We're more than on target for our business plan. Supporting my family will not screw that up for me."

"Are you sure?"

Damn, she's stubborn. Just like me. "What did I tell you?"

She takes a deep breath. "You have my back."

I lift an eyebrow. "And?"

She huffs a laugh. "And when you're old and infirm, I and all my future offspring promise to visit and not let you die bitter and alone."

"See? There you go. Fair trade."

She smiles. "Maybe not. We'll have our work cut out for us if you never get up the nerve to actually make a move on your girl," she says affectionately. "You should try telling her how you feel. Let her get to know the real you. She'll love you. Anyone who doesn't isn't worth your time anyway."

"I'm maintaining professional boundaries. Now mind your business."

She laughs, but lines of pain mar her pretty face.

"Make sure you tell her I said thank you for the amazing care package. I looked them up online, and those bath bombs she sent me were twenty-five dollars *apiece*. It was too much. But it was so sweet of her."

"She doesn't really think about money the way you and I do."

"Must be nice." She leans back and closes her eyes, a dent forming between her brows.

This conversation has shown me something I wasn't ready to face. My sister needs me right now. She's smart as hell, creative, and hardworking. But she's barely more than a kid herself. And life is kicking her in the teeth.

If I tell her I'm coming back for her, she's going to fight me on it, no matter how stressed and ill she's feeling.

So I rub my chin and say, "My job in Pennsylvania is nearly over, by the way."

Her brows pucker. "Really? Since when?"

I shake my head the tiniest bit. *Since about three minutes ago when I realized I don't have a choice.* "My client here prefers her security detail to blend in." That part is completely true. "She's more comfortable with someone who looks a little less—"

"Scary?"

"I am not scary," I say in exasperation.

Maddie snorts. "If you say so."

I look at my watch. Bronwyn should arrive any minute. I don't want her to catch me standing out here in the parking lot looking like I'm waiting for her.

Maddie's face lights in a sly grin. "Are you waiting for her?"

I scowl. "I have to go."

"I just bet you do," she says, smiling. "I'll talk to you in a couple of days. You can tell me more about your moving plans then." She sounds like I just lifted two hundred pounds from her shoulders.

"Will do. Take care of yourself, kid."

"I will." She hesitates. "I know you're not comfortable with sentimentality, but I have to say it. I don't know how I would have managed this without you. You're the best, Dean."

I clear my throat. "Right back at you. Call me if you need me."

She slumps a little and rubs her temple. "I will. For now, I need a nap."

When we've said our goodbyes, I make my way back inside and get myself comfortable in my usual seat—back to the wall with an easy view of the front and rear doors with just a turn of my head. Then I pull up the camera app on my phone to watch for Bronwyn's arrival.

Yeah, it looks a little like stalking. I watch her come, and I watch her go. I follow her at a distance when she drives back to her dorm to make sure she gets there safely. I track her schedule, and I keep an eye on her, even when my client is supposed to be my priority.

When she and her friends party, I stand in a dark corner and watch her move to the music. She smiles and tries to drag me onto the dance floor, always. And I'm the biggest hypocrite on the planet when I say, "That would be inappropriate, Ms. McRae."

I'm not going to be seeing that smile again for a good long while. A yawning emptiness stretches inside me if I let myself think about it.

Jack and, yes, even Neppy keep an eye out for her when she's working. But no one prioritizes her the way I do.

And that's not a problem. She doesn't need the level of security I've been providing. She's a waitress at a bar. Women do this job every day. In fact, most of them don't have a massive bear of a protective cousin in the background while they do it.

What I feel for her is futile right now anyway. Wanting Bronwyn McRae is like standing on the beach, watching the waves crest the shore, and trying to catch the ocean in my hands.

Maddie and Ophelia need me. There's no one else who can step in and do for them what I can.

And Bronwyn isn't my job or my responsibility. She's a fantasy. An emotional indulgence I can't afford. I'll make sure the bar is safe for her, and then I'll go.

The woman is an heiress. The only place I could have in her world at the moment is the same one this university does—one step up from a prank to irritate her father.

She loves to tease and flirt with me. Trying to get me to crack is a game for her.

But I'm not playing. I have a plan to put us on the same field eventually, but I'm nowhere close to being ready to make my move.

I watch on my phone as she pulls up to the back of the bar. She fusses with something on her passenger seat. Then she pulls down her visor mirror and fixes that pale blonde ponytail, checks her teeth, and smooths down her T-shirt before she's out of the car, locking up and shoving her keys into her bag and her phone into her pocket.

She makes her way to the back door, her ponytail caught in the cool spring breeze and flying forward to tangle around her face.

Her hair is so pale that in some lighting it looks almost white. I'm convinced the color is completely natural, because on days when she doesn't wear makeup, her eyelashes are the same color. Her blue eyes are huge and round, and when she graces the world with a smile, a dimple flashes in her left cheek.

She's more than a foot shorter than my six foot two, but she's got curves for miles.

She's beautiful and sexy as fuck. But I've known plenty of beautiful and sexy women. I've never felt as though they put a spell on me the way she has.

I tried not to let myself get friendly. To focus on my job and nothing else.

It didn't work, and that's my weakness to acknowledge.

I close the app and pretend I've been watching the game when the door from the kitchen swings open, and she enters the room.

Truth is, there are too damn many reasons for me to leave Blackwater. And my obsession with Bronwyn McRae is one of them.

2

F**kn' Perfect

BRONWYN

Dean's here. I'd be a liar if I said it isn't the first thing I check the minute I get to work.

His truck is out front, and I get that same thrill I do every single time I know I'm about to see him.

Maybe I'm a glutton for punishment. Maybe it's a weakness in my character. Maybe it's just straight-up hormones.

But happiness forms like a giddy bubble inside me every single time I see the man, despite his lack of overt encouragement. Dean is my addiction and my obsession, and I don't care who knows it.

He's been letting his hair grow into something more civilian looking. He's also lost the usual black suit since following Clarissa to Blackwater. The idea is to blend in with the other college boys in his jeans and hoodies. It's hilarious. Dean doesn't blend. He looks exactly like what he is.

Dangerous.

I thought I crushed on him in a suit and sunglasses, but casual Dean is next-level hotness.

He's the poster boy for the strong and silent type. So polite, holding doors open and calling me "Ms. McRae" and "ma'am."

But there's energy surrounding him, even when he's standing still, as though the real Dean Priester is leashed inside him. One of these days, he's going to let go of that chain. And when he does, he's going to push me against a wall, call me a bad girl, and then give me the biggest orgasm of my life.

He never smiles, but I swear there's one in his eyes. Clarissa says I can't possibly see a smile he isn't showing, but I do.

I park and glance over at the plant resting in my passenger seat. The poor thing is a little wilted, but I bought it that way on purpose. I'm going to sneak it into my dorm room to replace its dead predecessor. A beauteously healthy rabbit's foot fern wouldn't fool anyone that I've coaxed the dead one back to health. We have to have a transition period.

I pat the side of the pot. "You'll be fine. You'll see," I whisper encouragingly.

The plant, being a plant, says nothing.

I've taken to this deception because I refuse to admit that I'm utterly failing at plant parenthood.

When the first one died, Clarissa had suggested I replace it with a fake. As if I'd ever give up on anything that easily.

I'd swear there is some nefarious plot at work against me if I didn't know without a shadow of a doubt that I'm the plant killer. I'll water it too often. Then I swing the other way, and I won't water it often enough. I'll leave it in a place that gets too much sun. Or where it doesn't get enough.

The last time my ex-boyfriend (now friend) Louis road-tripped here for a visit, he'd taken one look at my struggling greenery and said, "Good thing you're not planning to have kids anytime soon. Jesus. How hard do you have to work to kill a fern?"

I laughingly quoted an internet meme back to him. "Did I kill it? Or did it just not have what it takes to make it in this fast-paced environment?"

But his words stung.

Now I'm replacing full-dead plants with half-dead doppelgängers, determined that this time I will prevail.

I check my reflection in the visor mirror, making sure I'm "Dean-ready." Then I head inside.

No one else would think so, but I can tell he's extra aware of me when I enter the front of the house. The way he's just sitting there in jeans and a black T-shirt and doesn't look away from the television to glance in my direction gives his secret away.

Dean always monitors the exits anywhere we go. Him pretending not to notice me? It's a dead giveaway that he does. It's my theory, anyway.

I work here because Jack needs help until he gets some staffing issues resolved. And from the outside looking in, I'm juggling all of it pretty well.

But I'm giving the same energy to a dead plant and remembering our regulars' drink orders as I am a research paper. It's exhausting trying to look like I always have my shit together.

But Dean has made these shifts not just worth it but the highlight of my day. Knowing he's going to be here when I'm working makes everything better.

I try to catch his eye as I deliberately sashay past him. Sadly, he never looks away from the television screen.

My cousin Deirdre is already here working behind the bar, her curly dark hair in a messy bun. She lifts a tattooed arm in greeting. "Hey, trust fund."

Dean hates when people call me "trust fund." Every time he hears it, his right eye gives an infinitesimal twitch.

I shoot a glance his way and... yep. He's leaning back in his chair, all man-spreader posture as he watches the television screen. No one would guess he's interested in anything besides the game. But he's squinting that right eye for sure.

A lot of my family from PA call me that. And since one of my cousins also goes to the same college, the nickname has infiltrated the school too.

My mother says it's a sign of affection, but it feels judgmental to me.

It doesn't do any good to tell Deirdre to stop. She just says I can't take a joke. So I pretend I don't care and give it back to her. "Hey, smooth criminal. How's it going?"

I don't think she's ever even been pulled over for speeding. But I call her that for the time Aunt Linda caught her shoplifting a Slim Jim at Sheetz when she was thirteen. It was all anybody talked about that entire summer.

If she's calling me "trust fund," she can suffer through the memory of her teenage folly.

Deirdre's nickname for me is just another reminder that I'm constantly straddling a line: trying to prove I'm not a spoiled brat to my family here and that I also belong in my adoptive family's world.

I was five when Arden McRae III married my mother and adopted me. He's the best dad. And if anyone ever had the nerve to say I wasn't his child to his face, he'd lose his mind.

But I'm also Steven Hunsic's daughter, though I never met him. I'm three years older now than my father was when he died. And I wonder sometimes if I'd known him if I wouldn't feel this sense of displacement. Or maybe I would. Who knows?

All I know is that I don't quite fit anywhere, though I would never, ever say that out loud. How ungrateful could a person get?

Grandmother Rose constantly reminds me of the immense responsibility I carry with the McRae last name. "Sit straight. Where did you find that clothing? Not so loud. Not so much energy, Bronwyn. That accent sounds positively uneducated. Arden shouldn't keep sending you back to the middle of nowhere for these trips if you can't maintain what you've learned while you're gone."

It's not just Dad's family either. My classmates at the private school I attended could smell the blue-collar on me, like it was rubbed into my pores. I couldn't have pretended to be someone else even if I'd wanted to.

I announced loudly on my first day of private school that "I never seen such a fancy school."

And when the kids all laughed, Clarissa Harcourt gave me a sweet smile, leaned over, and said, "Don't worry, you'll get used to it. Want to be friends?"

I did get used to it—and lots of other things besides.

But my Pennsylvania family's disdain for my unearned privilege, paired with Grandmother's dismissal of my loyalties here, leave me constantly feeling like I'm walking down the center line of a highway. I get hit by traffic coming and going.

"Hey," I venture, "by the way, next Wednesday there's a speaker coming in. Professor Robard says attendance is mandatory. Is there any chance you could cover my shift?"

Deirdre doesn't check her calendar, just starts wiping down the bar. "Oh, shoot. You know I'd love to, but Wednesday is out for me, I'm afraid. Tommy has a pool tournament."

"Maybe I could see if Tiff can cover for me," I say, heart sinking.

She flashes me a smile. "Sounds like a plan. Good luck."

Tiff has never agreed to a swap even once. Looks like my grade in Robard's class is about to take a swan dive. I paste a grin on my face. "It'll work out. One way or another."

She shoots me a thumbs-up while I straighten my spine and try to control the anxiety spiraling inside me.

And the best way to get my mind off stress? Operation: Flirt with Dean until He Smiles.

I sidle up beside him. "Heyyy, Dean. Looking gorgeous, as usual."

He stops watching the game and makes eye contact. A muscle flexes in his jaw, and he shoots a quick irritated glance at Deirdre before looking back at me. "You should tell Jack you're not working here on Wednesday night. Why do you put what everyone else wants above what you need?"

I don't know what to say to that, and I squirm internally until Dean seems to take pity on me. "Maddie really liked your care package, by the way. She says to tell you thank you."

My shoulders relax a little. "They're supposed to be good for pregnant women. I hoped they'd help her de-stress a little. You said she's been having a rough time."

He nods.

Then he reaches for his hoodie that rests on a seat beside him and pulls a paperback from the pocket.

When he slides it across the table toward me, my eyes light up. "The new Jim Butcher? I didn't realize it was out yet."

"I wondered if you'd picked it up yet."

I shake my head. "No."

He nods toward the book. "Take it. You can tell me what you think when you've had a chance to read it."

I snatch it up and shove it into the back waistband of my jeans since it would never fit in my pockets. "Thanks."

He glances down briefly, as though he can see through me to where I've stashed his paperback.

"I think I'd like that one back when you're done with it, Ms. McRae," he says. "It's my new favorite."

I smile. "Not a problem. So what can I get you tonight? Straub?"

"Yes, ma'am. Thank you."

"Someday you're going to call me by my first name, Dean."

He does the smiling-without-smiling thing, but he doesn't say another word. I fan myself with the tablet in my hand.

When I catch myself, I wink at him and play it off like it's a joke. "Keep sweet-talking me like that, Dean, and I'm going to start looking at engagement rings."

The smile that isn't a smile is gone now. There's something I can't quite read in its place. He doesn't break eye contact until the front door opens. When he glances in that direction, I head off to get his order.

Dean has been here every shift that I work for more than a month. He always stays until I leave and walks me to my car. Even if I'm the one closing. Those are my favorite nights, if I'm honest, when everyone except another employee or two is gone. He stays and sometimes helps mop the floors and wipe down tables.

And he listens to me.

I've never known a single other person who doesn't get overwhelmed or bored by my chatter eventually. But Dean doesn't. He watches me when I talk, and he asks questions in response to things I say. He acts like everything that falls out of my mouth is interesting. He's just... wonderful.

He's not much of a talker himself, but he does talk, despite what Clarissa thinks. I know he was shot in his left shoulder while he was in the military. And he told me that he and his friend plan to start their own cybersecurity firm.

Yes, he's very formal with me. But I know he likes me. Deirdre says he doesn't even come here on my nights off.

I'm turning back to take Dean his beer when I almost run straight into a bar patron who's gotten so close that he had to have been right up on me. I step back with a cheery smile and a "Whoops!" before my attention catches on the expensive shirt, and then the scent of a familiar cologne hits me.

I know who it is before I even lock eyes with him, and my gut roils.

Kevin Hallman, Grandmother Rose's—and, technically, my—financial adviser, standing close enough that I can tell he waxes instead of plucks his eyebrows.

He's so out of place that I shake my head a little just to try to make sense of it.

His smile doesn't reach his eyes. "Bronwyn. I found you."

His gaze flicks around the bar, then back to me. When his attention falls to my chest, he can't quite manage to hide a sneer. I'm not sure if he's looking at the bar logo or my boobs.

I have actively avoided dealing with the man in person for as long as I've known him. As a teenager, I didn't understand why he caused my hair to stand on end and my fight-or-flight to fire on all cylinders. I do now.

There's not a sincere bone in his body.

I clear my throat. "Why didn't you have your office call ahead if you needed a meeting?"

I suspect I know the answer. Kevin Hallman took my last email, which I'd cc'd to every relevant person I could think of, personally. He's not happy at all that I have an opinion on my own trust fund management.

Grandmother is my trustee, and that means she's the one I have to go through to have my voice heard. So I did. I recently also started my own version of an email campaign. I might not have any legal right to make decisions about these properties, but I can be a massive, annoying thorn in Kevin Hallman's side and put pressure on the right people to look harder at the man.

Two years ago, I decided it was time to take an interest in the financial reports associated with my trust fund. I'd had to field one too many questions from people in town, including my own aunt Teresa, asking me just what the hell my grandmother was doing. My answers of "I don't know" and "I don't actually have anything to do with management of the properties" only went so far before I began to feel like maybe I *should* know.

Then Kevin Hallman went from acting like a sycophant to being more obviously malicious. He wants me out of "his" business, even though it's very clearly "my" business.

"I was in the area, checking on some of the investments in person, and wanted to reach out to you while I'm here. I'd like to take you to dinner," he says with a sparkling smile.

He must be in his forties, though it's anyone's guess. He has that overpolished glossy look that comes with having had work done and regular appointments with an aesthetician.

And he's a liar.

He's never visited investment properties. It's nowhere close to his job description.

I lift an arm to indicate the bar at large. "As you can see, I'm working right now. But you can have your assistant schedule a meeting. I'm sure Grandmother and my father would like to be part of whatever conversation you want to have with me."

His jaw works, and I suspect he's gritting his teeth. "If you don't have time for dinner, can we take a walk outside? There are some important things I need to discuss with you about your grandmother. I have some concerns. I don't think you want to wait on this."

I suck in a breath. I'm going to have to hear him out, as much as I'd prefer to tell him to kiss my ass. "Now is not a good time, but you can call me tomorrow morning."

Color works up his neck. He's not liking my words, probably because he suspects I'll record any phone call he makes to me.

He's correct. I absolutely will.

He loses his grip on the polite mask he's been wearing and spits, "I heard you were working as a waitress in some dive. You can't even rebel like a normal person. You want to make stupid choices? Let the paps catch a shot of your tits in Cabo."

He looks around the bar, one hand gesticulating. "Why would anyone choose to work someplace like this if they didn't need to?"

I roll my eyes. "That's a stretch, my dude. You're going to have to come at me with something besides my preference for honest work over exhibitionism."

He shakes his head, a look of blatantly fake disappointment on his face. "Your grandfather should never have trusted you with this level of responsibility. You'll single-handedly destroy your entire legacy with this impulsive emotional behavior."

Every bit of air leaves my lungs. Then I suck it back in and my spine goes straight. If I were a porcupine, my quills would be quivering.

Grandfather Arden knew I loved this town. It's why he left the properties here to me when he passed away seven years ago. It's in trust for me until I'm twenty-five and, according to Grandmother, my "frontal lobe is fully developed."

I wonder if my grandparents assumed I'd outgrow ADHD. Joke's on them. I'm going to my grave neurospicy.

I don't know if my grandmother has talked about my diagnosis in front of this man or if he's just a raging dickhead.

He's the one destroying legacies. This town is about people. And he's bleeding them dry. Families who have held leases on Main Street for decades are being pushed out with over-the-top rent increases. He can justify it on paper because we're in a housing crisis.

He's convinced Grandmother I'm gullible and that her first responsibility is to look at my trust for its profit potential. He told her she has a responsibility not to squander my inheritance.

When the two of them look at Blackwater, they see numbers on a spreadsheet. I see Janet and Levi and DeShawn and all the others making a life for themselves with these properties.

"Agree to disagree," I say.

"Bronwyn," he says through gritted teeth. "Be reasonable."

He looks around at the "audience" of bar patrons and reaches to put his hand on my lower back. "I'm done with the games. We're going to have a real conversation. Now. Come with me."

I jerk away from him, Dean's beer order sloshing over my hand. "Don't touch me."

Kevin's face goes hard, and he grabs my bicep in a punishing grip. He tries to drag me toward the door as he hisses under his breath, "You're going to ruin everything, you stupid bitch."

I'm about to put this guy on the floor with his neck under my thousand-dollar boot, but before I even twitch in that direction, Dean is removing Kevin's fingers from my arm.

Dean doesn't let go of him, even after he's placed his own body between us.

"Take your hands off me," Kevin demands.

Dean tips his head and, in a rare show of sarcasm, quips, "That's what she said."

Kevin strains to look around Dean. "Bronwyn, tell your bouncer I'm allowed to touch you."

I'm leaning against Dean's broad back, and I shudder in revulsion at Kevin's words. Dean goes rigid in front of me, the muscles of his back tense. A split second later, he goes eerily relaxed and cracks his neck to the side.

Dean has released Kevin's arm and shoved him away, but he's still alert. Ready. "Bronwyn, what would you like me to do with this piece of garbage? Would you like to file assault charges?"

Kevin sputters.

"I—" Dean said my name. Angels should be singing a heavenly choir while I bask in the beauty of this moment.

Instead, Kevin Hallman has tainted it. More than any other thing he's just said or done, that's the one that most has me wanting to knee him in the balls.

I set Dean's order on the bar, wipe my hands on the short apron at my waist, and move around to stand beside him, eyes narrowed and hands on my hips. "You need to leave, Kevin. You're going to want to start looking for new clients, as well. Because once I tell my family that you threatened me, you won't be managing anything with the name McRae on it."

"I don't think you realize the position you're putting me in." He says it quietly, clearly conscious of our enraptured audience of bar patrons. "If your interference continues, I will be forced to have your competence evaluated. I have years' worth of evidence of your erratic behavior."

I didn't realize a human being was capable of lowering the physical temperature in a room, but at my side, Dean goes so flat and cold, I shiver in response.

3

Natural

BRONWYN

Kevin continues, oblivious, before I manage a single word in response. "You don't understand business. Stay in your own lane."

"And what's my lane?" I snap. "Sitting around a pool, sipping a blended coffee, and pretending I don't know there are real people with their names on those leases?"

The deep, furious red that had started in his neck has worked all the way up to his thousand-dollar haircut. A vein throbs in his temple. He nods his head in a shallow bob, lips pressed tight. "I'm giving you two weeks. You will leave this place, return to New York, and behave yourself."

Who does this guy even think he is, telling me where to live and what to do? "The fuck I will, you fucking piece-of-shit, creepy-ass creep."

Maybe that's not the most eloquent I've ever been. But I can't even wrap my brain around the sheer effrontery of him. He's not my parent. Not my boss. He's no one.

Then it dawns on me. Two weeks from now is when the first of the rent increases are meant to happen. He wants me out of town before anyone feels the impact and people start talking.

Kevin speaks very quietly. "If you don't, let me assure you that your grandmother has become very malleable in recent years. If I tell her a competency hearing is for your own good, she'll follow my lead." He smiles tightly. "She loves you, after all."

It takes me a moment to process. He's saying she's losing her mental acuity with age. That she would choose him over me. And I'd like to argue the truth of it, but she's become very fragile since my grandfather's death, both physically and mentally. She's eighty-three years old. And she's taken Kevin's side over mine many times.

If I'm honest? Ultimately, every time.

How dare he take advantage of her frailty?

Kevin Hallman is threatening people I consider under my protection. If he knew me at all, he'd have come at me with a carrot, not a stick. He'd have behaved *himself*. Because he sure as fuck will not get me to step in line for him.

I will burn this asshole to the ground before I let him hurt my grandmother.

And the people of this town? All his threats have just made me more determined to protect them.

I have to talk to Dad about this. Things are about to get hella messy.

The idea of a competency hearing is laughable. I'm not worried about that. My father will murder him if he tries it, if not literally, then certainly in court. But the man has to have been up to something seriously shady if he's come all this way to threaten me. It's obvious that he's panicking.

Meanwhile, Dean's done with this asshole. "It's time for you to leave."

He grabs Kevin by the back of his shirt, spins him around, and marches him to the door.

Kevin twists in his hold and shouts, "I'm going to enjoy it when you cry and beg me for my help, Bronwyn. Remember what I said. Two weeks."

Dean keeps walking with him, straight out the door and directly to his absurd cliché of a red sports car. Every person in the bar watches as we go.

They might not have heard all the details of our conversation, but they could clearly see the tension radiating between us and heard his last words.

One of our regulars, Jimmy Redder, a usually jovial guy in his fifties, actually grabs a basket of popcorn from the bar and tosses a handful of the stuff, hitting Kevin in the face with it as he passes. "Kick his ass, Dean. Nobody threatens our girl."

Dean doesn't kick his ass. He has way too much self-control for that.

He releases him, leans in, and, in a voice as cold as ice, says, "Bronwyn McRae is mine. I protect what's mine." He nods toward the car. "Now be on your way."

Kevin sputters furiously. Dean doesn't move or say another thing. He just watches, a promise of death in his eyes.

All that angry color drains from Kevin's face, like sand losing water at low tide, leaving him the color of chalk.

It turns out I'm not the only one capable of hearing words Dean doesn't say.

Kevin throws himself into his show-off car and peels out of the lot in a spray of gravel that no doubt dings his own paint job.

I don't realize a bunch of customers followed us outside until Jack shouts, "Show's over, folks. Get your asses back inside."

I turn to head through the door when Dean's hand lands lightly on my elbow. "Not you."

I glance up at him and force a cheerful smile. "Thanks, Dean. What a creep, right?" My voice doesn't sound right, and I fake a cough to try to cover it. The cold wind stings my cheeks.

As usual, Dean doesn't smile back.

"I have to get back in there and get you your beer," I say. "My treat tonight."

Still unsmiling, Dean simply says, "No."

Jack walks over and gives me a gruff side hug. "Take the night off. We're good here."

I shake my head, making a point to show my dimple. "I'm fine. Really. It's Friday night. You're about to get slammed."

Jack reaches out with his thumb and swipes an errant tear off my cheek. I duck away and wipe my face on my shoulder. "It's windy out here," I tell him.

"I know. You're tough as nails. Nobody's questioning it. But I don't want you here if that asshole comes back tonight. Go home. I'll see you Monday night."

Deirdre runs back out and hands me my purse, real concern in her eyes along with protective anger. "We're good, hon. I hope that dipshit comes back. I got my bat behind the bar."

I shake my head, but my lips curve for real at the image she's put in my head—Deirdre, wielding a metal baseball bat, hurdling over the bar and chasing down Kevin Hallman. He'd throw both his hands in the air and run screaming. I just know it.

"Okay. I'm going. Thanks." I untie the short apron from my waist and pass it to my cousin. When I take a step, I find myself forehead to nipple with Dean.

A muscle twitches in his jaw, just once. Then he indicates his truck. "We need to talk."

4

Somebody

DEAN

I open the passenger door for Bronwyn and wait. Her brows are furrowed, and her shoulders are tense.

I'm not feeling exactly relaxed myself.

I might look calm on the outside, but I'm seething with rage under the surface.

It took less than the span of a heartbeat for me to shove it down and ice that shit over. But in the in-between, I pictured all the ways I could kill that man. So easily I could have done it, and in the heat of it, I'd have enjoyed it. I wanted to do it.

But I'm a patient man. I always have been.

I don't lose control of my temper.

Bronwyn heaves a sigh, then starts to clamber into my vehicle. It's set a little high with no running boards. I don't need them, but it's a stretch for her. When I put my hands around her waist and give her a little boost, she makes a sound of surprise before she settles in her seat and reaches for the safety belt.

"So, you want to talk?" she asks when I settle in behind the wheel and hit the ignition. There's blatant skepticism in her voice.

I grunt.

She laughs, but it doesn't sound like she finds anything funny. It's borderline hysterical. If she breaks down right now.... Dammit, I don't know what I'll do if she cries.

"Stop that," I bark.

Her laugh cuts off like someone hit a switch.

A dull flush of guilt washes through me. "I didn't mean.... I wasn't telling you to shut up."

She picks at a loose thread on the knee of her artfully torn jeans. "It's fine. I'm loud. You're not the first person to tell me to be quiet."

The steering wheel creaks under my grip. "I don't want you to be quiet. I like it when you're loud."

"Sure you do." She turns her head and looks out at the trees as they blur past us. "Where are we going?"

"Somewhere we can talk."

"We can talk now."

"No, Bronwyn. We can't talk when I'm driving." Because if I hear something I'm very much afraid I'm about to hear, I'm going to turn this vehicle around, track down that guy, and finish him.

Her head swivels toward me. "That's the third time you've said my name, Dean."

I don't respond. I crossed a line tonight, saying she was mine. I know it. But even in retrospect, I can't regret it. I'd do it again.

I let the situation tonight become a turning point for us. There's "before" and "after." Maybe it was because I know I'm leaving. Maybe it was seeing another man try to control her. Or seeing her visibly upset.

I've never seen her need anyone. And maybe I'm wrong, but it feels like she needs me right now.

Doesn't matter why. She'll never be "Ms. McRae" to me ever again.

We lapse into silence, and she leans back against the seat, closing her eyes.

I tap the steering wheel and finally offer, "So we can go on up to the diner to talk, if you'd rather. Or, if you're not afraid to be alone with me, we can go back to my place."

Her eyes snap open. Then she's scowling at me. "If you were going to do something creepy, I think you'd have done it by now."

She has no idea the things I've done, and that's a good thing. But she's been traumatized. "Just making sure you feel safe."

She sniffles. Then she sniffles again.

Aw, hell.

Luckily, I'm pulling into the driveway of my boxy little one-bedroom rental house. I put the truck in Park and jump out, coming around to open her door. She's huddled there, still strapped into her seat belt, chin wobbling and eyes wet.

She makes way for me when I reach across to undo her seat belt for her. Then I gingerly pat her shoulder. "Shh. It's all right."

She launches herself at me and winds her arms around my neck and her legs around my waist, burrowing her face into my shoulder with a shuddering sob.

My heart seizes in my chest. Not once in almost two years have I seen her like this.

She's the one her friends cry on. She's the one who's all piss and vinegar and a stiff upper lip. Always making a joke of everything and anything.

If I hadn't told her I wanted to talk to her, she'd have gone around back, driven somewhere alone, and done this by herself in her car. Then she'd have wiped the tears off her face and gone back to her dorm like nothing happened at all.

How many times has she cried alone?

She's clinging to me, so I hold on right back and carry her toward the house, kicking the door closed behind me as I go. I rub her back gently, up and down. Slow and calm.

"I'm so sorry," she hiccups wetly against my neck. "It's just an adrenaline crash."

"Who is he?"

"Kevin Hallman. He's my grandmother's financial adviser, and, by extension, mine… at least until I turn twenty-five and manage my own trust."

"He's dangerous."

We're in the kitchen now, and I ease her onto a counter stool, patient as I wait for her to relax her stranglehold on my neck. She eases away slowly, in increments. And when she finally drops her arms and lifts her head, I stop my slow back rub and put a little space between us.

"Well," she announces, "that was embarrassing."

I scowl. "Don't be an idiot."

She laughs, exactly as I'd hoped she would, covering her mouth with the back of her hand. "From 'ma'am' to 'idiot' in one night."

"First name. Hugs. Insults. You've joined my inner circle." Her dimple flashes.

"Just… sit there for a second. I'll be right back."

"Where are you—"

I'm already back, handing her a roll of toilet paper that I snagged from the linen closet. I frown. "I don't have Kleenex. Sorry. This place is…." Not a home.

She unrolls a wad and blows her nose. "It's fine. Thank you."

I pull a saucepan from the cupboard and a whisk from the drawer. When I grab the milk from the fridge and chocolate from the pantry, she cranes to get a better view.

"What are you doing?"

"I'm making you hot chocolate."

She doesn't say anything else at all. After a moment, I glance back to see what she's doing because she's never quiet like this.

She's just... watching me.

I clear my throat. "You always order a hot chocolate. Did I get it wrong? You want coffee? Beer?"

"No. Hot chocolate is perfect." She sniffles again and wipes her nose with the rolled-up tissue in her hand. "Thank you."

When it's ready, I ladle it into a mug for her. Then I pull out a can of whipped cream and put a squirt on top.

The look on her face is pure stunned delight when I pass it over.

"What?"

She shakes her head, then takes a sip. "I never pictured you having a sweet tooth."

I shrug noncommittally. I don't have one, to be honest. I drink my coffee black. But Bronwyn likes sweet. I told myself I'd never have her in this space with me. But I bought her favorites anyway, just in case.

Not that I can admit to keeping chocolate and whipped cream in this house on the off chance she ever ended up hanging out here.

At my lack of response, she watches me over the rim of her mug. "Well, anyway, thank you. It's perfect."

I lean back against the opposite counter, cross my legs at the ankle, and brace myself there. I'm glad she likes the chocolate because she's not going to like this next part.

"I'll understand if you don't want to talk about it. But I'd really like to know more about the situation with Hallman."

She stares down at her whipped cream, then swipes a finger through it before it disappears between her lips. After a moment, she says, "You heard him. He wants me to stay in my own lane. Let him do whatever he wants with the properties in my trust. I've been making too much noise for him. And it's not just me wanting to be 'too nice.' There are discrepancies. Things that don't make sense. And his philosophy favors fast profit over a sustainable business model. He says I don't understand, but I do. More than he wants me to."

"You'll be contacting a forensic accountant?"

She frowns, troubled. "Definitely."

"What did your parents do when you told them about what he's been up to?"

"I haven't yet. Honest to God, until tonight, I still thought maybe I'd blown it out of proportion in my head. But his reaction is all the confirmation I need."

"You need to learn to trust your instincts better. He's trying to hide something, and he's getting desperate about it."

She shudders and sets her half-finished mug on the counter. Hopping down, she walks to the sink and peers out the window at the wooded backyard. The sun is going down, and the tops of the trees are tinged pink in the setting sun.

"He's going to destroy this town," she says.

"Maybe."

She turns toward me, hands clenched against the counter behind her and knuckles white. "I can't let him do that."

"Call your grandmother. Tell her what he's threatening."

She shakes her head. "You don't understand. And I don't expect you to, but I'm... an embarrassment. A disappointment. If I tell her, she won't believe me. She'll tell me to stop being dramatic to get my way."

Her grandmother sounds like a bitch. "Then talk to your father."

She nods. "I'm going to. But an investigation could take time I don't have. There are people here who will be affected by the beginning of next month. I have to stop him before then."

"And how are you planning to do that? You have four years until you turn twenty-five." I was there at her private party, acting as Clarissa Harcourt's security, on the night Bronwyn celebrated her twenty-first birthday.

She lifts her eyebrows and looks triumphant. "According to the terms of my trust fund, there are several conditions I could meet. If I became a parent, for instance. Or if I get married. Either of those would allow me to be in charge of my own trust fund. Obviously, parenthood is out. But marriage would work. Two weeks is completely doable. I just have to marry someone trustworthy."

If she'd tossed a glass of ice water in my face, I'd be feeling less shock.

She needs to talk to her family, not plan a wedding,

And who's she planning to marry? She's not dating anyone. I'd know, considering how much I watch her.

She nods to herself. "That's the answer."

I don't panic as a general rule. Panic gets soldiers killed.

But my heart rate kicks out of control at her words, and adrenaline floods my body.

She can't do this. If she marries someone else, then I've lost her for real and forever. I'm not stupid enough to think it would end up as some platonic friendship situation. Who could say vows to her, live with her, and not fall in love with her?

And she's... Bronwyn. She's all huge heart and sass. She's full of life and fun. In a word, she's irresistible.

She can't say vows with someone else or—

My brain won't even allow me to picture her in bed with some other faceless person without devolving into a jealous rage.

"This town isn't your responsibility." I know even before I say it that she won't believe it. I even understand her feelings about it.

"Yes it is. If I can protect the people here, I have to do it."

"Do you even know what to do with these properties once you're in control of them? That's a huge responsibility."

She scowls. "I'll hire advisers and employees who do know, just like Grandmother. The difference is I'll choose someone who also cares about people."

I straighten from the counter. "Who exactly are you planning to ask to marry you?"

Her laugh sounds flirty. Sassy. "I don't suppose I could convince you?"

I don't react visibly to her question. I'm processing it. Trying to determine whether this is more of her teasing game or if she's serious.

"I could pay you. Two hundred thousand up front and a hundred thousand every year until I'm twenty-five for staying married."

I should be offended. But I'm not. I'm just... elated that she isn't kidding.

When I don't respond to her quickly enough, her shoulders droop in apparent dejection. "I guess I could pay someone else. Or maybe Louis would do it."

Oh, Louis would do it. He'd fall all over himself for a shot at her. How she's oblivious to the way her "friend" wants her, I have no idea.

"I'm going back to New York. No later than the end of April," I say, because she needs to know.

Her head rears back at my apparent non sequitur. "Clarissa didn't tell me that."

"She doesn't know. I decided earlier today. If her husband doesn't want me, I'll find another gig."

"Why?"

"Maddie is going to need someone there when the baby comes."

Her expression softens. "That makes sense."

"Yeah. But the thing is, I can't leave you here to marry some random person. You need someone you can trust. And that someone has to convince people that it's real. I told Hallman you were mine. I implied that we were together. Marry someone else, and he'll be more likely to try to prove it's fraud."

She clears her throat. "What are you saying, exactly?"

"We have witnesses. We've been together every night you've worked for over a month." I'd deliberately taken day shifts so I was available in the evenings to do just that.

Her brow furrows.

I continue, on a roll. "I never leave until you do. As far as anyone at the bar knows, you could have been going to my place afterward. We have history. We've known each other for years. I could even say that you're the reason I agreed to the job here." I could say it because it's true.

She nods eagerly. "Yes."

Her pulse has picked up and is beating a visible tattoo in her neck. Her breaths are rapid, and she rubs her palms on her thighs.

I was never going to play her games. I still don't want to.

She's so far above me, it's a joke. Marrying her alone doesn't change that. I would still have zero leverage besides maybe a general sense of gratitude from her. There'd be nothing to keep her with me after she got bored with me.

I don't have an exciting life. Moreover, my sister and niece are going to be a big part of it. Maddie lives in my house. She needs me around for a while.

That's a lot for anyone to handle, let alone someone playing at marriage. I don't know how long Bronwyn will give me before she's done.

But what are the odds, without her current situation, that I could have any part of her?

Plans solidify in my mind. Her lawyer will create a prenup, I'm certain. If she's serious about getting married, I'll be serious about making it difficult for her to walk away.

The fact that she'd be marrying me for the purpose of financial gain means she can't divorce me if I won't cooperate. At least, not officially, and not without legal, social, and financial consequences from exposure of the secret.

She can still physically leave, obviously. But we'd be tied to each other in a way that would make it difficult for her to move on from me permanently.

If I make sure there are penalties for infidelity in the prenup, it would mean if she gets lonely, she'd believe she has to come to me. Sex with her husband or no sex at all. It's just… insurance against getting my heart destroyed. And that seems fair.

It'll be too late for her family to stop us. Too late for them to convince her I'm some nobody with nothing to offer. And I won't have to worry about losing her to some nepo baby in the meantime.

I can stick to my original plan, but with the added benefit of knowing I have her on a legal leash. I'll have four years to convince her to love me.

If I can get a cohabitation requirement written into the prenup, we'll have forced proximity *and* fidelity.

That's a stronger foundation than a lot of marriages. God knows my own mother never hung around for long and wouldn't know loyalty if it bit her on the ass.

Bronwyn is impulsive, and I'm taking advantage of that instead of trying to steer her back to a more sensible and moderate approach to her problem. If some dick did something like this to my sister, I'd want to kill him.

But I won't hurt Bronwyn. I'll worship her. She doesn't have to know that I wouldn't actually expose the truth.

If I were a better man, I'd be helping her brainstorm other ways to handle this situation.

But I'm not a better man. I'm a cunning bastard.

"Keep your money. I don't want it," I say.

She nods, then smiles. "Hey, I get it. It was worth a shot."

"I'll take a favor instead. Nothing on paper that anyone can point to as transactional. We can decide on the favor later." It's a salve to my pride so she doesn't realize I'm so far gone for her that I'd do something like this just to be allowed to call her mine.

Her smile drops and is replaced by a look of dawning incredulity. "Are you for real?"

I look around for something I can use for my proposal. Reaching for the loaf of bread behind me on the counter, I unwind the twist tie. Then I drop to one knee.

She makes a sound in her throat I think might be of disbelief.

"May I hold your hand?"

She tentatively stretches out her shaking left hand, and I wind the green tie around her ring finger, making a little bow on the top. "Bronwyn McRae, will you do me the great honor of becoming my wife?"

5
We're Not Friends

BRONWYN

I thought he'd respond to my request with his usual "That would be inappropriate, Ms. McRae," the same way he did when I teased him last year that he was secretly in love with me.

But I wasn't teasing him this time. Dean is the only person I would ever marry. And if that makes me silly or impetuous or just plain hopelessly romantic... I don't actually care.

I'm freaked out about Kevin Hallman. But I'm not so freaked out that I don't see that I have other options. When I came up with the marriage idea, it was based solely on the fantasy of marrying Dean.

His initial lack of reaction had me bluffing about finding someone else just to save face. Then I threw in a bribe, which I'm not proud of.

But it worked. He's being smart about not accepting payment that would leave a paper trail and trusting me to keep my promise of a favor later.

He's still there on one knee, utterly patient as my thoughts no doubt skate across my face.

He's seriously asking me to marry him. With a bread tie.

A bubble of optimism rises inside me. It's not like he doesn't know what he's getting into with me, right?

Besides, I know he likes me, at least a little. Maybe not enough to marry me—okay, not even enough to date me—before I offered money. But I knew he was coming to Jack's every night just for my shifts, and he feels responsible for my safety—he's commented on it a couple times.

But there's no way he'd have gone for this if he didn't at least have *some* feelings for me.

I slide my phone from my pocket and snap a pic for posterity. He starts scowling the second he realizes what I'm doing, so he looks grouchy as hell in the photo. It's adorable.

I should be thinking this through better. But no, thank you.

After all, in the pro column, I present Dean Priester.

In the negative column... *I got nothin'*. I freaking want this man.

Maybe my PA relatives are right, and I'm a spoiled brat. Maybe I'm the blueberry girl from Willy Wonka if I say yes—greedy and selfish and taking horrible advantage of his kindness and sense of honor.

And maybe my New York family is right that I need to calm down and not be so impulsive all the time.

But I need to keep Blackwater out of Kevin's hands. And I'll be a good wife. I'll make sure Dean doesn't regret our marriage.

"*Girl, do you ever use that brain of yours for anything besides holding up your ears?*" Grandad Miller's voice fills my mind from the time I climbed a tree, got stuck there, and when my cousin Marie ran the quarter mile back to get him, I tried to shimmy down on my own.

I slipped, and when Marie and Grandad huffed their way back to me, Grandad running so fast he had to hold his pants up with one hand, I was dangling upside down, hanging with one foot stuck in the crook of the tree. He caught me just as I slipped out of my shoe and plummeted toward the ground headfirst.

"*The girl is impulsive. One day, she'll get herself into something it takes more than that dimple of hers to get out of. You're not strict enough with her, Arden.*" Grandmother Rose on any number of occasions.

Dean's expression says he's in no hurry. He's giving me all the time I need to make a decision.

I am going to marry Dean Priester.
God help us both.

He sees the moment I decide, something like satisfaction settling behind his eyes.

"Tell me you like me first," I demand. I shouldn't make him say it, but I need to hear him actually admit it.

His expression doesn't change, but his shoulders relax, and he smiles just a little on the inside where only I can see it. "I like you, B."

He gave me a nickname. I love that for us.

"I like you, too, Big D." I pause. "That is a terrible nickname. Forget I called you that."

"Forget what?"

"Perfect."

"Is that a yes?" he asks.

"Tell me you *like*-like me. I can't marry someone who doesn't."

Those warm hazel eyes of his go hooded and lazy. "I like-like you," he says.

"Just to clarify, I'm talking about kissing."

His eyes close for two whole seconds. When he opens them, he says, "I'm going to be blunt, if you don't mind a little bad language."

I dip my chin and lift my left eyebrow. "Please use bad language with me, Dean. I'm begging you."

His lips twitch, but his voice is dead serious when he says, "You're smart. You're funny. You're loyal. And you have excellent taste in urban fantasy novels. I admire the hell out of you."

I press my lips together, my smile a little shaky as a lead weight takes up residency in my chest. Obviously, I misinterpreted things and pushed him for too much. As far as brush-offs go, he's being very kind.

I can't believe he thinks "hell" is bad lang—

"And I want to do a lot more than kiss you, Bronwyn. I want to make you feel so good that your legs shake when I fuck you."

Oh. My. God.

Dean doesn't.... He never.... This is....

My brain is just firing half-formed thoughts in a chaotic swirl. My breath leaves me in a whoosh, and I clench my thighs against the hot rush of lust that pulses through me.

I pull myself together before I melt onto his kitchen floor in an embarrassing puddle, squinting at him through one eye. "I *knew* you were checking out my ass."

Dean almost gives me a real smile. With his mouth and everything. "Does that mean you'll marry me?"

"Yes."

His knee cracks as he rises to stand. "Most people seal this kind of bargain with a kiss."

My heart thuds painfully in my chest. I've been flirting with Dean for so long. I've talked a big game. Now it's time to live up to my own hype.

I clear my throat and tip my head back to look at him. "I can't reach you up there. You have to come to me."

He smooths some strands of hair that have come out of my ponytail, tucking the stray pieces behind my ear. His eyes follow the path of his fingers across my forehead, around my ear, then back to trace my cheekbone. Cupping my face, he rubs his calloused thumb over my bottom lip, then leans down. Closer, closer, until I feel his breath skate across my mouth as he murmurs, "Close your eyes, B."

He smells so good. It's not expensive cologne or some exclusive grooming product. He smells of regular body wash you'd buy at Target and laundry detergent, with some masculine tang of his own that sets my hormones dancing.

Then his mouth is on mine.

He's gentle at first. No real tongue, just a soft press of his lips. Then he sucks lightly on my lower lip.

My eyes drift closed all on their own, and when my mouth parts on an indrawn breath of pleasure, his tongue delves inside to tangle with mine.

I meet him enthusiastically, wrapping my fingers in his short hair and yanking him to me.

I try to remember to be cool about this. But when I dial back and move my hands down to rest on his biceps instead of tugging his hair, he reaches up and puts them right back where they were.

I tighten my grip, and he groans low in his throat.

My phone buzzes in my pocket with a text alert. We ignore it. It buzzes again. Then again. Finally, Clarissa's ringtone alerts me to an incoming call.

He draws back. "Tell her you're spending the weekend at your grandparents' place."

I haven't hit the Connect Call icon yet, and I glance up in surprise. "Why shouldn't I tell her I'm with you?"

The phone is still jingling its cheery ringtone.

"What are your friends going to say if you tell them you're marrying me to take control of your trust fund?"

"That I'm making a mistake."

He waits for me to work through my thoughts.

"Listen," I huff, "Clarissa doesn't have any room to talk."

The phone has stopped ringing, and now another text comes through. I look down and see a string of them.

Clarissa: Are you okay?

Clarissa: I heard about the guy at the bar.

Clarissa: Now I'm getting worried. Answer your phone. I know you left Jack's.

Clarissa: You need to text me before I start calling hospitals and the police station.

Clarissa: Who is harassing you with New York plates? And how bad did you fuck him up? (Not a criticism, btw)

And people say I'm the dramatic one.

I'm ready to type a response when Dean's phone rings. He answers, "Hello, Mrs. Harcourt-Mellinger. How can I help you?"

Silence as he listens, and then he says, "I do know where she is."

He looks down at me, eyes narrowed just the slightest bit.

I mouth, "Tell her."

He nods in response, but I get the definite sense that he doesn't approve. "She's here with me now. I was at the scene of the incident, and everything is fine."

Clarissa's pitch changes in the background. Then Dean says, "Yes. We're at my place."

He continues speaking to Clarissa. "I don't mind at all. I'm happy to give her a hand."

He moves his grip from my waist down to my butt and gives it a little pat and a squeeze.

I laughingly mouth, "You're bad!"

He rolls his lips between his teeth and looks at the ceiling.

After a moment, he says, "Have a nice night, ma'am."

When he hits the red icon, I tap him on the chest. "I thought I was the bad one and you'd be the one spanking me."

He frowns slightly. "Do you *want* me to spank you?"

"*Yes, please.* But only if it doesn't actually hurt." The words come out breathless, but they're loud and clear.

His eyebrows lift.

Heat floods my face. "Is there such a thing as a spanking that doesn't hurt?"

His expression is so gentle that my throat clogs with unexpected emotion.

He searches my eyes and runs his knuckles lightly across my jaw. "I could never deliberately cause you pain. But a sexy swat to your ass? That I can do."

He pokes his tongue into his cheek briefly before he mutters under his breath, "Just enough to make it bounce."

Who is this? Not the man who stands at the front of the car with his hands folded in front of him and says, "Good night, Ms. McRae."

For almost two years, I thought this man was hot. But I had no idea. It was like looking at a ghost pepper when you've never tasted anything hotter than a jalapeño and thinking "You know what? I bet that's spicy." But you have no idea until the first time you bite down that it's going to strip three layers of skin from the inside of your mouth and renovate your sinuses.

Just like that pepper, I think I may have sorely overestimated my ability to handle Dean. But if I go up in flames, I can only believe I'll do it with the words "Worth it" falling from my lips.

He eases away from me. "You should probably text your friend now. If she's already heard, then someone from the bar is spreading it around."

He pauses for a moment before he says, "I don't think you should say anything about our marriage to anyone until it's a done deal."

I frown. "Because they'll try to talk us out of it?"

Unease niggles at me.

He lifts his right shoulder casually. "If you want to, then go ahead. Call your parents too. But the sooner we get this done, the better. We should fly to Las Vegas tonight."

6

Emperor's New Clothes

DEAN

She was right to call me Big D. That's exactly what I am.

A huge irredeemable dick.

My original plan was a long game.

But then I saw this opportunity. And with barely a thought, I jumped on it like a grouse on laurel. I manipulated her into not talking to a single soul before we got on the plane.

Every minute, I keep expecting her to pull back and question my motives.

It's 10:00 a.m., and Bronwyn has disappeared into a spa in our hotel lobby. She already found her wedding dress in the Dior store; it's currently hanging on the back of our hotel bathroom door, hiding inside a zippered bag. The bouquet of red roses she had the hotel staff procure for her currently rests in a silver ice bucket on the corner table in our room.

I crack my neck and contemplate the doors to the Cartier store, also found in the lobby of our hotel.

I need wedding rings. And I need a new box for the engagement ring I've been carrying around since last Christmas. It's battered and worn, both from constantly being carried in my pocket and because I have a tendency to rub my thumb over it.

But I can't let her see that I've had her ring for months. She doesn't know how obsessed I am, and now is not the time for her to find out.

This past December, when she was Christmas shopping with Clarissa, I'd seen Bronwyn stop short and stare in a store window with a sort of longing smile on her face. She'd pointed out a ring to her friend and said, "It's so beautiful."

She was the one who was beautiful: the wistful look on her face, her blue eyes sparkling, her cheeks and nose painted pink by the wind, and her blonde hair curling out to frame her face under a cherry-colored winter hat.

I could immediately picture the ring on her finger, and I wanted to be the man who put it there.

It was also forty thousand dollars.

The price tag had me breaking out in a cold sweat.

Every time I imagined finally making my move on Bronwyn, I'd pictured myself further along, with my new security company thriving. I had plans.

But sometimes you have to strike while the iron is hot. That was the ring. So I went back the very next day and bought it for my girl.

I don't have as much financially as I planned to, but I saved the majority of my paycheck for years while I was in the military, I've made some good investments, and I tend to be frugal in general.

I have simple needs.

The truth is, any kind of unrestrained spending immediately gets my back up. It reminds me of my mother and the way she'd disappear for months or years at a time, then return with a mountain of gifts while promising she was absolutely never leaving us again.

She did that over and over. Until, when I was seventeen, I'd finally refused to speak with her at all. My father told me not to be stubborn and just take the things inside. It was the first and last time I remember ever just giving in to rage. I'd picked up the box holding a brand-new gaming computer and monitor, intending to carry it in and shove it in a closet. Then I found myself kicking the shit out of the thing until it was just a shattered mess of plastic, metal, and broken glass.

It was the last time my father had allowed her back into the house.

A dignified-looking black man in a three-piece suit that probably cost as much as my first car clears his throat. "Welcome. How can I be of assistance?"

I've moved inside the store, and I'm just standing there, blocking the entrance.

I fold my hands together, widen my stance, and dip my head toward a glass display case. "I'm getting married."

Half an hour later, I'm in the waiting area of the spa where Bronwyn asked me to meet her.

I don't know exactly what happens in these places, but when she emerges through the double doors, she looks relaxed and not at all like someone who's only sleep last night happened while sitting upright in a cramped plane. She's also stunning, but that's nothing new.

When she sees me, she does a happy little wiggle, as if the excitement in her body has to find its way out somehow.

She turns to an older woman in black scrubs who's escorted her to the door. "What did I tell you? Is he not the most gorgeous man you've ever seen in your life?"

She's not saying anything different from the way she's constantly flirted with me. But I'm starting to *believe* her.

The way Bronwyn looks at me? I feel as though she's hearing the things I don't say.

The woman smiles at me, then back at Bronwyn. "You're a lucky lady," she says.

"You don't know the half of it."

Bronwyn reaches for my hand, and we walk together to the elevators, then down the long hallway to our hotel room. She keeps randomly taking a step that turns into a skip. Then she pulls herself back together… only to let out a burst of energy a few minutes later. She's humming under her breath beside me as I unlock the door and hold it open for her.

We have a lot of things left to do. Our ceremony is scheduled to take place in two hours. I still haven't talked to her about a prenup yet. I have to give her the engagement ring. And neither of us has really slept in about thirty hours. Now is not the time to be imagining peeling those black yoga pants off her—

She reaches out, hooks her hands around my belt, and pulls me into the room with her. When she pushes me back against the door, I go willingly, just watching her, waiting for what comes next.

Her gaze travels over me as she chews on her perfectly manicured thumbnail, one hand still pulling at my jeans.

She's visibly excited about marrying *me*. This may have started out as a way to get her hands on her trust fund. It may even still be her primary motive. But her hand isn't wrapped around my belt because of a contract.

She cups my neck with the other hand and pulls me down.

My mouth meets hers, and I try to be a gentleman. For about three whole seconds, I attempt to be polite.

But she's a grenade, and my lips on hers pulled the pin. She's out of control, and I'm not far behind.

I devour her, my hands roaming everywhere. Up under her shirt to skim the planes of her back. Her waist. Her hips. Her *ass*. I can't even wrap my brain around the sheer privilege of it.

My phone alerts me to an incoming email. I've never wanted to ignore anything more in my life.

I pull away, and Bronwyn sighs with clear disappointment. Her enthusiasm lightens my irritation with the distraction a little. We just have to get through this next part, and then we'll be back in this room with rings on our fingers and documents signed. Officially man and wife.

I can manage to control myself long enough to deal with the prenup and get a real engagement ring on her finger.

She shoots me a mock annoyed glance but steps away at my "Sorry. We have to deal with this."

As I confirm receipt of the contract in my inbox, she walks over to the bed and throws herself backward onto it. Periodically, she gives me an up-and-down look of longing, then sighs dramatically in apparent despair.

I'm so used to maintaining a formal attitude with her and hiding my reactions that I realize I'm doing it even now. For the first time, I give myself permission to just *laugh* with her. "You are cute as hell."

She stills, wonder written all over her face. "You have the most beautiful smile I have ever seen."

My ears go hot, and I clear my throat. But I couldn't stop smiling right now if I tried.

When I don't say anything, she changes the subject. "Considering you're busy scrolling through your emails instead of ravishing me against a door, it's a reasonable assumption that you're not all that into me."

I set my phone on the table and crawl over her, bracketing her with my arms. "You are the sexiest woman I've ever seen in my life. And if we didn't have to make sure that our marriage is legally secure so someone like Hallman can't hurt us, you and I would already be naked."

She chews her lip. "Fair."

I'd kiss her, but that's dangerous territory at the moment. We don't have time. So I sit up and go for the Cartier bag, waggling it back and forth like a hypnotist. "Guess what I have?"

"Oh my gosh, Dean, is it the new Patricia Briggs book?"

I fake consternation. "That's not supposed to release for another six months."

She snickers and snatches at the bag. "Show me our wedding rings."

I hold it out of her reach and pull out the first of two boxes. I end up pressing the ring box tightly against my thigh so she can't see that my hand is shaking when I pop the lid open.

Her mouth drops open. "You are never going to believe this, but that is my dream engagement ring."

"So you like it?"

"I love it."

"Good."

Her face scrunches the tiniest bit. She looks like she wants to say something.

"Yes?" I ask.

Shaking her head, she gives me one of her brilliant smiles. "Nothing."

She holds out her hand, complete with green bread-tie bow. "Gimme my ring. Leave the bread tie. I'm sentimental."

I slide the Cartier diamond on next to its ignominious partner. "I know."

7
Come and Get Your Love
DEAN

I'm sitting on a padded wooden pew in the cheery waiting room outside a quickie wedding venue on Fremont Street. It's decorated with neon signs and kitschy Andy Warhol-style art on the inside. But we're in Vegas. I'm not sure I expected anything else.

Not that there aren't nice places to get married here. I asked her if she wanted me to try to get us into the wedding venue at The Bellagio. Her response was a horrified "No! If we get married at a quickie place on The Strip, I can convince my friends and family this was a lack of impulse control. If we do somewhere like The Bellagio, they'll be heartbroken that they weren't invited."

She lapsed into silence after that, and so had I. Mostly because her words had landed like a sucker punch. "*This was a lack of impulse control.*"

As if that wasn't the very reason I'd convinced her not to tell anyone where we were going in the first place.

I shove the thought away and straighten my tie.

This place is nice enough. It's not some cathedral or expensive hotel like Clarissa Harcourt's wedding, but everything looks clean and new. It's tacky but fun.

I wonder how many weddings they perform here that even last a year.

Bronwyn and I will last at least *four* years. On paper, anyway. I made sure of it with that prenup. The financial penalties against her if she initiates divorce within that time frame or is unfaithful are straight-up predatory.

I was concerned that a cohabitation clause that forced her to live with me was pushing too hard, under the circumstances—after all, this isn't a normal marriage. Her lawyer had said it could be a problem if one of us were called away for work or school, so, I'd allowed him to change my demand that we live together 100 percent of the time to a clause that indicated that we had to sleep under the same roof at least once every two months.

I need to give the appearance that I'm not interested in restricting her freedom, despite the fact that I most definitely am.

She'd smiled as she signed the prenup. As if I weren't acting the part of The Sea Witch, and she, The Little Mermaid, as I gave her a contract designed to leash her for the next four years.

She crosses one slender leg over the other. Reconsiders, then switches legs. Her dress is knee-length, and silk rustles with her agitated movements. The dress is, according to Bronwyn, "ivory with champagne accents."

She looks straight out of some movie about the 1940s or 50s. Her hair is in a vintage style with blonde curls cascading down her back and the front rolled away from her face. She's wearing a little net veil attached to a tiny hat, and she has on cherry red lipstick. Her collarbones and shoulders are showing, and the dress tucks in at her waist and flares out with layers of netting underneath.

When she'd stepped out of the hotel bathroom, I'd almost swallowed my own tongue. The reality that I was about to marry this woman nearly stole my breath.

Sitting beside me with her knees together and her ankles crossed, she fidgets with her pearl necklace and drums her nails on the upholstered seat.

An attendant comes to tell us it's our turn, and we both stand abruptly.

Bronwyn laughs and pulls out her phone. "Selfie."

I crouch down with my face next to hers and try to look pleasant.

"You look like you're marrying me under duress," she says in mock reproof.

"I'm smiling."

"Oh my gosh, Dean, you are not." But she says it in that same way she usually speaks to me—with rampant affection in her tone and a healthy dose of amusement.

I look at her, and she sighs happily. "There it is." And she snaps the picture.

I kiss her cheek for another shot.

She puts her phone into a pocket in the seam of her dress as the young man pulls the doors open.

When she steps forward, I grab her hand. "Wait."

She looks back at me quizzically.

For a moment, I just stare at her—my conscience fighting a battle with the strategic, manipulative asshole who lives inside me.

Then I move her hand up to take my arm as if chivalry were my intention all along. "Time to say 'I do.'"

• • • ● • ● • • •

"Bottoms up."

She licks the salt, slams a shot of tequila, and bites the lime.

I'm not drinking, just watching her as I lean back in my chair in the hotel bar.

I frown. "Top-shelf tequila doesn't need salt or lime. You're just ruining your own experience."

She shakes her head at me like I'm the one wrecking the perfectly good bottle of alcohol. "It's a vibe, dear husband."

"Are you trying to get drunk?"

She's always the life of the party, but I've never seen her actually trashed. Instead, she's typically the one mothering her friends when *they're* wasted. Her change in mood this evening is concerning. I can't help but wonder if she's realized she made a deal with the devil when she signed that prenup.

She freezes in the process of reaching for the bottle and blinks at me. "I have no intention of getting drunk," she says. She looks back down at her shot glass. "Wait... we *are* having a wedding night, right?"

"I think it's probably a good idea from a legal standpoint. Just in case anyone questions if the marriage is real, Mrs. Priester."

She winks. She might be the only person who has always been able to tell when I'm kidding. "Good thinking," she says. "Very strategic. Well, then, I'm not getting drunk."

I hadn't realized there was a boot on my chest until I feel it lift.

"So...." She props her chin in her palm. "Why do I have to become a Priester? Why don't you become a McRae?"

She's startled me. Again. And I don't have a good answer.

The idea of me somehow carrying on the Priester lineage, as if it's some great family legacy, strikes me as almost laughable. But I won't be Mr. McRae. It would look like I was trying to use our connection for the social and business advantages it would provide.

She slumps a little before reaching out and placing her hand on top of mine. "Can I be honest?"

"Yes."

She sighs. "I'm kind of stressed right now."

I clench my hand and pull it from under hers. I wrap it around my sweating water glass, take a long swig, then set it down.

She nods wisely. "You're stressed too."

I'm not stressed. I'm guilty. There's a difference. "Tell me why you're stressed."

She leans toward me, alcohol forgotten. "First, there's the Kevin Hallman thing. We have to be back in New York by Monday, and then I have to be at my lawyer's office and get everything rolling. And then I started thinking about how I'm going to break this whole thing to my friends and family. Their feelings are going to be hurt that they weren't invited."

She eyes the tequila bottle and pours another shot. "The worst part is, my parents won't be mad. They'll be disappointed in me, you know?" She swallows her drink but seems to have forgotten about the lime wedges.

I'm still scrambling to think of some comforting thing to say when she asks, "What's Maddie going to say when she finds out?"

"She's probably going to scream in excitement."

Her face fills with relief. "Really? Will she like me?"

I frown. "Who *wouldn't* like you?"

She snorts. "Plenty of people."

"Those people have horrible taste and don't count." I'm not even kidding.

She shakes her head the tiniest bit, but she gives me a smile. "Do you have any other family?"

I shake my head. "My mother is alive, but I haven't had contact with her in years. My dad died a couple years ago. It's just me and my sister. She's the only family I have who counts."

Her expression changes subtly at my words. Then she reaches out and puts her hand on mine. "You and Maddie have mine now too."

She doesn't understand that most people don't share her enthusiasm or openness.

Her family is going to hate my guts.

I try to pull the conversation back on track. "You're thinking of this like you've deprived them of a big wedding. But that's not what they missed out on. This is more like a contract."

She frowns down at her shot glass and shoves it away. But not before it's blatantly obvious to me that she'd rather pour herself another drink.

Dammit. I shouldn't be reminding her that this is all about her trust fund.

She wiggles a little in her chair, then rests her elbow on the table and her chin on her fist. "If that gets back to Grandmother Rose, I wouldn't put it past her to report it to somebody as fraud and sue me to take trusteeship away from me."

"Who would she report it to? You're using it to gain access to your own property."

She leans back and huffs. "I don't know. Somebody. I googled it. Technically, getting married for the sole purpose of financial gain is considered marriage fraud." She flops backward in her chair, arms dangling loose, and stares at the ceiling. Her ladylike crossed-ankle posture is long gone. "We're criminals. Embarking on a life of crime."

I pinch the bridge of my nose. "You're not defrauding anyone."

She shakes her head mournfully. "Tell it to the judge, Deaner. Here's the thing. You said it isn't a regular marriage, and that's true. But they have to think it is."

I reach for the tequila and take a huge swig straight from the bottle.

A big old house full of rowdy kids, a swing on the porch, and *Bronwyn*.... That's my secret fantasy. To have a ridiculously "regular" marriage with this amazing woman.

I didn't have the worst childhood, but I didn't have a good one. I grew up as an Army brat. No living grandparents or extended family who were involved in our lives.

My father was angry and cold. And my mother was gone most of the time. When she was around, she was manipulative and critical. She used her version of love as a weapon.

Maddie and I didn't have what I'd consider a "home." We were always moving. When my father deployed and my mother wasn't around, we were pushed onto other families as a favor to my father. He paid them to keep us.

So yeah, I want what I never had. I want to live in the kind of house you stay in for the rest of your life. And I want to fill it with loud kids who know Bronwyn and I are always there for them. A life full of chaotic consistency.

"We'll figure it out, B. It won't be a problem."

She searches my eyes and seems to gain some reassurance from whatever she sees there. Her smile feels like she's wrapping me up in affection, as she appears to shake off the glum mood she's worn like a blanket since we entered the bar.

A server stops by our table. "Congratulations!" he says, clearly taking in her dress and my suit. "What can I get for you folks today?"

I nod my thanks. "Can you bring my wife some water?"

Bronwyn does a little shimmy in her seat, and with big eyes, she mouths back at me, "My wife," and fans herself with her left hand.

I smile at her and shake my head. But I'm not going to pretend I didn't get a massive sense of satisfaction from saying those words.

"Of course. Anything else?"

We ate before we came into the bar, so at least those two shots of hers didn't land on an empty stomach. But I tip my head toward her in inquiry just in case.

"Hello, Jason! I'm Bronwyn," she chirps, reading the tag on his shirt. "How is your day going?"

Jason grins at *my wife* and gives her a subtle once-over. I'm pretty sure the sconce lighting strikes a sparkle off his perfectly veneered teeth. The guy looks like Cupid just hit him with an arrow. "It just got better," he says with a shit-eating grin.

The chair creaks as I adjust in my seat, and he remembers I exist. He shoots a nervous glance at me over his shoulder and clears his throat.

That's right. She's gorgeous. And sweet. And you are never, ever getting anywhere near her.

He gives me a sharp nod. Bronwyn can tease me about not talking all she wants. Seems to me that most people understand me just fine.

"Ooh, is there any way I can get something chocolatey?" she asks.

I wince at the thought of chasing tequila with chocolate, but the waiter is already happily agreeing. When he turns to go, I clear my throat. "Can you make sure it has whipped cream?"

Bronwyn beams at me like I just threw myself in front of a bullet for her. "Thank you."

Jason's whole face softens, and he looks back at Bronwyn like she's the most adorable thing he's ever seen. When he hurries off to track down her order, I huff a laugh into my water glass.

"What?"

"You dazzle everyone you meet."

She shakes her head with a smile. "Not you. For a year and a half you called me 'Ms. McRae.'"

"Bronwyn, I was definitely dazzled."

She gives me a little smile, but I can tell she's not entirely convinced. "I did think you liked me."

I nod. "You were right."

She taps a nail on the side of her shot glass. "A lot of the guys I've dated pursued me hard in the beginning. They see the money, and they think I'm fun, I guess. But as soon as they got to know me, they realized they'd bitten off a little more than they could chew."

I lean forward in my chair and brace my forearms on the table. "All that tells me is those men were weak."

She laughs and winks. "Doesn't matter. I swore off all other relationships the day I met you."

Sure you did. When I don't say anything to that, she squints at me and says, "Side-eye."

"You can't just squint straight at somebody, say, 'Side-eye,' and think you gave side-eye."

"It's metaphorical side-eye."

I smile, and she dimples back.

When Jason returns with her order, she lifts her drink in a toast. "To your big, strong muscles, Dean."

I huff a small laugh and tap my glass against hers.

When a band starts their sound checks on a small stage near the gleaming dance floor, her eyes light up. "Oooh, Dean. You have to dance with me."

I shift a little as I admit, "I don't dance."

Her face scrunches in disappointment. "Not even once? It's our wedding day."

"I'm not good at it."

Her expression clears. "That's the amazing thing about dancing. You don't have to be good at it to have fun."

"If I step on your short-person toes, I'll break them."

She snort-laughs. Then she laughs at her own laugh. People at other tables glance her way, smiling in response.

Finally, she says, "If you try to step on me, Dean, I promise I'll dodge and weave."

A man wearing a red-sequined tuxedo speaks into the microphone. "Hello, beautiful people. Welcome to Las Vegas! My name is Raoul, and I'm going to tell you a secret."

Bar patrons glance toward the man onstage, and after a little pause for effect, he continues. "You already know Las Vegas is a place for dreaming. Maybe you're hoping to hit the jackpot. Maybe you're looking for love...." His drummer starts a beat. "Maybe you're looking for both."

His head bobs as the bass player starts a familiar tune. He nods to a woman in a "Roll Tide" T-shirt. "Whatever happens when you go home to Alabama, remember what it feels like to know the future is wide open. That's the secret. You can take it with you."

Bronwyn stands and starts to back onto the dance floor, urging me to follow with a crook of her finger. She gives me a smirk.

When the man onstage launches into the first verse of "Come and Get Your Love," Bronwyn tilts her head to the side and tries to coax me to join her.

I glance at the ceiling, then right back at her. I wasn't kidding when I told her that I can't dance. But I wouldn't be able to keep the smile off my face even if I tried.

She calls, "Come on, Dean."

I shake my head, but I stand up.

A guy in the crowd shouts, "Dance with your wife, man!"

I move out to stand in front of her. I don't dance, but I put my hand on her waist and watch her move. My wedding ring glints as I use the other to push back a strand of her hair that's worked loose from its pins.

A crowd of people have joined us.

When the song ends to a smattering of applause, the music transitions to something slower. Bronwyn cuddles against me and weaves the fingers of her right hand through my left, putting the other on my chest. "Just sway, Dean. That's enough."

I press my right palm against her upper back, the silk of her dress slick under my fingers, her body warm against mine. I don't lift my feet, but I sway my upper body a little as I hold her.

She lays her head on my chest. And I'm so caught up in the feel of her against me that I don't even notice what song the band is playing at first. When I do, I flex my hand involuntarily and pull her even closer.

I'm not a superstitious man. I don't believe in omens.

It doesn't mean a thing that we're dancing on our wedding night to "Till Forever Falls Apart."

8
Till Forever Falls Apart

BRONWYN

I wobble a little as Dean and I make our way down the corridor to our hotel room, and he tightens his hold on my hand, shooting a concerned glance my way.

"Don't worry. Those shots wore off an hour ago. It's the shoes. You try wearing stilettos for hours. You'd get wobbly too."

Comprehension lights his features. Then he sweeps me into his arms.

I wrap both of mine around his neck, my bouquet of red roses dangling from one hand, and laugh.

His lips twist. "Why do you wear those torture devices anyway?"

I shrug. "They're pretty."

"Nothing is pretty if it causes you pain," he growls.

"D'awww!" I run my finger over his bottom lip. You'd think a man like Dean, one with such rugged features and that sharp, square jawline, would have lips to match the rest of him—hard and sculpted. But Dean's are soft and full.

He sucks my finger into his mouth, his tongue curling around the digit. The lust that's been on a low boil for hours erupts into molten lava, spilling over until I'm lost in it. Overwhelmed.

I hang on to his wide shoulders as he unlocks the door, and then we're inside our hotel room.

There's one dimly lit floor lamp in the corner. Dean kicks the door closed behind us, and I reach out to secure the deadbolt.

Then his lips are on mine, and I melt into him.

This is my fourth kiss from Dean. I can't wait until I've lost count. Until we've kissed so often that no one could keep track. Fifty years of kisses every day. More even than that.

He sets me on the bed, then crouches on the floor and reaches for first one shoe, then the other. He pulls them from my poor swollen feet and tosses them over his shoulder to land somewhere behind him with a soft thud.

Massaging my foot, he frowns at my red pinkie toe. "People don't have feet shaped like those shoes."

"I don't want to talk about my shoes."

I'm leaning back on my elbows, one leg straight and the other bent. He slides both hands up my right calf, over my knee, and up my thigh. His fingers come to rest mere inches from my panties.

"How is your skin so soft?" he mutters.

He guides me to my feet, then very carefully removes my birdcage veil. He sets the hat on the table behind him.

One by one, he pulls every pin from my hair until it tumbles around my shoulders and down my back. He combs his fingers through it, his gaze trailing over my hair, my eyes, my mouth.

So patient. So methodical.

I reach up and remove his tie, then unbutton his shirt. I'm not methodical at all, but I can tell he doesn't mind.

I push his suit jacket from his shoulders, and he shrugs it off. Then I'm yanking his shirttail from the waistband of his black trousers.

"You should be an underwear model." I slide my palms down his abs.

He shakes his head. "You haven't seen the shoulder yet. It's grisly. I'm warning you. And I'm not.... I think you see me differently than the rest of the world does."

He walks behind me and lifts my hair to drape over one shoulder. Then he finds the hook and eye at the top of my zipper. Unlatching it with calloused fingers, he drags the closure down, his warm breath a whisper against my spine, until the dress sags loose around my shoulders.

"Fuck me," he breathes when he catches sight of what's beneath it.

He moves to stand in front of me, and I let the dress slide down one arm, then the next, finally stepping out of it entirely.

His shocked gaze shoots to mine, then back to my body, then to my eyes again. "*This* is what you had on under your dress? The entire day. You...."

"Do you like it?" I wish I could snatch the question back. I want him to think I'm confident, not desperate to impress him.

He takes in the little ivory-and-rose-pink number, with its bow that rests right at the top of my butt crack and its floppy little lace "skirt" that hides nothing over the sheer thong that hides even less.

The matching bustier laces up the back in crisscrossing straps, and the flirty bra cups hint at burlesque without going quite that far.

He sits down hard on the edge of the bed, almost as if he's forgotten that he intended to be standing. He wipes a hand across his mouth and blows out a breath. "I like it."

Then he wraps those big hands around my waist and draws me in to stand between his spread thighs. His eyes catch mine, and the trepidation there takes me by surprise. "You're too pretty to touch."

"I'm definitely not."

I reach up to tug on the bow that holds the bustier together, and he grabs my wrist gently. "Let me? Please." His voice is hoarse.

I drop my hand, and he pulls the bow loose. If I thought his reaction to the lingerie was gratifying, it's nothing on the moment he pulls the bustier away and reveals my naked body.

I'm not perfect. My breasts grew quickly in puberty, and I have some stretch marks to show for it. I'm short-waisted, and my stomach isn't completely flat. I don't have a thigh gap. It's not something I spend time worrying about one way or the other.

But the way he looks at me... I feel beautiful.

"The first day I met you, Clarissa's father asked the two of you to come into his study to introduce me. Do you remember that?" he asks.

It may seem like a strange question under the circumstances, but I get it. Because I do remember. He'd shaken my hand and said, "Nice to meet you, ma'am," but he'd had the same look on his face that he does now.

"Yes."

"I wanted to know everything about you. What made you laugh and what made you cry. What your favorite season was. What your kiss tasted like. What you read and what you listened to."

"You know all those things now."

"I do." He narrows his eyes. "Though I don't think it counts when you won't pick a favorite color or season. It's cheating to say 'all of them.'"

His hands skim my torso until he's cupping my breasts, thumbs gliding over my nipples. "But it doesn't matter. I learned those answers, and I just have more questions. I'll never reach the end of you."

My abdominal muscles tense in a visible clench, and the corner of his mouth lifts in a crooked smile. Then he draws me against him and into a lush kiss that leaves my thoughts incoherent. Or maybe that's the feel of his hands as they roam my body.

It's as though he wants to touch every inch of me. Like he can't get enough. One hand on my breast, the other kneading my butt cheek. Then his right hand skims up over my clavicle and loosely circles my neck before sliding up into my hair. The fingers of his left hand trail down my thigh, then back up.

He holds me to him as he slants our heads first this way, then that.

He's slow but never tentative. There's purpose in every caress.

I press myself against him, shoving his shirt from his shoulders. The gnarled yet overly smooth texture of his shoulder draws my attention, and I pull back to see the part of him that he referred to as "grisly."

He grimaces. "I can wear a shirt if it bothers you."

"The only thing that bothers me is how much pain you've experienced." I press a kiss against the angry, shiny skin.

He pulls me flush against him, then lies back and rolls us until I'm lying beneath him.

The hard steel of his cloth-covered erection nudges against my clit, and I groan at the sensation. He kisses me, and I rest my palm on his smooth-shaven cheek.

There's a sense of unreality to this moment. Yesterday, I was walking into Jack's thrilled to see Dean's truck in the lot. Now, his ring is on my finger.

He moves down my body, taking one aching nipple between his lips to suck and flick. He holds my other breast, lightly pinching. I push up against him, seeking friction.

"Take—" I gasp at the delicious sensations he's lighting up inside me. "Clothes... take off...."

Dean lifts himself away just enough to remove the last of my lingerie and then slides even farther down, trailing open-mouthed kisses across my abdomen as he goes.

"Take off your clothes," I say.

"Has anyone ever told you you're a patient person?"

"No!"

He winks. "Didn't think so."

Then Dean Priester's mouth is on me. My *husband* has his mouth on me.

And it is glorious.

Slippery, firm flicks of his tongue. Then he's sucking my clit as he eases first one finger, then another inside me.

An orgasm is building, building. I squirm and writhe beneath him, a hot flush painting my chest and cheeks.

I clutch the comforter beneath me as I push up against him, and Dean's free hand settles over one of mine.

I turn my palm upward, and we hold on to each other. The next time I clench my fist, it's with Dean's fingers wrapped tightly around my own.

My abdominal muscles tense in anticipation of the oncoming storm. Pleasure floods me, sweeping me away in a current of release. He never stops what he's doing, but he looks up to watch my reaction, easing me through it and down, holding my eyes with his own.

I don't have to push him away when I become too sensitive. He's so focused on me that he already knows.

He slides up over me, and I fuss ineffectually with his belt buckle, the mechanism strange and backward to me.

He kisses me, slow and deep, then rises to his knees and puts his hands over mine on his buckle. He indicates the nightstand. "I put a box of condoms in the drawer."

He's kicking the remainder of his clothing off as I stretch across to open the drawer in a move that is anything but graceful. He holds me steady by the waist to keep me from falling completely off the bed and onto the floor. After what feels like minutes but is probably only fifteen seconds, I have the shiny packet in my hand.

Then I wiggle out from under him and give him a gentle push to lie down on his back. He leans back, his expression intrigued.

When I get a good look at his hard dick, my eyes shoot wide, and my brows creep up my forehead.

Whatever he sees on my face has concern flooding his. "B?"

"You're very *proportional* with the rest of you."

"If it doesn't feel good, we'll stop at any point. You just say the word."

I nod. "Thank you. But I'm not worried, just admiring."

His cheeks turn adorably pink.

I'd like to pull some slick move and open the condom packet with my teeth. Unfortunately, I don't trust myself not to accidentally tear a hole in it that way. So, I fumble with the thing and tear it open exactly like someone who technically knows how to do it but has never actually put a condom on another person before.

I sneak a glance up at Dean to find he's looking back at me with something like awe in his hazel eyes.

He makes a sound low in his throat. "Can't believe I get to touch you."

I run my thumb over his full lower lip before dropping a lingering kiss there. Then I stroke him. Once. Twice. Three times. Satin-soft skin glides over a core of iron. I roll the condom over him.

He watches me with hazel eyes that glitter in the dim lamplight, reaching out to caress my body in sweeping strokes. I straddle him, and he leans up to bring my nipple into the warm cavern of his mouth.

I writhe against him, the desire for more... and still more... building once again.

I position him at my center and drop my weight. He doesn't go in easily. My body is ready, but I haven't been with anyone in years.

He catches me by my hips, slowing my trajectory, and grunts. "Don't hurt yo—"

I push down and bottom out. The head of his cock bumps against my cervix, and I grit my teeth, aching from the tight stretch.

"Oh fuck. Yes," Dean grinds out, slamming his head back against the pillow. Then he spanks me in a kind of heavy, pawing grab, except he doesn't lift his hand away afterward. He holds on and kneads my ass.

"We're going to have to make some rules here, angel. You're not allowed to hurt yourself on my dick," he growls.

"It doesn't hurt." This is just enough sting to ignite my nerve endings but not enough for me to call it pain. My brain is buzzing, and I imagine this is what it feels like to be drugged.

I gasp and hold still for a moment to catch my breath. To savor the insane fullness.

My heart is as overwhelmed as the rest of me. Because... *Dean*.

He's looking at me like this is the start of *everything*.

He puts his warm hand on my abdomen and trails his thumb down to rub circles against my clit. I clench around him in a rush of wet pleasure.

And then I move. I'm almost frantic, but I can't find it in me to be anything else.

Dean leans up to take my nipple into his mouth once more and flicks it with his tongue. He wraps his arms around my middle in a bear hug and pulls me down against his body. The tang of his skin is salty on my tongue as I lick the place where his neck meets his shoulder and breathe him in.

His heart thuds strong and steady against me as my knees dig into the crisp cotton bedding beneath us. He holds me still and fucks up into me.

I revel in the way he's taken control of my pleasure. I'm going to come again. The realization shocks me.

I sob against his neck and place my hand against his smooth-shaven cheek.

Turning his head, he kisses my palm, then rolls until I'm beneath him.

I look up with a soggy smile.

He searches my eyes with his own, his expression so tender my chest aches. "You okay?"

I nod. "Yes."

He kisses me long and deep as he moves within me. He's being careful, that big body rolling over mine in an undulating wave of pure, decadent pleasure.

I buck against him, clutching the hard muscles of his ass as he flexes against me. "You don't have to be—" I gasp. "—gentle."

I don't have to say it twice. He leans back on his knees and hooks his elbows under my thighs. Then he powers into me.

My own hand creeps down toward my clit before I realize what I'm doing. I catch myself just before I do something truly embarrassing.

He shakes his head. "I'd give anything to watch you play with your clit while I fuck your wet pussy."

I go for it with greedy fingers, and Dean grunts in approval. The tension is still building. He leans down to take my mouth in a carnal kiss, bending me like a pretzel, my knees beside my ears.

He fucks me and grinds into me... and then I'm coming so hard that colors spark behind my eyelids. My legs are shaking, and a cry escapes my throat.

Dean rides it out with me. Then he leans back and repositions me so my legs are framing his hips once more. He moves over me, forearms bracketing my head, and thrusts once, twice.

His body goes tight against me, muscles tensing, his cock flexing and impossibly harder inside me. He orgasms, and I'm overcome by the strange desire to *comfort* him.

I don't analyze the thought, just hold him against me, one hand buried in his hair, the other clutching his broad back.

It feels too soon when he pulls away, and we both groan as he leaves my body.

He drops a kiss on my temple. "I'll be right back," he murmurs, then pads to the bathroom.

He returns a short while later with a warm cloth and towel. After he's washed me, he climbs into bed beside me, pulling the comforter over the two of us.

He wraps his arms around me, and I snuggle in, trying to squirm one of my legs between his hair-roughened muscular thighs.

He rumbles a quiet laugh. "That is a serious level of trust you're expecting from me."

"Hey, you put a lot more than your *thigh* between my legs."

"Yes, but I'm delicate," he deadpans.

I snicker, burying my face in his neck and breathing in the woodsy, masculine scent of him. He draws me even closer, though he doesn't make room for my leg. Instead, he slides one of his between mine so we're plastered as closely together as two people can be.

I fight sleep as long as I can, purely because I don't want to miss a moment of how this feels.

My fantasies were nothing on the reality of his smile. His arms around me. This connection that feels so much more than physical.

I've had sex. And it wasn't this.

I don't know what tomorrow will bring. This weekend feels like a moment out of time, but we'll need to rejoin the "real world" soon.

Dean and I can build a beautiful future. I know we'll have challenges, but my family will love him when they get to know him, and I'm excited to have a sister-in-law.

I wonder if Maddie will let Dean and me help with the baby. I love kids, have been babysitting my younger cousins since I was fourteen. And sometimes we make a heck of a mess and drive my aunts crazy, but no one can say their kids don't have fun with me.

Gah! I'm going to be the cool aunt. It's my new mission.

Dean's house is small, so I'm hoping he and Maddie might be willing to consider moving. Maybe I can get us something closer to my parents' place.

I know our marriage is in its infancy, and we did this backward—we got married, and now we're, hopefully, going to build a relationship.

He said I dazzle him, but I don't want that. It implies infatuation. And that never lasts.

I want the Dean who knocked on my dorm room door when I took a mental health day three weeks ago and asked if I wanted to go for a hike and talk, or if I just wanted him to get me some pizza and ice cream. The nerdy Dean who gets that deep down I'm a super big dork, too, and asks what I think about the difference between hard and soft magic systems in urban fantasy novels.

I drift to sleep absorbed in the way Dean feels wrapped around me and reminding myself not to expect too much too soon.

· • • ● • ● • • ·

A phone vibrates in the quiet darkness of the room, and Dean stirs beside me. He reaches for the bedside lamp, then scrambles through his discarded clothing until he finds it. Sitting on the edge of the bed, he answers with a neutral "Hello," no indication that he's been pulled from sleep in his voice.

There's a pause while he listens, and then he curses under his breath.

I sit up, wrapping the sheet around me, and take in the stunned expression on his face. Then he hangs up, dials a number, and waits with eerie stillness, his face like stone, until someone picks up on the other end of the line.

"Yes, my name is Dean Priester. I'm calling about my sister, Maddie. Madison Priester."

He closes his eyes as he listens, and I scramble from the bed to kneel at his feet, holding his free hand in both of my own.

His eyes screw tight, and he gives a sharp shake of his head. "The baby? My niece?" A pause. "Yes. I'm—" He looks around the room almost helplessly. "I'm on the other side of the country right now. I have to book a flight. I'll be there as soon as I can."

He pulls the phone away from his ear and looks down at it with a dazed expression before he presses End Call.

"What happened?" I can't manage to lift my voice above a whisper.

He scrubs a hand down his face, then stalls with his palm over his mouth. I clutch his free hand.

He finally drops his hand from his mouth. "Maddie's in a coma. It's too early, but... they said her blood pressure was too high. They did a C-section to try to save the baby. But Maddie hasn't woken up from surgery."

He looks at me incredulously. "She's nineteen years old. How does it make sense for her to have high blood pressure?"

I shake my head. "I don't know."

"I need a flight out now." He begins a search on his phone, then growls. "There are no direct flights tonight. I can't even get a connecting flight until our already scheduled one tomorrow evening."

"Let me deal with that. I'll have us in the air within an hour or two at the most," I say.

While Dean drags on clothing and starts throwing our things into our bags, I call my father.

He answers on the first ring. "Bronwyn? What's wrong?"

I shudder. "Hey, Dad."

"Baby? It's the middle of the night. I can't hear you. Are you safe?"

"Yes." I'd forgotten about the time difference. I'm on the opposite side of the country, after all.

I clear my throat. "Dad, I need a private plane out of Las Vegas to New York. Right now. As fast as you can."

There's a beat while the words bounce around in the air between us. Then they land with a crash as he goes straight into rapid-fire interrogation. "Are you safe?" he repeats.

"Yes."

"Are *you* in Las Vegas?"

"Yes."

"Are you in trouble?"

"No." If I were in less of a hurry and more awake, I'd have come up with a better way to break this to him. "I married Dean Priester. But we just found out his little sister is in a coma back in New York. She was pregnant, and they did a C-section, but the baby's too early."

Dad draws in an audible breath, pauses, and seems to recalibrate before saying, "Shhh. It'll be all right."

I'm very much afraid it won't, but I'm not manifesting that energy into the world by saying it out loud.

"Can you get us in the air?"

"I'll take care of it."

• • • ● • ● • • •

The flight home is tense. Neither of us speaks much.

Dad is waiting with a car and driver at the airport. He opens his arms when he sees me, and I rush forward into his familiar embrace.

"Ah, baby. What did you do?"

I don't have the energy to answer him.

"Where are we taking you, Dean?" Dad asks over my head.

I stiffen in my father's arms and pull away. "I'm going with him."

Dad's silver hair glimmers in the overhead lighting. He's wearing his glasses, which he only does when he's tired or putting on his intimidating lawyer persona.

He'd better be tired. Because the absolute last thing I will tolerate is anyone putting Dean through the wringer right now.

Dean's attention rests on me as I stand there with Dad's arm still around my shoulders. He shakes his head slowly. "I'll go straight to the hospital. You go home with your father and catch him up on everything. Get some real rest."

"No." I move away from Dad and pull both of Dean's hands into my own. "I'm going with you."

His hands tighten briefly. "This isn't your problem." He lowers his voice so only I can hear. "You didn't sign up for this. You have to deal with Hallman. I have to—"

"The stuff with Hallman can wait," I say with a scowl. "I have time."

I can't read his expression when he says, "No. That's not part of my plan."

"Plans change."

He shakes his head slowly.

"Why can't I come with you?"

My persistence is clearly making him irritated. This might be the first time I've ever seen him show frustration with me. "We can't build something on top of stress like this. When things are easier, we'll figure it out."

I step back, releasing his hands.

"If you need me for anything or there's any problem with the legal end of things, call me. I'll be there. If there is even a hint of anyone saying fraud, you let me know. When my sister has recovered and life is back to normal, you and I can start over."

I don't want to pretend the last eighteen months didn't count. I don't want to forget about one amazing day and night in Las Vegas when the future stretched out in front of us like an endless sea of joyful possibilities.

"Dean, please let me come with y—"

Dad draws me back against him and holds me tight.

Does he see what I do when I look at Dean? So much pain and doubt and fear hiding behind cold, stoic resolve.

He doesn't. He can't. Because my father's voice is hard as steel and dripping with rage when he says, "I'll get you to the hospital, Priester. And you'll stay away from my daughter."

I turn in his arms. "Dad, no. He's just upse—"

He holds both my shoulders and leans down to look me in the eyes. It's the exact same move and expression he used on me when I was a kid and balked at facing an intimidating opponent in the dojo. "My daughter doesn't beg any man for his trust or affection. You're a McRae." His voice is quiet but intense.

My eyes are hot, and I can't control the muscles in my face.

I nod, and when I turn my head to look at my husband, I've wrestled myself back under control. I square my shoulders and put on the mask. Forcing myself to smile, I say, "Okay, Dean. We'll give each other some space."

The relief that blooms across his features is a blade so sharp that, at first, I barely feel the cut. For a few seconds, I don't even register that my heart is bleeding out onto the pavement beneath my feet.

I step away from Dad and remove my wedding rings. I pull Dean's hand into mine and place the rings on his palm.

For the briefest moment, a flash of something I don't recognize joins the cocktail of emotion behind his eyes. Then his expression shutters and his face goes flat. He closes his hand into a fist with my rings inside.

I kiss his knuckles and say, "We'll keep this weekend quiet for a while and avoid the drama. Need to know only. You can give those back to me when you're ready."

He hesitates, then shoves the rings into his pocket, wraps one arm around my back, and cups my skull with the other hand, holding me against his chest.

His heart pounds beneath my cheek, and my own matches the rhythm in painful longing, until he murmurs, "I'll see you soon."

I nod, and he leans down to speak against my mouth. It's not a kiss; it's a promise. "We signed a contract."

9

Ceilings

BRONWYN

My mind won't let me rest, though my body is exhausted. Besides, I know my parents will be waiting to ambush me with questions the minute I venture downstairs anyway.

My thoughts are consumed with worry about Dean and Maddie and the baby. I texted him about an hour ago, reminding him that if he needed anything to let me know and to ask if there was any news.

He didn't answer my question. He'd simply responded, "Thank you."

After a quick shower, I throw on some comfortable clothing and go downstairs to join my parents in the home office the two of them share.

I tap, then push open the double doors, only to encounter a "family meeting." My parents and both of my older brothers are lying in wait. The only member of what I call "the ruling council" who's missing is Grandmother.

They probably thought she'd be too scandalized—or maybe just too tired—to deal with me.

Gabriel, never one to take anything too seriously, is sprawled in a leather club chair, his light brown hair tousled like he just casually ran his hand through it. I'm well aware that it's the result of a great haircut and judicious use of product.

He has one long trouser-clad leg propped on the other, an ankle resting on the opposite knee. He heaves a dramatic sigh. "I can always count on you to divert parental attention.

You make my little transgressions look like"—he smirks, raising his eyebrows—"little transgressions."

I shake my head at Gabriel, then make eye contact with my parents. "I'm about to tell you some things you aren't going to like. Before I do, you need to know that all of it, every bit, was my idea. Dean is a good guy, and you're going to leave him alone. What he's dealing with right now is a nightmare. If I find out any of you have so much as breathed in his direction, I will never forgive you."

Mom flips her honey-blonde hair over her shoulder and props a hand on her hip. "If he didn't do anything wrong, he doesn't have anything to worry about," she says in an irritated tone.

"If you don't promise to be nice to him, I'm not telling any of you anything."

Dad looks ready to spit nails.

Henry leans back and sits on the edge of the massive desk. He folds his arms across his chest and peers at me through wire-framed glasses like I'm growing in a Petri dish.

I cross my own arms, squish my lips together, and prepare to wait them out.

After approximately fifteen seconds of stubborn silence, my mother caves first. Dad gives in immediately after, as he usually does. And my brothers? They're basically giving me the "Whatever, just stop being stubborn" treatment.

As I expected, they aren't happy to hear about Hallman.

"Wait," Mom says, "so you married the Mellingers' driver so you'd have access to your trust fund because of your grandmother's financial adviser?"

She sounds bewildered, as she should, because it's ridiculous. My dad is going to deal with Hallman before the man even has a clue what hit him. And if he's done anything criminal at all, he's almost definitely going to prison.

Before I can answer, however, Dad speaks up. "No. She used Hallman as an excuse to manipulate the Mellingers' employee into marrying her because she wanted him."

I scowl. "It sounds bad when you say it like that."

Gabriel snorts and mutters over his coffee cup, "That's because it is bad."

"Shut up."

"You started it."

"I did not start it," I growl.

"Knock it off," Mom snaps. "We're talking about your marriage, and the two of you are squabbling like five-year-olds."

She shakes her head. "Please tell me you didn't trick this poor man into marrying you."

"*Trick*," I say defensively, "is an overly aggressive word. He likes me."

Dad takes off his glasses, rubs his eyes, then places them back on his face. "We can get started on the paperwork for an annulment."

"Nope."

He grits his teeth. "A divorce, then."

"Also no. We both signed a prenup, and whichever of us initiates divorce will experience a deliberate financial apocalypse. So forget about my marriage and let's focus on getting the trust straightened out as quickly as possible and getting someone in there to figure out what Hallman has been doing, because he is shady as heck."

The use of "heck" instead of an appropriate swear word is a nod to my father's delicate constitution.

"I can get you out of that contract, one way or another."

"I don't want out of it."

Dad's eyes are wild. "You tried to trap him and caught yourself instead?"

Mom's huff of laughter seems inappropriate in the extreme.

When Dad turns on her with an incredulous expression, she says, "I can't help it. This all sounds a little familiar, doesn't it?"

"That was entirely different."

"How was it different?"

"You were in love with me."

I flinch. Dad would never hurt me on purpose in a million years, but wow. Yeah.

I pull my phone from my pocket to obsess over that last text.

Dean: Thank you

That's it. Nothing else.

Suddenly, I can't stand to be here after Dean shoved me away. I don't want to listen to the judgment or the pity. I need to be where nobody knows what an absolute mess I've made of things.

I push my phone back into my pocket and look up to see, once more, all eyes on me.

"Dad, do I have to be here for the trustee status change or any of the rest?"

His gaze softens. "No. I can take care of it. Baby, I'm sorry this didn't work out the way you'd hoped."

I shrug and force a smile. "Nah. I'm just racking up life lessons, right? But I have things I have to do back at school."

• • • ● • ● • ● • • •

Leaving is my excuse to text Dean one last time.

Me: Are you sure there's nothing I can do? I'm heading back to school. But I can stay. Just say the word.

He leaves me on Read for what feels like forever before he finally replies.

Dean: I'll take you.

Me: You can't leave your sister and niece.

I watch those three dancing dots for a long time until his message comes through.

Dean: Maddie didn't make it. The baby is in the NICU. I want to drive you back to Blackwater.

Oh God.

• • • ● • ● • ● • • •

Henry and Gabriel are long gone when Dean arrives at the gate. I refuse to allow my parents to even greet him.

He kisses my cheek and tosses my bag into the back of his rental car.

"Are you sure you should be driving?" I ask. "You have to be exhausted."

"I'm fine. I have to get my truck and pack up the house in Blackwater anyway."

"I'm so sorry about Maddie."

He gives a tight nod. "Thank you."

I wrap my arms around his middle. He stands there, stiff and unmoving, until something snaps inside him and his arms clench around me in a hold that's almost vicious in its intensity.

It lasts only seconds before he's pulling away and opening the passenger door.

The drive is long and quiet. He's not in the mood to talk, and my usual chatter feels disrespectful and inane under the circumstances. I ask about funeral plans, the baby, if there's anything I can do, then lapse into silence when it becomes clear that he doesn't want to discuss any of it with me.

As we near our interstate exit, I place my hand on his thigh. "Will you let me help with the arrangements?"

He squeezes my hand lightly before he once more grips the steering wheel. "The best thing you can do is take care of yourself so I don't need to worry about you too. I don't want anything from you except that. Let it go. Please."

I draw my hand back into my own lap. "Sorry."

He nods once.

He doesn't take me to my dorm. He takes me to Jack's, around to the empty back lot where my car still sits. How has it been less than forty-eight hours since he told me to get in his truck?

When he cuts the engine, we sit there for a long time. It's started to rain, and the windows fog in the thick humidity of his vehicle. A deluge beats against the windshield. It feels like gunfire. We're safe in here, but the moment I open—

He steps out into it, his door thunking closed behind him. His hair and T-shirt are plastered to him by the time he makes it to my side of the car, cold water running in rivulets down his face. He doesn't brush it aside or shield his eyes.

He bends down to kiss me, and I wrap my fingers in his wet hair, shivering as I pull him to me. But the kiss is no more real than our marriage. Who can kiss and cry and breathe in the rain?

When he backs away and gives me his hand, I take it and force myself to step into the thunderstorm.

"I'll come back for the funeral," I assure him.

His jaw flexes before he says, "I don't want you there."

And now I'm grateful for the rain. I can hide in it.

He's in so much pain. There's no fixing it, I know that, but I could hold him while he grieves. I could make sure he eats and sleeps. I could handle the little things so he can concentrate on the big ones.

But he doesn't want that from me.

How, in the space of one day, did I forget that I'm not a real wife? This was a contract. He even tried to remind me of that at the hotel bar, but I was blinded by what I wanted. And I confused the fact that he was a guy who liked me and wanted to have sex with me with someone who wanted a life with me.

I nod. "If you change your mind, even just want someone to take your mind off it, call me. We don't have to talk about anything shitty if you don't want. Just call, okay?"

Brow furrowed, he gives a jerk of his head that someone, somewhere, might consider a nod.

I walk to my car without looking back. He follows with my bag, and when I hit Unlock on the fob, he opens the passenger door to put my luggage on the floor.

He turns back toward me. "Why do you have a dead plant in here?"

I crane my head around and, sure enough, the poor fern gave up the ghost while sitting neglected on the front seat of my car.

I don't know what killed it. Lack of water? Too cold overnight?

"Hand it here," I say.

He passes me the box. The rain creates a muddy mess, dirt splattering from the pot and all over the front of my jacket and the back of my hand. I walk to the dumpster, lift the lid, and toss the whole thing inside.

10

Going Under

DEAN

I go back to my place in Blackwater long enough to shower, change, and pack up the things I'll need. I contact HR and send slightly more personalized emails to James and Clarissa, though I don't go into specifics.

When my mind tries to veer off track and force images of my sister or the baby into the forefront, I ruthlessly squash them and focus on the practical things I need to accomplish.

The packing. The organizing. There's so much to finish at the house if the baby survives—*when* the baby survives. I need to call my lawyer to make sure she doesn't end up in the foster system.

And I need to deal with Hallman. Concentrating on what I need to do for Bronwyn is practical. It's something I can do right this minute.

Hallman's cybersecurity is shit. I make it into his systems and his low-rent private detective's computers in no time flat. And I don't like what I find.

The photos he has of Bronwyn....

There are even some of the two of us. When I look at them, I don't see how everyone doesn't know how I feel about her. There's a long-distance shot of me walking her to her car after closing at Jack's. I'm slightly behind her, and though I'm not touching her, I'm looking down at her with my hand hovering mere inches from the small of her back, as if I desperately want to do so.

When I find the photos taken by drone through the window of her dorm room when she was undressing and an upskirt shot that appears to have been taken by either a friend or a date, my decision is made.

As far as the finances go, I'm not an accountant. But I do know how to find things people want to hide. And Hallman has been hiding a lot. More than enough to put him in a federal prison.

But he grabbed her. Threatened her and violated her privacy. I'll need to report the breach in our security to our team, as well. After all, Clarissa shares a room with Bronwyn. Hallman didn't have any photos of my client. But the fact is, he could have.

For now, I pick up my phone.

• • • ● • ● • • •

Five hours later, I pull up to the gates at Bronwyn's family estate. The security guard on duty checks my ID, then wands me. When he finds my sidearm and the knife strapped to my calf, he shakes his head and narrows his eyes. I don't even blink in response.

He mutters under his breath and returns to the security booth to speak to, I assume, my father-in-law. He returns and, with a sour expression, opens the gate. "Watch yourself."

A man wearing a suit and an earpiece escorts me to a home office on the ground floor. Arden McRae III is looking out a window at the darkened landscape. His youngest son, Gabriel, is pacing in front of the cold fireplace. Bronwyn's eldest brother, Henry, is leaning against a bookcase cleaning his wire-framed lenses with a soft cloth.

When I enter, he puts the cloth in his pocket and fixes his glasses on his face. Then he waits and watches. None of us say a single word.

I toss a manila envelope full of photos on the desk. Arden strides across the room, picks it up, and looks through it. The only indications he gives of the rage growing inside him are the vein that throbs at his temple and a narrowing of his eyes.

"I didn't include the ones where she's unclothed for obvious reasons. I've scrubbed what I can remotely, but I'm going in to get the hard copies."

"How much do you want?" Arden asks.

"Nothing. I'm telling you because if this were my child, I would want to know."

Henry dips his head to the side and eyes me curiously. The man's features are refined: sharp jawline, cheekbones like cut glass, a divot in his chin. Light brown hair and freckles.

I've been told I look intimidating. Henry McRae doesn't. He looks mild-mannered and professorial. But his eyes say something very different.

"I've seen that prenup," he says. "You're a shady fucker yourself, Priester."

True enough. But I want to make one thing clear. "I don't want her money."

"What *do* you want?"

Every single fucking thing else.

When I don't answer, Gabriel grins. He looks absurdly cheerful under the circumstances. "We're not worried. You'd have an unfortunate accident before it ever got that far."

I shrug my right shoulder. "Fair enough."

Arden's eyes light with something that could be reluctant amusement, but there's no telling if my words have caused his reaction or if he simply really enjoys the idea of killing me.

Finally, he sobers and gives a small shake of his head. "Going in alone? No backup?"

"It won't be a problem."

"Your sister just died. You're emotionally compromised. You could get sloppy."

I want to punch him. To tell him to shut his fucking mouth.

There's no hint of emotion in my voice when I say, "There's a time to mourn and a time to get to work. Soldiers know this."

"Your sister wasn't a soldier."

Images of her in that hospital bed threaten to drag me down. Her last words to me happened in a phone call, and I don't remember exactly what they were. Something about needing a nap. I've tried *so fucking hard* to remember.

"I can't do anything for my sister right now. But I can make sure Bronwyn is safe from any asshole who tries to hurt her or blackmail her. And I don't *get* sloppy."

Gabriel straightens. "We're going with you."

"Hallman is not making it to prison," I warn.

Arden walks to the fireplace, crouches there, and turns on the gas. He drops the envelope with its contents into the flames, then watches as it catches fire with a *whoosh*.

"People like Hallman usually scurry off somewhere with very few consequences at all. Do you know why?" he asks.

"Pressing charges is bad for business," I acknowledge.

He watches as the last of the envelope and its contents are consumed. "That's right. It means admitting that we allowed someone to get the drop on us. It lowers public confidence. If we can't safeguard our own assets, let alone the safety of our family members, how can we do so for our clients?"

I could make excuses. Hallman was slick, no doubt about it. But he's right.

"I don't care about public image," I say.

"You wouldn't," Arden replies, and I can't tell if that's admiration in his tone or if he just thinks I'm an idiot.

He rises and moves to what, at first glance, merely looks like part of the mahogany finish on the wall. He slides it aside, revealing a gun safe, then reaches inside and starts strapping on weapons. He looks at his sons and gives a jerk of his head.

Henry makes his selections, checking the safeties and ammunition. He lifts his head and, with a single raised eyebrow, asks, "Who's driving?"

"I am," I say.

Gabriel smiles. "Shotgun."

• • • ● • ● • ● • •

I drop them back off at the mansion just before sunrise, all of us frustrated as hell. We stand just outside my SUV, and I shove my hands into my pockets.

Kevin Hallman panicked after his trip to Blackwater. Maybe it was Bronwyn's refusal to cower or give in to his demands. Maybe it was my implied threat.

Either way, he was long gone by the time we'd made it to his home and office.

"Without the man himself, there's no way of knowing if we got it all," Gabriel grumbles.

"A USB slipped into a pocket is all it takes," I agree. "I'll try to track him, but his departure was way too fast and efficient for me to think he's left a trail. He's an asshole, but he isn't stupid. He knew what he was doing when he chose to target Bronwyn and her grandmother."

"It might have even been a bit of a thrill. Take on the McRae family while believing he wasn't *really* taking on the whole family. Thinking the women were a weak link. Until he realized that isn't how we operate," Arden says.

I nod. "He didn't count on that seventeen-year-old girl growing into a savvy woman who couldn't be coddled or threatened."

"He's realized his mistake. I doubt he's even still in the country, let alone using his own identity. If he surfaces anywhere, we'll be waiting," Henry says.

I get into my vehicle and close my eyes briefly, forearms on the steering wheel as I try to put myself in the right headspace.

The McRaes have turned to go inside the house when Henry walks back and raps on my passenger window. I lower the glass and look at him with bleary eyes.

He leans down and rests his arms on the door, peering in at me. "When was the last time you slept, Priester?"

I shake my head. I have no idea. My wedding night for about an hour, maybe?

He sighs. "If you think you'll fall asleep behind the wheel, grab a bed here."

"I'm fine."

"I assumed you'd say that. But my conscience is assuaged."

"Who the hell uses the word *assuaged*?"

"Obviously I do. By the way, that offer doesn't mean I like you or ever want to see you near my sister again."

"You're breaking my heart, Henry," I say sarcastically.

My brother-in-law grimaces. "You're managing that just fine on your own."

11
Stick Season
DEAN

I pull a beer from my fridge and pop the top, then move into my living room and lower myself into the big, ugly chair that Maddie always says I should burn.

There's a sense of unreality to the world. For weeks, I've been going through the motions.

My baby sister is gone. But that's just a story someone told me. Her bedroom is still full of her things. Her water glass is still sitting on the end table. It left a ring in the wood because she didn't use a coaster. And then the water in the glass evaporated entirely as it sat there, day after day.

Now it's covered in dust. And I won't touch it.

She's not gone if I don't touch it.

As long as her things are the same, I can function. She's just at work. She'll walk in that door after a long shift, and I'll ask her if she was raised in a barn and remind her to use a coaster next time.

I'm a plate glass window with a chip out of it. I look fine, but tiny cracks are spreading. And little by little, reality is creeping through those fractures.

Every time it does, I patch the crack. I ice it over.

When Bronwyn wrapped her arms around me, I heard the glass creaking, threatening to explode in a shower of jagged pieces that would have ripped us both to shreds.

I can't have her here when I'm like this. Her kindness, alone, would be my undoing.

And still, when I'd told her not to come back for the funeral, the voice inside my head was begging her to say she was my wife and wasn't leaving.

I scrub a hand over my eyes and huff a laugh at the thought. We've never even lived together. Our only real date was our wedding day. And I'm wanting her to fight to stay.

I'm so damn tired that I don't even make sense to myself.

I used to have PTSD nightmares a couple times a month, reliving those days in the desert. But after Maddie died, the dreams changed. Now I can't make it more than a few days without a nightmare.

Phee is holding on. The first time she drank from a bottle after they were able to remove her feeding tube, I wanted to pump my fist and holler in celebration.

Then I remembered that her mother was gone.

How a person can hold joy in one arm and grief in the other is baffling.

I'm also very aware of the burden I'd be placing on Bronwyn if I pulled her into this with me. She'd end up with two choices: martyr herself for me and Phee... or take off in self-preservation.

But I didn't count on how hard it would be to try to go back to who we were before that weekend.

I lean back against the armchair in my dark living room, get comfortable, and open the security camera app on my phone.

I'm not supposed to have access to the cameras I installed at Jack's the week after Maddie passed. It's an invasion of privacy, particularly since Jack doesn't know I can log into his cameras.

I installed them as a favor, but I don't provide security monitoring. I'm not even in a position to offer that service until Jacob and I start our business, which is fine since Jack isn't interested in having anyone monitor his bar, anyway. Understandably so. Two nights ago, I didn't realize that Bronwyn had left work early, and I logged into the new interior cameras during closing hours. I got a view of Jack's pumping ass that I could have happily lived my entire life without seeing. Apparently he *really* likes his new upstairs tenant.

It should have convinced me to mind my own business, but there's no way I'm not staying dialed in as long as Bronwyn is still waitressing there.

Now that I'm home for the night, I'm about to indulge in my favorite pastime: spying on my wife while she's working.

I check inside the bar first, immediately able to spot her in the crowd. Her hair is like a beacon. Tonight, she's got one of those high ponytails that makes me want to wrap it around my fist.

She's smiling at her customers, her dimple on full display. But there are lines of stress near her eyes. She's carrying tension in her shoulders, and I wonder if she needs anything or if that asshole professor, Robard, is still giving her a hard time.

I don't want to think her stress could be because of me. The whole point of staying away from her was to prevent that. But maybe she'd like to talk. It wouldn't hurt to check in with her after her shift.

I click out to the back lot cameras, if only to convince myself that what I'm doing has any legitimate purpose besides feeding my addiction.

What I see there has me pulling up Bronwyn's contact immediately. I dial her number, but she doesn't pick up. Not surprising—Jack's is packed, and she's hustling. If she even heard her phone, she probably didn't bother to see who was calling.

But she needs to pick up.

I don't leave a voice mail. Instead, I start texting her. I'll continue to do so until those alerts drive her crazy. In the meantime, I call Jack.

Me: B. Don't go out back. There are bears out there.

Me: Bronwyn. There's a mama bear out back.

Me: B, LOOK AT YOUR PHONE. THERE ARE BEARS BEHIND THE BAR

Me: BRONWYN

Me: B

Me: BEARS

Me: WOMAN LOOK AT YOUR DAMN TEXTS

Jack picks up with his customary corny "Yell-o."

"Hey, it's Dean. Just checking how those cameras are working out for you."

Me: BRONWYN MCRAE READ YOUR TEXTS.

"Working great, buddy. How you been?" Jack asks.

Me: BEAR. TEXT ME.

"Good, good. Listen, I just wanted to double-check something. Can't remember if I linked up both rear exterior cameras to your app or one. Do you mind taking a look?"

"You got 'em both working just fine."

I grit my teeth before I say, "Thinking I might have set one of them on a temporary schedule. Could you just take a look?"

I watch Jack through my own camera access as he pulls it up. "Sure thing."

He peers at his phone for a moment, then scrubs a hand through his beard. "You know, Dean, that's an interesting coincidence. There's a mama black bear with cubs right there next to the rear exit."

"That is a coincidence. Hey, I got another call coming in. Have a good one."

I hang up just as Bronwyn pulls her phone from her back pocket and starts reading her texts.

Her eyes widen, and then she looks around the bar, as if I'll materialize from thin air.

Me: I told you to text me back.

She startles, then looks around the bar again.

Me: I'm not there. I'm on Long Island.

Her head turns toward Jack as he holds up his phone and makes an announcement to the bar at large.

Bronwyn looks like she's fighting a smile as she looks back at her phone.

My Wife: You'll never believe this, but there's a BEAR behind the bar.

Me: Keep it up. I like your sass.

She bites her thumbnail before she replies.

My Wife: You already told us to check the cameras every time we go out.

Me: Do you remember to do that?

She pulls her ponytail over her shoulder and twirls it around her finger as she texts back with a smirk on her face.

My Wife: I almost sometimes do.

Me: Yeah, I know. Do better.

My Wife: Is this where I say "yes, sir"?

Through the slightly grainy footage, I watch as she fans herself with one hand, then tugs the collar of her T-shirt away from her neck.

I'll be damned.

Me: Does it make you wet to call me sir?

She shoots a furtive glance around the bar before texting back.

My Wife: If it's you, then yes.

It'll only ever be me.

12

Could Have Been Me

BRONWYN

"So he's not working right now?" I ask, setting my margarita on the little table beside me.

Clarissa folds one long leg under the other as we both sit on the sofa in her media room. Janessa is curled in the chair to my right. And Franki is sprawled on the floor with the giant purple "movie-watching" pillow she brought herself and her miniature dachshund, Oliver, who's stretched out on her back like he's a seal sunning himself on a rock.

I'm here at Clarissa's Brooklyn Heights brownstone for some much-needed bonding with my best friends, yes. And, supposedly, we're going to be watching the Keira Knightley version of *Pride & Prejudice* for the five hundredth time.

But now that classes are done and we're back in New York, I'm also dying for an "accidental on purpose" run-in with Dean. Will he act differently in front of others? Or is he going to pretend that I'm still Ms. McRae to him?

I told him I wouldn't say anything to anyone about our marital status until he was ready, and aside from immediate family and the appropriate legal counsel, I haven't. My mother blabbed to my grandparents. So now some of my cousins in Blackwater know, but I tracked them down and swore them to secrecy.

Dean transferred to Clarissa's husband's detail when he came back. But I saw James heading out to some meeting this evening when I arrived, and the guy behind the wheel was not my husband.

"You made me promise not to talk about him even if you begged," Clarissa reminds me.

"I've changed my mind upon reflecting on new information," I say.

She shakes her head. "That's not how it works."

I scowl at her and pull out my phone.

She eyes it suspiciously. "What are you doing?"

"Since you're not going to be helpful, I'm consulting other sources."

"What other sources?"

"I'm texting Dean."

Janessa rolls her eyes. Clarissa and Franki both shout, "No." And Oliver barks at me.

"That number is for business use only," Clarissa says firmly.

I'm not texting his work phone. Was I born yesterday? I'm contacting his personal line. As *if* I'd have even half of the conversations we do on a phone owned by James.

I snort. "And I want to know all about his business. Namely, is he still working or is he on his leave of absence yet."

"This is coercion. You know I'll tell you what you want to know purely so you won't harass my employee."

I lean back and pat my hair into place. "My daddy didn't raise a quitter."

Since the bear incident, Dean and I text a lot. And I was sure he'd said he was scheduled to work tonight.

Janessa narrows her dark eyes at me. "This crush you have on a man who barely even talks to you is getting a little sad. For all you know, he has a wife stashed away somewhere."

I choke on my drink.

Clarissa pats my back and frowns at Janessa, giving her the hand across the throat signal to cut it out. Janessa flips her long brown hair over a tan shoulder. "What? He isn't worth your energy."

I scowl and point a finger at her, then curl it back in. Finally, I mutter, "Yes he is. And just because you're not there when he talks to me doesn't mean he never does. He likes me."

Janessa huffs in disbelief, and I love the girl. I really do. But I also want to pull up one of our wedding pictures and shove it in her face.

Clarissa gives in, clearly reluctant to share but unwilling to listen to us bicker over it. "Dean just started paternity leave."

Franki gasps. "He doesn't just have a wife. He has a wife and child! Bronwyn, you have to leave the guy alone."

Oliver jumps off Franki's back and gives another quick and surprisingly deep bark in solidarity.

I put my hands in the air. "The baby is his niece. He's raising her after her mother died in childbirth, and the birth father didn't want anything to do with her."

There's stunned silence, and then all three of my friends start talking at once. When the chaos dies down, Franki says, "Poor Dean. And that poor baby."

It truly is devastating. I might squabble with my brothers sometimes, but I know beyond a shadow of a doubt that if I lost one of them, I'd never be the same. And Maddie was his baby sister. He felt responsible for her. In many ways, he helped raise her. At least until he left for the Army at the age of eighteen.

Finally, Franki asks, "But how do *you* know this?"

Janessa says, "She probably stalked him."

"He's my friend, and he told me. Tell me again why you and *I* are friends?" I demand.

"Because if you did stalk him, I'd be your alibi. And if you ever call me in trouble, I'll bring the rope and shovel."

"That's so sweet, " I admit.

Franki lifts onto her elbows and says, "I think you have a very warped perception of sweet."

I shrug. Maybe she's right. When I realized Dean was spying on me at the bar, I should have been infuriated. Instead, I got a full-on case of the warm fuzzies.

I focus on what this paternity leave means for Dean. "His niece must be out of the hospital and home now."

"That makes sense," Clarissa says.

"I should take him a baby gift," I say.

Another cacophony of shouted "no's" pelts me from every direction.

"Why not?"

Clarissa is the only one who knows I went away with Dean for that weekend in April, though she doesn't know I came back a married woman. She reaches out and gently squeezes my hand. "Maybe he needs space."

Janessa tosses the throw pillow she's been hugging onto the floor and stands with her hands on her hips. "You know what we need?"

We all look at her expectantly.

"We need," she says with raised eyebrows, "a girls' trip. Get out of the city. Hell, let's get out of this country."

Franki nods. "It's a good idea. Clarissa's hardly been anywhere. And you need to get away from your obsession, Bronwyn. We'll tour Europe. Let's go have fun!"

"You'll have to count me out this time," I say.

Clarissa shakes her head. "No. It has to be all of us."

I can't go. If Dean is home on paternity leave, he probably really needs some help right now. When my cousin Marie had her kids, she was exhausted. I babysat just so she and her husband could sleep a little. I can do that for him.

I know he said not to visit, but I won't be making things harder. I'll help. "I can't go to Europe. I have to get everything straightened out with my new property managers and financial adviser."

Janessa says, "I can't believe all that crap Kevin Hallman pulled. And then to just disappear so he didn't go to prison? Can you even imagine how long it could have gone on if you hadn't realized he was up to something?"

"I wish they'd caught him, though," I say.

Franki shifts and runs a hand down Oliver's back. "I'll bet he rues the day he crossed you."

I squish Franki's cheeks, careful not to hurt her. "You are so freaking cute. I hope Hallman rues the day."

She nods, her cheeks still squashed under my palms. "I'm sure he does."

"I hope he's on a beach somewhere and not plotting revenge. Deirdre said he was really scary at the bar that night," Clarissa says worriedly.

I sigh and release Franki's face. "Nah. He's scurried off. We'll never see him again."

"I don't know," Janessa muses. "The man was just one giant ego. He's going to be looking for someone to blame for his scheme falling apart."

I shudder. "I hope you're wrong."

"Are you sure you can't come with us?" Franki wheedles.

"Europe won't be the same without you. It has to be the four of us," Janessa says.

"If I can't make it, I'll be there in spirit. You can FaceTime me every single day. Five times a day."

I pass Clarissa her margarita and lift my own glass. "To Kevin Hallman ruing the day."

Clarissa lifts hers. "To the best friends anyone has ever had."

"Now I need to change my toast. Yours was too nice," I say.

They laugh, and I clear my throat and lift my glass again. "To the friends who pretended they spilled water on me in second grade so Jolene Harding didn't figure out I peed my pants. You girls are the real deal."

We all cackle like hyenas. Then Franki lifts her glass. "To friends I'd trust with my life."

Janessa points at me and Clarissa. "But not my tequila."

My laughter is a little guilty. I've kept a lot of secrets from them over the years, mostly about my family. But this feels different and somehow weirdly personal. They already don't approve of what they think is my "crush" on Dean. I can just imagine what they'd say if they knew I not only slept with the man but *married* him, then was ditched by him the same weekend.

13

In A Perfect World

DEAN

It's three o'clock on a Thursday afternoon. Phee will start screaming again in approximately three hours if my calculations are correct. For now, she's blessedly asleep in her crib.

Her pediatrician says she has an "immature nervous system." All I know is she doesn't sleep for more than a few hours at a time, tops. Has to be fed just as often. And she screams bloody murder if she's awake and not being fed or carried around.

I'd throw myself in front of a train for Phee, if necessary.

But I also feel like some kind of medical experiment. Sleep deprivation is a literal torture tactic, and I can see why.

My texts with Bronwyn feel like I'm another person in another world.

There's the shitty world where my sister is gone and I'm a jackass.

And then there's the person I used to be. Our texts make me feel like I'm still that man. The one who smiled and almost danced.

But when I put down the phone, that man no longer exists. I'm lying. Showing Bronwyn who I would have been for her, not who I am.

I close my eyes on a long blink.

I wake half an hour later, still sitting in the same position, when my phone vibrates on my thigh. It's Bronwyn texting. But it's not our usual flirty banter.

My Wife: Open your front door

My pulse kicks up before I realize what a bad idea this is.

I haven't had a shower in two days. I sniff-test my pits and my breath. *Dammit.*

My phone vibrates again.

My Wife: I didn't want to ring the doorbell in case the baby was sleeping

I lunge out of my chair, absently rub my aching shoulder, and throw open the door.

She's standing there smiling, a gift bag slung over one arm and some kind of food in an insulated carrier held in both hands.

For a moment, I just stare at her, absorbing the sight. She's wearing navy high-waisted shorts with buttons on the front like a sailor, wedge-heeled sandals, and a kind of short, wide-necked sweater that hangs off one shoulder. Her collarbones show, and they're as sexy as her smooth, toned legs.

I've well and truly lost it if I'm standing here in a spit-up-covered T-shirt, gym shorts, and two days of scruff on my face, pining for this woman's collarbones.

"Heeey, Dean."

A little knot unwinds inside me. I clear my dusty throat. "Hey, Bronwyn."

She holds the carrier a little higher. "Can I come in?"

I look back inside, then say, "It's a mess in here."

She shrugs. "Not here to see your house, big guy. I'm here to see you."

I'm a mess in here too.

I'm almost surprised by the amusement I feel at the thought. But just standing here with her changes me on the inside.

She sighs happily. "There it is."

"What?"

She shakes her head with a smile and says, "My hands are full. Kiss me hello."

I bend at the waist, give her a quick peck, then take the dish from her and back away.

Phee's asleep. I can spend time with Bronwyn for a couple of hours if the baby doesn't wake up early. I take the insulated bag to the kitchen and set it on the counter as she kicks off her shoes by the front door and follows me.

I shoot a furtive look around at the general clutter, which I'm normally on top of, and at how cheap this whole place must look to her.

But when I glance back at her, she's not even looking at my kitchen. She's looking at me.

I get caught in her pale blue gaze for a long moment, then glance back down at the dish. "What's this? It smells like an Italian restaurant."

"Stuffed shells. They keep really well. If you don't finish these, you can freeze them."

I open the bag and lift the lid.

She winks at me. "I have exactly three dishes I know how to cook, and they all involve pasta and cheese."

"Wait... you made this yourself?"

"Yes, but in case this makes you suddenly think I'm a domestic goddess, the other two recipes have the exact same ingredients. The only difference is the pasta itself and whether I stuff it, layer it, or stir it all together with a spoon."

"You're a pasta and cheese specialist. Own it."

She smiles, and I'm struck stupid by how sweet she is. "Thank you. I've ordered more takeout than I care to admit since Phee came home from the hospital."

She beams at me.

"Are you staying to share it?" I ask. "Phee is probably going to sleep for a little while, yet."

"I would love to."

I'm uncomfortably aware of the picture I present. "Would it be okay if I keep this warm in the oven and take a quick shower first?"

"I wish you would," she says.

I snort. "That bad?"

"That is not what I meant. I just want you to do whatever you need to."

I turn on the oven and slide the glass dish inside. "Can I get you anything first?" I open the fridge. "I have water or—" *Shit.* "Unless you're in the mood for baby formula, it's water."

"Not a big fan of baby formula myself." She sticks her tongue out in disgust.

As I fill a glass with ice and filtered water, a thought strikes me. "How did you know where I live?"

She takes a sip before she says, "I'm sure you must have mentioned it."

"I'm sure I didn't. Even the care package you gave Maddie came through me. You didn't mail it."

She mumbles something under her breath.

"Say that again." Now I'm just teasing her, because I heard her loud and clear. "You did what now?"

She makes her confession in a rush. "You had mail in your house in Blackwater with your permanent address on it. And I accidentally saw it and accidentally memorized it."

I laugh. Out loud. "You little snoop. That mail was in a drawer. Are you stalking me?"

She clears her throat, then says delicately, "I'm not spying on you. I just like to know where you are and what you're doing at all times."

That sobers me a little, though I know she meant it as a joke. Because I *have* been spying on her.

"Give me your phone."

When I raise my eyebrows, she passes it over with an intrigued expression. She smirks a little when I type in her security code without asking her for the number.

We both know she once told Clarissa her passcode in my hearing.

When I'd scolded her later—"Ms. McRae, you shouldn't tell other people your security codes"—she'd rolled her eyes.

"I didn't tell other people. I told Clarissa and you. You want to poke around in my phone, handsome? Go right ahead. All you're going to find are the pictures I take of your ass and texts telling everyone that you're the love of my life."

It was hard to remember not to smile. Somehow I'd managed it and reminded her that we had a professional relationship.

But when she left her phone in the back seat of Clarissa's car that very same day, I did "poke around" in it. I didn't read her texts, emails, or look at her photos. But I did put a location tracker on it so I know where she is all the time.

I told myself it was so if anything happened to her, I'd be able to find her. I enabled crash detection too.

But she's back living with her parents for the summer, and I'm still checking the thing a couple times a day.

When I gave her back her missing phone that day, she narrowed her eyes playfully and said, "Well? Did you poke around in it?"

I looked her straight in the eye and said, "Yes, ma'am. There's a tracker on it now. If you lose it again, let me know. I'll find it for you."

She gave me a slow smile and said, "I already have Find My Phone."

"Then consider it insurance."

"Did you look at my pictures?"

"No, Ms. McRae. I did not."

She winked. "That's too bad, Dean. There was a surprise in there for you."

She clears her throat, and I glance up at her as she watches me curiously.

I nod down at her phone. "Do you realize you have 189 unread text messages?"

Her expression goes blank, and then she gives a sheepish lift of her shoulder. "It's just ads from stores. That kind of thing."

"Not judging here. Just curious."

"I open your texts."

I smile a little and pull out my own phone.

"What are you doing?" she asks.

"I'm connecting us so you always know where I am."

Her mouth falls open.

"There. Now I can always find you, and you can always find me. In case of an emergency."

She takes her phone back and looks at the icon with disbelief. When she taps it, a map shows with both of our dots overlapping. I labeled my dot "Husband" so she doesn't forget me while I'm busy getting things under control here.

"Am I allowed to know where you are? Because of your job?"

"If I'm on duty and security is an issue, all I have to do is temporarily disable it." I show her how to turn it off.

"It shows battery life too, so if you forget to charge your phone, I'll remind you." I say it as though I'm teasing her. I'm not. It's been driving me insane to see how she forgets to charge it. But since she likely didn't realize I was actually using the app for more than the purpose of finding a lost phone, I could hardly text with a reminder to "charge your phone."

She sniffs. "You may remind me if you don't do it in a judgmental tone."

"I would never do that." *Does she think I don't realize that she has ADHD and routine tasks are harder for her to remember?* Probably. She never talks about it with anyone, and I'm not about to try to force that conversation. She'll tell me when she trusts me enough to do so.

"So it's basically like Find My Phone?"

"If Find My Phone had Crash Detection Alerts and a messaging system on it. Most of these apps work off the same principles. This one automatically disables tracking if your battery drops below 6 percent in order to preserve function of the device. Some others disable tracking at 10 percent battery life."

When I hand her phone back, she moves closer to hug me, and I back away with a hand up. "I can't wait to get a hold of you, but I need that shower."

"I don't care."

"You will once you try to snuggle up against me. Give me ten minutes."

I leave her sitting in the living room, dinner in the oven, and take the fastest shower of my life. Then I head to my bedroom, shut the door, and throw on a new pair of gym shorts and a T-shirt before stripping the bedding. After I've replaced the sheets and pillowcases, I look around to make sure I haven't missed anything.

This room is mostly clean. There's a basket with some laundry in the corner, which I shove in the closet. Cleaning my bedroom was probably wishful thinking, but if she wants to come in here after dinner, I don't want to be caught with laundry in the corner.

When I walk back into the living room, those concerns fly straight out of my mind.

She's pulled the casserole dish from the oven and set my small dining room table. It's not fancy. There's no candlelight or wine, just my plain white dishes and some water glasses. I don't even own fancy napkins, so she's folded paper towels under our forks.

She moves to stand by the table, barefoot with her hands clasped a little nervously in front of her.

I pull her chair out for her, and she sits, one leg tucked beneath her, and reaches for her fork.

She watches me intently until I've taken my first bite, then relaxes at the look on my face.

"This is incredible," I say.

"I hoped you'd like it."

I finish the bite I'd already shoveled into my mouth. "Who doesn't like Italian food?"

She chews her lip. "You never know. I've heard there are even people who don't like chocolate."

I freeze for a moment, then rally. "Really? What kind of weirdo doesn't like chocolate?" I take a quick drink of water.

She lifts her hand. "No accounting for individual taste, I guess."

"Talk to me about the trust fund situation," I say and dig in to my meal.

She talks as I listen and eat.

When she's done explaining how she chose her new adviser, she shudders. "Kevin Hallman is such a toad. I can't believe he had photos of me. It feels so violating."

I frown. I wasn't the one who told her about those photos. If it were up to me, she'd never have known about any of it.

She sighs. "It's probably good that he skipped town. If he were still here, my dad would have—" Her eyes go wide, and she swallows. "He would have... been *concerned* about it."

I nod. "It's good that you have a father who feels concern for you."

"Right."

She's too fucking cute. "I *know* about your father, B."

Marcus Harcourt had shared information with me when I started working for him. Approximately sixteen years ago, Arden was the prosecuting attorney for a case against the head of a New York crime syndicate. When Arden couldn't be bought or threatened, the syndicate came after Arden's family.

My father-in-law didn't cower or hide his family in WITSEC. He's a McRae with all the money and resources that entails. Instead, he built his own army and systematically eliminated every member of the syndicate until there was no one left to challenge him.

Marcus liked Bronwyn's father. More importantly, he trusted him and looked at the man's reputation as another layer of security for Clarissa.

Bronwyn goes rigid, her fork suddenly resembling a weapon more than an eating utensil. "Did he or my brothers threaten you?"

"No."

She relaxes, then immediately tenses again, leaning forward. "Did they have someone else threaten you?"

I reach out and put my hand over hers, coaxing her to release her weapon of tined destruction. "No one threatened me, angel."

My in-laws and I have an understanding. I don't betray, hurt, or traumatize my wife. They don't bust my kneecaps or arrange for an accident. It's a perfectly reasonable agreement.

"If anyone does, you tell me."

I can picture it now: me running to Bronwyn to tattle on her big, mean father and brothers.

She pauses, concern in her gaze. "How are you holding up? You must miss your sister horribly."

I grunt. "I'm fine."

Another pause. "What's the stay-at-home-dad life like?"

"Phee and I are still adjusting."

"Anything I can help with?"

Ha. "No."

After a moment of silence, she nods at my now-empty plate. "Do you want seconds?"

I shake my head, holding eye contact and pushing my chair away from the table.

She gives me a slow smile and tilts her head to the side. "Did you miss me, Dean?"

"Yes."

"We've been married for six weeks, and we've made love once," she says.

"It's a travesty.," I agree.

Sex with each other or not at all. That's the rule in our prenup. I wouldn't have been sleeping with anyone else, regardless. I haven't even looked at another woman with a hint of interest from the first moment I laid eyes on her.

I have just enough time to brace before she jumps into my lap and wraps around me like a monkey.

It's hard to kiss and smile at the same time. We keep bumping our teeth together. I fill each of my hands with a plump ass cheek, stand, and carry her to my bedroom.

Kicking the door shut, I cross the room and lower her to the center of the bed. She gives me a saucy smirk and wiggles out of her sweater. Today's bra is a combination of completely sheer fabric and ivory straps that crisscross, barely covering her pretty pink nipples. It's somehow both demure and raunchy. My girl likes her lingerie. The sight of it has my already-hard cock almost painful with arousal.

She tugs at my waistband, and I rise to my knees to remove my shorts. She starts to take off her own, then freezes as her attention snags on something behind me.

Suddenly, she's on her knees, too, curiosity firing behind her eyes. She points at the wall. "What is that for?"

I don't have to turn around to know what she's talking about. In my rush to clean up in here, I didn't even think about what the walls look like. They're covered in sound-dampening foam panels, similar to what you might see in a recording booth.

"It's so I don't wake up the baby if I get too loud."

It took me dragging myself out of two of my nightmares to the sound of her screaming to realize I was probably yelling in my sleep. I'm surprised the neighbors have never called the cops, frankly.

So I'd slapped the panels on the wall, and it's working fine.

"Who are you bringing in here that you're worried about getting loud with?" she demands.

I'm not about to start discussing my nightmares right now. Talk about a mood-killer. "You're *jealous*?"

"Why is that funny to you?" She crosses her arms under her breasts, plumping them up into two perfect pale globes.

She drops her arms and snaps her fingers under my nose. "Stop looking at my boobs when I'm mad."

I turn my attention from her gorgeous tits to her face. She is definitely pissed. "I promised you I wouldn't be with anyone else, and I meant it. I'm a married man."

Her suspicion softens into confusion. Then her eyes light on the instrument in the corner.

"*Oh*. Your guitar." She smiles a little sheepishly. "Did I act like a hag for no good reason?"

This woman. "You acted possessive. I liked it."

"You're nuts."

"You like me anyway."

She presses her body against mine and wraps her arms around my neck. "I like you *because*, not *anyway*. And for the record, I consider myself a married woman. Even if we are weird."

If I wanted to lie to myself, I'd call the feeling running through me right now satisfaction. But it's relief, pure and simple.

I drag my fingertips lightly over the curve of her ass and up her back. When I hit her bra, I flick the catch open. She pulls her arms through the straps.

"Does this mean I'm allowed to look at your breasts again?"

She laughs. "Yes."

I drag the cups away and toss the bra. My mouth waters when her nipples are finally revealed.

She puts her palms on my face. "I went to the doctor and got an IUD. If you want to skip the condoms...."

My eyes fly wide, and I nod enthusiastically. "Fuck yes, I want."

She reaches to draw the zipper at her hip down, then slides out of the shorts and thong at the same time.

I finish yanking off my own clothing, my cock bobbing between us. I breathe in the scent of her as I lay her down. She's floral and feminine and turned-on woman. Bronwyn's clit pulses beneath my fingertips, her gorgeous pussy slippery and swollen.

I want to lose myself inside her. Inside my *wife*.

I'm playing with fire by letting her in this house and bringing her into my bed. I'm pushing the limits of what I'd decided we were "supposed to do" while my life is still such a chaotic disaster.

I don't give one single fuck.
I am happy to burn.

14
I See You
BRONWYN

I gently push him backward and work my way down his chest and abs, trailing wet kisses as I go. I've barely taken the hard length of him into my hand and licked a stripe up and over his cock, barely even begun to close my mouth over him, when he's pulling me up and under him.

"We don't have time," he mutters.

My thoughts scatter into the ether as he props one forearm beside my head and uses his other hand to work me toward an orgasm. His thumb circles my clit, and he fits first one, then two fingers inside me, scissoring them to stretch me.

He watches me as I ramp up higher and higher. His hazel gaze is hooded, but his attention is laser focused.

Breathing hard, I thrust up in time with his movements and lift a hand to his face. "I need you."

He turns his head to kiss my palm, then rests his forehead lightly against my own. "Let me play a little first, angel. I have to get you ready."

I nod, and he kisses my temple. "How many?"

"I... what?"

"How many times do you want to come before I fuck you? Give me a number."

I can't think beyond his hands on me, his hard body against mine. The smell of him. The feel of silken skin over toned muscle.

"B?"

"Once. Don't make me wait for more than that."

He groans as my clit pulses beneath his thumb and I flutter around his fingers. "That's it. Almost there."

He keeps going, leaning down to nuzzle my neck. The tension builds higher. Higher.

I bite my lip and punch down against the mattress with my free hand.

"That's my angel. Come for me. Give it to me." His voice is a rumble against my skin.

My body clamps down on his fingers, spasms of electric pleasure tearing through me until I've lost the ability to think or speak.

I'm still shaking when he pulls his fingers from my pussy, sucks them into his mouth with a barely audible groan, then fits the head of his cock to my entrance.

He doesn't plunge inside the way I expect him to. He pauses right there, pressed against me but not pushing forward. "Are you sure?"

This is just one of the reasons I'm obsessed with this man. It's that core of honor and gentleness and kindness behind his stoic facade.

He's horny as hell, but he's waiting for me. Double-checking that I'm all right without a condom.

"Yes. *Please*."

He eases into me, an inch at a time, and we groan together. He fills me so completely that everything else falls away. There's only Dean inside me.

He stills, waiting for me to start moving, to give him a sign I'm ready for more.

I'm not yet. Not quite.

He tips my chin up. "Kiss."

I do. His jaw is square and rugged, his body huge and hard. But his lips are plush, and his kiss is decadent. Sensual.

I feel owned and I love it. When I push up against him, encouraging him to move, he does.

He drops his head onto the mattress beside me and groans.

I meet his rhythm. We're loud, the sound of our bodies slapping together in time. His bed creaks. But it doesn't matter.

I lift my head and lick a path across his collarbone. His rhythm doesn't falter for even a moment, but he lifts his upper body just enough to look down at my face. He smiles and huffs out a breathless laugh.

Then he drags his open mouth over my own collarbone before working his way up to kiss and suck at my neck.

"Perfect," he mutters against my skin. "You are so damn perfect."

He shifts a little, obviously adjusting to take pressure off his left shoulder.

I squirm and push at him with a smile, and he rolls off me, his expression intrigued.

"Lie on your right side," I say.

He rolls into position, and I fit myself against him face-to-face, lifting my left leg over his thigh.

"Mmm." He props his right arm under my head and slides his cock home.

I wrap my arms around his neck and hold on as we move together. He grabs my butt and squeezes, guiding me with it. Our movements are slower and gentler. And when I orgasm this time, it's gentler too.

When he comes, the arm beneath my head flexes, and he moves his hand up to cradle my nape in the palm of his hand.

We lie like that for a long time, still connected. He doesn't have to rush off to clean up a condom this time. He stays, just holding me against him.

I lie there, feeling sated and cherished, as he runs his fingers lightly up and down my back.

Eventually his cock softens, and we're no longer entwined. His arms are still around me, but they're looser, his breaths deeper and slower.

A glance at his face shows me exactly what I expect to see.

Dean has fallen asleep, and I'm glad. He looked so completely exhausted when he opened that door. Even his color wasn't quite right.

He needs rest, and I'm going to make sure he gets it.

I'm going to take care of him and Phee, and he'll see we don't need to wait to be together.

I'm careful and slow as I slide out of his bed, lifting his arm and ducking beneath it.

Grabbing a folded comforter on top of his dresser, I arrange it over him carefully. He doesn't react at all, sleeping so heavily that he doesn't even twitch.

His phone and the baby monitor are both on the nightstand right beside him. If either one makes a sound, he'll be awake in an instant.

I grab them both, then pick my clothing up off the floor. I carry my bundle into the bathroom in the hallway and clean up as quietly and quickly as possible.

After putting the leftovers in the fridge for later, I get to work in his kitchen, washing dishes. His house isn't dirty at all, so it doesn't take me long. Then I move into the living room, where a basket of clean laundry needs to be folded. They're all Phee's things, and my heart squeezes at the cuteness. Teeny tiny little onesies and cotton pants. Pajamas and thin blankets and burp cloths.

I try to picture giant Dean with his big, calloused hands, folding an itty-bitty T-shirt. Better yet, holding Phee wearing that T-shirt. *Gah! So sweet!*

I find a glass that I missed earlier, so I gather it up and make quick work of it. Then I search for something to use to dust. I'm no sooner done with that and finished washing my hands when I hear a rustling, then the very distinct newborn cry coming through the monitor.

I hustle down the hallway, hoping Dean's soundproofing works both ways. When I peer in and get my first look at Phee, my heart melts into a puddle. She's smaller than Marie's babies were at this age, but she looks healthy. Her little face is red as she hollers and kicks inside her swaddle sleeper.

She has an apnea monitor, and it takes me a hot second to figure out what it is and how to use it. I'll have to be careful to remember to turn it back on when I get her back to sleep.

I pick her up gently and carry her to the changing table. When I unswaddle her, she does the most freaking adorable little stretch I've ever seen in my life and briefly stops crying to peer up at me.

I smile at her and kiss her little fist as she waves it around, then change her diaper. She's already fussing again before I've managed to get her back into her yellow cotton one-piece.

"Oh, I know. You're starving, aren't you?" I soothe, cradling her in my arm, careful to support her head. "Let's go find you a bottle."

Dean is an organized guy, and I can easily see his routine. He already has bottles prepared. They only need to be warmed up in the machine he keeps on the counter for that purpose.

While the bottle warms, I sway with her and sing the handful of baby songs I know. Jack's son, Little Max, always liked the "Apples and Bananas" song. Phee isn't sure what she thinks. She routinely stops squalling to look at me with intense navy-colored eyes before she starts up again. Luckily, it doesn't take long to get her bottle ready.

When I've tested the temperature, I tease her little rosebud mouth with the nipple and laugh when she attacks it like she's been starved to within an inch of her life.

I sit down on the sofa with her while she drinks, looking up at me with wide eyes.

She is the sweetest thing. Her hair is so fine and pale that she looks bald at first glance. Her eyes are huge, and her nose is the cutest little squish.

I'm not sure at her stage of development how well she sees. Marie said something about newborns only being able to see at very close distances. And though she was born six weeks ago, developmentally, she seems younger, probably because of her preemie status.

She smells like a combination of baby shampoo, formula (which frankly smells gross), and some distinct scent that I swear nature gives tiny humans specifically so adults become obsessed with the desire to cuddle and care for them.

When she finishes the bottle, she's already beginning to drift off. I lift her to my shoulder and burp her carefully. When she does, she spits a mouthful of formula vomit all over me; it runs straight under my sweater and down my back.

I snort. "My bad, baby girl. I forgot to use a burp cloth."

She coos and burrows into me.

There, now. That wasn't so hard.

I carry her back to her crib, but the second I try to swaddle her and lay her back down, she kicks and screams in outrage.

"Okay, okay. How dare I try to lay a sleeping baby down?" I tease her.

She stops crying the moment I pick her back up.

"I have to change my shirt, but my things are still in my car. With my luck, I'd end up locking us both outside if I went out to get something, so I'm going to have to find something of Uncle Dean's."

It's easy enough to see that Phee's nursery was also Maddie's bedroom. Aside from the addition of baby items, it doesn't seem like anything has been changed. Even her Kindle is still sitting on the bedside table, the case covered in stickers.

I'm certain she has clothing in the closet here, but I'm not touching that. It feels too intrusive.

Phee's fallen asleep again on my shoulder, but the moment I attempt to lay her horizontal, she flails and whimpers.

"All right. I got you."

I hold her until she's limp once more, then, keeping her snuggled against me, carefully open Dean's bedroom door.

He hasn't moved a single inch.

Tiptoeing to his dresser, I hit pay dirt immediately, finding rows of T-shirts neatly organized in the top drawer. Internally, I chuckle at the sight. He has them rolled, not folded, and color-coded: white on the left, gray and navy in the middle, and black on the right.

Someday, I'm buying him a red or yellow shirt, just to watch him scramble to figure out where to put it.

I creep back out of his room with a gray T-shirt clamped in my free hand.

We spend the evening with me walking her, singing to her, feeding her, and basically ceasing to exist as anything except her personal handmaiden.

She yaks formula all over herself at one point when I don't manage to burp her as thoroughly as I thought I did. Later, she has a diaper that explodes up her back and makes me gag through tears of laughter. So freaking gross.

She has a little bathtub that fits in the big tub, and after the diaper situation, a bath is definitely required.

By eleven o'clock, I fully understand why Dean looked so completely wiped out when he answered the door. Little Miss is demanding.

She's settled after I clean her up, and once she's fallen asleep, she allows me to lay her in her crib. I hover over her and go online on my phone to make sure I've got the apnea monitor working correctly, then wash her laundry. She wakes up again about two hours later. And on and on it goes. I end up sleeping on Maddie's bed so I'm next to the crib.

There's not a peep from Dean's bedroom. I check on him a few more times, but he's basically dead to the world.

• • • ● • ● • ● • •

At 7:00 a.m., I'm sitting cross-legged on the sofa with Phee sleeping on my lap when his bedroom door opens. He sounds like he's in a hurry coming down the hall. He pauses at Phee's doorway, and when he doesn't find her there, he says, "Bronwyn."

I look up just as he stomps into the living room and looms over us like some gladiator ready for war.

He's disheveled, but his color is better, and some of those lines that were bracketing his mouth have eased.

"You look better," I say.

"You don't. Did you sleep at all?"

I clear my throat. "A little."

"Where are the baby monitor and my phone?"

I nod toward the end table. "There. I didn't want to wake you. I used Maddie's bed when Phee slept so I'd be near her."

He freezes. Then he swallows. "You slept in my sister's bed?"

"I... yes. I didn't think that would be a problem. I wanted to be near Phee if she needed me."

"I didn't ask you for any of this." He lifts Phee into his arms and begins to pace. "You shouldn't have taken the monitor or my phone. You shouldn't have let me sleep."

"You were tired. I didn't mind taking care of her."

"*I* mind."

I lift my hands helplessly. "Why?"

"Because I have two lives. I have responsibilities and things I have to take care of. And I have you. You're separate."

"I don't understand what you're saying." I stand beside him, and he stops moving to scowl down at me.

"You're the bright spot in my day, Bronwyn. Every day."

Before the warm feeling that engenders takes root, he rips it away. "I can't have you here. Not yet. You're—"

He stands arrested, his attention on the end table. I'd already told him the baby monitor was there, so I'm not certain what he's looking at.

Then he glances around the room and into the kitchen.

He screws his eyes closed and speaks through gritted teeth. "You cleaned up in here too."

"Yes."

He looks like I stabbed him in the heart. "I need you to go. Now. I'm glad you stopped by. I want to spend more time with you. I'll find a regular babysitter. We can get a hotel room, just the two of us, as often as I can manage. But not here."

"I'm...." I'm not a "hit it and quit it," but I am a fuck buddy. One who doesn't deserve a real place in his life.

What did he say? He has two lives.

Phee is his real life, and I'm his night out away from it all. She's his home, and I'm his vacation rental.

I force myself to smile as I reach for my bag and phone. "Phee puked on my sweater. I'll have to get your shirt back to you another time."

He jerks his head. "Keep it. I like knowing you have it."

"Sure. Okay." I'm sliding the strap through the buckle on my sandals, anxious now to leave before I embarrass myself.

"I'll find someone to watch her soon. I already have an agency lined up for when I go back to work. We could see each other again in maybe three days? We could have dinner," he says.

"Dinner and an hour in a hotel room?" I ask.

He doesn't answer, just watches me warily.

I can hear my father's voice in my head. My grandmother's. *"Remember you're a McRae."*

I smile. Hard. "That sounds amazing, but I actually promised my friends I'd do Europe with them this summer. You know how it is. Girls wanting to have fun."

His jaw flexes before he says, "Yes, I know all about that."

"Great."

He drops a kiss on my temple. "The calendar reset when you spent the night here, but don't be gone too long."

The cohabitation clause in our prenup. Of course.

"No worries, Dean. I'm not about to violate our *contract*."

15
You Don't Know

DEAN

Bronwyn pulls away and gives me a smile. Then she's gone, and I'm standing here with Phee in my arms wishing she'd walk back in and say, *"Forget it. You can't make me go. You need me."*

And if she did that, she'd be right.

The door remains stubbornly closed. And the fractures inside me spread.

When I saw what she'd done.... It was a stupid water glass. I should have cleaned it up the same weekend Maddie passed.

It was pure sentimentality, the way I couldn't stand to move or change any of her things.

Then in one single night, Bronwyn swept in and...

She stripped the sheets from Maddie's bed. When I'd looked in the room, there was different bedding entirely. She slept in her bed. She cleaned off her nightstand and put her things away.

The water glass was the last straw. Except what was I supposed to say? *"How dare you wash a water glass?"*

She didn't even know what she'd done.

The pressure in my chest breaks loose in a spasm of agony that shakes my whole body.

I knew Bronwyn was going to do this to me.

I need to stay numb.

But Bronwyn didn't just crack the glass of my composure. She took a sledgehammer to it.

Phee in one arm, I grind my other palm against my eye socket.

The sound that tears out of me is one of a wounded animal. It startles Phee awake, and she whimpers. I try to stop the jerking spasms racking my body and shut my mouth.

Shove it down. Shove it back.

But I can't.

"Be a man." That's what my father always said. Being a man meant shove your shit down until it gave you a heart attack at fifty.

I turn my back to the door and slide down to sit on the floor.

Phee begins to wail in earnest, and I rub her back. "Shhh. Don't—"

I drop my head against the door, and I stop fighting it. Because it's unbearable, and I can't do it anymore.

Phee cries with me, and, in this moment, it almost feels right. Because she lost her mother. A mother who would have cherished her. Adored her.

And that's worth crying over.

Maddie deserves these tears. Phee deserves them. So do I.

I can never let Bronwyn see me like this.

She thinks I'm strong.

Before deployment, I stood in a line while my commanding officer barked, "Look left."

I'd done as ordered and gotten an eyeful of the back of Ramone Vasquez's head.

"Look right," he ordered.

I turned toward Jacob Turner.

Expression grim, he continued, "One in three of you are going to die. Those are the numbers. Make peace with it."

But it was supposed to be me. *It was okay if it was me.*

Now I can't even face my own death without fear. Because what would happen to Phee if I weren't here?

I stay where I am until I'm sweaty and wrung out.

Phee eventually settles, and I lift my knees, feet flat to the floor, to give her an incline to rest on.

"We're going to be okay, kid."

She sucks on her bottom lip, and her eyes drift shut. I rest my head back against the door once more.

And when I finally haul myself up, I start to pack Maddie's things. Over the next week, I go through it all, saving anything I think Phee might want someday and keeping a few sentimental items for myself. Then I donate everything that can be donated and throw away what can't or isn't worth saving.

Maddie is dead.

It's raw and real and in-fucking-escapable, no matter how much it hurts. There is nowhere to hide from it. Not even in my sleep.

This isn't like our mother and father— here, then gone, then back again.

Subconsciously, I'd been waiting to be told it was all a mistake.

I'd been living in denial and shock. I didn't believe it.

Until Bronwyn ripped the curtain back on the lies I'd told myself and made it all too fucking real.

16

Come Back, Be Here

DEAN

August, Six Weeks Later

I've had a constant low-grade pressure in my chest since Bronwyn left for Europe.

The lack of enthusiasm and formality in her responses to my texts and calls have me almost desperate to get *my* Bronwyn back. The one who flirted nonstop for the first twenty months I knew her. The one who acted like everything I said and did was something special.

Bronwyn hasn't initiated a single conversation since she left.

Until, that is, bright and early (my time) when she sends me a photo.

I almost fumble my phone onto the kitchen floor when it comes through.

What. The. Fuck.

She's spending the day on a beach in the South of France with her friends. And she isn't wearing a bikini top. In the photo, she's blowing me a kiss.

Me: Where's the rest of your swimsuit?

My Wife: I thought you liked my breasts

I grit my teeth.

Me: I more than LIKE them. What I don't like is how many fucking people are seeing them

My Wife: James was fine with it. If he doesn't care, then why should you?
Me: I guarantee James Mellinger cares if his wife is half naked on a beach
My Wife: Clarissa and I FaceTimed him, and he doesn't

Jesus Christ. This just gets better and better.

Me: Are you saying my boss has seen you like that?
My Wife: Yes.

I wait for her to elaborate. To say something to diminish the impact. To follow up with a "J/K" or tell me the photo is fake.

She doesn't.

Maybe James Mellinger really is cool with the world seeing his wife's tits. Maybe I should be too.

I'm not.

Me: You win.
My Wife: What is that supposed to mean?
Me: You wanted to make me jealous, and now I'm jealous.
My Wife: This is a beach in the South of France. NO ONE has a top on here

Thirty seconds later, she sends another photo. She's wearing a long T-shirt dress, but she's not smiling in this one. No mischief lights her eyes.

My Wife: Happy now?

I rub my eyes. I have no right to act like this. And I hate that she did something she didn't want to do just because I'm a jealous dick.

This is the first time she's reached out to me in six weeks, and I slapped her down for the *way* she flirted with me.

It nearly kills me to type the words, but I do it.

Me: I'm an asshole. Wear what makes you happy, and I'll try not to fantasize about blinding every other person on that beach.

· • · ● · ● · • · •

Two days after that debacle, I open an email from James's assistant. In it, she's asking me to go to France for a week, starting immediately.

I look over at Phee as she lies in the new baby swing that Bronwyn had delivered the day after she left.

She's already three and a half months old and grown what feels like an insane amount to me. I could swear sometimes that she's a quarter of an inch taller in the morning than she was when I put her to bed. I had to move her up to the next size of diapers a week ago. Every ounce she gains is cause for celebration. She's still underweight, but her size is close to her "adjusted age" when you consider her due date.

She knows me now. She calms sometimes just at the sound of my voice. And she looks up at me like I hung the moon. She makes the funniest little faces. Even when she's angry and looks like a grouchy little old man, she's adorable.

She remains a terrible sleeper and a very demanding infant. But the swing keeps her happy for long enough that I have breathing room for things like cooking meals when it's not safe to be holding her.

Among other things, Bronwyn's overnight stay hammered home to me that I needed to take better care of myself. No one was awarding prizes because I was parenting Phee with no help and no breaks.

I hired the nanny agency I'd discussed with Bronwyn. There are two women who watch her for me. Her primary nanny, Anne, is a woman in her fifties with grandchildren of her own. The other, Sonia, is a little older than I am and decided after more than a decade in the profession, that working in health care was not for her.

One or the other is usually here for a few hours a day—long enough for me to go to the gym and run any errands I need to. I also made an appointment with a therapist at Veterans Affairs to see if I can try to get a handle on the PTSD, and what the doctor at the VA diagnosed as clinical depression and anxiety.

Progress there has been slow. I'm shaking the worst of the depression with the help of therapy and meds, but the PTSD shit is stubborn as hell.

The doctor gave me meds to make me sleep. I don't take them if I'm here alone with Phee, but I've had a nanny stay overnight a couple of times when I've gotten to a point where I couldn't function from lack of sleep.

Between the two nannies, there'll be plenty of coverage once I start working again.

When I contacted the agency, I'd discussed the nature of my job and that I could be called away at a moment's notice.

I'm not supposed to be back at work yet. But I need to see Bronwyn.

Five minutes after I reply, James calls me. "You're on a leave of absence. That email was sent to you in error."

"With all due respect, I'm more than ready to get back to work."

He pauses for a moment, then says, "HR will probably have paperwork for you. I'll have them reach out. I need you in the air ASAP."

"Is there a specific threat to your wife?"

He makes an irritated sound. "You could say that. My wife and her friends arrived in Paris yesterday for the last week of their vacation. Clarissa contacted me an hour ago. She'd snuck past her security. Franki, Janessa, and Bronwyn were all falling down drunk and hooking up with strange guys in the hotel bar. One guess who instigated the whole thing. There's your threat. Keep Bronwyn McRae in line."

• • • • • • • • • •

I knock on her hotel room door before I've even officially reported for duty.

She's sharing a suite with Janessa, who opens the door. She's around five foot ten with long brown hair and tan skin, though she's looking more than a little pallid this morning.

Janessa rubs her temple. "James is really not a happy camper if he's sending out the big guns."

At my stony expression, she waves a hand. "I don't understand why James pins the blame for everything that ever happens on Bronwyn. But don't you dare give her a hard time. She's already been on the phone with her father for half an hour, and Gabriel showed up here two hours ago."

She squints at me. "That means her player brother who never met an alcoholic beverage he wouldn't drink or an unrelated adult woman he wouldn't screw showed up here, pounding on our door at 6:00 a.m. with the unmitigated hypocrisy to call his *sister* irresponsible."

She flings the door open wider. "Bronwyn likes and respects you, so you can come in. But don't you dare hurt her feelings."

Sometimes it's a good thing when people expect you to just stand there like a sentinel. It means Janessa doesn't wait for a response from me.

She closes her eyes against the glare of a sitting room that has the curtains drawn and only a small table lamp turned on. "I," she says, holding up one finger, "am going to puke. Again. Then I'm going back to bed."

She gestures to a doorway. "Bronwyn is sleeping. You can wait in the hallway or in here."

She goes through what must be her own door, muttering about Clarissa being a tattletale and James being a bully. Then the door closes with a snick.

The sound of Paris traffic is muffled but ever-present. The room smells subtly of some expensive French perfume, and there's a large arrangement of fresh flowers on a fancy table set under an equally elaborate mirror.

Partying in Paris, hooking up with other guys, probably from her own social sphere—from the outside, it all makes sense.

But I'm not convinced. How many times did I see her out with her friends? How many parties and shifts at Jack's? I know how she has fun with her friends. And this doesn't track.

It would be stupid to take a blowtorch to whatever we have based on hearsay from my boss, who has an axe to grind. Impulsive. *Emotional.*

I tap at her door. When I don't get a response, I ease it open. Her bed is empty, and the sound of running water floats from her bathroom.

There's a thunk, like a shampoo bottle just hit the bottom of a bathtub, and, in a perfectly ridiculous English accent, she announces that it's only a flesh wound.

Monty Python quotes aside, she sounds very energetic for someone who's supposedly recovering from a hangover.

I knock on her bathroom door with a knuckle. She turns off the water, and a few seconds later, she opens the door, a white towel held to her breasts.

She looks straight ahead, then slowly rakes her gaze up my body until she reaches my face.

I look like what I am today: black suit and tie, pressed white shirt.

Her eyes flash with happy excitement, then dawning understanding. Her lips tighten. Finally, a mask of composure descends over her features, and she gives me a cool smile.

She brushes past me and heads for her open suitcase. "You're not supposed to be working. You took three months of paternity leave, not six weeks."

My own heart had lifted for all of two seconds when I'd realized she was glad to see me. Now it lands somewhere near my stomach with a thud. "James's assistant didn't realize I was on leave. She contacted me to come to Paris."

She snorts. "Clarissa doesn't need more security. She just needs to cooperate with the team already here."

I have the sudden realization that I'm about to hurt her feelings. "James thinks you need someone to keep you from causing trouble."

My words land like a rock in a puddle. There's a shocked moment while she absorbs the impact. Then she whirls to face me. "*Me?* I've spent this entire trip trying to keep *his wife* from going off the rails. She's completely lost it. All those years of repression.... Now, she's rebelling like a fifteen-year-old sneaking into her parents' liquor cabinet."

"Who is Clarissa rebelling against? It can't be her husband. She has that man wrapped around her little finger."

Bronwyn frowns at me. "Dean, on her father's orders, you all treated her like she was a five-year-old instead of a twenty-year-old woman. She's rebelling against all of *you*. She's got years of resentment built up over being treated like an asset instead of an autonomous person."

I scowl at her. "When I came to work for Harcourt, Clarissa was already an adult."

Bronwyn looks at me skeptically and crosses her arms over her chest. "So you didn't report back to her dad every time she varied her routine or sneezed or dared to smile at a man?"

I look at her incredulously. "You're joking. I reported security threats. It was never my job to *police* her."

"Well, the team that's been on her since she was a three-year-old didn't get that memo. She's been more than policed. She wasn't even allowed to date before she got married. The only reason she didn't fire the lot of them was because she loves them like they're family."

So many things suddenly become clear.

"And she *is* rebelling against James, whether she realizes it or not," she continues. "He's another man who thinks he knows what's best for her. She loves him, and he loves her. But that is seriously fucked-up."

She's right that he loves her. Clarissa wears her heart on her sleeve, and her feelings for her husband are obvious. James is more reserved, but it's impossible not to see how he feels about her. That woman is everything to him.

I don't have a personal relationship of any kind with James or Clarissa. I have professional boundaries, and Bronwyn is the first and only time I've ever crossed them. But I do very much *like* my employers.

James can come across as cold. But fuck, so do I.

Suddenly, I almost desperately hope Clarissa and James figure their issues out. In some strange way, it feels like if they can do it, then so can Bronwyn and I.

"What happened last night, B?"

"My friends got trashed, and absolutely no one listens to me. Ever. Is that what you want me to say? *That nobody respects my opinion or gives a shit what I say.* Even my best friends." The look she levels on me is cold as ice. She's including me in her accusation.

"You're angry at me," I say.

Her back straightens, and she dips her head. "Maybe I am."

"Does it help that I'm sorry I was a jealous dick?"

She scowls. Then she shakes her head and turns back to her suitcase, pulling out plain cotton underwear that is most definitely not the lingerie I've come to expect from her.

She drops the towel and yanks the panties and then a matching bra on with stiff movements. "You can go home to Phee and tell James I refused your services. He can't keep a bodyguard on me without my permission. It's fucking stalking."

"He'll just send someone else."

"James Mellinger can be a Grade-A douche canoe," she seethes. "Let him send someone else. I'll get rid of them too."

I grit my teeth. "Is that what I am, then? Just a bodyguard here to harass you?"

"You said yourself that this is a *job*, Dean. And since I don't need or want a babysitter, there's no reason for you to be here. Don't worry. I'll tell James you tried super-duper hard to make me to be a good girl." She says the last sentence in an annoying imitation of Marilyn Monroe.

I wrap my hand around the back of her neck. "Do you honestly believe I left Phee at home and cut my leave short because I wanted to come here to *work*?"

I trace her cheekbone with my thumb. "I'm here to see you."

Attempting to tease her out of her bad mood, I parrot back the comment she made when we had dinner together at my place, "We've been married for nearly four months, and we've made love twice."

My hope was that her eyes would soften and she'd respond with a flirty, "It's a travesty."

Instead, she rears back like I slapped her before she regains her dignity and responds stiffly, "I'm sorry you're horny, but you wasted a trip. I can't be just your.... I'm not a...."

I know exactly what she's implying, and I don't like it. "You're not a hookup. You're my *wife*."

She shakes her head and says, "I don't feel like your wife."

Cold washes through me, and I back away and head for the door. My hand is on the knob when she asks, "Where are you going?"

I look back. She's standing in the center of the room now, cheeks pink from the heat of her shower, hair in wet strands, her hands clenched in fists.

"You don't want me? I'm gone." I sound so fucking casual. There's no sign of the turmoil seething inside me.

She marches toward me and grabs my arm, attempting to pull me back to face her. I give her a flat stare that's made more than one grown man cry.

Her face puckers, but with anger, not tears. "You're the one who showed up here wanting a fuck buddy."

Air has never felt so good in my lungs. I wrap her wet hair in my fist and search her eyes. "You're not listening to me. You're not a hookup. Do you understand that you're my best friend? You could never be *casual* for me."

Her eyes fill with tears, and she swipes at them as if they embarrass her.

I twist my lips to the side before I finally shrug. "I *only* want you."

Something of the Bronwyn I know peeks through when her expression turns calculating. She lifts one eyebrow. "What if a supermodel was like 'Oooh, Dean, let me buy you a drink. And you can come up to my hotel room to make sweet, sweet love'?"

I lift an eyebrow right back. "I'd dry heave in disgust that someone other than you would dare to look upon me with lust. Obviously." My words are an exaggeration, but lack of loyalty is the last thing she ever needs to worry about with me.

"As you should," she says approvingly.

The tension seems to drain out of her as she leans forward and rests her forehead on me with a sigh. I try to act cool about the fact that she lets me put my arms around her. No big deal here. Not like I want to collapse at her feet in gratitude.

"Am I staying?" I ask.

She nods silently against my chest.

"Do you want to talk about last night?"

She sighs. "I spent the whole time trying to herd Franki, Janessa, and Clarissa like drunken cats."

I hold her head against my chest and rub her back. "Janessa told me about your father and brother."

She wraps her arms around me. "Why would they believe James before they asked me?"

"I don't know."

I'd have been blindsided if it had been true. And my thoughts on the matter weren't solely based on my gut. My *gut* wanted to remind me of the lack of fidelity between my own parents.

But logic said it would have been a drastic departure from her pattern of behavior. She's loyal to the bone. She's had the same best friends since she was a *six-year-old*. And in almost two years, I've never seen her break even the smallest promise.

She tips her head back to look at me suspiciously. "Do you think I'm irresponsible?"

Impulsive? Yes. But irresponsible? "Bronwyn, I don't think I've ever known anyone who takes on more responsibility than you do. You married me so you could take care of a town. You mother Clarissa—"

She starts to speak but stops at my raised eyebrows.

"You mother Franki too. You'd probably mother Janessa if she'd allow it. You even mother Louis Larrabie. Jack needs help? You help. You constantly put your own needs last. You'll work yourself to exhaustion before you ever let someone down."

I brush her damp hair from her forehead. "You're plenty responsible."

She goes for my belt, wrapping her fingers around it and pulling me even closer. "Who's watching Phee?"

"A nanny."

"It must have been hard to leave her."

It was. I've already called to check in and have the nanny FaceTime with her for me. But I say, "I don't want to talk about Phee right now."

I hesitate. "I *am* sorry I was an ass about the beach. My jealousy has nothing to do with you doing anything wrong."

She nods. "I know. It has to do with your own insecurities."

I lean back a little to look down at her. "Excuse me?"

"It's based on your own sense of powerlessness, insecurity, or lack of self-worth."

I lift my eyebrows. "Is that right? It can't just be based on the fact that I don't like other people *checking out my wife's tits*?"

"Listen, I don't make the therapy TikTok videos. I just watch and learn."

"If you saw it on social media, it has to be true," I say sarcastically.

"I watched them because I get jealous. But if it's happening to you, too, I'm going to encourage you to spend some time in self-reflection."

I snort, then frown. Then I purse my lips. Finally, I relent. "I'd rather you tell me to self-reflect than watch you change anything about yourself, including your clothing, for another person. Not even for me."

She sighs. "It's hard. I want to respect your feelings."

I have no words to explain how the very idea of admitting that I even *have* feelings that could be hurt strikes me as somehow both unmanly and manipulative. "Don't respect someone else's feelings at the cost of your own boundaries."

She plays with my lapel. "Clarissa already had her top off. I figured if I took mine off, James would either see that everyone was doing it or blame me, not her.

"Then when I was topless, I thought about how all those people could see me except the one person I wanted looking at me. So I sent you the picture. Besides, I wasn't going to pretend I hadn't taken my top off. Sooner or later, the truth always comes out."

Her hair is wet, and her back is damp and naked beneath my palm. The longer I stand here with her body tight against mine while she talks about sending me photos, the harder I get. I shift my lower body away from her so I'm not poking her with my dick when we're trying to have a real conversation.

I might be an ass, but I don't want to be *insensitive*.

She just shifts right along with me. "You seem distracted."

"Do I?"

She smirks. "A little."

"Bronwyn, you're rubbing against me in your underwear while you talk about sending me a picture of your tits. I'm doing the best I can with what I have to work with."

"Why am I such a sucker for your sweet talk?" she asks.

If she wants romantic declarations, I'm going to have to work up to that. I'm not good with words. So I bend down and kiss her instead.

After a moment, she leans back with a smile, grabs hold of my tie, and waggles her eyebrows. "So, I've got you for a week in Paris, huh? Not the worst honeymoon I can imagine."

17

What A Time

BRONWYN

James contacted the hotel and demanded they move my room to the same floor Dean is staying on and away from his precious wife. The better for my "guard" to keep an eye on me and to diminish my "terrible influence" on Clarissa.

I couldn't complain too loudly because that would look fake, given my known crush. So I pouted just enough to look miffed. Which, to be fair, I *am*.

Even my own father wouldn't have the arrogance to contact a hotel and threaten to buy the place and fire every employee in it if they didn't bow to his wishes. But James doesn't care what anyone thinks. He gets what he wants and everyone else can suck it.

In this case, though, what James wants also makes it easier for me to spend time alone with Dean.

I didn't understand why Paris is considered a romantic city. It's congested, I don't speak the language, and the locals are very much not impressed with the tourists crowding their home.

Then Dean arrived, and he flipped a switch for me. Paris is the City of Love.

We manage a surprising amount of alone time, disappearing into the crowds.

He holds my hand as we wander the streets.

We sit outside at a café and drink coffee from tiny cups.

He makes a face as I coax him to try pain au chocolat. "Mmm."

I eye him suspiciously. "Do you like it?"

He washes it down with a mouthful of bitter coffee, his ears pink. "Delicious."

I nod in satisfaction and shove the rest of mine toward him. "Well, I, for one, am completely full. You can have the rest."

He looks at it and shakes his head regretfully as he pats his flat midsection. "One is enough. This body is a temple. Have to treat it like one."

I snicker. He says things so completely deadpan. My friends all think he's so serious all the time.

He pulls out his phone. "There's some kind of specialty yarn shop here. It's supposed to be good for fabric artists. They sell fancy wool, probably from llamas hand-fed brussels sprouts and artesian water. Do you want to check it out for your projects?"

I smile. First, because he called me a "fabric artist" when really I just knit basic things like hats and blankets. And second, because he's freaking adorable. "I would, indeed, like to check it out. Have you been to Paris before?"

He shakes his head. "No, but the internet is my friend. You seem pretty comfortable here."

I shrug. "Not really. I know a very small area. But I've been shopping in Paris with Grandmother and Mom since I was... oh, maybe twelve?"

He snorts, even as we rise to start down the street to seek out the amazing yarn he's googled for me. "You say that the way someone else says their mother took them to Costco."

Heat rushes into my face. "Sorry. I don't mean to sound snotty or something—"

"You didn't sound snotty. You're just from a different world than the rest of us."

"I.... Sorry."

He's about to say something else when a couple teenagers get a little close to us in the street.

Dean veers to put his body between me and the boys, shooting them a cold look when they skim their eyes over me and lean in to say something to each other in laughing French.

The boys turn serious and give him a respectful nod as they continue past.

I nudge Dean with my elbow. "Overprotective much? I can handle myself. And it's the middle of the street."

He looks at me indulgently and kisses my forehead.

I narrow my eyes. "Now you're looking at me like I'm a three-year-old who just yelled, 'I'm a ballerina.' I'm not kidding, you know. I've had a lot of training."

"Don't take it personally, angel. This is part of the job."

When we find the boutique, I browse while he stands beside me and checks his nanny cams.

He looks at those cameras obsessively. He FaceTimes the nannies multiple times a day as well. A phone call or text isn't enough for him; he needs to see exactly what's going on with Phee.

"Are you worried about her?" I ask.

He shakes his head. "Just keeping things under control."

He says that, but he looks like a man who hasn't slept in a week. And while I'm enjoying every second with him, I'm almost glad this trip is winding down. The guilt that comes from having pulled him away from Phee gnaws at me.

I hold a skein of incredibly soft yarn in a pretty teal color close to his face. He lifts an eyebrow.

"Just trying to figure out whether I should make your scarf in green or blue or green *and* blue," I say. "To match your eyes."

His lips quirk. "I don't wear scarves very often. They're even easier to use as a weapon than a tie. And you know how much I hate having to wear one of those in this job."

"Yikes! Good point. A hat it is. To keep your sexy ears from turning red."

His ears turn red, and he squeezes my butt. "Hats are good."

• • • • • • • • • •

On our last day, I peer at Clarissa over my sunglasses and say, "I hope this doesn't ruin any of your plans for the fall semester, but I don't think I'm going back to BSU."

She stops right there in the hotel lobby to turn wide green eyes on me. "What? Why?"

Beside me, Dean tenses.

"My dad is making noise about me transferring to an Ivy League school. You know how he feels about me graduating from a state school."

That's a fib. Dad hasn't said a word about me transferring schools. In fact, I'm pretty sure he *wants* me back in Blackwater, far away from Dean. But I'm trying to set the stage with Clarissa so she doesn't question why I stay in New York near Dean when we get back.

Clarissa wraps an arm around my waist. "I hope you can change his mind. I found the cutest house online. It's white brick with blue shutters and those dormer windows on the roofline. But it won't be the same without you there."

The irony doesn't escape me that not long ago I was the one coaxing her to come to Blackwater.

This trip is winding down, and I can't help but feel a little melancholy about it. Things are changing with all of us, and it's a little bittersweet. Franki flew home the same day Dean arrived. That miserable night seemed to suck the joy out of her, and Paris lost its sparkle. She's headed back to Los Angeles to live with her mother, and Janessa left yesterday to give her time to prepare for her transfer to a college in Milan.

If I don't go back to Blackwater with Clarissa, the four of us will be scattered on the wind. It was bound to happen sooner or later, but it still feels like it crept up on me.

We enter the elevator, and I pop my sunglasses to the top of my head. When Clarissa, and her bodyguard, Sasha, are ready to exit at their floor, I say, "Oh, I forgot that I wanted to check out that little shop next door. Dean will escort me. I'll see you at dinner."

Clarissa leans toward me and whispers, "Don't make things hard for Dean. The man is just doing his job."

I beam at her and bat my eyelashes. Behind me, where she can't see, I lift my leg and run the top of my high-heel-clad foot over his calf.

"Dean doesn't mind when I make things hard. He can handle me," I say in a normal volume. "Can't you, Dean?"

When I turn my head to look up at him, he's just standing there, stance wide, hands folded in front of him. His face doesn't show a flicker of emotion. "Yes, ma'am. Ms. McRae is not a problem."

Clarissa eyes me with more than a little suspicion. She is very, very close to figuring out, if not the whole truth, at least *some* of it.

She says, "Have fun shopping," and for the life of me, I can't tell if she means "shopping" or what we'll actually be doing.

When Clarissa starts to walk down the corridor, Sasha stops the elevator door, taps her own earpiece, and nods at Dean's lapel. "Don't forget to turn it off this time."

The elevator closes on Sasha's smirk.

Clarissa and I have been best friends since first grade. Sasha has been her personal bodyguard for more than half of that time.

She's a tall, fit black woman who takes no shit. During our teen years, she confiscated everything from liquor to vapes to condoms from me when I'd decided to try to "educate" Clarissa on the ways of the world.

She knows. And she isn't ratting us out. That's more shocking than the fact that she knows what we've been doing.

I turn slightly horrified eyes on Dean. "What did she hear?"

He fusses with the equipment. "Nothing much. Maybe thirty seconds of... maybe thirty seconds."

I press the number for our floor. "Dean!"

"Okay, maybe four minutes. Five at the most."

"*No.*"

He runs a finger under his collar. "I was distracted."

I lean against his chest and beat my forehead there a couple times in embarrassed laughter. "I can't believe Sasha is letting that go."

He puts his hands on my shoulders. "She's not. You're a conflict of interest. I told her I'm moving up my plans for the new company. I'm resigning my position with the Mellingers within the next six months, and I've promised to never accept an assignment on Clarissa's detail in the meantime."

My laughter dies. I made him leave his job. I did that.

"Do you need money? Let me invest. I'll be a silent partner."

"I don't need your money." He sounds stiff and offended.

"I'm talking about investing in my own husband's business. Stop making it sound like I'm trying to offer you a handout."

"It doesn't sound like a handout. It sounds like you're trying to buy me."

"Screw you." I stab at the button to go back up to Clarissa's floor. I'll hang out with her until dinner.

He wraps his hand around mine. "This is our last day together before we're back in the real world. Are we really going to waste it fighting over money?"

"Just because we'll be back in the States doesn't mean we can't still see each other."

He lifts his eyebrows a little and blows out a breath with a small smile. "I'll be busy, but I'll make as much time as I can. At least a couple nights a week. Maybe more. We could do dinner together before I go home for the night. I could work it into the regular schedule."

He sounds like he's figuring out the details in his head. Trying to squeeze me into the periphery of his real life.

Of course. I'm the vacation. Phee is home.

This feeling? It's the same one I get when my cousins call me "trust fund" and when Grandmother reminds me to "try to remember you're a McRae."

But somehow, this is worse. It's sharper because when I'm with him, he makes me feel special.

But he has a lot on his plate. And he considers me one more thing to juggle.

He's not even being unreasonable. I understand that. If I look at our wedding as our first date, what I already want from him sounds ridiculous. But knowing that doesn't change the way I feel.

I can't do it his way. I've always been an all-or-nothing kind of person. Give me a hobby? I will hyper-fixate on that sucker until I've mastered it. Find a show I like? I'm binge-watching six seasons in three days.

I can't do an hour here or there every few days. I'd give it a week before I talked myself into all the reasons why it would be a good idea to show up on his doorstep with an overnight bag like a Stage Five Clinger.

So I say, "I'm not sure how things are going to go with my dad. I'll probably be back in Blackwater with Clarissa. But I'll come visit. Or we could meet halfway?"

His expression tightens. "You won't have any trouble convincing your father. Just remind him of how many miles there will be between the two of us."

I nod and swallow the lump in my throat. "That will work. Definitely."

When I'd made the excuse to Clarissa to be alone with Dean, I'd expected playful, raunchy sex.

Instead, we're somber as we walk down the corridor side by side. The back of my hand brushes his, and he reaches out subtly to entangle his fingers with mine.

When my hotel room door closes behind us, he guides me backward until I hit the wall. He kisses me, a hand wrapped in my ponytail, guiding my head this way, then that.

His kiss is rougher than he's ever been. There's a bite of desperation in it, and I'm right there with him. This is an almost animal need to claim each other, and emotion clogs my throat, even as he drops to his knees and lifts my leg over his right shoulder, then shoves my skirt up. "Hold this."

I do, more than a little turned on by the bossy tone he's using. I'm not sure he even knows he's doing it. He's just so focused on the task at hand that he's not thinking about what he says or how he says it.

He runs a knuckle down the seam of my sex over the red silk of my panties. "You and your lingerie."

He gathers the fabric, tugging and pulling it, using it to tease my clit.

I gasp and clutch at his hair with my free hand, and he looks up at me with the expression of a starving man. "That's right. You hold on to me."

He tugs my panties to the side and crouches to eat my pussy, licking and flicking as he eases a finger into me, then another.

He's watching my reactions, and I yank his hair too hard when I come against his mouth.

Then he's standing and freeing his cock. He's still dressed—for that matter, so am I—as he lifts me in his arms, my butt balanced in his big hands. He nudges me, and I reach down to fit him to my entrance. Then he drops me onto his dick with a snarl.

This is no gentle easing into anything. This is rough and frantic fucking. He shoves me back against the wall, one hand holding me up, the other braced above my head.

"*You. Are. My. Wife.*" He punctuates every word with a rough thrust of his hips.

"Yes." I lift my hands to frame his face. His eyes are wild, his expression feral.

He leans down to growl directly against my ear. "Don't forget it."

"I won't," I promise. *How could he think I would?*

"I'm going to make everything perfect for you."

I wrap both my arms around his head. "I don't need perfect. I just need you."

He thrusts deep and hard, then keeps me there, pinned and full, as I orgasm on his cock. He jerks inside me in response and tenses against me.

He doesn't move away in the aftermath and speaks quietly against my hair, "You deserve perfect."

There's no such thing. There are devastating tragedies. There are accidents and illnesses and disappointed hopes and a million things that no one could possibly control or predict. There is only meeting those challenges together and finding happiness and comfort during the hard times.

He pulls back and his hazel gaze burns into mine. "Give me time. Let me try."

I drop my head to his shoulder and hide my tears. "I'll give you time," I whisper.

18
Rock You Like A Hurricane

DEAN

Late October, Bronwyn's Senior Year

James is spending the weekend with his wife in Blackwater. Which means, when I'm not on duty, I'll be spending the weekend with mine.

I haven't seen Bronwyn in person in more than a month. We both make time for weekends away when we can, but our schedules are busy. Between getting ready to transition out of this career, laying the groundwork for my own company, and making sure I'm giving Phee as much time as I can, I'm spread thin.

Phee is six months old already. She sits up in a high chair now. She babbles and pretends to have conversations. She eats cereal, mashes banana into her curly blonde hair, and loves bath time.

And she loves *me*.

She might be exhausting, but God, she's worth it. She's smart, stubborn, affectionate, and funny.

I know we'll be ready to try to be a family with Bronwyn soon. I just have to get the nightmares under control.

Phee's still a little behind developmentally. Her doctor has been discussing setting her up for evaluations with a physical and pediatric occupational therapist. We'll have to get through that first too.

In the meantime, I sneak around with my own wife like she's a dirty little secret. More than anything, that's the part I can't stand. The secrecy is her idea, but it's like wearing a sock that keeps sliding down my heel. I fucking hate it.

When James and I arrive at the house that Clarissa and Bronwyn share, I stand outside the car, hands folded. I watch as James and Clarissa run up to each other, grinning like a pair of lovesick fools.

He gets to touch her right there in the driveway and nobody even blinks. He throws her over his shoulder and jogs up her porch steps while she shrieks with laughter and sneaks a squeeze of the man's ass.

I stand still, expression flat, and wait as Bronwyn barrels her way down the steps and up to me.

One of their housemates, Sydney, is sitting in a rocking chair on the front porch. In other words, we have an audience.

Bronwyn wants to launch herself into my arms; I can see it in the way she has to force herself to stay in place. Instead, she bounces on the balls of her feet and clasps her hands together.

Her breasts rise and fall against her sweater as she breathes a little fast in excitement. "Heyyy, Dean."

Removing my sunglasses, I put them in the breast pocket of my suit jacket and murmur, "Hey, Bronwyn."

I wait for her to say something else, but she doesn't. She just stands there, looking like sunshine itself. So beautiful.

I barely move my lips when I say, "What do you think would happen if I just grabbed you right here and kissed you in front of God and everyone?"

I thought it would make her laugh, but it dims her mood a little.

She answers quietly, her back to the house. "I think, unless we're actually going to be together all the time, everyone would call me an idiot. Since I'm not interested in being lectured, we'll just have to wait until we're alone for kissing."

I put my sunglasses back on and swallow. "I'll be at the Blackwater Inn. I'm back on duty at 7:00 p.m. I'll be in my room until six thirty. Text me when you get there."

She drifts toward me, and I move subtly into her space so our bodies brush gently as she moves past me and heads for her car. When she reaches her door, she holds up her keys and shouts back to Sydney, "If anyone asks, I'm staying at my grandparents' this weekend."

Sydney lifts an arm in acknowledgment, and then Bronwyn is gone.

• • • ● • ● • • •

Seven o'clock comes too soon. Clarissa and James are headed to Jack's Place. Their whole friend group will be there. And so will my wife.

It's not ideal. This is the exact scenario that Sasha was concerned about—and, if I'm honest, so am I. Namely, I'm there to protect James. But my wife will be in that bar. If there's a threat, Mellinger and his wife are not my priority. Bronwyn is.

Bronwyn is already here when I arrive with my client. She's wearing jeans and sitting at the bar, one stiletto-clad foot propped on the barstool, the other dangling down.

She's flexible as hell. All those dance classes she probably took growing up, I guess. I force my thoughts away from exactly how flexible she was an hour ago.

I have a job to do, so I take position and watch the room.

James seems off. The guy is strung as tight as a bowstring.

I'm always alert, but his behavior has me scanning the crowd even more thoroughly than usual, wondering if there's something he knows that I don't.

When the band comes in through the back door and Louis starts to set up on the small stage, I fight a sneer.

I hate that little shit.

I don't expect Bronwyn not to have a past, but Louis is such a smarmy prick. He's also Kevin Hallman's first cousin. I'm well aware that we can't choose who we're related to, but I don't trust him.

Besides, he only plays these gigs in Blackwater because they're an excuse to be near Bronwyn. He's obsessed with her.

I'm a hypocrite because so am I. Far worse than Louis, truth be told. But the difference is, Bronwyn wants me.

I scan past the band and across the crowd, evaluating threats. There's a rowdy group of frat boys in the corner, but they don't appear to have taken note of my client. And if they did, they'd probably offer to suck his dick for the "networking opportunity."

"Check. Check." Louis practically makes out with the mic, his mouth right on the thing.

Why does he talk like that? He's trying to sound like he's from Seattle, not New York City. Fucking tool.

A throat clears. I don't have to look to know Bronwyn has moved to stand beside me. Yeah, I noticed her in my periphery. But that's not why I know she's there. I just feel her. She's gravity drawing me to her.

"Ma'am," I say.

I know without glancing down that she's dragging her collar away from her neck and fanning her face.

Weird? Maybe, but considering I go hard as a rock when she calls me "sir," I'm not here to judge.

She steps behind me and surreptitiously squeezes my ass.

"Behave, woman."

Her laugh makes everything inside me fizz like champagne.

"I'll see you later, Dean," she says.

"Yes you will."

It irritates me that Louis actually has a good voice. But at least the music doesn't suck as the night goes on.

Bronwyn hangs out with her friends. She dances. James loosens up. And the night isn't all that different from any other that I've spent in this bar, wishing I could kiss my girl on the dance floor.

Louis speaks into the mic. "Going to slow things down with a song for the one who got away." He launches into a heartfelt version of "Dancing On My Own."

Jesus Christ, the man sounds ready to cry. Two women at a table near the stage actually hold their hands against their chests and sing along with tears in their eyes.

Bronwyn keeps chatting with her friends and doesn't even notice he's singing to her. I take petty satisfaction in that.

He'll be hooking up with one or both of those women near the stage tonight anyway. He does it every time: makes a play for my wife, and when it doesn't work, he drowns his sorrows in random pussy.

Pathetic.

Clarissa signals to her own bodyguard that she and Bronwyn are headed to the restroom. Against my better instincts, I don't watch their progress. James is my responsibility, not the women.

And then it happens. A feminine scream. A shout and derisive male laughter. My boss is headed across the bar like an angry bull.

The other bodyguard on duty, a blonde named Beth, has Clarissa behind her with her back to the wall.

With a glance, I take in the entire scene. Clarissa has had a drink thrown in her face, at the very least. There are those six frat boys, all drunk and cheering on their friend, who's getting the absolute shit pummeled out of him by my boss. The others are either heckling Clarissa or *threatening my wife.*

Bronwyn is right there with her finger in the face of one of those frat boys, screaming up at him.

My lip reading is giving me "You fucking dick," though I can't hear her over the chaos in the bar.

I yank him away just as he takes a swing at her and slam him against the wall. He slides to the floor, then scrambles to get up and come at me. I point a single finger and bellow, "Stay down."

He does.

Bronwyn is still in the middle of it all. She snatches a phone out of one of the guys' hands and slams it against the edge of a table.

This time I grab two of the shitheads coming at her, one in each fist, and lift them off their feet by their polo shirt collars. I shake them like a terrier with a rat, then toss them at their friend. "None of you move."

Jack's handled two of the others, but I can't get to Bronwyn before the last polo shirt guy has pulled back a fist, aiming straight for her face. Somehow she manages to dodge him, and he staggers. Deirdre nails him in the arm with a metal baseball bat before he can follow through with another attempt at a haymaker.

The guy staggers away, holding on to what I'm guessing is a broken arm, and the two women high-five each other.

I scowl at Bronwyn. "Get behind Beth. Now." Clarissa's bodyguard is armed and trained within an inch of her life.

Then I move past my wife to try to get my boss off the prick who assaulted Clarissa before he kills him.

It takes both Jack and me to pull him off. I've seen this kind of thing before. James isn't aware of anything happening around him. Right now, he could take a knife wound and it would barely register until he started to bleed out.

His only focus is on the fight.

Clarissa is panicking, trying to get out from behind Beth to get to James. Her white blouse has gone completely transparent from the beer poured on her.

"James." I never call him that to his face, but I'm trying to get him to actually hear me. "Let him go. Your wife needs you."

He stops punching, but he doesn't release the asshole, so I go on. "You're scaring Clarissa. Get. Your shit. Together."

His head snaps straight to his wife. Then he lets go with a shove, yanks his own shirt off, and pulls it over her head. He drags her into his arms and starts rubbing her back and muttering something none of the rest of us can hear.

Beth's already called for backup, and she and Jack are demanding to see people's phones and offering what sound like bribes with James's money for videos to disappear.

James is signaling that we're leaving, so I head in his direction. I grab Bronwyn around the waist as I walk past, lifting her completely off her feet when she resists. I carry her out the door with us, because like hell am I letting her stay while those guys are still here.

"What are you doing?" she demands.

"I'm thinking about spanking your ass. For real, not for fun. What the hell was that?"

She folds her arms across her chest as I carry her across the gravel parking lot. "I hope you realize that the only reason you're carrying me anywhere right now is because I'm allowing it."

"You're not staying here to pick a fight with those guys when I'm not here to protect you."

"Is that right?"

I set her down and guide her with a hand on her elbow so that if James or Clarissa looks back, our interaction doesn't draw attention. "Sit in the front with me."

She scowls but doesn't take off as I open the back door for Clarissa and James. When I open the passenger door for her, she doesn't move.

I lean down and speak close to her ear. "You've never seen me lose my temper, Bronwyn. That's because I can count on one hand the number of times I've done so in my life. But if you don't sit your pretty ass in that car, I'm going back inside the bar to make sure that not one of those guys is capable of even holding his own dick to piss for a very long time."

"That's fucked-up, dude. It's coercion."

"Get in the car."

She gives me the finger, then gets in and crosses her arms. I reach over and connect her seat belt.

"Are you seriously angry with me?" she asks incredulously.

"Yes," I hiss through my teeth, then close the door.

Taking a deep breath, I go around to the driver's side, then slide into the driver's seat. Starting the car, I pull out of the parking lot and head back to the house.

"What was I supposed to do?" she demands as soon as we're moving.

I double-check that the privacy screen is completely engaged before responding. "You're supposed to let the professionals handle it."

"You were too slow."

I gnash my teeth like a rabid dog. "I wouldn't have been too slow if I wasn't having to do damage control on you at the same time. You should have gotten behind Beth with Clarissa and stayed there."

"They were trying to livestream Clarissa while she was traumatized and wearing a transparent beer-soaked shirt."

"Your first responsibility is to your own safety. *Godammit*. Bronwyn, you're a civilian."

"You don't know me at all if you think I'd hide behind another person when one of my friends needed my help."

"It's not cute to act like a feral chihuahua attacking a pit bull. You were a distraction to those guys. Nothing more."

The crazy woman huffs out an annoyed laugh. "Please. I had it under control."

I have to fight not to punch the steering wheel. "You had nothing under control. You're a five-foot-tall woman attacking men who easily weigh twice what you do."

"Five foot one. And I was defending, not attacking."

I take a deep breath through my nose. "I don't care about your extra inch right now."

She growls. "That's rude, Dean. Don't act like you earned your height. You won the genetics lottery. That's it. Of all the people in my life, you're the last one I'd have ever believed would make a short joke."

Dammit. "I'm not making fun of your height."

"Jokes are only funny when you're punching up. Otherwise, they're just bullying."

I glance her way to determine whether she's jerking my chain. She's definitely not.

"Now you find something to smile about?" she demands hotly.

"I'm not smiling."

"You're smiling inside."

"You just told me short jokes were punching down," I bite out. "It's not my fault you're funny. And, for the record, I'm still furious."

She makes a sound like something you'd hear from a T-Rex in a Jurassic Park movie. Then she twists in her seat and stares out the window until I pull into the drive.

"Do you need anything from the house before we go back to the inn?"

She shakes her head with a jerk. But when I open first her door, then the back door for James and Clarissa, she follows me inside the house and slams around in the kitchen until I'm ready to "drive her to her grandparents' house."

It takes me a while to debrief, and I hope it's enough time for Bronwyn and me both to cool our tempers. However, she continues to give me the cold shoulder even after we're back in the car.

When we finally arrive at the inn, she breaks her silence. "I've had a lot of training, Dean. Short of one of them pulling a gun, none of them was a real threat to me."

I rub the back of my neck. "I'm glad you know some self-defense. But the first rule any decent instructor would have taught you is not to go looking for a fight. The moves they teach in those classes are designed to give you an opening to escape, not teach you how to subdue someone."

"You're telling *me* what the instructors teach in self-defense classes?"

"Because you didn't use your common sense," I explode in a flurry of angry words. "You got involved in a *bar fight*. We're lucky you didn't end up in the hospital."

She slides her lower jaw to the side. "Is that right?"

"Yes."

She points to a stretch of lawn on the far side of the inn. It's littered with a few picnic tables and strung with Edison bulb lighting overhead. "Tell you what. We'll take it out there. If you can put me on my back before I put you on yours, you can call me a chihuahua all you want."

"I could have you incapacitated before you even tried to poke me with your keys," I say.

She shoves open her car door. "Prove it."

She ditches her high heels at the edge of the parking lot, then marches barefoot across the lawn, her breath fogging and her nose pink from the cold.

I stand by the car with my hands on my hips. "I'm not wrestling with you unless we're naked on a bed," I call.

She turns around and walks backward, giving me the "bring it" hand gesture as she narrows her eyes. "Pussy."

I scrub my eyes, then squint at her. "Is this a kink? You want me to chase you down and pin you in a public place?"

She scoffs. "I want you to try."

I can have her on the ground in about two seconds flat. And I can do it without hurting her. That's not a problem. "Just remember this was your idea."

"Enough talk, big guy."

I barrel down on her like a freight train. I'll do a leg sweep, but I'll catch her and guide her down gently. Then I'll come down on top of her and cage her under me.

Except when I sweep my leg, she's not there. And when I grapple to get a hold of her, she slips away before I can even get my bearings.

And then I'm wheezing, the cold night dew soaking through my clothing, as I stare up at the patchy network of cloud cover, stars, and string lights overhead.

She straddles my chest, grabs my hands, and "pins" me to the ground. Eyes sparkling in the yellow-orange wash from the artificial lighting, she drops a kiss on my nose exactly the way I do to Phee. "Gotcha."

I roll, taking her with me, until I'm the one on top, stunned and proud of her and grinning like a loon.

"Just so you know, I let you roll me over," she says in a pious voice.

"How do you know how to do that?"

There's a dent of confusion between her eyebrows and sadness in her voice when she says, "I'm a *McRae*. I wanted horseback riding lessons and dance classes. I got gymnastics, mixed martial arts, and firearm training. My father has always been determined that we could defend ourselves."

She looks at me with a question in her eyes. "Sometimes you seem like you know things about me that I never told you. I could swear you notice everything. Then other times you have blind spots when it comes to me about things you should already know."

I frown, not comprehending.

"I told you I had martial arts training. Not just tonight but lots of times. You knew I taught self-defense classes back home. It was like what I said skated right over your head.

You were determined that I had to be who you thought I was, and nothing I said changed your opinion."

I shake my head, not in disagreement but in disgust at myself.

I've been trained not to do things like that. But with Bronwyn... sometimes I can't help it. "I thought you meant you were helping out someone else who was teaching self-defense. I thought...."

Her brows furrow.

"You didn't take dance classes?" I ask. Because she is an amazing dancer.

Her smile is wry and gentle. "No, Dean. I didn't take classes to learn how to dance."

"You want to show me how you did that?"

I understand the mechanics. She used my own center of balance against me. What I don't understand is how she got the drop on me.

She sighs dramatically. "I could show you, but then I'd have to kill you."

I lift my eyebrows and smirk. "I think I can handle you."

She gives me a tiny push. "Once you know, I've given you the advantage. It's mostly about taking your opponent by surprise. Speed counts. You obviously outweigh and outmuscle me. Someone my size has to fight differently than someone like you who can rely on power. I can't take you down with my strength alone."

I stand and offer my hand. "Teach me your ways, oh short and mighty one."

She grabs my balls and gives a gentle squeeze. "The McRae family has a motto: 'Love hard. Remain loyal. Fight *dirty*.'"

19

All Too Well

BRONWYN

Early April

I whip open the doorway to the house on Martha's Vineyard and wait for my husband as he pulls into the gravel drive. He steps out of his SUV with a bouquet of red roses exactly like the ones I carried a year ago on our wedding day.

He gives me a grin and jogs up the short walkway, coming to a stop one step below me as I stand on the brick stoop. It puts our faces almost on the same level.

Dean is always sexy, but he looks *happy*. And that is everything.

I expect him to kiss me immediately, but he just stands there and lets his gaze travel over every inch of my face. Then he does that thing with my hair, running his fingers across my forehead and tucking the windswept strands behind my ear. The ocean breeze is just this side of frigid this time of year, but the sun is warm.

I close the distance, and he meets my kiss. Then he wraps his arms around me and swings me in a circle before depositing me back on the small stoop.

He steps back and looks at the house, with its gray shake siding and black shutters, its widow's walk and abundance of gleaming windows. He shakes his head in mock reproof. "This place is ridiculous."

I squirm a little at the criticism. "It's not costing us anything. It belongs to a friend of the family. And it's not that bad. It only has seven bedrooms."

His lips twitch. "Well, since it only has seven bedrooms...."

"The views are gorgeous. I thought it would be nice."

He puts his arms around me once more. "I'm only interested in one view, and I'm looking at her."

• • • ● • ● • • •

"I don't want you to go," I say, peering out through the curtains at the rolling lawns and the waves breaking over the pebbled shore.

Dean's packing his bags.

He sighs. "I don't have a choice."

I know that, but... "This weekend was nothing but a tease."

The shuffling and rustling behind me stops and Dean wraps his arm around me, his forearm resting against my collarbone as he pulls me back against his body. "We spent time together. That makes it a great weekend for me."

I slide out from under his arm and move away. He tenses at my rejection, his jaw flexing.

"I'm tired of sneaking around," I say.

"Then stop doing it. Keeping us a secret was your idea, not mine. I've only kept my mouth shut because it's what you wanted."

I throw my hands up. "I know that. But it wasn't supposed to go on this long."

When I gave him my rings back, I'd assumed it would be a couple weeks. Maybe a month. Instead, it became our permanent reality.

I know he cares about me. If I needed him, he'd find a sitter and be here in a heartbeat. But he also doesn't want me to fully be part of his life.

"How's Phee doing?" I ask abruptly. "She's a year old now."

He frowns. "She's good."

I wait for him to elaborate. He doesn't.

"Have I given you the impression that I don't like children? Or that I wouldn't be kind to her or—"

"Of course not," he says, sounding exasperated.

"Then show me her picture! Tell me something cute she did. Hell, tell me how she's teething and miserable! Tell me that she's sleeping through the night... or that she isn't."

He walks back to his duffel and zips the side compartment closed. "How did you know she was teething?" he asks tightly.

"I was taking a guess because my cousin's kids all started between six months and a year. Guessing is all I do with you."

He clenches a shirt in his hands before shoving it into a cotton laundry bag. "I said she's good. She smiles and giggles and throws things on the floor just to make me pick them up."

"Is she catching up on her milestones or—"

"You want to know that PT and OT come to the house? They do. You want to know that she's allergic to soy? She is. I'll tell you when things are calm."

"I don't need things to be calm—"

"Why do you do this? You wait until we have fifteen minutes left together to pick a fight. Every time."

"I'm not picking a fight. I'm telling you I need more from you."

He runs a hand through his hair, then leaves it clasped around the back of his neck. "I can't win with you. There's no right answer."

"Am I asking for so much? Give me a little bit of your life. You know everything about me. You know what I ate for breakfast on Tuesday. Why can't I have some of that from you?"

He rubs his jaw. "You want to know what I ate on Tuesday?"

I grab a pair of clean socks from the bed and throw them at his head. He catches them—of course—and puts them into his suitcase.

"Don't be literal," I growl.

He watches me for a long moment, then heaves a breath and reaches into his pocket to retrieve his phone. He swipes around on the screen.

I frown. Then my phone dings with a text alert, and I pick it up from the table.

He's sent me a photo of Phee sitting on a brightly colored play mat and smiling joyfully at the camera. Her cheeks are round and rosy. She's filled out—she looks positively sturdy now. Her hair is still wispy blonde, but it's turned curly and a little darker.

"She's beautiful."

He smiles a little, but there's sadness in it. "Yeah. She looks a lot like her mother."

Our anniversary will always be a strange blend of love and loss, though Dean has never said he loves me. We found each other. Phee entered the world. And Maddie left it.

He clears his throat. "She talks now. Some words. She says 'hungee' when she wants food."

My chin wobbles, and I smile. "That's freaking adorable."

"I'll send you a video the next time she does it. It's cute."

I nod eagerly. "Please. Or you could FaceTime me."

"I'll send you a video."

"Okay."

He hesitates. "I decided to have her call me Daddy. I wasn't sure in the beginning... but I'm her father. The only one she has. I feel like her father, I mean. She's my child. And I want her to grow up knowing she has a parent."

I swallow and blink the moisture from my eyes. "That's wonderful."

He looks a little unsure. "Yeah? You think that's okay?"

I wrap my arms around his middle. "Yes."

He hugs me back and rests his chin on top of my head. "This is a good idea. You should know about the happy parts."

If he thinks those words are a comfort, they aren't. He acts like offering me a glimpse of what amounts to a curated Instagram feed is some kind of gift.

"You can tell me about the parts that are hard too. I don't need your version of social media branding."

He doesn't say anything, so I go on. "How are plans for your business going?"

"Good."

That's it. Just "good."

"You don't want to talk about it? I tell you every detail ad nauseum about school and my property managers and my grandmother calling me an 'upstart.'"

His jaw tightens. "I'm glad you have a sense of humor about that, because I don't find her attitude funny."

"She's eased up a little since the Hallman thing, at least."

He straightens his arm to look at his watch. "I have to go, angel."

I tighten my grip, as if clinging to him is in any way about to change the part that comes next.

He tips my chin up. "Kiss me until next time."

I lift my head and push down the part of me that wants to rail at him. The part that wants to kiss him but also wants to beat my fists against his chest and tell him I can't do this.

He's giving me more than he ever has. But it isn't enough. I'm still on the outside looking in.

I kiss him. Then he pulls away and picks up his duffel.

He walks toward the door, then turns back, his expression intense. "To hell with the secrets. Just tell them."

I shake my head. "Text me when you get home. I'll be watching your dot on my phone until you get there safely."

He gives me a crooked smile. "Now you know how I feel all the time."

I wish I did.

20

Breathe Me

DEAN

One Month Later, Last Week of Bronwyn's Senior Year

"Slow down. I can't understand what you're saying."

I'd known something was wrong before I picked up the phone. Bronwyn never calls me when I'm working. Her voice is so high-pitched and frantic that I'm struggling to understand her.

"Clarissa. I told you she refused to go see a doctor for her cramps. She collapsed on campus. Completely unconscious…" She's still talking even as a security alert comes through my phone. "…took her in an ambulance. No one at the hospital will even tell us what's happening because we aren't related to her—"

"Breathe, angel. She's at the hospital now?"

"Yes."

I've already parked illegally in front of Harcourt Tower with the blinkers on. When one of the security guards approaches me, I toss him a set of keys. "Don't let anyone touch that car. We'll be out of here within five minutes."

Alarm lights his gaze. "Everything okay, Mr. Priester?"

I give a sharp shake of my head as I stride through the building and straight for the elevators to swipe my security badge. "Not even close."

Bronwyn sobs into the phone.

"Do you have someone with you?" I ask.

"Sydney is here. And Jeanine."

"Okay. We'll be there soon. Just watch my dot on your phone."

"I will. I love you."

I freeze for precious seconds I can't afford to spare. Then I say gruffly, "I have to hang up now."

"Okay. I... okay."

The elevator doors open, and I enter James's outer executive offices, where chaos already reigns.

James barks at his assistant, "Get Dean to bring the car around. Contact our pilot to file a flight plan—"

"I can do it faster," I say.

He turns his head toward me, obviously just noticing me for the first time.

"Traffic into JFK is crawling right now," I continue. "Construction. I can get us there faster by car if I break a few traffic laws."

He's jabbed the elevator button before I even finish speaking.

• • • ● ● ● ● • • •

I screech to a stop in the ambulance parking area long enough for James to throw himself out of the car. Then I park and take off for the hospital at a clip.

Bronwyn has clearly been watching for me, because she meets me before I even find my way through the security checkpoints and into the waiting room.

Wrapping my arms around her, I hold her head against my heart. "Any word?"

"No. They took James into a private room to talk to him. That can't be good, right? Why would they do that if it wasn't bad?"

"Not necessarily. There are privacy laws. It could just be because they don't have permission to share that information with anyone else."

She takes a deep breath. "Okay. Yes. Okay. That makes sense."

"Are you ready to go back inside?"

She shakes her head against me, then seems to rally and pulls back, nodding. "Yes."

When we make it through security, she reaches for my hand. I can't help but wonder if she realizes she's done it. But I don't point out what it may look like to the people sitting in the waiting room.

She pulls me behind her as we enter the large surgical waiting room, then lets go when Jeanine sees our hands and gives her a mildly concerned look.

Clarissa's personal chef probably thinks I'm just comforting Bronwyn in a crisis. The security personnel she latched on to in a moment of need.

Seeing them treat her like she's delusional for having feelings for me chaps my ass. I want to stake a claim on her. To ask these assholes how they could believe anyone could resist her.

I don't, though. Because it isn't what Bronwyn wants. And I have less than two weeks left in the Mellingers' employ. Bronwyn is also right that it would cause more than a ripple there.

My boss is going to be less than happy when he figures out he paid me to go to France last summer to guard my own wife.

On the other hand, I definitely kept her busy and "out of trouble." As far as I can see, I did what he wanted me to. I just had more fun doing it than he'd planned.

Two of Clarissa's personal security are here. I don't know if it's evident to the others, but they're both rattled. I'll need to talk to them soon.

For now, I sit in a blue upholstered chair with a metal armrest between me and Bronwyn. I slide my left foot over so it's resting against the side of her right one.

We both have shoes on. Her legging-clad calf rests ever so slightly against my own trouser-covered leg. No skin-to-skin contact. It isn't enough, but it's something.

She types on her phone.

My own vibrates, and I take it from my pocket.

My Wife: Did you make arrangements for Phee?

Me: Yes. I called while I was driving. Her regular nanny is staying with her.

My Wife: Will Phee be upset with the change in routine?

Me: She'll be all right.

Me: Do you need anything? Food? A drink?

My Wife: Just you

I press harder with my leg.

She sniffles a little beside me. Scrambling for something to distract her, I text her a video of Phee "dancing."

She's not walking yet. The physical therapist says it's not a problem. Lots of thirteen-month-olds, including ones who weren't preemies, aren't ready at that age. He says she's almost there, though.

In the video, Phee is standing, holding on to the sofa. She bounces her little butt up and down and bobs her head but never lifts her feet from the floor.

My Wife: She dances like you

I send her a meme that says "Fuck you very much."

And when I look back at her, she's no longer on the verge of tears. She glances at me with a quiet smile and presses her leg to mine.

Later, a doctor and an administrator enter the room, making their way over to our group.

The doctor speaks first. "Mrs. Harcourt-Mellinger is out of surgery and awake. She asked us to share that she experienced ovarian torsion as a result of a cyst. We did need to remove the entire ovary. However, we expect an uncomplicated recovery."

The administrator adds her own information. "She's with her husband. He's asked that you give her some time to rest. If she's feeling up to it, she'll be accepting visitors tomorrow."

That's good news, and I blow out a rough breath, meeting Clarissa's bodyguards' relieved gazes.

Bronwyn's roommate, Sydney, mutters, "Surgeon *and* administrator. I guess it's a different world when you're a billionaire. James says, 'Jump,' and the world says, 'Would you like me to finish with a backflip?'"

They ignore her comment.

Bronwyn scowls and turns to me. "Can James do that? Keep us out?"

My look is sympathetic. "He can. He's her husband."

A wave of gratitude washes over me. *Thank God Bronwyn is my wife.* If anyone tried to keep me away from her? I would lose my goddamn mind.

21

Quarter Life Crisis

BRONWYN

Early September

"You don't like it?" I ask in disappointment.

Dean's quiet on the other end of the phone as he scrolls through the photos I've sent.

I'm standing in the governor's drive of Great-Aunt Gillian's house in Blackwater. My grandfather's sister once lived here for a season of her life, and it's been a vacation home of sorts for the McRae family ever since. I have a lot of happy childhood memories here. I inherited this property as part of my trust fund, and now that I've graduated and have the time, I'm excited to get to work bringing it up-to-date and filling it with new memories.

It started out as a classic Georgian mansion. An older home, yes, but lovely.

It's in need of renovations, but it sits on a hundred acres, with hiking trails through the woods and a lake in the distance. It even has an old barn that was once used for community theater on the property. It's been defunct for more than a decade, but I have a dream of revitalizing all of it.

And even though it doesn't really suit the architecture, the back of the house opens onto a huge porch perfect for rocking chairs and a porch swing.

It's a little bit of a mishmash of styles, but it has character.

And I'd really hoped he'd love it.

Finally, he says, "It's… big."

"I don't think it's too big, though. We have to be getting to a place soon where you feel ready for us all to be a family. Phee's almost a year and a half old."

He doesn't say anything in response, so I fill his silence, barreling straight ahead. "Even if we're only here for major holidays, between my family, Phee, and any future children we might have, I think it's lovely. You said you wanted a place in the country someday…."

He's silent for a long time, and I realize I let my mouth get away from me again. Maybe I'm assuming too much about what our relationship means to him.

But I'm getting to a point of frustration and impatience that I find harder and harder to control. I'm like a dormant volcano. All the villagers are sleeping peacefully in their beds while I'm seething under the surface. Soon, I'm going to burn this thing to the ground.

I've thrown myself headlong into several projects. Not just this house but opening the youth center here in Blackwater. I'm modeling it after the one on Long Island that I spent so much time at as a volunteer, but with obvious tweaks based on the fact that this is a rural community and has different needs.

It's been an ambitious project, to say the least. But it's not enough distraction to keep me from chronically missing Dean. I even miss Phee, though I only know her through Dean's stories and videos. I live with the constant ache of homesickness.

Dean finally speaks. "The security system there looks circa 2000. Who's taking care of that for you?"

"I haven't gotten that far in my plans—"

He growls. "Unacceptable. I'll make the arrangements. You're not planning on staying there while renovations are going on?"

"Why does it sound like you just asked me if I'll be sleeping naked on a pirate ship? I'll be fine."

"I don't like it. You need to bring in a team to maintain security on a place that size. You're not safe there."

"If we were living together, you'd have a vote. But we're not." I say it just to be contrary. I know he's right, and I plan on taking care of it. But lately I can't seem to resist poking the bear.

I swear I can hear him grinding his molars through the phone.

Finally, he asks, "You don't think you'll be lonely living out there in a big house in the middle of nowhere?"

"It's not the house that makes me lonely." I rub the back of my aching neck. I need a massage. This tension is unbearable, and my head is killing me.

There's a pause, and then he says, a little gruffly, "I miss you too."

I grit my teeth against the steel band of pain squeezing my head and working its way down my spine. "Obviously not enough."

"I'm working on things to get us there."

"Whatever," I say tiredly.

"Bronwyn—"

"I have to go."

"You'll be at the hotel tonight." I can't even tell if it's a statement or a question.

"Our conjugal visit," I quip.

I can picture his expression clear as day: jaw flexing, brow furrowed.

"It's not a conjugal visit. You don't want to fuck, we don't fuck," he says. "But, Bronwyn... you always want to fuck."

"You know what? I can't do this."

I hit End Call and nearly throw my phone across the driveway but manage to rein it in. I can just imagine the talk it would cause if one of the construction crew caught sight of me. The last of them are leaving for the weekend, and I lift my arm in a friendly wave as they file out of the driveway in their work trucks.

Hide it all. That's been my mantra now for way too long. Smile and act like everything is fine. But I can't maintain the illusion that I have my shit together anymore. Even my body is rebelling. My head aches. There's a strange tingling across my skin, and my arms and legs have pins and needles, like they're falling asleep.

I dig through my purse for the headache medicine I stashed there this afternoon before I remember that I'm not due for another dose for at least two hours. So I swig from my water bottle instead and head back toward the little cottage near the edge of the woods.

In the past, the cottage was used to house staff. Dave, my foreman, left a note for me to take a look in here and let him know if I'd be updating this space as well. He says it's structurally sound but, as he put it, "uglier than sin dipped in misery."

As I pass through the small kitchen, a manila envelope on the table catches my eye. My first name is printed on it in block letters.

I flip the catch, pulling out the contents, my reactions slow. They're photos of the main house in its current state. I assume the crew were using them as reference for something.

There's a note attached, but all it says is "Nice place."

There are also three photos of me in here. One of me on the back porch, one where I'm speaking with the foreman, and one of me walking down toward the lake.

Maybe I was caught in the foreground and whoever took these thought I'd like a copy.

I flip the envelope over, looking for any hint of who left them here, but there's nothing. Even as fuzzy as it is at the moment, my mind goes to Hallman and the photos my father said the man had taken of me, but I dismiss the thought. No one has heard from him, and I can't imagine he'd be stupid that. *What? No sense.*

My thoughts are sluggish, and I feel like there's something I don't understand. I can't think.

So sleepy. And nauseous. Head hurts. Can't think.

I move toward the cottage door before I realize there's no way I can walk back to the house feeling like this. I turn the lock, then shiver with a chill. I drag myself back to the sofa, but I feel dizzy. Confused. I need to call Dean. Tell him I can't make it tonight. Maybe 911. Maybe Dad or Dean. Or.... But my phone is in my purse all the way across the room, and I can't....

22

Not Gonna Die

DEAN

She's not coming.

I've been checking her tracker app for the last hour, and she hasn't even left her property. Her phone battery is at 14 percent, but she's ignored my reminders to charge her phone, which is completely unlike her.

On the other hand, we've never argued the way we have been lately. She's frustrated and sick of waiting, and I don't blame her. But my nightmares are out of control. On the nights Bronwyn and I spend together, I fight sleep every minute.

In France, I left her in our bed to sneak back to my original room to sleep for a few hours at a time away from her.

It's one thing to stay awake for a night or a weekend. It's another entirely to go more than a couple of days without sleep.

I've been working on something called Image Replacement Therapy. I try to control the dreams. Turn that vision of combat in the desert into a day at the park, Bronwyn and me pushing Phee on a toddler swing.

It doesn't work. No matter how hard I try or how much meditation I do beforehand, I can't convince myself that the day in the park could possibly be real.

Only death is real.

Her last location pinged at a little cottage a short walk from the house. I watch Bronwyn's unmoving tracker dot. She's now at 12 percent battery life, and unease skitters up my spine.

I head for the parking lot. She's not meeting me halfway? Then I'm going to her. And if she doesn't let me in, I'll spend the night on her damn porch. It's under the same roof, so I'm calling it cohabitation. She's not dissolving this marriage without a discussion.

She's not dissolving it *with* one either.

I'll work harder. I'll get it figured out. Whatever it takes, I'll do it. But she can't leave me.

The drive is taking too long. A half an hour into it, and I'm mentally rehashing every text I sent and every voice mail she's ignored for the last two hours. She may stop making the first move. She may be stiff and formal when she gets angry, but she never ignores me like this. Ever. It's the one thing guaranteed to shove me over the edge.

I'm still more than a fifteen-minute drive from Blackwater when the app no longer gives notice to "Remind My Wife To Charge Their Phone." Her battery is dying. Maybe it's already dead.

And I don't know why that realization has me hitting the gas when I'm already speeding, but my first assumption—that she's punishing me—feels wrong.

At the entrance to Bronwyn's property, I'm met by a wrought-iron gate. The security system on it is child's play.

I don't even bother with the intercom, just open the thing and let myself in.

I don't slow when I pass the main house. Her car is parked in the governor's drive, but the lights in the house are all completely out. If she forgot her phone in the cottage, then we'll laugh about how I rushed straight there later. But I'm not wasting time until I find her.

When I pull into the cottage's cracked and weed-choked drive, it's clear there are no lights on here either. There's no response when I ring the doorbell. Not a flicker of activity, and I'm no longer concerned that she's leaving me.

She's been here with construction crews full of strangers in and out constantly. They probably have keys to her house—

I rattle the door handle, but when I find it locked, I don't finesse it; I kick in her door.

I perform a sweep of the house, turning on lights and calling her name as I go.

I'm leaving the kitchen when I hear a voice just above a whisper coming from the room to my right.

"Dean."

I'm beside her on my knees and reaching to take her pulse before I've registered that I moved.

She's on the sofa, so still that it's frightening. Normally she moves and fidgets even in her sleep.

"Bronwyn. What's wrong? What happened?"

She won't open her eyes. Maybe she can't. She moves her forearm in a bizarrely slow motion to cover her face. "Head hurts. Neck hurts."

"I'm turning on the light in here, angel."

"No," she croaks.

"I have to see you better."

I flick on the lamp, and for a moment, I can't breathe. She looks like a wax doll.

"What else besides your head hurts?"

She doesn't say a word.

"Is this a migraine? You don't get migraines."

No response at all. She barely looks like she's breathing. Her pulse is thready and erratic. Her mouth hangs open, and she lies limp as I lift her eyelids to check her pupils. Both of them are blown wide, and her skin is hot and dry under my fingertips.

My mind is playing out any number of scenarios, all of them horrifying.

"No. No. No. No. Bronwyn. Angel, please."

I'm juggling my phone, calling 911 and telling them to send an ambulance and meet me halfway, even as I stand and lift her. She flops in my arms, completely boneless. Until, without even fully gaining consciousness, she vomits over both of us.

Jesus Christ.

I'm not swearing. I'm praying.

There's no time for cleaning up. I run with her in my arms to the car. I'd put her in the back seat, but Phee's car seat is there in the center, and I don't have time to remove it. Instead, I recline the passenger seat as far as it will go and lay her down on it.

She makes a sound, but her lips don't move. I race around to the driver's side and jump in, hitting the ignition button as I slam the door, then peel out and head for the hospital.

"Dean."

"Yes, angel."

"Somethnn's wron."

"You'll be okay. You'll be fine. Almost to the hospital."

She doesn't say anything to that.

"Bronwyn, wake up."

I'm driving with one hand on the wheel and one on her pulse.

"Dammit, do not fall asleep. Did someone give you something? What was it?"

Nothing.

She lives more than half an hour away. I flag the ambulance on its way toward her place, and we pull over to transfer her into their care. Another EMT is checking her pupils. "Shit. Bronwyn?"

He knows her. Of course, he does. Everyone in this town does.

"What's wrong with her?"

They ignore me and move her into the ambulance, the doors closing behind them just as my wife starts to seize.

I arrive at the hospital at the same time the ambulance does, and they immediately start wheeling her away.

"How long did that seizure last? Is she conscious? Where are you taking her?" I demand.

"I can't answer those questions right now," a nurse answers.

"I'm going with her."

"Are you a relative?" she asks skeptically.

"I'm her husband."

The look she gives me is pure irritation. She jerks her thumb behind her at the gurney where Bronwyn is disappearing down the hall. "I know her. I don't know you."

I dig into my pocket and pull out the box, the one that's now just as beaten up and worn as the first one was. I flick the lid open. "These are our wedding rings." I pull out her wedding band and show the nurse our names and the date inscribed inside. "She is my *wife*. No one is keeping her from me."

"Come with me."

I'm shown into a room with glass walls where Bronwyn is lying unmoving. Someone is taking her vital signs. Another nurse is cutting away her soiled clothing. A masked woman hands me a plastic drawstring bag and clean scrubs, pointing to an attached bathroom.

For half a second, I consider just staying there, covered in sick. But the look the woman gives me has me moving into the bathroom to clean up. They won't let me stay the way I am.

I wash and change in record time, then hover near the end of her bed.

There's a young female nurse with red hair and pale skin standing on one side of her bed, her mouth and nose covered in a mask, and a thin man with brown skin and a white jacket on the other, his face covered as well.

I stand at the end of her bed and hold her bare ankle.

The doctor mutters, "Damn," under his breath.

"What's wrong with her?" I bark.

He turns to me, and I see his name badge says Dr. Patel. "Mr. McRae... I'll need a spinal tap and MRI to confirm, but this looks like meningitis. We won't know for certain or what type until we've run some tests."

Bronwyn makes a sound, and the doctor doesn't wait for my reaction before he's asking her questions. "Bronwyn, when did you first notice the rash?"

When she doesn't respond, he looks at me. "How long has she had it?"

I shake my head. "I don't know."

I didn't even know she had a rash until the nurse cut her shirt away.

"It's important. Did she have it last night? Is it new today?"

I run a hand over the top of my head, gripping like I can produce the knowledge of something I don't know by sheer force of will.

"I wasn't here."

"Has she been ill? Symptoms of the flu or a sinus headache?"

"She's had a sinus headache for a week or so. But it wasn't bad. She said it wasn't a problem. Seasonal allergies."

He nods, then dismisses me with a glance.

A woman with curly brown hair runs into the room full-bore. She looks a lot like Deirdre, so she has to be Bronwyn's cousin, Marie. I hadn't thought about the fact that she's a respiratory therapist in this hospital, but she's obviously in the middle of a shift.

Dr. Patel leaves the room to do whatever it is he has to do next. A phlebotomist wheels in a cart before setting up an IV in Bronwyn's arm while the nurse is filling Marie in on her cousin's condition.

Someone hands me something made of paper to put on over my clothing. A mask that looks like a duck bill. Latex gloves.

When she finally notices me, the look Marie gives me over her face-covering is grim. "So you're 'the stealth husband.'"

I frown.

"She's going to be Life-Flighted out of here," she says.

I blink, my eyes hot and throat dry.

"You need to call her parents. If you don't, I'm going to violate all sorts of HIPAA and not give a flying fuck about it."

I jerk my head. "Of course I'll call them. Or... I can give you permission to call them, right?"

"Yes."

"Do it." I look at the nurse. "I give her permission to call them."

Marie takes a shuddering breath.

"What else? What else can I do?" I ask.

"Pray it's viral and not bacterial."

She leaves to make the phone calls, and I put on the protective gear and hold Bronwyn's hand. I can't feel her skin through the gloves. I fixate on that one thing. *If I could just touch her skin, she'd be okay.*

Dr. Patel returns to stand beside her gurney and nods toward the door. "Mr. McRae, you'll need to leave the room while we do the lumbar puncture."

Bronwyn has been mostly out of it when they've asked her questions. But, in response to his demand, she grips my hand and slurs frantically, "No, Dean. *Please*. Please stay. Don't leave me again. Can't watch you drive away. Can't."

Still holding her hand, I crouch beside her so my face is level with hers and brush her hair back from her forehead. I wipe my wet face on my shoulder. "I'm here, angel. I will *never* leave you."

The doctor's dark gaze lands on mine. "If you remain in this room, you need to be rock solid. You're her support, not the other way around. You pass out or hit the floor, you're staying there until we're done with our patient."

Bronwyn knows half the people in this hospital from volunteering here. Dr. Patel obviously likes her. And he's not impressed with me.

"I'm solid."

He rolls her onto her side and guides her into a fetal position.

I glance back at the doctor when he murmurs briefly to the nurse, catching a glimpse of the wicked-looking needle and the cloudy fluid he's extracting from her spinal cord.

Bronwyn hasn't opened her eyes voluntarily since I found her on the sofa, but she whimpers, "It's too bright."

"We'll turn the lights back off for you again as soon as Dr. Patel is done, sweetie," the nurse responds.

I lift my free hand and hold it over her closed eyes.

"Thank…," she attempts, then simply doesn't finish the sentence.

"Hold very still, Bronwyn," Dr. Patel says.

She doesn't move at all, her hand lax in mine.

As soon as he finishes, they take her for an MRI. I stand just outside, and it seems to go on forever. If the light through her eyelids hurt, I can't imagine what the sound of that machine is doing to her.

Then we're back in her room in the emergency department, waiting for a helicopter.

When the flight crew arrive to take her, Dr. Patel stops me, handing me a prescription and a stack of papers. "You'll need to take this and follow the quarantine protocol I explained earlier."

At my blank expression, he nods at the papers. "It's all written down for you if you don't remember."

I frown. "I need to be with my wife."

I can't be away from her. Never again. I don't know how I'll manage it, but I have to figure it out. The way we've been living has been so stupid.

For the first time, the doctor's expression is sympathetic. "You won't be able to do that. When she's feeling well enough, she can call you. She'll be in isolation."

"If she's contagious, I've already been exposed."

"Nice try."

Racing out to the parking lot, I jump in my car and drive to the hospital she's been taken to, a larger one near Hershey, PA. But when I get there, her family greets me in a solid wall of "Don't even think about it."

They've flown here and brought their own security with them: three guys, each as big as I am.

"Where is my wife?"

The doctor, a white woman with light brown hair and glasses, shoots a nervous glance at my father-in-law, then straightens her spine. "I'm sorry, sir. I'm not authorized to share information with you regarding Ms. McRae's condition."

"She's my *wife*."

She looks at Arden McRae III one more time, then turns back to me and says, "I'm sorry."

When she walks away, I glare at the man in front of me. "Did you buy the people in this hospital or threaten them?"

He lifts his chin and gives me a glacial once-over.

"I vote for both," Gabriel says in a lazy voice.

"I'm not leaving," I insist.

Arden assesses me. "Stubborn."

I say nothing.

"You found her. For that, I'm not having you forcibly removed from this hospital. But you've been playing with my little girl's heart. And I don't like it."

"I would rip my own arm off before I hurt her."

Whatever he sees on my face has him tipping his head to the side, expression intrigued. After a moment of his focused attention where, I suppose, he expects me to crack under his narrowed gaze, he indicates a room behind him. "We're waiting in there. We don't know anything yet."

I shake my head. "I can't be close to other people."

He contemplates me for a moment, then says, "It's a large room. You can have one side. We'll take the other."

23

Please Stay

DEAN

We file into the private room I'd guess is reserved for VIP families.

And we wait.

Periodically, we receive reports: She's in a negative pressure room, which means that her room is isolated from the air supply of the rest of the hospital to avoid contamination. She's on both antiviral medication and antibiotics through her IV. She had another seizure. She's conscious, but not fully lucid. They suspect the infection is bacterial. She asked for me. They let her know I was here.

Midway through the next morning, Charlotte, Bronwyn's mother, pats me on the shoulder and hands me a cup of coffee, a single-serve bottle of orange juice, and a brown bag containing a bagel. "I know you don't want to take the mask off around us, but you should at least eat something."

I clear my throat. "Thank you, ma'am."

Her eyes crinkle at the corners, though she doesn't really smile. "Thank *you*. The doctor said the only reason she's still with us is because you found her so quickly. She wouldn't have lasted the night." Her voice catches on the last sentence, and she smooths shaking hands down her thighs.

She sits down with two chairs between us, angles her body toward me, and finally says, "Dean, when you found our daughter and brought her to the hospital, you were exposed."

"I feel fine. I'm taking the prescription they gave me." If she's going to tell me to leave, I can't. I'll wait somewhere else, away from other people. But I can't *leave*.

She nods. "That's good. Is your daughter with a babysitter right now?"

"Yes." I wonder if Bronwyn told her I adopted Phee.

"If you fall ill, who will take care of Phee?" she asks.

I swallow. "The babysitter...."

We both know that if I were incapacitated for any length of time, the state would step in. Phee would end up in foster care. I have to force myself to stay still and not rock in place from pure dread at the thought.

"I want you to look at me and hear what I'm saying to you."

I hadn't even noticed that I'd been staring at my own hands. When I glance back at her, Charlotte's expression says she doesn't want to hear another word of my nonsense.

My mother-in-law's eyes are wet, but her voice doesn't waver. "I want you to know that if anything happens to you, that little girl has a family in us. *She will be safe with us.*"

I sit there. Rigid. Unmoving. I'm a hiker in an avalanche zone, tensing against the slightest sound. Afraid even to blink in case some small movement on my part starts a domino effect of emotion I can't control.

When I can finally speak and move again, I dip my head. "Thank you, ma'am."

My phone alerts me to an incoming call, and when I glance down I see James Mellinger, of all people, lighting up my phone. I excuse myself to take the call and step into the hall.

"How can I help you Mr. Mellinger?"

"What's wrong with Bronwyn? And stop calling me Mr. Mellinger. I'm not your boss anymore."

I frown. "How do you know *anything* is wrong with her?"

Charlotte planned to contact Bronwyn's friends later this afternoon, but she hasn't done it yet.

"I'm hoping there isn't and this is a stupid prank. But someone calling himself a 'disgruntled employee' has contacted my office asking for you. The messages sound ominous, Dean. So clue me the fuck in to what is going on with her, and how you even know anything about her life, whatsoever."

"Send me those messages."

My text alerts, and I scan the screenshots he's sent with growing rage.

"That *motherfucker*. Is he still responding to messages?"

There's a muffled pause, then James says, "It seems so."

"It's Kevin Hallman. If he did something to cause this, we need to find out exactly what he did and how. Other people could be in danger."

I explain the details as succinctly as I can.

"The team is on it. We're having Trayvon pretend to be you. We're also contacting the FBI. Now, explain to me why Hallman thinks you care about Bronwyn's health. Better yet, explain to me why you're even at that hospital in the first place."

At this point, I no longer care what James thinks. If he even looks at my wife unkindly, I'll fucking kill him. It's as simple as that. "I'm here because we're together."

Silence. Then James says coldly, "You asshole. Did you hook up with her in Paris?"

"We were married before I ever went to Paris."

Another pause, longer than the first. "You had a responsibility to keep me informed of conflicts of interest that could present a threat to my wife," he says silkily. And there is no missing the threat in his words.

"Which is why I transferred away from Blackwater and refused jobs that would force me to choose between Clarissa's safety and my wife's."

There's muffled sound, then James says, "I'm handing the phone to Trayvon."

Trayvon speaks. "Kevin Hallman wants 'credit' for her illness. He doesn't know the details of exactly what is wrong with her. He keeps making jokes about "the plague" and claims he was inside her house. He says he contaminated her water bottles with rodent urine and droppings. He says he 'took a chance and got lucky.' The FBI will be in touch."

I scrub a hand over my eyes.

"This guy is obsessed with the idea of revenge. He's not acting like he has anything to lose," Trayvon warns. As if that wasn't patently clear to me already.

When we've gone through everything we need to, I head down the hall to inform her healthcare team of the new information. Then I return to the waiting room to tell my in-laws.

Henry immediately begins working on his laptop and arranges for round the clock security for Phee. Hallman doesn't seem to know anything about my private life, thank God. He still thought I worked for James. But if he found my home or child....

Arden and Charlotte leave the room shortly after to find a nearby bed to crash in and a place for Arden to meet with his team.

I finally sit back down and do my best to eat and drink the food Charlotte provided earlier without removing my mask.

Gabriel is sprawled in a chair on the other side of the room and to my left. Henry is seated directly across from me, working on his laptop.

Henry doesn't appear to be paying attention to either of us. But when Gabriel reaches inside his jacket and pulls out a flask, dumping a generous amount of the contents into his paper coffee cup, Henry closes his computer and just *looks* at his brother.

Gabriel rolls his eyes. "Don't be a judgmental prick, Henry. This is a stressful situation. There's nothing wrong with taking the edge off a little."

"Hmmm."

Gabriel stands abruptly and toasts the two of us with his coffee cup. "Gentlemen. I'm taking a walk. It's stuffy in here."

Henry watches him leave, then turns his attention on me.

I'm not a talker. At least not with anyone besides Bronwyn. He can stare at me all he wants; it's not going to get me to start spilling my guts to the man. I lean back, cross my arms, and wait for him to say whatever it is he wants to get off his chest.

He smiles a little at my attitude. Then, apropos of nothing, he asks, "Do you know what beer goggles are?"

"Yes."

He waits for me to say more, but what the hell else is there to say to that?

He sighs. "Have you ever worn them?"

"No."

"Hmm." He looks out the window.

It's a beautiful, sunny day. I hope if Bronwyn's room has a window that it has blinds. The daylight has to be killing her head—

"Gabriel wears beer goggles a lot." He purses his lips. "Not beer, actually. He likes the hard stuff. But it's the same effect. Another nightclub, another woman he can't stand to look at the next day."

"Why are you telling me your family's private business?"

His brows lift a little. "*Your* family's private business."

"What?"

"You're a member of this family."

I almost laugh out loud at that. Fucking ridiculous. They weren't even going to let me know what was happening with Bronwyn until I refused to leave.

Henry smiles at me blandly. "I've decided you're a misunderstood person."

"I don't need anyone to *understand* me."

"I think you do." When I don't reply, he leans back, and I could swear I see pity in his eyes. "Ah. I see."

I don't want to ask this know-it-all prick what he sees. Suddenly, I'm grateful for the mask I'm wearing. It's hot and uncomfortable, but it's also excellent camouflage.

I pull out my phone and check my nanny cams for the hundredth time. Phee is eating in her high chair, laughing and smearing applesauce in her hair.

When Henry doesn't say anything else, my curiosity eventually gets the better of me. "What do you think you see?" I ask, my voice full of irritation.

He looks back up from his laptop, for all the world appearing to have forgotten I was even here. "Oh. Yes. So, I'm thinking... absent mother." He appears to be mulling it over. "Or maybe even worse than absent."

At my cold expression, he nods, smiling a little.

"Let's see. Bitter father," he continues as if he's working it all out in his head. As though he didn't read it in a report somewhere seventeen months ago when he was threatening to murder me if I did his sister dirty.

"You weren't allowed to have feelings," he says. "They weren't manly. Only anger was manly."

"I don't have a problem with anger," I state honestly. Because he may have made some correct guesses about my upbringing, but he's coming to some dead-wrong conclusions. My father was a fast fuse, but I promised myself I would never be like him. And I'm not.

"I'm aware. You have admirable self-control. So much, in fact, that I wonder if you even realize you have feelings at all."

"Okay, I'm done listening to you." I keep my expression flat.

"You imagine your daughter will always see you as a poor substitute for the mother she lost. You're even okay with it because that's how you see yourself."

His words make me deeply uncomfortable.

"You have abandonment issues."

I scoff. "Are you done?"

"No. You love my sister."

I huff, but it only sounds like a laugh. Inside, it feels an awful lot like despair. "Who the hell wouldn't love her?"

"Have you ever told her that you love her?"

"Words are just words. They don't mean anything."

"They mean a lot to some people. My sister has always been one of them. She can't hang up the phone without saying it and hearing me say it back. And I'm her brother, not her husband."

At my blank expression, he shakes his head in disappointment. "She's said them to you, hasn't she? And you're so uncomfortable with the words that you ignored them. And slowly... she stopped. Because the way you brushed them off hurt her."

He scoffs. "You've been so concerned with staying in your own comfort zone that you constantly force my sister to live outside her own." He spreads his hands. "Selfish."

At my horrified expression, he smiles a little. "It's just three little words. My sister needs them. Maybe even try them out on your daughter. The more you say them, the easier they get."

He stands and stretches the kinks out.

"Why are you telling me this instead of warning me to stay away?"

"Because I've decided you're not a lost cause." He cracks his neck to the side. "I'm taking a walk. Text me if there's any news."

I move to the window and wait for him to take his ass out of this room.

If Bronwyn was feeling hurt or rejected, why wouldn't she have told me about it?

Right. Because I expect her to share everything when I share nothing.

Henry stops at the threshold and looks back. "You know, I wonder," he muses, "how you'd see my sister if you took off your fear goggles."

I stare after him as he goes. Fucking Henry with his "observations" on my psyche.

I asked Bronwyn once why she always put what other people wanted ahead of what she needed. Then I turned around and did it to her myself.

I know what I have to do. I just don't know if I *can*.

Henry hit the nail on the head when he told me I've been wearing fear goggles. Because the idea of exposing myself to her makes my stomach knot into a hard ball of dread.

I clear my throat and try to say the words out loud, feeling sheepish and silly. "I lo—"

I scrub my hand down my face, then pull out my phone and text Phee's nanny.

Me: How's everything going?

Anne: Just fine. She's a happy ball of energy today.

Me: ...

Me: Tell her Daddy loves her.

Anne: Will do.

And I breathe.

I've no sooner shoved my phone back into my pocket when a FaceTime alert comes through.

I answer, and a nurse in full gear with his face and hair covered asks, "Dean?"

"Yes."

"Your wife would like to speak with you."

Then he's holding the phone for Bronwyn.

"Heyyy, Dean," she says, her voice barely a whisper. Her eyes aren't open fully.

"Hey, Bronwyn."

"Thanks... for coming for me."

"Always."

She holds a hand over her eyes. "I need you to do something."

"Anything."

"Need you to leave."

"Anything but that," I say.

"You can't get sick. Phee needs you."

I shake my head.

"I'm starting... to feel better already. I'll be here a couple of weeks. I'll be sleeping. Use our house in Blackwater to quarantine. Then go home to Phee."

The fact that she's speaking at all is an improvement, but "better" is relative. She's still in danger. "I can't."

"Sometimes we don't see each other for a month at a time. This... no different."

"We can't keep living like that. Staying away was the biggest mistake of my life."

"All you'll do is sit outside and wait. If you end up sick, you'll... expose my family too."

She's right.

She closes her eyes fully, and a tear snakes down her cheek. "Please. I'm tired. My head hurts. Say you'll quarantine...worried. My family will make sure you're okay. I need to know...."

I cover my eyes. *Is this what I did to her? I sent her away. Over and fucking over.*

When I can finally manage it, I drop my hand to find she still hasn't opened her eyes.

"I love you." It just falls out of my mouth.

My mother threw those words around like confetti, and they meant nothing. My father never said them. Not in my hearing, anyway.

But Bronwyn needs the words. And they're true.

I called it infatuation. Obsession. Addiction. Anything but what it actually was.

"I love you so much. I can't live without you, B."

She doesn't open her eyes or answer, and after a beat, the nurse says, "She's sleeping now," and disconnects.

24

If You Love Her

BRONWYN

I vaguely remember bits and pieces of the first week.

Dean found me at the cottage. I may have thrown up on him. He held my hand. He covered my eyes.

I think I asked him to leave when the infectious disease specialist started talking about contagions and vulnerable populations.

He came back and brought me clothes and my phone, plus a pillow and blanket from my own bed.

The last part I only know because one of my nurses, Ivan, told me it was my hot husband who brought them.

I managed a smile at that.

I'm on the mend, but it's the worst headache of my life. It's ever-present and agonizing. At first, I don't really notice that I don't have much strength in the left side of my body. My thoughts are still confused. I forget words easily or my train of thought, and my face sometimes feels like I have no control over it.

I've cried a few times randomly for what seems like no reason at all, as though my body simply took over and made me sob when I wasn't feeling sad. But I barely remember it.

They gave me a port since I'll need high doses of intravenous medication for a while even after they release me from the hospital.

My abdomen is black and blue from the shots they give me.

But everyone here is kind, even if they do, understandably, come in, do what they have to do, and get out as quickly as possible.

There's something new from Dean every day. A sleep mask to cover my eyes. Flowers. A soft robe.

The room is filling up with deliveries from my family and friends too.

I'd never tell them, but Dean's are my favorite.

The fact that I've kept him a secret has become ridiculous. At the very least, I need to tell my friends.

And if they say some things I don't want to hear? I'm strong enough to defend my position.

Before this happened, I was reaching a breaking point. But I've realized something that changes things for me.

Dean loves me. I heard him say it. I almost remember it. But even if I hadn't, I felt it. I can work with that.

No more of this stoic, "you only get to know about the good parts" nonsense. Just… no more. "Fish or cut bait," as Grandad would say.

I was scared to demand a marriage because I thought crumbs were better than nothing.

But they aren't. Crumbs leave you starving and feral, like a neglected dog kept outside on a chain. They turned me into someone I didn't know and didn't like.

But now I know. Dean needs me. He will *always* come for me.

I'm done accepting the status quo with us. I'm a mess right now, and I won't do anything while my brain still hurts nonstop. But soon.

My head and my neck hurt, and looking at a screen makes it worse. But a nurse has helped me FaceTime Dean, my parents, and brothers a couple of times already, though I don't remember days or how many times or what we said.

But I finally feel awake and fully aware.

I pick up my phone, which some kind aide or nurse plugged into a charger and left on the wheelie table beside me, and open my texts.

Dean: You fell asleep. You didn't hear me. But I love you.

Dean: I love you.

Dean: Just so you know. I LOVE YOU.

Dean: I love you.

Dean: You keep forgetting things. I'm reminding you here, so you can look at it and see it anytime you need to. I love you.

It hurts to laugh, but I do it anyway. It reminds me of the bear incident.

Me: Just checking. Dean Priester, are you saying you love me?

Dean's response is instantaneous.

Dean: Yes. I love you.

I FaceTime him, and he picks up. He doesn't say anything, just looks at me, smiling without smiling.

"I love you too," I say.

His expression turns very serious as he nods. Then his lips twitch. "Say you love-love me."

My hair is matted in a greasy mess against my head. My skin is waxy. My eyes can only open to partial slits because even the natural daylight through the window hurts.

But I smile and say, "I love-love you."

He grins. "I knew you were checking out my ass."

I lean back, and my eyes drift closed.

"Still wiped out, huh?" he asks.

"Yes."

"Will you remember this time?"

"I will. I'm waking up more. Time is functioning normally again," I say. "My thoughts are clearer."

"Good."

"When I get out of here, am I moving in with you, or are you moving in with me?"

"I'm coming to you. I can work from anywhere most of the time."

"Really?" I breathe. "That easy?"

He snorts. "You think this was easy?"

"I guess not. But since I don't understand why you didn't want to be with me in the first place, I don't know why this changes anything."

"I can't lose you." He takes a breath. "I didn't want to be a burden to you. Phee and I, we'll make your life harder. And I couldn't figure out how not to do that. But seeing you like that.... I could lose you in an instant. You were alone. Like my sister. And some things will be harder with me, but at least you'll never be alone again."

I don't like that sentiment at all. As if all he's worth to me is a warm body in case of an emergency.

"You could never be a burden," I say.

He just smiles with that look he gets on his face when he thinks I'm being "sweet."

"The doctor says you might be ready to leave the hospital in a couple of weeks." He looks up, as if he's doing calculations. "But you'll still be recovering for a while. Phee and I are moving into the pool house at your parents' place for now, and you'll be right next door in the mansion. Your house and a security team aren't set up in Blackwater, so you'll have to stay with your parents while we work through that."

"Oh." It makes sense, but it's disappointing.

"Just until you're stronger. The doctor said when you do go home, you'll still have an IV and need nursing care. You'll need physical therapy. Probably occupational therapy too. She's a really active toddler. She could hurt you."

"I'm not worried about that, but she can't be near me until I complete all my medications. I won't feel like it's safe for her, until then."

"Yes. There's that, too."

"And then we move back to Blackwater?"

"After we've found Hallman and after we have as much security on that estate as your parents have in New York."

"You could stay in my parents' house with me. Phee wouldn't need to come near my room."

He hesitates, then says, "I need to sleep in the pool house."

My eyelids drift closed all on their own. "I'm too tired to argue with you. I'll kick your ass about this later."

He huffs a laugh. "I love you, B."

I don't open my eyes. "I love-love you."

• • • ● • ● • • •

The next night I text him at 2:15 a.m. I don't do it so late on purpose, but my days and nights are all mixed up, and I've freaked myself out.

I figure he won't pick up the phone until morning. Then he'll see a missed text.

Me: How many people do you think have died in the bed I'm sleeping in?

FaceTime rings. I should have known he'd pick up no matter what time it was.

He's turning on a lamp and sitting up when I accept.

He lifts an eyebrow. "None. Zero. No one has ever died in your bed."

I shake my head slightly, then press my palm to my temple. "That can't be accurate. They don't replace the bed just because someone died in it."

"Your father probably paid for a brand-new bed."

"Nope. I don't believe you. Because *I* bet he didn't think of it. If he thought of it, he would have. But he didn't."

He squints. "What's that noise?"

I squirm, then flip the camera to the television and back again. "*Supernatural*. It's a marathon. I've never watched it before. It's got a hot guy named Dean. Reminds me of you a little, except he's more...."

Dean's chest puffs out. "He's more what?"

I wave a hand. "Actor-y."

"Why are you watching something you know will freak you out?"

"I can't even really watch it. The screen hurts my head. Mostly I'm just listening to it."

Dean's eyes smile. "I love you, weirdo."

"Love you too."

"Are you still freaked out?"

"I'd like to say no."

A text alert comes through.

"I sent you a link to one of my playlists. I use it to try to center myself and relax before I sleep."

"Wow. I didn't realize you were such an enlightened guy, Dean."

I was kidding, but something tightens in his expression.

I try to backpedal from what he obviously took as criticism. "This is way cool. Thank you. I'll turn off *Supernatural* and listen to this."

"It's just something to try. To make it easier to sleep."

"If it works for you, I'll give it a shot."

"It doesn't work exactly. But it doesn't hurt."

"Do you have trouble sleeping?" I ask, surprised.

"I was already awake when you texted."

"Oh."

He's been rubbing his shoulder on and off the whole time. He does it so often that I'd almost wondered if it were habit. "Your shoulder keeps you awake?"

"Among other things. Tell you what. You turn off the television, I'll turn on the playlist, and we can both chill out as we fall asleep."

I roll over and prop the phone beside me on the pillow. Music plays through the speaker. It's a sort of soothing instrumental thing with nature sounds in the background. Nothing I'd have ever imagined Dean listening to in a million years.

He's smiling back at me as my eyes drift closed. "Happy thoughts, B. Sunshine and picnics. We'll sit on your back porch and drink sweet tea. At Christmas we can take Phee together to pick out a tree..."

Dean, who no one seems to think talks at all, keeps talking. His voice grows quieter and soothing as he tells me about a day at a park and pushing Phee on a toddler swing. He tells me to imagine it, pushing the swing while Phee laughs.

I fall asleep that way, phone clutched in my hand and Dean's voice wrapped around my heart.

25
Long Way to Go
BRONWYN

October, Four Weeks Later

"This is the worst idea you've ever had. Just sit down and tell him that this is your boundary," Clarissa says, plopping her empty margarita glass onto the counter. "Take it or leave it."

I prop my cane against her kitchen table. Everything in her house in the Hamptons is white, white, white. Occasionally, there's a splash of some foamy green or gray-blue.

It's lovely, and it suits her.

But I can't help but want to go at the place with about five different colors of paint.

Because Clarissa and I? We are not the same.

"Please," I scoff. "This is far from my worst idea."

She grimaces in acknowledgment.

My expression matches hers because *ugh*.

At the same time, we both say, "Prom night."

But she refuses to be distracted for long. "I don't think it's a good idea to play games with your husband. Honesty is one of the foundations of a healthy relationship. You have to learn to talk to each other."

"Dean's been playing games since Day One. He low-key stalks me. I'm just going to match his energy. He has to think it's his idea."

She shakes her head. "What if you asked him to go to couples therapy? Would he try that? He loves you. He's just worried about you."

I huff. "If he'd move into my parents' place with me, I'd let this go for another month or so. But since he won't sleep under their roof, I'm out of patience. I'd have done therapy six months ago. Now, I'm just done. My way is going to have that man not just moved into my house in Blackwater, but *belligerently* moved in. He's going to go all 'You are my wife' and think he did something when I agree and 'allow' him and Phee to live with me."

"You're still not wearing your wedding rings."

"He tried to give them back to me, and I said he can put those rings on my finger when he's living under the same roof with me, and not before."

She winces. "Ouch. Harsh."

"He's a big boy. He can take it."

"An ultimatum didn't exactly get James on board."

"They are very different people."

She turns on the blender, and I watch, mesmerized, as she once more turns Clase Azul tequila into margaritas.

When she turns the blender off, I say, "I can't believe we're doing this. Isn't this, like, the most expensive tequila in the world?"

She shrugs. "I think it was a great idea. You were right. If we want to drink it in margaritas, then we should." Her face puckers up, on the verge of tears.

This is why I'm here tonight of all nights. It's their anniversary, and James sent her a case of tequila that probably cost close to half a million dollars. Because he loves her even though he has his head up his butt too.

"Men are dumbasses," I state matter-of-factly.

She shakes her head in exasperation. "Now you sound like Janessa. Don't call them names. It's not true, and all it does is create an 'us against them' attitude. When you're married, there's not a winner and a loser. Either you're both winning together or you're both losing. You're one team."

I look at her with a bemused smile. "When did you turn so *wise*? You're some kind of relationship guru now."

She gives a sad huff of laughter. "If that were true, then I wouldn't be living here, would I?"

"You and James will figure things out."

She sniffs and pats at the tears on her cheeks with delicate fingers.

I wave both my hands at her. "Bring it in. Gimme a hug, Harcourt."

A couple of months ago, I'd have jumped up and thrown my arms around her. But I'm still a little whiffy, my head still has a constant low-grade ache, and I'm unsteady on my feet.

Clarissa hugs me, then gracefully eases into the chair beside me. How she manages to do that when she's already tipsy, I'll never know.

I'm a flopper—lotta energy, not always a lot of grace. It's so cute that Dean thinks I'm a good dancer. Or at least he did. Not sure how long it'll take to get my balance back.

Clarissa is on her second margarita, and I've had a few sips from mine in solidarity.

"I'm being too hard on you. Dean said you're just supposed to sit and relax."

"I'm sitting and relaxing," I reassure her.

"I still can't believe anyone could do what Hallman did." Clarissa sways a little in drunken horror. The tequila is beginning to take effect.

"Henry believes he's reacting to a 'narcissistic wound'. The man's choices aren't logical. Basically, there's nothing too far for him because he feels justified and victimized. I think he was hoping to affect my whole family."

"It was attempted murder."

"The only advantage I can see to something like that is how hard it would be to pinpoint as a crime. Go bragging about it, and you've just thrown that away. His messages said he thought it was a long shot that I'd even drink from one of the bottles, let alone get sick from it. He thought it would be something 'fun' to screw with the bottles I drink from, and my infection was a 'lucky break.' His real purpose was to frighten me by leaving the photos. But once it was done, he couldn't resist gloating."

"He needs to die."

My eyes shoot wide. Not because I don't agree, but because *Clarissa* said it.

She shrugs. "Don't care. The world will be a much better place without him in it."

"Forget about him. We have more important things to worry about. We've both been through it this year. But look at you, all recovered. I'll get there too."

I point at Clarissa's margarita and change the subject. "According to Dean, we're committing a crime against good tequila," I say with a grin.

"I still can't believe you've been married to him the whole time. It's a good thing you almost died or Janessa would have stopped talking to you for weeks."

I snicker. "You are so drunk. I hope you remember tomorrow that you said that."

She slaps both of her hands over her mouth. I think she's going to laugh.

Instead, she wails, "I didn't mean it. It's not a good thing you almost died."

I lean forward to rub her back. "Awww, honey, this is why you're not supposed to get drunk when you're sad. I'm only teasing you."

She sniffs. "I'm worried your plan could backfire, Bronwyn."

I shrug even as I tighten my arms around her. "It's a chance I have to take."

26

Dancing Queen

DEAN

Five Days Later

Bronwyn *left* me. Through a text message.

My Wife: Not doing this anymore. I love-love you, but no more hotel hookups. I won't be your fuck buddy.

I'd barely started a text reply when her next words came through.

My Wife: I'm taking my dot off your phone.

She ignored my texts that followed. She sent my calls to voice mail.

Unlike the last time when she didn't show for our weekend, I know exactly what she's doing. She thinks she shut off the tracker on her phone, but she obviously didn't remember how to disable it. I'm guessing she just removed the icon from her home screen without uninstalling the app.

While she was in the hospital, I installed a state of the art security system and hired a full team for her house in Blackwater myself. So I watch her progress on the locator app as she makes her way back to Pennsylvania. Then I access the estate security system and watch Henry park the car and carry her bags inside for her.

I watch her make herself a cup of hot chocolate in the kitchen and chat briefly with one of the staff. Watch her walk with her cane and mug onto the back porch and cuddle up on the swing. Then I listen as she talks out loud to herself, debating her next step.

I'm lucky, honestly, that she chose one of the more public places where the security cameras are located. If she'd had her little self-talk session in one of the bedrooms or a bathroom, I'd have been screwed.

As it is, she's seated right there, front and center. And loud and clear.

"Just do it. Block him. If he doesn't want to live with you, it's time to cut him loose." She hovers over her phone, then sets it on the swing with a clatter.

She appears to be repeating some mantra in her head. Then she says it out loud. "I deserve a real marriage. If he doesn't want one, then he needs to get out of my future husband's way."

What the actual fucking *hell* is she saying? Did her friends tell her this shit? I bet it was *Henry*. That prick decided I was a lost cause after all.

Two seconds later, she picks her phone back up and decisively swipes around on the screen. "You made a fool of yourself over him long enough."

She's blocked me. I don't even need to check to know it.

My gut tightens at the realization that I was the one who pushed her to this. Oh, it might have been Henry's idea—I wouldn't put it past him at all—but she'd never be thinking about finding a new relationship if the one I'd been giving her was enough for her in the first place.

She's called herself my fuck buddy before, and I've argued with her about it. But if I've been making her feel like one, then that's how she feels. Telling her she's wrong is worse than pointless. It's dismissive.

She tried to talk to me about this last week when I tried to schedule a weekend away for just the two of us. She'd told me then that she didn't want to continue with the status quo. I'd insisted it wasn't time, yet. Not with Hallman still in the wind and her recovery incomplete. And she'd replied, "All or nothing, Dean."

But I hadn't realized she'd actually meant *nothing*.

I think I can manage Phee with her. As long as I don't expect Bronwyn to take on childcare tasks, it should be mostly fine. But I haven't figured out yet how I'm going to sleep in the same house with her without letting her see how weak I am.

I wake from those nightmares with my face and pillow wet. I don't know exactly what I'm shouting out loud, but I know what I say in my dreams. I scream and beg like a fucking pussy.

"Fear Goggles."

We were on a hamster wheel, and she got tired of it. But she didn't just jump off the wheel—she knocked the whole cage over.

I have to get us all living under the same roof.

Visions of sneaking out to sleep on the porch or in my car fill my head.

I could tell her she snores, then take one of the spare rooms for myself. I could bring my guitar and cover the walls with the soundproofing.

No. That isn't going to work.

It's one thing to keep my own secrets. It's another to gaslight her and make her feel bad about something that's my own fault.

I'm going to have to tell her about the dreams and that I have to sleep in another room. I'll put up the soundproofing. It'll have to be enough. I'm out of time.

With a satisfied expression on her sweet face, Bronwyn says, "Alexa, play 'Dancing Queen'."

Then, on a beautiful fall evening, with colorful foliage all around her, she stands, leans on her pink cane, and starts to dance, wiggling her butt to the beat.

And I pack my bags.

27
The Last Time
DEAN

The security guard hasn't taken his eyes off me as I stand just outside the entrance to the youth center Bronwyn opened in Blackwater. I give him a nod, adjust Phee's warm weight in my left arm, and press the security buzzer.

A tinny female voice responds. "Can I help you?"

Here goes fucking everything.

"Yes, ma'am. You can tell Bronwyn McRae that her husband is here to take her home."

She got a ride here from security this morning because she's not even cleared to be back behind the wheel. She shouldn't be at work at all.

It's pretty obvious from the look on the guard's face that he doesn't like what he just heard.

I looked over the plans for the physical security for this building when she opened it. But she hired a local company for the guards themselves. In other words, I don't know this guy.

I tip my head in his direction. "That's right, rent-a-cop. I'm Bronwyn McRae's husband. Make sure you have a beer after work and whine to *everyone* about how she's taken."

He rolls his eyes. "Do you spend your entire existence thinking that every man on the planet wants your wife?"

I suck on my teeth. "Of course not. Women want her too."

He gives a reluctant huff of laughter and shakes his head.

Phee conked out hard on the last leg of the drive. She woke when I finally got her out of her car seat and bundled her up. Now she's alert but not fussy, busy taking in the scenery, her attention caught on the big clock, the buildings and signs, the pedestrians as they pass us.

She shifts against my shoulder, and I glance down at my watch. It's chilly, but I'm not worried. Phee is wrapped in a red blanket that Bronwyn knitted for her. I've got on a navy fleece jacket and deliberately chose to wear one of the hats she made for me.

Just a little reminder of who we belong to. I haven't worn my wedding ring outside the house, but I can put her hat on my head. It's a physical reminder that she cares.

Bronwyn isn't going to keep me waiting for long anyway. Not after the way I just exposed our relationship to what amounts to the whole town.

When I lift my eyes toward the building, I catch a glint of blonde hair and a bright red coat as she makes her way down the stairs.

I eye her cane with concern. She's overdoing it, and she looks wobbly as hell. Her security is two steps ahead of her, but Austin isn't watching to make sure she doesn't whiff it down the stairs. He's watching for potential outside threats.

I'm getting this woman home. Now. She can rail at me about it later, but it hasn't even been six weeks.

Austin nods at me as he opens the bulletproof reinforced glass doors, and Bronwyn follows behind.

I wait for her face to light up, for her expression to go sly and flirty. I wait for her "Heyyy, Dean."

It doesn't come.

Her ice-blue gaze alights on me. A blow to the chest, though she hasn't laid a hand on me.

When her attention skims over me and lands on Phee, her expression softens, and she reaches out as though to rub her little back.

She pulls away before she makes contact and shoves her fingers under her armpit, as if to stay warm in the October chill.

Bronwyn turns to Austin. "I'll catch a ride home with Dean. You can head back. Thanks."

He dips his blond head. "No problem."

Bronwyn walks toward my car. I follow, putting some distance between us and the guard.

I hover a hand near her elbow to steady her in case she trips or her leg gives out.

She turns, finally, and meets my gaze. "You realize there's no going back from your announcement. This isn't like the hospital where you can threaten people with privacy laws and my family name. You may as well have shouted ''we're married' into a bullhorn on the fifty-yard line."

"I have no intention of 'going back.'"

She narrows her eyes at me. I mirror her expression.

Then I cover Phee's ear and press her against me so the other is muffled against my chest. Turning my head in the general direction of Main St., I bellow, "Bronwyn McRae is my wife!" as loudly as I can.

It's so out of character for me that Bronwyn's eyes shoot wide in shock, and Phee squirms against me. She lifts her head and looks at me curiously. I smile at her and wiggle my eyebrows. She giggles.

A few people in the distance look our way, startled. One lifts a hand in greeting.

Bronwyn is trying really hard to scowl but only half managing it. "You're an a—"

She stops herself and glances at Phee, then rephrases. "You're like a kid with a toy. You don't want me for yourself, but you want to make sure no one else has a shot at me."

I shake my head, long and slow. "You know that's not true. I'm like a kid with a cookie he was saving for later." My eyes trail down her body. "I licked it. Now it's mine."

She closes her eyes, slaps a palm across her mouth, and stands there for so long that I start to wonder if I just made a major misstep.

I'd rehearsed a speech for this moment. If I could have remembered it, I'd have given it. But the second I saw her, I went off script.

She doesn't drop her hand, but, thankfully, humor laces her tone when she says, "Stop trying to make me laugh."

"I figure if you laugh, maybe you'll forgive me."

The whole time I'd packed up the SUV, placed my phone calls, and made arrangements to work remotely, I'd been focused on one thing: get it done and get to my wife.

I didn't let myself consider that Bronwyn might not want me anymore.

She didn't even cry after she blocked me. She didn't mourn the loss of us.

She danced.

Now I feel it, standing on this sidewalk in front of a public building downtown surrounded by potential witnesses.

She told me she loved me. And she left.

She drops her hand, and her expression has moved from humor to concern. "I don't need to forgive you."

"Bronw—

"You didn't do anything wrong. I had to make a decision about what I could live with. I couldn't do breadcrumbs anymore."

She's not even angry. Anger I could work with. Anger means she still cares.

"No more cohabitation weekends. We're just together. All the time. Forever," I agree.

She squeezes my hand, but she doesn't throw herself into my arms. "How did you know I'd be here?"

"I ordered a cup of coffee at the diner and chatted with your aunt. I didn't even have to tell her I was looking for you. She assumed I knew where you were, what you were doing, and that you're being, in her words, 'stubborn'."

Technically, that's only true because I needed an alibi. I'm not ready to tell her she didn't disable her tracker. If she runs again, I don't want her to know I can find her.

Bronwyn snorts. "Lovely."

She's not admitting to it. Maybe she doesn't even realize she's feeling it. I have some experience with that. But something in the tightness of her mouth tells me she *is* angry.

Phee wiggles around and beams at Bronwyn. She's spent some time with her in the last week, but always with me there and careful that she doesn't put any demands on her physically.

She puts her hand on my cheek and asks eagerly, "Mom-win, Daddy?"

I give her a wink. "Yes."

"Mom-win is pwitty!"

Attagirl. I'm no expert on other kids her age, but I'm certain my kid is a genius. Her speech is pretty clear for an eighteen-month-old, and she has a memory like a steel trap.

I grab her little hand from my cheek and pretend to nibble her chubby fingers, partially because it's what I always do but also because I'm fairly sure it's going to make Bronwyn melt into a puddle. "Yes, Phee Bee. Bronwyn is very pretty."

Phee giggles in response, and Bronwyn actually puts her hand on her chest as her eyebrows rise in the middle. If I listen really, really hard, I can almost hear the echo of her mental "*Awww.*"

That's right, Bronwyn. My kid is cute as hell. She doesn't fight her diaper changes, and she doesn't scream if you forget to cut her toast into triangles. She's all cute, all the time.

Just like I'm all sexy and in control. All the time.

For once in my life, I play the dad card with Bronwyn. "Can we get her settled in at our new house? We've been on the road for hours. She needs to stretch her legs."

Bronwyn's eyes light up in admiration. "Oooh, you're good. Just when I think you're about to go all caveman...."

I blink at her innocently.

She wiggles her eyebrows at Phee. "Your daddy is smooth. Did he tell you to call me pretty?"

Phee claps her hands. "Yes. Mom-win pwitty."

I look directly into my little traitor's face. "Side-eye, kid. Side. Eye."

And Bronwyn laughs.

28

Liability

BRONWYN

Dean looks tired and stressed, and I feel like a bitch.

But I'm looking at it as relationship surgery—you have to make some cuts before the healing can start.

He doesn't show emotional vulnerability very often. He's always the strong one. The stoic man who hides everything. Even his smile.

I worried he might get bossy. Haul me over his shoulder and try to seduce me into bed. Not that I would have allowed that.

Instead, he looked like I'd gutted him. He pulled himself together fast, but I saw it.

Dean brought Phee with him. I wasn't sure about that part. I worried that he might just show up on his own and I'd have to send him back to New York.

When I saw his car full of his things, I almost threw myself at him and blabbed my confession.

Something in his expression stopped me at the last second. Because we are so close to having it all, but we've been close before.

Until he's ready to break down those walls with me, all my confession will do is give him an excuse to go back to what we were.

So I need to stay the course. Getting him and Phee here is only the first phase of the plan Henry annoyingly dubbed "Operation Save the Stealth Husband."

Dean is going to murder us all when he finds out. But maybe he never has to know that part.

He peers out the dining room window. Phee is in a portable high chair munching on a snack, and he occasionally refills her tray with cereal puffs.

She's drinking her milk from a sippy cup, looking first at Dean, then at me with curiosity. She keeps saying, "Mmmm," every time she takes a bite, then watches to make sure I smile when she does it. She's the cutest kid I've ever seen.

She slams her sippy cup on the tray and yells, "Down!"

Dean shoots me a glance, then swoops in to unstrap her. He speaks to her so quietly that I can't hear his words. She pats his face and smiles at him.

A kind of helpless pain skates behind his eyes. I blink and it's gone.

I put my arms out for Phee. "I can watch her while you bring in the rest of your things."

He shifts her away from me. "No. She's a handful. You relax."

"I want to do it."

"I'll take care of her. I don't expect you to do that."

"Because she's a handful?" I ask quietly. "Considering people say the same thing about me, I'd think you'd find me uniquely qualified." I force a smile.

He runs his thumb over my cheekbone, then dips it down to skim my dimple. "You're still recovering, angel. I'll take care of everything."

"You're standing here in our kitchen, but I'm still dangling," I say.

His brows knit. "What?"

"You kept me dangling on a hook for almost a year and a half," I explain. "But then I realized I don't need to be perfect or do every single thing that every person asks me to out of fear of being unlovable. Either you love me or you don't. And that includes"—I wave a hand—"whatever that was we were doing."

He looks like I slapped him. "You were afraid I wouldn't love you? B, I *do* love you."

I nod seriously. "I *was* afraid you didn't love me. Not anymore. Now you just have to figure out how to believe I love you."

He runs a hand over his chin. "We need to talk."

I look at him hopefully. "Yes?"

He glances away. Swallows. When he looks back, he gives a quick jerk of his head. "Not in front of Phee. She listens to everything. We can talk after she's down for the night."

29

Just Us

DEAN

I start Phee's bedtime routine around eight o'clock. I expect her to fuss at being in a different place, but after I feed her, let her wear herself out exploring, and give her a bath, her eyes are drooping before I finish singing the first verse of "Hey There, Delilah."

Bronwyn disappeared downstairs while I was giving Phee her bath. I heard her speaking to both a man and a woman. The front door opened and closed several times. If my hands hadn't been full of soapy kid, I'd have checked the security cameras.

But I heard her laughing, and I'm pretty sure the male voice was Jack's, so I wasn't concerned about her safety. Though she's massively overdoing things. The doctor only removed her port less than a week ago.

But I also understand. She was tired of waiting. I was the same way when I was recovering, impatient as hell with my own body.

Bronwyn comes upstairs just as Phee is falling asleep.

She's standing in the doorway to the guest bedroom, peering into the gloom with those sensitive pale blue eyes of hers. She watches as I lay Phee in the crib that I set up for her after dinner.

When I've successfully settled her into bed, I marvel over her for a moment, smoothing her curly hair back from her forehead. She makes my chest ache in the best way possible.

I wait to be sure she's really asleep and won't jerk awake or fuss.

She's out like a light, so I straighten and turn toward the door.

It's time for that talk I promised Bronwyn.

My wife flips her hair over her shoulder and turns away, walking down the hall toward the stairs. Her cane plugs into the floor with every step.

She's changed into a pair of yoga pants and a fitted T-shirt. I'm distracted by the curve of her ass as she walks in front of me. It's been *two months* since I've seen my wife naked, let alone touched her. Granted, she was recovering for most of that time, but—

She glances back and catches me ogling her ass.

I attempt to affect an innocent expression, and she rolls her eyes. "Stop looking at me like you're a lion stalking his dinner."

"Seems to me you got that backward. There I was, minding my own business, living out my dreams of munching on grass like any good zebra does"—she snorts in disbelief—"and there you were, pouncing on me every chance you got."

She flinches at the reminder of how she'd relentlessly flirted with me when we met, then straightens her spine and gives a stiff jerk of her chin.

My words must have sounded like an accusation.

She said she made a fool of herself over me. But that's not how I remember it. Being the object of her affection was like swallowing sunshine.

"I'm terrible at flirting," I admit. "My words always come out wrong. I liked that you—"

"Maybe I was the lion," she cuts in, "but I'm done chasing you. If you want me, you're going to need to do more than stare at my butt and expect me to jump into your arms in gratitude for a little attention. Those days are over."

She mutters something, and my heart stops. When it starts again, it pounds painfully in my chest.

I move into her space before I even have time to question myself, wrapping my hand beneath the silk of her hair and around the back of her neck.

My mouth is against her temple as I whisper hoarsely, "You are not pathetic. You're perfect. I didn't give you enough. I know that. But it was never because you deserved less than everything."

She's changed her shampoo since the last time we were alone together. It's a kind of citrusy floral scent now, and she smells good. She always does.

But some part of me hates that new shampoo because it reminds me of how much time and distance exists between us. How both of us have been living our lives away from each other.

My fault. Always my fault.

Relief floods through me when Bronwyn doesn't try to pull away from me.

She moves closer, our bodies just inches from each other, and places her palms on my abdomen. She sighs, breathing me in the same way I'm doing with her.

Then she's pushing me away. "We're not ready for that yet. You start touching me, and my brain shuts off and my hormones take over. I need...."

Her eyes trail over me. And yeah, I feel it too.

I can hardly breathe with how much I feel it. Not sex. Or not *just* sex. I need her skin against mine. I need her heartbeat and warmth. The skim of her breath over sensitized nerve endings. The sound of her voice. Her laughter. Her sobs of pleasure. The scent of her. The taste of her. I need to fill myself with Bronwyn until, for just those moments, I forget that we're two people. We're just who we are together.

I wrap my fingers around hers and squeeze gently, then we turn to the stairs.

She's wobbly on her feet and hanging on the banister as she takes the steps one at a time.

"I can carry you," I say.

She waves a hand. "Don't fuss."

She wants us to fill this house with a family. I want to cover her in Bubble Wrap. I'll be damned if I can figure out how to do both.

I'm preparing myself to tell her that I'll need a separate bedroom when we enter the living room.

I look around in confusion at the bags and boxes that currently fill the space, spilling into the hallway like the chaos after a hurricane. It's all washed in the golden glow of wall sconce lighting and table lamps. It looks like a Target store vomited the baby aisle straight into Bronwyn's previously artfully curated space.

I scowl when we enter the room, distracted from my initial plan to talk to her about my nightmares. "What is all this?"

She crosses an arm around her middle and says, "If I'm going to be part of Phee's life, the house has to be child safe. She needs to be comfortable here."

I have no idea why my throat won't let me push out any words. It's like someone's sealed my voice off behind a trapdoor.

She fills my silence. "Marie has a four-year-old and a two-year-old. She helped me figure out what I'd need. She and Jack went and picked it up for me."

She gives a little shake of her head. "This isn't everything. I'll need to buy some things online. I can't really get everything in a town this small. This is just a start, you know." She rushes to a pile of bags on one of the blue velvet sofas, digs through it, and holds up two overstuffed handfuls of cardboard and plastic packaging. "These are rubber things to stick on corners. They're for coffee tables and counters, that sort of thing. Not that she can reach counters, but just in case, so she doesn't get hurt." She sounds delighted by the idea of them, as if those little pieces of silicone are the invention of a genius.

I nod again, and she digs through more bags, showing me each item as she goes. "Cabinet locks. Outlet covers. Ooh, I got gates for the stairs. And I ordered some rugs for the bare hardwood. And Grandma Miller said I can have the rocking chair from their front room, so we'll have that for naps by tomorrow morning."

She's speaking faster, excitement evident in her tone and the energy of her movements. "There's a new high chair in the kitchen, but I haven't put it together yet." She indicates some boxes by the door. "I saw the diapers you used, so I got more of those. Two sizes. Marie told me to get these bottles because she swears by them, but I wasn't sure if she still took a bottle."

I shake my head and clear my throat. "I managed to get her completely moved over to sippy cups about two months ago."

She looks impressed. "That's awesome. Good job, Dad."

My heart does a weird flip in my chest at her praise.

Jacob, my friend and business partner, is a single guy who looks at Phee like she's a cute but entirely incomprehensible and exhausting puzzle. The extent of his commentary can be summed up in one sentence: "I don't know how you do it, man."

It took forever for the pediatrician's office to stop asking if I needed to call Phee's mother anytime I betrayed the slightest hint of being unsure about what I was doing.

I finally looked the doctor hard in the eyes and said, "If you can't remember that her mother is dead, then put an alert in her chart. And don't ever ask me that question again."

The nannies try to mother me along with Phee. They're nice ladies, but they hover over me and tell me everything I'm doing wrong. Sometimes their advice conflicts with each other. Sometimes it conflicts with my gut, and I insist we do things my way even though I'm not any kind of expert whatsoever.

Bronwyn's sincere, uncomplicated admiration makes my throat ache. I don't know if I hate it or love it.

She's oblivious to the mess she's making of my insides. She *left* me. Now she's got all this shit here trying to do what exactly?

"It's not a big deal," she says, referring to her purchase of unnecessary baby bottles. "Whatever Phee doesn't use, I can donate to the women's shelter."

I try to remind myself that spending this kind of money is nothing to her. But she's packed this room full of virtually anything a new parent of a toddler could need. She's spent thousands of dollars.

"This is too much."

She waves it off. "It's really not. It just looks like a lot because it's all in one place and still in the packaging."

I scan the bags and boxes. "She doesn't need a two-foot-tall teddy bear or a princess tent or all those toys either. She doesn't need more clothing. She has plenty."

"Oh, I'm sure—"

"You're not buying us," I snap.

30

Outsider

BRONWYN

For a moment, I still have a smile on my face. Then it slides away like honey off a hot spoon. I blink rapidly, press my lips together, and square my shoulders.

His words hang in the air between us. A flash fire that lasts only seconds but leaves scorched earth in its wake.

He reaches for me but lowers his hand when I back away.

"I'm sorry. I didn't mean that," he says. "This was kind of you. I know you're not... I don't know how to...."

I'm done.

My gut reaction has always been to let him get away with this shit. To go somewhere and lick my wounds. But that has gotten us nowhere, and I'm fucking *tired*.

"Is it because I have more money than you do or because you don't know how to accept kindness?"

"I'm working on it," he mutters.

"I didn't ask you if you were working on it," I snap. "I asked you if it bothers you that I have more money than you do. Because you've accused me of trying to buy you more than once. And I'm done pretending you aren't hurting me when you do it."

For a moment, he just stares at me, stricken. Then he says, "I don't know the answer to the kindness question. And admitting that I feel uncomfortable having less money than you makes me sound like an ass."

"As opposed to accusing me of trying to buy you. That doesn't make you sound like an ass at all." I've never spoken to him like this. Dean and I don't fight with each other. Not really. We usually just say, "Whatever," and then don't talk to each other for two days. Then we come back together and pretend nothing happened.

But he's not going anywhere. He's not leaving me. He loves me. That's not changing just because I call him out.

"What if the situation were reversed?" I ask. "If you'd been the one with a trust fund waiting for you? That would be okay, right? Because you're the man. Man provide. Man hunt and make fire," I grunt in my best interpretation of a caveman.

He looks torn between amusement and offense. "It's not about being sexist."

"You're right. It's probably a lot bigger than that. Male ego is just a piece of it."

I walk toward the kitchen, my limp more pronounced than ever. "The first time I came back to visit Grandma and Grandad Miller after my adoption, I was so excited. Five years old, and I'd missed everyone here so much.

"I couldn't wait to see my cousins. Marie was eleven. She walked in the room, rolled her eyes, and said, 'I guess you think you're hot shit, now.' Then she turned around and left."

At his scowl, I shrug. "We were kids. Don't go hating on my cousins for things they did when they were children. You aren't acting any better than they did, and you're a grown-ass man."

He swallows hard.

"My point is that I get it. I wasn't born a McRae. I don't act like them. I don't look like them. But I'm not a Miller either. I didn't work for what I have."

My voice shakes as I continue. "I don't think I'm better than *anyone*. But it would be really freaking nice if the man who says he loves me loved *all* of me and not just the parts that make him feel good about himself."

He stands as still as a statue.

I rub my eyes. "I'm grabbing some water. Do you need anything?"

He shakes his head. "I'll get it for you."

I move into the kitchen, and he follows.

"I don't need help," I say.

He stands in the casement doorway of our large modern kitchen and leans there, hands shoved in his pockets, eyes following me like I'll disappear if he looks away.

I start to fill a glass with water.

"My parents...."

I turn toward him and wait. Whatever he has to say is obviously difficult.

He clears his throat and tries again. "Neither of them was around consistently. And it was honestly better when they weren't there. My mother left. A lot. From my understanding, the first time was when I was around six months old. She couldn't handle.... She said I was too much for her. She came back when I was a toddler. Sometimes she'd stay for a few months. Sometimes a year.

"My father took her back every time. But he was angry. He blamed Maddie and me. I know now that she was leaving with other men, but she told Maddie and me that if we were good, she'd stay. And we were never good enough. At least when my father left on deployment, we knew it was his job.

"Every time my mother returned, it was like Christmas morning. I'd come home from school, and there she'd be—no warning, no call ahead. At least not one to Maddie or me. She'd just be there, smiling at us. She loved us so much. Look at all the things she bought us while she was away."

"Oh, Dean...."

"And you know, as a kid, her return was this wonderful thing. But she was toxic as hell. It got to the point where when I saw a stack of gifts, expensive or otherwise, it set my teeth on edge."

I wrap my arms around him. "I hate her. If I ever meet her, you'll have to hold me back because I will beat her ass."

He squeezes me. Then my words must sink in, the juxtaposition between them and my gentle hug.

When he stops laughing, he rubs my back and says, "The things my parents did don't belong in my relationship with you. You've never done a thing to deserve being painted with the same brush. My reaction was subconscious. I'll do better."

"Just like that?" I ask skeptically.

"I'm aware of it now. I'll deal with it."

"Hmm."

"Your whole family uses '*hmm*' like a threat," he says, and I can tell he's only half kidding.

"Hmm."

"Bronwyn, you are not funny."

"Oh come on. I'm very funny."

He squints at me in our silly version of side-eye that isn't side-eye at all.

"You know, there's something called immersion therapy," I tell him.

"Bronwyn," he growls.

"The more you're exposed to real generosity, the kind that asks nothing in return? The easier it'll get to receive it."

"Woman—"

"Practice makes perfect," I say blithely.

He huffs a laugh. "You're a pain in the ass."

"You love this pain in your ass."

His eyes crinkle at the corners. "I really do."

I pull away and turn back to my water. "Is that what you wanted to talk to me ab—"

The glass doesn't so much slip out of my grip as my left hand simply stops working. I've been pushing things way too far today. My head is aching like crazy, and my muscles feel like they're nothing but spaghetti.

My vision blurs, and the glass shatters on the floor, water splashing onto the hardwood.

I rub my neck. "Shoot."

When I turn to grab a dish towel, the room spins, and I have to release my cane and lean against the kitchen cabinets.

"Whoa. Easy." Dean's got his arms around me and a scowl on his face. "Too much. You were supposed to be resting."

I dip my chin in a slight nod. "Yes. Maybe a little too much."

He lifts me into a bridal carry.

"I have to clean the floor."

"I'll get you upstairs, then come back and take care of it."

My eyes drift closed.

"B, are you okay? Do you need a doctor?"

I lift my lids briefly, then snuggle into him, my face pressed against his neck. "Just tired and achy."

He strides for the stairs.

When he lays me on my bed, I barely open my eyes as I mumble, "Will you hold me tonight? Miss you."

He brushes my hair back and kisses my forehead. "Yes. I have to take care of the kitchen first."

"Love-love you."

He takes an audible breath. "Love-love you too. I'll be right back."

31

Mr. Loverman

BRONWYN

I wake to the sight of Grandma Miller's face six inches from my own. I jerk back against the pillow as she straightens up with a smile, then turns her head, curly salt-and-pepper hair bouncing with the movement, to shout out my open bedroom door, "She's awake!"

I'm awake because she woke me up.

I sit up and blink gritty eyes, taking in the sunshine that's flooding my room. "I... what time is it?"

"Eight o'clock in the morning, lazybones."

I throw myself back against my pillow and pull my comforter over my face. "Grandma," I complain, voice muffled through the fabric. "I'm tired."

"Well, then, why are you awake?" she asks in a tone that tells me she's genuinely perplexed.

She pats my shoulder as I hide beneath the blankets. "You just rest some more. Go back to sleep."

I snort a laugh at that. But not out loud because I wasn't born yesterday.

I'm not sure what she's doing, but she's clattering around with something.

She tsks before saying, "When was the last time you organized your closet? It's a disaster in here. And you haven't put your summer clothes away yet."

I pull the blanket from my face. "Grandma, I'm barely moved in. Besides, I'll forget I have them or where they are if I put them away somewhere."

She shrugs, eyebrows lifted. "Well, it's not the way I'd do it. But you're an adult. You have to do things your own way in your own house. But I don't know where your husband is supposed to fit his things."

Shoot. She's right about that.

I close my eyes and affect a little snore. Nothing too fake-sounding.

"You are tired. Poor thing." She keeps clattering around, talking to me the entire time.

I finally give up, pulling the blanket off and turning to sit at the edge of the bed.

"Oh good, you're up! I can never sleep once the sun's up either!"

I rub my temples and scan the room for my cane. Technically, I'd be fine to go to the bathroom without it, but I feel steadier with it until I can get the strength in the left side of my body back up to speed. I tend to trip over my own feet easily.

I vaguely remember Dean helping me get ready for bed last night. He'd undressed me like I was a child, and I was so sick and tired that I'd let him.

I'd pointed at my closet for nightwear, but he'd pulled his own T-shirt off and settled it over my head. Then he'd eased me back into bed and covered me with the blanket.

I'd fallen asleep immediately but roused briefly when he returned with my cane and a baby monitor in hand. After he placed the monitor on the nightstand, he climbed in beside me, tucked up against me, and I slept.

I'm a little bummed that I fell asleep so quickly and so soundly that I didn't really get to savor being in his arms. The bed is cold beside me, so he's obviously been awake a long time. I'm surprised I didn't hear Phee wake up through the baby monitor if he got up with her.

There's my cane, leaning against the end of the bed, right where Dean left it for me. His shirt falls nearly to my knees as I stand.

Grandma hovers around me, putting her hands on my elbow and back, like she's going to guide me to the bathroom. She's an inch shorter than I am.

I snicker. "What are you going to do if I fall? You'll just end up a grandma pancake on the floor with me."

"I'm stronger than I look."

"I don't need any help. I'm all better now," I assure her.

She follows me into the bathroom anyway as I do my business, talking to me about last month's 100-Mile Yard Sale as if we're sitting around the kitchen table while I pee and then take a quick shower.

When I'm brushing my teeth, she circles back to Dean. "Your young man didn't know where you wanted the rocking chair."

I speak through a mouth full of minty foam. "Wherever he says to put it is fine."

"He's a big one, isn't he? I'll bet he knows how to lay pipe."

"What?"

"You can tell when they know their way around plumbing. It's good to have a handy husband."

I look down at her innocent face, yet again six inches from my own.

I am approximately 78 percent sure that she's referring to literal home construction and not *my* plumbing. "I can pay someone to install any sink I ever need."

She backs up, and I put away my toothbrush and walk to the armchair in my bedroom.

Grandma moves to my dresser in the closet, shouting through the door as she finds a bra and underwear for me, "Just because you can handle your own plumbing doesn't mean it isn't nice to let someone else take care of things for you."

"Grandma!"

She pokes her head out of the closet and turns wide, innocent eyes my way. "What?"

She returns and points at my little side table. "When you were in the shower, he brought you hot chocolate and a blueberry muffin. Wasn't that thoughtful?"

I'd already noticed that and had three sips of chocolate while she was rooting through my lingerie drawer. And yes, it was thoughtful.

I sink down on the edge of the bed, mug in hand. He made it exactly the way I like it, and the muffin is still warm.

"That baby is adorable. She reminds me of you, Bronwyn. The blonde hair. Yours wasn't curly, though. You looked bald until you were four years old. Everybody thought you were a boy."

Grandma opens my closet door. "I think you should wear a dress today."

She pulls out two choices: a long cotton dress with a fitted bodice that shows a little cleavage and a looser denim Louis Vuitton micromini. Either one is guaranteed to drive Dean out of his mind.

"You choose, Grandma."

This way I can truthfully say Grandma picked my outfit so he doesn't get the impression that I'm trying to look sexy for him. But I also absolutely want him half feral with lust.

"He cooks. Did you know that? Your grandfather can't boil an egg. There's something very hunky about a man who knows how to cook."

I shimmy the cotton dress down over my hips and frown at her. "You do know our marriage is kind of... it's sort of...."

I don't even know how to explain it.

She blinks at me. "It seems to me you already did the hard part of getting him down the aisle. It'd be a pity to let a perfectly good marriage certificate go to waste."

I grin. "I think you're right."

"He changes diapers." She says it like a chess player would say "checkmate."

She shakes her head with a grimace of disgust and mutters, "They didn't make men like that when I was your age. They would have sat around naked and starving before they lifted a finger in the house if there was a woman there to do it."

"Grandma, you're not exactly painting Grandad in the best light."

She huffs. "We didn't know there was any other way. And now look what you've got. A hunky man cooking and changing dirty diapers. Bringing your breakfast up here like you're some kind of princess."

She does a little burlesque shimmy. "All those muscles." She sighs. "I guarantee the man changes his own brakes."

"I don't need a man, Grandma. I'm a strong and independent woman," I say, partially to tease her and partially because it's true. I don't need just any man. I need Dean. And if I can't have him, then I don't want anyone.

She sniffs. "I'm just saying, there's no reason to make the poor man sleep on a sofa, is there? You didn't even give him a bed upstairs, Bronwyn?"

Frowning in confusion, I look at my bed, where I'm quite sure my husband was cuddled up to me when I fell asleep, then back at my grandmother.

"Poor guy. Huddled on the sofa. He's too big for that. It probably aggravated his injury too. Those scars look awful. I thought you were raised better than that."

I snap my mouth closed when I realize my jaw is just hanging open.

"Can't you give him a chance? It seems to me that he's trying really hard. And he really loves you, Bronwyn. Grandmas can tell these things."

"I will definitely give him a chance."

She beams at me. "Wonderful. I'll go let him know."

"Wait—"

Annnd Grandma's gone.

I finish dressing and hurry after her but draw up short at the baby gate newly installed sometime this morning.

I'm fidgeting with the mechanism, trying to figure it out, when Dean appears at the bottom of the staircase.

I wave at him with forced cheer. "You stay there. I'm fine on my own."

He opens the bottom gate, climbs the stairs in a jog full of way more energy than a morning like this deserves, and stops on the step just below me.

I'm still fiddling with the stupid childproof mechanism. The fact that my senior citizen grandmother managed it without even uttering one of her "Oh dear Lords" while I stand here shaking the thing like I'm trying to mix a flipping martini is, frankly, embarrassing.

I contemplate throwing a leg over and trying to jump it like some kind of turnstile criminal, but Dean scowls. "No."

"I wasn't going to do it," I bluff. "I was just thinking about it."

His lips quirk, and his warm hazel eyes never break contact with mine as he reaches down to hold my hand. He slides it over, then moves my thumb to the latching mechanism and presses it in with a slide.

The gate swings open under our combined grip, and Dean reaches out to pull me into his arms. I waffle internally, trying to decide whether I should let him.

I don't need the man to carry me around. But it would mean I was in his arms again.

"I can handle the steps by myself."

"Where I'm from, we call that cutting off your nose to spite your face," Dean says patiently.

I can hear Phee squealing in laughter and the rumble of cheerful adult voices from the family room.

I sigh dramatically, then lean into him. "Fine. If it makes you happy, go ahead and cart me around like a sack of potatoes."

He lifts me into a bridal carry. I think he's *smelling* me.

"You're the sexiest potato I've ever seen," he says.

"I'm not *a* potato. I'm the whole *bag* of potatoes."

He chuckles under his breath and starts down the stairs.

I lay my head down and cram my face in that place right where his shoulder meets his neck. And I smell him too. Because we're both psycho obsessed weirdos.

When we get to the bottom of the stairs, I lift my head. "What time did my grandparents get here?"

His expression turns mildly uncomfortable. "Around seven. They have the security codes, I take it."

"They're on the approved list. What did my grandmother do to put that look on your face?"

"She took me off guard. That's all."

"But how exactly did she do that?"

He glances toward the family room, then back at me, his cheeks pink. "I'd rather not talk about it."

"Did she wake you up with her face six inches from yours?"

Dean's eyelid twitches.

Ha. Then my eyes widen. "Oh Lord, tell me she didn't get in your face when you were only in your underwear."

He squirms. "Gym shorts. But commando under the shorts, so...."

I can't help it. I let out a sound that's a combination of horror and delight. Because I know what those gym shorts look when he just drags them on, and they hide nothing. The good news is, I guarantee Grandma really didn't notice. She'd have been too busy looking at his scars and trying to figure out how to save my marriage. But Dean doesn't know that.

"Did she sit right next to you on the sofa and start talking to you about your skills with plumbing?"

His expression turns sour. "I'm 90 percent sure she was referring to actual construction. Don't make it sound dirty."

He's giving her even better odds than I did.

"Grandma's a sweetheart. It's best to just let her do her thing."

His expression is amused. "She's you in another fifty years."

"Ha! No," I sputter.

He shrugs. "If you say so."

"Do you want to talk about why you were sleeping on the sofa instead of beside me or even in one of the rooms upstairs?"

His eyes shift again, away and then back. "Not... no."

Okay, then. One thing at a time.

I rub my neck and look toward the kitchen.

"What do you need? I'll get it for you," he offers.

"Tylenol and water. But I'll do it myself."

"No. You'll rest, and I'll bring it to you."

"You should put me down now."

He grunts, and his arms tighten. We both know he isn't carrying me because I need it. In fact, I should be building these muscles back up, not babying them.

"I don't want to put you down," he mutters.

I hide my face against his neck one more time so he doesn't see my smile.

"Are you manhandling me?" I tease.

Dean puts his lips against the shell of my ear and murmurs, "I know exactly how to handle you."

His touch is temptation enough. But those words aren't playing fair. Goose bumps pop up on my skin, and my vagina clutches at nothing like the horny little hoebag she is.

I pull slightly away and remind myself to be strong. It's not time for that yet.

Without another word, he carries me into the family room and deposits me on the chaise end of one of the sofas.

Grandad Miller is seated in a recliner, Grandma on the arm, watching Phee with indulgent smiles on their faces. They turn at my arrival, and Grandma lifts one shoulder, smiling at Dean flirtatiously. Then she wiggles her eyebrows at me approvingly.

Henry stayed at my grandparents' place last night and must have come with them this morning. I can't imagine what time Grandma must have woken him up.

He's seated in the other armchair, leaning forward, forearms propped on his knees as he engages in what appears to be a rather intellectual conversation with Phee, who's standing in front of him gesticulating wildly.

He hands her back a toy. "I see exactly what you mean. If the pieces aren't aligned correctly, it would be incredibly frustrating."

She bobs her head, blows a raspberry, then says, "Fusstayng."

He nods seriously. "Very frustrating."

"Henry, she's a baby, not a grad student." I laugh.

He scowls over at me. "There's no rule that I have to use baby talk with her. I looked it up."

Dean chooses that moment to prop my feet on a set of throw pillows like I'm an invalid. He studies me, then grabs a blanket from a basket by the hearth and returns to drape it over me.

I gape at him. "What are you doing?"

"The doctor said to rest."

"The doctor said to listen to my body, not to lounge around 24-7."

"You've had a busy few days," he argues. "Henry agrees with me that you should stay off your feet today."

I shoot my brother a suspicious look. "So you two are friends now?"

They speak in tandem.

"No."

"Absolutely not."

"Now, boys," Grandad cuts in.

They both turn to him respectfully and wait for him to continue.

He rubs his whiskery chin, looks from one to the other, then mutters, "Don't be a-holes in front of the women and children."

They both nod in agreement, as if he just spoke the wisdom of the ages.

I just roll my eyes because what does that even mean? "How about neither of you act like a-holes in front of anybody, male or female?"

Dean changes the subject. "Where do you keep your Tylenol?"

When I explain, he heads for the kitchen. Phee toddles after him, then races ahead, giggling.

I turn to take in my brother. Henry is leaning back in his chair and smiling at me blandly.

I scowl at him. "What are you doing?"

He does that lazy-lidded look that drives me crazy. "I don't know what you're talking about."

"You're up to something. I don't need your help. You're making things worse, not better."

He rolls his shirt sleeves with meticulous neatness. "I sincerely doubt that."

"I can manage my own marriage. Stay out of it, Henry," I hiss, "or I will kick your manipulative ass."

"You can't even kick my ass when you're healthy. I don't fall for your tricks. And, frankly, today you're too weak to kick much of *anything*."

I shake my head in disbelief. "How can you be so... rigid about everything else and then so flexible with your morals?"

He twists his lips to the side. "I'm not flexible with my morals. I have a great many hard limits. Within those parameters, I have a sliding scale to evaluate cost-benefit."

He spreads his hands as if presenting evidence. "And now your husband is carrying you from room to room, plumping your pillows, and, most importantly, not annoying me. Cost." He waves his hand as if he expects me to join in. "Say it with me: benefit."

I don't like it. Not one bit.

Dean returns with Phee running just ahead of him. She barrels straight for Henry. When she puts her hands up, he leans over, picks her up, and places her on his knee.

I shove down a shameful wave of jealousy. "Henry, sometimes you're a real jerk."

Phee looks at me, back at Henry... and then perfectly mimics my expression and tone. "Jerk."

I glance at Dean, knowing he's got to be furious with me for teaching Phee that word. But he doesn't seem angry. He looks smug.

My brother makes an exaggeratedly sour expression. "Uncle Henry. Not 'jerk.'"

"Unca Jerk."

I snort, covering my mouth with my hand. Phee beams at me, basking in my apparent approval.

Henry narrows his eyes at me, then looks back to Phee. "Hen..."

"Hen...," she mimics.

"Ree."

"Ree."

Henry smiles encouragingly. "Uncle Henry."

"Unca Jerk!" she crows with a giggle. The little stinker knows exactly what she's doing.

"I will not be verbally abused by precocious toddlers, Ophelia," Henry says mildly.

She throws herself toward him and plants what looks to be a very sloppy kiss on his lean cheek.

Poor Henry appears to be disconcerted. "Yes. Well."

"She really likes you, Henry," Grandma says.

"She also likes to finger-paint with the contents of her diaper if you don't get to her fast enough," Dean mutters.

Henry rises fluidly from his chair, then very gently places Phee on my lap while making a great show of "dumping" her there.

Phee giggles and reaches for me, her small hands wrapping around a section of my hair. Pure joy bubbles up inside me. "Hey there, baby girl."

Dean looms over us, and I glance up defensively. "I'm just holding her."

He takes a deep breath through his nose. "It's not a problem, Bronwyn."

"Mom-win!" Phee squeals happily and yanks hard on my hair.

I wince with an "Ouch" even as I laugh at her enthusiasm and peel her little fingers away.

Dean freezes solid beside us. Then, without a word, he picks her up and marches straight out of the room. He no sooner makes it to the hallway when Phee squeals in outrage and attempts to squirm out of his arms. He just keeps going, telling her he'll take her outside to play in a little while.

"What in the world?" Grandma cranes her neck as if she can see around corners and up the stairs. "That was very odd."

I clear my throat, but the lump there doesn't want to budge. For the first time, his refusal to allow Phee to "inconvenience" me makes sense. It's not about me at all. It's about his bitch mother who made him think he had to be perfect. That a child could be responsible for an adult's behavior and rejection.

He thinks it's about what I can handle. What will be "too hard" on me.

It's really about a man who's afraid he and his child are unlovable.

This pain in my chest isn't just for me anymore. It's for all three of us. Operation: Save the Stealth Husband is a bigger job than I ever imagined. And it's even more important than I thought it was.

There's a travel mug full of ice water and a bottle of medication on the side table. Dean must have set them there before "rescuing" me from Phee's hair pulling.

I swallow two pills and lean my head back with my eyes closed. If I concentrate hard enough, I can keep the tears from escaping. And if I can't? I'll claim a headache.

Henry walks past me, patting me like I'm a dog as he goes. It's his very own awkward expression of brotherly reassurance.

"I think," he says softly, "your husband needs all the help he can get."

32
Chosen Family
DEAN

Bronwyn has a big-ass house. She also has a big-ass patio and a big-ass front lawn, various outbuildings, and a huge backyard that leads to acres and acres of wooded property.

Yesterday, I'd thought it was all too much.

That was before her mother's parents showed up and Henry McRae decided it was his job to "keep an eye" on me.

Turns out this property isn't big enough. Because everywhere I go, that fucker manages to find me.

He actually reminds me of Bronwyn with that unrelenting determination. Except where she's charming and irresistible, he's a pain in the ass.

Henry is swiping through a text conversation beside me. "Is there some reason you have your things in my bedroom?" he asks conversationally.

I frown. "You don't have a bedroom here."

He glances up from his phone. "Seriously? I've been coming here on vacation for most of my life. Your shit is in my bedroom."

Phee is toddling through the backyard, collecting random bits of fall foliage and showing them to me. Occasionally, she tries to eat something, and I have to swoop in and distract her from it.

Henry kicks his foot through the brown, red, and yellow leaves. "There are perfectly good outdoor toys in the garage, you know. There's no need for her to touch leaves and sticks."

I shake my head. "A little dirt won't hurt her."

Henry nods briefly. "I'm certain you're right. Otherwise, Bronnie would never have survived childhood."

The thought amuses me, as does his use of Bronwyn's childhood nickname.

He holds up his phone and waggles it at me. "Have you and Bronwyn worked out where you'll be staying when you come back to New York?"

"We're not coming back," I say. "Our home is here."

"You're thinking like a man who doesn't know how to diversify assets."

"I know how just fine. It's still wasteful."

He shrugs. "You're probably right. Besides, I'm sure my father will prefer it if you spend the major holidays in his home."

I know damn well that my expression is flat, but somehow Henry still knows he hit a nerve because he smirks.

He swipes a few items on his phone, then gives the side button a double-click while holding the camera up to his face. "The two of you also own a modest four-bedroom in the Hamptons near my parents and Clarissa Harcourt-Mellinger. Phee will enjoy spending a couple months in the summer on the beach, I'm sure."

He turns the phone screen toward me. "Oh, look. It has an age-appropriate physical development center in the backyard."

I shove the phone back toward him. "It's called a swing set."

"That's ridiculous. It has a lot more than just a swing."

I rub my temples. "When did she buy a house in the Hamptons?"

"She didn't. I bought it—" He consults his phone. "—sixty-seven seconds ago. It's a wedding gift for the two of you."

He smiles without showing his teeth, and I really, really do want to punch him in the face.

"What is wrong with you people?" I mutter.

"Quite a lot, actually. We can explore that another time, perhaps."

"What are you—"

"Circling back, I need you to move your things out of my bedroom. I don't know why you didn't just put them in the same room with your wife. But I need that space. I always stay in that room."

"You can deal with the inconvenience. Find another open bedroom."

"That won't be an option," he says cryptically.

"Then you can go back to your grandparents' or stay at the Blackwater Inn."

His lips turn up at the corners. "Would you like to take a bet on that outcome?"

No I fucking would not.

"Have you ever seen a honey badger?" he asks apropos of nothing.

I pull some leaves from Phee's fist just before they make it into her mouth.

"Badder," Phee yells.

Henry nods. "If you'd like to see how one acts when defending its territory, tell my sister I can't have my bedroom because you want to sleep in it. She has two settings: fight or flight. I promise she'll head straight for 'fight' when it comes to defending me."

His grin is outright feral as he slides his phone back into his trouser pocket. "Well, I'd love to continue to stand here in the dead grass and leaves and pretend to enjoy myself in your company, but I have things to attend to."

He claps me on the shoulder awkwardly—thankfully my good one—and pushes his glasses back up his nose. "Good talk, brother."

33

This Love

BRONWYN

Dean fills my water tumbler twice and checks to see if it needs to be refilled two other times.

He keeps bringing me food. Constantly.

He brought me the stack of new books he found on my nightstand "in case you get bored" and my knitting bag in case I wanted to work on the baby hats, booties, and blankets I make for our local hospital NICU.

Now he sits down on the sofa with me, lifts my foot into his lap, and sorts through the small basket he brought with him.

My jaw falls open as he removes cotton pads and nail polish remover. Then, without a single word, he picks up my foot and begins to remove the chipped, grown-out pink polish from my toes.

"What are you doing?"

"You hate when your polish chips. I'm fixing it for you."

I haven't done a thing with polish since before I went into the hospital. I removed the stuff from my fingernails at Mom's, but I have a very slight tremor, just enough to make painting my toenails impossible.

"I was going to get a pedicure next week."

"You can still do that if you want. But you won't have to look at janky toes in the meantime."

"I do hate it when my toes get janky," I say.

"I know."

My grandparents have gone home, and Phee is napping upstairs. My brother disappeared after giving Dean and me a weirdly significant look and announcing loudly that he would be in the study working "for the next four hours."

Dean is quiet as he removes the old polish from my toes. Then he uses a nail file and a cuticle pusher. When he fits me with a toe separator and pulls out a bottle of base coat, I can't stay quiet any longer. "How do you know how to do this?"

He glances up with a slightly sheepish smile. "YouTube. I know a lot of guys wear nail polish, but I never did. You're my first attempt to use the stuff."

"You're trying to seduce me."

He looks up again, this time with a frown marring his brow. "I'm seducing you with smelly chemicals?"

"You're *not* trying to seduce me?"

"I always want to. But specifically this second? I'm just trying to make you happy."

His hands are warm and steady as he holds my heel in his palm and applies fresh polish to my toenails. He concentrates completely on his task, his tongue poking out the side of his mouth as he works.

Whether he's trying or not, I. Am. Seduced.

Finally, after he completes the last toe and puts everything back into the basket, he says, "I have to talk to you about something."

He moves to sit next to me and scrubs a hand through his hair. "I haven't been fair to you. From the very beginning, I didn't realize I was layering my experience with my own parents over top of us. But you're not my mother. And I'm not my father."

He shakes his head. "I don't have to be my father."

He reaches for my hand. "When you see the shit show that my life is, B, you're not going to want any part of it."

"You know everyone has their own personal shit show, right? You just painted my toenails because I couldn't."

"It's not the same. That's not your fault."

"You don't believe I could love you as much as you love me."

"I want to believe it."

I growl at him, but I don't let go of his big, stupid, beautiful hand. "But you don't?"

"Every time I told you to go, what I wanted was for you to say you were never leaving."

I frown. "You were testing me?"

He stands and looks at the doorway, then at our clasped hands. Abruptly, he plants his butt back on the sofa. "It wasn't a conscious thing."

No matter what he says, it was a test. And I failed.

He looks around the family room, taking in the framed photos, the crocheted afghan Aunt Teresa made me for my birthday, the shelves holding worn books that I've read a hundred times, the stereo in the corner and stack of old CDs I inherited from my father, and the baby toys that litter the space already.

His voice is rough when he says, "I should have been talking to you, not pushing you away."

He leans forward, pulling his hand from mine and lacing his fingers together, looking off at nothing in particular. "The reason I didn't want to live in the same house is the same reason for the soundproofing on my walls. I'm a noisy sleeper."

My eyebrows creep to my forehead. "Seriously?"

"I talk in my sleep."

He rubs his forehead. "There's no point in downplaying it. I'm loud enough that before I put up the panels, I woke up Phee. They used to be dreams about combat, and that was.... It was bad. Memories mostly. And then my sister.... The shoulder starts bothering me. In my sleep, I don't know what's real and what's a memory. Phee and you. It's a mess."

He shoots me a concerned look. "I'd wake you up. I'll have to sleep somewhere else. I'm sorry."

"Does sleeping with me make it worse, somehow?"

He shakes his head. "I don't know. I've never actually slept with you."

At my confused frown, he rubs his forehead and confesses, "I don't sleep when we're together. Even in Paris, I used to sneak out and sleep in my own room for a few hours. You're a heavy sleeper or I'd never have gotten away with it."

My lips part in an indrawn breath of surprise. "*Why?*"

He gives a quick jerk of his head. "Because I don't want you to see me like that."

Oh, Dean. "Whatever you say in your sleep, whatever you do, that's not going to change how I feel about you."

"I think it'll work better if I sleep in my own room."

I promised myself I'd tell him how I was feeling. No more smiling while I bleed. "I won't fight you on that. But it hurts my feelings."

He glides his fingers across my forehead and behind my ear, tucking my hair away from my face. He swallows, his jaw flexing, brows drawn tight, and rubs his thumb over my jaw. "We can try it. Maybe with you there, I won't.... We can try."

Hope hurts. No one ever tells you that. My chest aches with it. So close to everything and so afraid to believe in it.

He puts both hands in my hair, holding my head as he leans closer and searches my eyes. I'm caught in the striated green-gold of his. "I love you. And I am all in, B."

I breathe, just so I can get a whiff of his soap and the salt of his skin. I crave the taste and texture of him.

I slide my fingers over his jaw. "No more secrets, Dean?"

His ears turn red. "I... I'm...."

Okay. Baby steps.

Besides, I have some secrets of my own.

I sway toward him, and that big chest of his heaves out a breath.

He digs in his pocket and pulls out a small box. I'm not surprised to see our rings inside when he flips the lid open.

"What happened to the box?"

"I've been carrying it in my pocket every day for the last eighteen months."

I barely have time to register surprise at his words before he's pulling my engagement and wedding rings from their little velvet bed and sliding them onto my finger. "You're mine. And I'm yours."

I nod, my chin wobbling. "Yes."

He turns my hand over and places his ring on my palm. Then he holds out his left hand. It's not shaking. He's solid as a rock as he stands there and waits for me to put it on his finger.

I press my lips together. "Don't break my heart. I'm trusting you with it."

He straightens and squeezes my hand. "I need you to keep letting me know if I'm hurting you. I'm not good at guessing."

I nod but say, "No more testing me. No more manipulation."

"Agreed."

I slide the gold band on his finger and swallow.

"I can't fuck this up," he mutters, flexing his hand before clenching it into a fist.

I kiss his wedding ring. "We won't."

34

So Easy

DEAN

Bronwyn leans toward me, her breath hitching.

I know what that hitch usually means, but I confirm anyway. Because we've been through a lot, and I'm assuming nothing.

"Can I kiss you?" My voice is a rumble, and she shivers at the sound of it.

Then she wraps her arms around me and presses her lips to mine.

I kiss her slowly. Gently.

Heat prickles behind my eyelids, and I squeeze them closed hard until I've got that shit under control.

I nip at her bottom lip. When she shivers again and gasps, I lick inside, tangling her tongue with mine.

It's just a kiss. One of so many we've shared. But every time, she takes me by surprise. I get caught in a riptide of not just sensation but *feeling*. There's no time passing, no world turning, only her mouth and mine. Her body and mine. There's only the beating in my chest that says this woman *is* my heart. My soul. My everything.

She yanks roughly at the hem of my shirt, attempting to drag it off my body.

There was a time, way back in the beginning, when she used to try to be "demure." As if I'd find her clothes-yanking, hair-pulling, back-scratching enthusiasm anything but hot as fuck.

I lean away just far enough to reach back and pull my shirt over my head.

"God, you're beautiful," she says.

I shake my head and look at her with narrowed eyes. "I'm not, and you know it."

She runs her fingers over my cheekbone, my jaw, my lips, the planes of my chest and abs. "You're not *pretty*. But you're strong and solid and steadfast. You're not a painting in a museum. You're a mountain range."

I don't understand how she believes that. I'm just a man, and a flawed one at that.

Then she smirks and makes a grab for my belt.

I smile back, then shift her, laying her on the sofa beneath me. She's an all-you-can-eat buffet, and I haven't had a meal in months.

She moves, then laughs. "I don't know if my polish is completely dry. You'll have to do it all over again."

I give her a crooked grin, then lift her foot and kiss her ankle. "Leave that to me."

I cradle her left leg and position her silky-smooth calf along the top edge of the sofa back. She is a perfect temptation beneath me, legs splayed wide and her breasts straining against the confines of her neckline.

"I like this dress." I run a palm up her muscled thigh.

She sighs and melts for me, even as she breathes, "It's the cleavage, isn't it?"

"Among other things." With deft fingers, I pull the skirt up to her waist, exposing her white lace panties. I tweak the little satin bow and run a knuckle along the damp seam of her pussy.

"Mmm," she hums in response.

I eye the buttons on her dress with approval. One by one, I work each closure free, slowly revealing her upper body.

"Did I say I like this dress?" I ask in satisfaction. "I meant I love it."

I slide her bra straps from her shoulders and use my teeth to pull the stretchy lace cups down to make a perfect frame for her plump breasts.

She throws her head back against the armrest and gasps in pleasure when my mouth closes on her hard nipple. I'm absorbed in the feel of her. Her taste. Her scent.

I suck. Lick. Hold her in my palms and flick my thumbs across those gorgeous peaks.

"Fucking hell. You're a masterpiece." I push her breasts together, my focus trapped on the picture we make: pale pink-tipped nipples and paler skin framed by my big rough hands. I pinch her nipple the way she likes, just hard enough to make her grind her pussy in search of friction.

She drags one of my hands down to where she needs it, pushing up against my palm.

"You're soaking wet, you dirty girl."

Her voice is a breathy laugh. "Always so polite with your 'please' and 'thank you' and 'yes, ma'am.' And then you say things like that."

I pause, unsure. "You don't like it?"

The first time I'd said, "Bounce that pretty ass on my dick," she'd orgasmed so hard her knees had given out. But if she feels like I don't respect her or—

"The way you talk is freeing. It makes me feel like I could ask you for anything."

I draw her into a kiss, her lips clinging and damp, before saying, "That's because you *can*."

Then I slide down her body to position my face right there at her pussy. Lifting her right leg to drape over my shoulder, I wrap my arm around her thigh, my forearm anchoring her pelvis in place.

I move her panties to the side and wet my lips. "Damn, you make me hungry."

I glance up to catch her eyes. "Put your arms over your head, angel."

She lifts them slowly as I return my attention to her slippery clit and use my thumb to tease her.

"Grab the armrest," I say quietly, my eyes on her pretty pussy.

She shifts slightly, and her breath catches as my hot gaze skims up her body.

My voice simmers with warning when I growl, "Now, hold on."

My first taste of her is heaven. Like sex and home, and I want to drown myself in her wet heat. She's slippery and swollen. Welcoming.

And it's been so long.

She's soft everywhere down here, except for her little clit as it peeks out from beneath its hood.

My cock is hard as steel, tucked painfully behind my zipper. I release my dick and wrap a hand around it, stroking slowly even as I throw myself into my self-appointed task.

Three orgasms for Bronwyn.

And they don't count if her legs don't shake and she doesn't sob out my name.

I've seen porn where the guy just sort of hovers there and flicks a woman's clit with his tongue. And I'm not telling anyone how to do their job, but that shit isn't going to fly for my girl.

There is no hovering happening here. I am all in, devouring her pussy like I'm gunning for a blue ribbon at the county fair pie-eating contest.

I suck her clit and she squeals, bucking against my face. She's almost there already.

I slide my hand down her abdomen, across that tiny triangle of trimmed blonde hair just above her slit. She told me once that she kept that little patch for me. Because it turns me into a damn animal.

It's still there, ready and waiting for me. That means something.

She knew we weren't over. We both fucking knew.

Thank God.

I trace my thumb over her clit exactly the way she likes and fuck into her with my tongue.

She's building. Building. And I settle in to give her what she needs.

Bronwyn comes the first time, her thighs quivering as she sobs my name. "*Fuck*. Dean. Yes."

I lift my head to wink at her. "That's one."

She pulls at me, trying to drag me up over her. "You're not doing the counting thing when we haven't been together in months!"

"No?"

"No!"

At first the clatter in the hallway doesn't register in my lust-addled mind.

Then I hear the confused voice of an elderly woman standing in the large casement doorway of the family room. "Oh my heavens!"

The back of this sofa is to the doorway and has us mostly covered from view. The only thing they'd see, I think, is Bronwyn's bare calf propped there, her hands on the armrest above her head, and my feet hanging over the far end. But that bare leg and my feet are... well, there's no *guessing* at what we were doing.

Another woman's voice. "Rose? What's the ma—" she manages before her words cut off on a squeak.

And I know I'm not trapped in molasses. I know full well that I'm moving at normal speed. But as I lift my head over the sofa back and turn to look their way, it feels like a slo-mo reel in one of the Matrix movies.

Five sets of eyes are staring at me.

Time finally rearranges itself, and I snap into action, sliding up and over my wife, shielding her body from view in case anyone comes all the way into the room.

The crowd in the hallway comes back online, tittering and scrambling to get out of the hallway, some scurrying back toward the front door, some to the stairs. No one seems to know exactly where they're supposed to go.

Another set of footsteps approaches. "What's going on here?"

Charlotte, Bronwyn's mother, says, "Arden, stay where you are."

Arden is *Arden* and keeps right on walking.

"Just tell m—"

There's a pause. Absolute silence broken only by the faint ticking of the grandfather clock in the hallway.

Bronwyn can't see anything from where she is. For that I'm glad.

"Eep," she wheezes beneath me.

I glance down, easing my weight off her slightly. "Sorry."

Her father makes a strangled sound in his throat.

I swallow. "You can put your arms down now," I whisper. Because, *shit*, they can definitely see her hands back there.

Face so red, I swear the heat of it is seeping into my own, she lowers her arms. Unfortunately, one bare leg is still propped on the back of the couch. I lean for the throw blanket while still keeping her covered. The idea is that she can pull her leg down once I've got the two of us out of the danger zone.

"Get off my daughter," Arden thunders.

I lift my head over the back of the sofa and scowl at the man in question. "Leave."

Bronwyn reaches up and slaps her hand over my mouth, dragging my face back to stare into her wide eyes. She starts praying beneath me. "Hail Mary, full of grace—"

I peel her fingers away and kiss her knuckles. Without lifting my head, I point to the stairs and bellow, "Go to your rooms."

They all jump into action, luggage and overnight bags clattering behind them as they make a beeline for the bedrooms, some returning from the front door, some already halfway there.

Arden says, "Upstairs. I'm going upstairs now."

I call behind them, "And don't wake the baby."

The low-key cacophony in the hallway and on the stairs immediately becomes a subdued whisper of sound.

Bronwyn squirms beneath me, and goddammit, my dick is still hard. And she's right there. My cock could be inside her with one quick slide.

She puts her palms on my chest and gives a little shove.

I back off in resignation. "Just tell me one thing, little wife."

She bats her eyelashes and gives me an innocent look. "Yes?"

"Exactly how many people have you given security clearance for this house?"

***

I'd believed the gigantic dining room table was an affectation.

Turns out, it's barely big enough to handle a family dinner.

Silverware clinks. Throats clear. And absolutely no one says a word.

Even Bronwyn's maternal grandparents, who returned after this morning's visit just for this meal, are silent.

The elderly woman who'd prayed to the heavens at the sight of her granddaughter's bare calf is Bronwyn's paternal grandmother, Rose McRae. Hours later, she hasn't yet fully recovered from the shock, as she regularly sneaks sideways glances at me and flaps her cloth napkin to cool her face.

Also at the table are Charlotte and Arden; Bronwyn's friend and former housemate, Sydney Walsh; and her friends Franki Lennox and Janessa Fontini.

Clarissa and James are the only two who aren't here—though apparently not for lack of an invitation. Clarissa is currently heading up some writer's convention in Spain.

Henry and Gabriel are both here. And there are also several cousins and two small children, in addition to my Phee, in attendance.

Oh, and Louis Larrabie.

Yes. *That* fucking Louis Larrabie.

It's been exactly seven minutes since I last remembered how much I hate Henry, but watching Louis breathe near my wife is an excellent reminder. I can almost admire my brother-in-law's creativity. He wanted "my shit" out of "his" bedroom and found a way to make it happen, but inviting Louis, too? That is some petty bullshit.

"You didn't need to cook for us. We brought extra staff so we wouldn't be too hard on you," Charlotte finally ventures.

"Dinner is excellent, as always," Arden agrees. "But you really didn't need to feed us, baby."

He follows his praise to his daughter with a steely-eyed stare my way.

I could be wrong, but it feels like Arden punched those consonants on the word "baby" a little hard, given that Bronwyn is a grown woman.

But I get it. Honestly, it's beyond my imagination to picture Phee as an adult, let alone married. The man is clearly struggling.

Bronwyn gives him that big, beautiful smile of hers. "I'm afraid I can't take the credit for this one. Phee and I just sat at the counter and helped a little. Dean did most of it."

"I just know how to follow directions when the cheese and pasta expert speaks," I say.

More than once, I've thought that Gabriel reminds me of an unaltered, untrained golden retriever. He's twenty-five, so old enough to know better. But clearly he doesn't care as he says, "Nice. You know, Dean, I didn't take you for a guy who likes to cook. I'd have thought you'd prefer to eat out."

He lifts his wineglass in a salute.

There's a beat. Just a moment that hovers in the air while everyone absorbs that comment.

And then chaos ensues.

Charlotte whisper-screams, "Gabriel *Allen* McRae, what is wrong with you?"

Gabriel represses his grin like a guilty kid, raises his eyebrows, and shrugs sheepishly. "It's funny."

Maybe it is. But I'm not stupid enough to laugh about it in front of my mother- or father-in-law.

Grandmother Rose flaps her napkin harder.

Bronwyn's friends are snorting and giggling, falling over onto each other like they can't even stay in their chairs without the support of the other.

Marie starts singing under her breath something about "gittin' it and hittin' it."

Louis's face is red, his square jaw flexing and his shiny white horse teeth bared. A vein throbs in his temple, and well-plucked blond eyebrows furrow. The looks he's been sending Bronwyn and me are alternately full of longing and seething hatred.

Phee starts banging on her high chair tray, face smeared in red sauce, just to join in the melee.

Pretty much every person at the table begins either laughing or scolding someone for laughing about the events of the afternoon.

Henry, on the other hand, pulls his phone out of his pocket and completely zones out of the conversation around him.

"Henry," Arden sighs.

He doesn't even look up.

"Henry," Arden repeats louder.

When Bronwyn's brother finally glances up, Arden tilts his head down in a "we've talked about this" move. "We don't use our phones at family dinners."

"Acknowledged, but this is an emergency situation."

"What kind of emergency?" Bronwyn asks.

Henry doesn't look back up from his phone. "Shopping. I need a black light. Immediately."

"You prissy diva."

Henry puts his phone away and looks down his nose at his sister. "It's not prissy to be concerned about accidentally touching something that's been contaminated by—" He sends a covert glance toward Phee, then looks at me over his glasses. "—shenanigans."

"You're the one who told us we'd have privacy because you'd be in the office," she says hotly.

"To encourage you to talk to each other, not to soil public surfaces."

"You make it sound like we were getting it on at a bus stop," she retorts, voice rising. "This is our *home*. You brought everyone here for a surprise house party without warning us. When was there time or opportunity for Dean and me to do *anything*?"

"How do I know what you've been up to with the stealth husband?" Henry asks sourly.

"Stop. Calling him. The stealth husband. And you probably know the same way you know everything else about him. Because you stick your nose everywhere, Henry. Just mind your own business for two whole minu—"

"Quiet," Arden says. "Bronwyn, you're getting loud."

She shrinks back, chewing her lower lip, and starts shoving food around on her plate.

I wait for her to stand up for herself. She doesn't.

Henry, the asshole, is right. Damn him.

She goes into "fight" mode when she's defending others. But she doesn't defend herself. Instead, she retreats.

Before my eyes, Bronwyn dons a mask. She straightens her spine and drops her chin. She almost looks posed, as if she's waiting for a photographer to snap a picture.

And she doesn't say another thing.

Nobody notices. Not one person here sees the spark go out of her eyes.

Conversation has picked up around us as she sits quietly, her hair swinging forward to shield most of her expression.

I lean toward my father-in-law and say quietly, "Apologize."

Arden frowns. "I beg your pardon?"

"You just shushed my wife like she was a barking dog. Apologize to her. Now."

Arden sits for a moment, clearly dumbfounded. Then he looks at his daughter.

Bronwyn squeezes my arm and murmurs, "Please don't. The least I owe them is to try to remember to use my inside voice."

I keep my own voice quiet as I say, "This is your *home*. It should be a safe place for you, not a place for others to dictate your behavior."

She sucks in an audible breath.

I pull her hand up to my mouth and kiss her knuckles. "I will defend you, Bronwyn. Against anyone and anything. Please don't ask me not to."

She squeezes my hand and shakes her head a little. She thinks since the status quo is normal that it's acceptable. I know exactly what that feels like. But it seems to me that I'm not the only one who needs a little help now and then.

She pulls away, smoothing the cloth napkin on her lap. "It's not their fault. Believe me, they had their work cut out for them when they decided to try to turn me into a McRae."

Someone male sucks in a harsh breath. When I look back, all three McRae men wear identical looks of horror. Her mother has a softer expression—one of sympathy, maybe.

Grandmother Rose, seated just on the other side of Bronwyn, lays down her napkin at last and reaches a gnarled, veined hand over to give Bronwyn's a pat.

"You are my child," Arden says, voice gruff. "There's no 'turning you into' anything. There isn't a single thing on this earth that you could do or not do that would change that. I apologize if I ever made you feel like you needed to earn your place in this family."

She shakes her head. "You did nothing wrong. It's not your fault."

Arden frowns. "You're an amazing person, Bronwyn. You're wonderful exactly the way you are."

She squirms a little, looking both pleased and doubtful.

"You've got a heart like the ocean. You're awe-inspiring. I couldn't be more proud of you."

Bronwyn answers with a watery smile. "Thank you, Dad. But the roar of my surf does get a little loud sometimes."

Arden's eyes crinkle at the corners. "It does."

Henry nods at his sister. "You can't expect the ocean to sound like a pond. Who would even want it to?"

"I have something deep and meaningful to add too," Gabriel cuts in.

When everyone looks in his direction, his eyes go innocently wide. "I didn't mean right now," he says, pouring himself a second glass of wine. "I'm not telling you how much I love you in front of all these people. I'm shy."

When the laughter dies, Arden turns to Bronwyn. "I've been treating all three of you like children in need of correction. I forget that you're grown adults."

Charlotte looks at her children helplessly. "It was just a shock. That sort of thing should happen behind closed doors. And you're still recovering, Bronwyn."

Arden reaches for her hand.

Grandma Miller scoffs. "As if your father didn't catch you and Arden *doing it* in your car."

"We were trying to find somewhere with a little privacy. It was the middle of the night."

"It sounded like some poor animal was trapped and dying," Grandad Miller says grumpily.

"Don't exaggerate," Charlotte says, taking a delicate sip of wine.

"Mom," Bronwyn gasps. "Seriously?"

"It was dark. And it was down the back lane. *No one* should have been there."

Henry makes a retching noise, which Phee immediately imitates.

Franki smiles. "Aww, come on, Henry. I think it's cute when old people are still sweet on each other."

Henry's lips twitch in response. His eyes skate away, then back. He looks almost bashful, which, categorically, he is not.

Arden's back straightens in manufactured affront, and he shakes his head at Franki. "Hurtful words, young lady. Hurtful words."

"I hate to say it, Mom, but I think you've lost the moral high ground here," Gabriel says, laughing. He throws an arm around Franki's shoulder and leans down to whisper something in her ear.

She grins in response and pats his hand in a hearty "there, there" gesture.

Henry's attention seems to snag on the place where Franki has her hand on Gabriel's. His face shuts down, and he turns back to his dinner.

"Moving on." Charlotte smiles. "Tomorrow we're having a small party for you two. Just family and close friends. Henry took care of all the arrangements." She smiles. "We're here to support our daughter and her new family."

Henry shovels a forkful of lasagna in his face and keeps his attention fixed on his plate.

Arden looks me dead in the eye. "Hope you like big families, because you and Phee are part of one now. No getting out of it. You're in it for life."

And goddammit, I'm coming down with a virus or something, because my throat hurts too much to do anything but nod.

35

Darkside

BRONWYN

Dean's doing that thing all tall guys do: standing in the doorway to my bedroom with his arms above his head, just resting there against the doorframe.

They do it on purpose, just to make us salivate. No one on this planet can convince me they don't.

His T-shirt lifts just enough to show off a sliver of his flat stomach and those V-shaped muscles at his hips. "There aren't enough bedrooms," he says.

I sigh dramatically. "Oh no. I guess you'll have to sleep in here."

He drops his arms and reaches for a duffel bag just out of view. Then he winks. "How did that happen? My stuff was conveniently sitting right there."

I laugh as he closes the door behind him, tosses his bag on a slipper chair in the corner, then sits down next to me where I'm stretched out on the bed.

He swallows, rubs a hand over the back of his neck, and says, "I'm going to stay here tonight."

For the first time, I notice that he's tense. I understand. It's worse than just sleeping beside me. This house is full of people. Even the living room is being used to house overnight guests.

I didn't miss his phrasing. He's planning to stay awake all night.

"I should have told my family to leave or sleep somewhere else."

He frowns. "I told you not to do that. Do you know what I would give to have my sister be able to surprise me like this? They mean well."

I sigh. "They do. But I'm definitely telling them next time they need to call ah—"

An angry howl erupts from the baby monitor, and Dean freezes. Then he closes his eyes briefly before pulling himself away. "She's not normally so clingy. She's usually a good sleeper, I swear."

"I wouldn't mind if she were a terrible sleeper. Mom says I wouldn't stay in my own bed all night until I was seven. And it's completely understandable if she's a little thrown off schedule. She's in a new place and was introduced to a lot of strangers today."

He nods as he heads for the door. "All of you together *are* a lot."

I smile at the understatement. This wasn't 'all of us' by any means, but he'll learn.

The baby monitor is still in here, volume set low, and I can hear him as he enters Phee's room.

"Hey, pretty baby. Why the tears?"

Her crying stops almost immediately, and she says, "Up, Daddy."

I hear shuffling as he lifts her. "Can't sleep, huh?"

"Sing."

"More?"

"Sing Phee Bee."

He huffs out a laugh and launches into a rendition of "Baby, I Love Your Way." I'd caught a tiny snippet of this routine last night, but this is something else.

His tone is beautiful. He has to change the song a little because his voice is deep and a little husky. I don't know much about music, but his version gives me goose bumps. I haven't heard him play the guitar yet, but now I'm obsessed by the idea of it.

At a tap on my door, I call, "Come in."

Louis pops his blond head inside with a smile. "Hey, bestie."

I don't know why he calls me that. We're not besties. I was a little surprised to see him on Henry's guest list at all. We're friends, yes, but we're not what I'd consider "family weekend together" close.

I always feel like I'm having to ignore a certain awkwardness between us. And it only got worse when Kevin Hallman disappeared, leaving behind rampant evidence that he'd been stealing from not just my trust fund but several of his other clients' as well.

Since Kevin and Louis are first cousins, I'd expected either an unpleasant confrontation about it or for him to stop talking to me entirely. Instead, he'd shrugged and said, "Not my problem."

Louis is looking at me intently with a weird smile that doesn't match his eyes.

"Hey, Lou. What's up? You have everything you need?"

"I found a sofa in the living room." He doesn't try to hide his distaste. "Not the family room."

I roll my eyes and smile. "Whatever."

He clears his throat. "I saw Dean heading into one of the other rooms."

"He's with Phee."

"Good." He moves ridiculously fast to sit beside me on the bed, exactly where Dean had been just a few minutes ago. When he reaches for my hand, I shrink back against my pillows in alarm.

Clarissa always says Louis carries some kind of torch for me. And I've always thought she was seeing something that wasn't there.

There was that thing a few years ago when Louis tried to get me to hook up with him. But he'd laughed my rejection off, then turned around and tried to get with Janessa two days later.

He ended up bringing another girl we knew to our Christmas party and making out with her in front of everyone. So obviously his interest in me was nothing special, thank God.

But there's something in his expression as he holds my hand and leans toward me on my bed that has me seriously starting to freak out.

"I have to tell you something."

"Nope," I say. "You definitely do n—"

"I love you."

I gulp. "Friends love each other, Louis. That's normal. I love Clarissa, Franki, Janessa, and Sydney too."

I'm trying to give him a graceful out by listing so many people. A way for him to backtrack and not lose face.

But Louis doesn't want it. I can see that he has no intention of making this easy on either of us.

He's also pissed off. Finding out I was married has offended him.

And unlike the way my other friends were hurt that I didn't *tell* them about my relationship with Dean, he's offended by the fact that I *have* a relationship with Dean.

He doesn't care that I'm happy, only how it affects him. He was upset when I told him I was staying with my parents after I got out of the hospital too.

As he put it, "Then what's the point in me agreeing to play at a shithole like Jack's if I can't stay with you when I'm here?"

I'd ended up giving him the security codes and letting him stay at my house even though I wasn't here.

But afterward, when I'd thought about it, I'd decided the new me didn't need to give Louis free access to my house just because he was pouting. When I told him so, he said I was overreacting. That I always do. And that it was my own insecurity that made me question him. He didn't really think Jack's was a shithole. He *didn't* only play gigs here because of me, and I was full of myself if I thought that.

I'm annoyed now that I kept giving him chances to be a good person. He is a full-on douche canoe coming in here and making a love declaration to a married woman.

"No, Bronwyn. I love you," Louis insists.

I shake my head in frustration. "We're friends, and I'm also a woman. So it's natural for your mind to turn in that direction, but it's not—"

"Don't tell me how I feel," he says hotly.

"Then listen to me when I tell you how *I* feel. I only see you as a friend. And right now, I don't even see you as that. No one who really cared about me would try to hurt my marriage."

"That's not true. You're not giving me a chance because of that neanderthal."

Inside, I flip a switch. Before that sentence, I still felt some awkward embarrassment. Now Imma cut a bitch.

"You just called my husband a neanderthal?" I ask pleasantly.

He crams his lips together and flexes his jaw. "I don't believe any of this. He's not your husband. He's the fucking chauffeur. You think I don't remember that he was Clarissa's driver? He trapped you and tricked you. This is fraud, not a marriage—"

"I love him, you snobby-ass dick," I say, giving my temper the reins.

Louis's handsome face twists into something ugly. "No. You don't. Everyone knows that's a joke."

He moves closer still, and I shrink back as far as I can go, inserting a hand that's all "Stop in the Name of Love" between our faces.

He keeps coming, so when he speaks, he does so with his words muffled against my palm. "Just give me a chance, babe," he begs. "I know prom night sucked for you. But I've had a lot of experience since high school. I can rock your world now."

Then he fucking licks my palm.

I yank my hand back in revulsion, and he lunges forward, attempting to press his entire body down on mine. I cry out in pain when I jerk my head backward.

I twist away from him. "Louis, stop."

My reflexes are slower than usual, and my muscle tone isn't what it was, but I'm going to fuck this asshole up regardless.

Dean rips him away from me before I get the chance.

My husband doesn't shout. If someone didn't know him well, they may even think he was bored. Just a bouncer at a bar, escorting another drunk asshole to the door.

But his words tell a different story, as do his eyes. "You're dead."

Louis wriggles away from him, backing toward the door, and Dean allows it.

"You can't touch me. I'll have you arrested for assault. And then I'll sue and take everything you've ever owned and everything your crotch goblin will ever own," Louis says, clearly taking Dean's threat for hyperbole.

But something tells me Dean is 100 percent serious.

I've hauled myself up to stand without my cane, but I'm mad enough to ignore it. I push myself right there in between the two of them with my back to Dean.

"My husband saved me from you." I poke Louis in the chest with a hard finger, right on the X-shaped eye of the smiley face screen-printed on his band T-shirt.

Dean puts his hands on my waist and unceremoniously lifts me straight up, then places me back on the bed.

"Saved you from me? Do you even hear yourself?" Louis scoffs. "Dean is the one you need saving from. After what he did to you? Trapping you in this marriage?"

Louis shifts, rubbing his arm that I'm pretty sure Dean didn't even touch. "I'm going to have bruises from this asshole."

Wobbly assed balance or not, I am kicking Louis's ass.

I slide back in front of Dean and say, "I'll give you bruises, you gaslighting dick weasel." Then I pop Louis with a solid right hook straight to the mouth.

He reels back and squeals like a piglet.

I sway a little because my left leg isn't as strong as I instinctively expect it to be. The punch wasn't as powerful as I would have liked, and my knuckles hurt. But I know better than to flinch or check my hand while he's still looking at me, dazed but utterly furious.

I adjust into a ready stance, compensating for my left leg.

Once more, my husband picks me up and deposits me on the bed.

I scowl at him, shuffling to stand slightly behind him and to the side. I'm not lounging on the bed while Louis is still in this room.

Dean moves into my space, his breath skating over the shell of my ear as he warns, "Easy, angel. Let me handle this."

"He doesn't get to talk about you and Phee like that," I seethe.

His features soften a little, but his brows lift. He reminds me sternly, "Stay here. And next time, don't warn your target that you're about to punch him. You're telegraphing."

"Excuse me. I'm not back to 100 percent yet."

"Which is why you're letting me handle this."

I promise nothing, but I do retreat physically. Addressing my words to a pouting Louis, I say, "You need to leave."

He glares at me. "You're a bitch. The guys in my band have all said so. I defended you, but they're right. You never appreciated me."

He wiggles his jaw back and forth, his lip split and bleeding, before saying, "Your loss. Go ahead and play house with the Mellingers' driver and his annoying crotch fruit. I'll watch for your divorce announcement. Maybe I'll take you back then. But don't count on it. He's going to leave you with nothing."

"Were you ever my friend, or were you just pretending to be nice to me thinking I was going to eventually have sex with you? Because that sucks, man."

His attention skates behind me. Then he turns back and sneers, "You mean have sex with me *again*. You should be grateful I'm even willing to give you another chance after all your crying and whining the first time."

The muscles in Dean's back go hard and tight beneath the thin fabric of his T-shirt.

There's some shuffling and throat clearing happening from my doorway. We've drawn an audience. Unsurprising, really.

I cover my eyes and take a breath, then drop my hand. "Louis, get out of my house and lose my number."

Louis turns to the crowd that's peering in the open doorway. Franki must not have been able to see over the men because she's crawling between Henry's knees to get a better view.

"I have witnesses," Louis says, indicating my nosy family and friends. "They all saw you and the hulk assault me."

"Is that what we saw?" Gabriel asks Henry mildly.

Henry shakes his head, his mouth twitching in a disapproving grimace. "That's not what I saw. I heard my sister scream, 'Stop hurting yourself, Louis.' And when I got here, I saw Louis punch himself in the face and say he was going to frame Dean for it."

"That's exactly what I saw too," Gabriel agrees.

Franki pipes up from between Henry's knees. "Me three."

Louis whines, "I thought you were on my side, Henry."

Henry narrows cold eyes at the asshole. "You thought wrong."

Face red, Louis brushes past me, slamming into my shoulder as he goes. I'm not fast enough to avoid him and didn't expect him to be so stupid.

Motherfucker, that hurt. I stagger and Dean steadies me, then lunges for Louis, shoving his arm behind his back and up toward his shoulder blades.

Louis snarls back at me, "I was the one who uploaded that video at Clarissa's wedding and started the hashtag, by the way. Just thought you should know, you stupid cunt."

Louis was the asshole who turned Clarissa and James into the #ialmostdo meme. The realization hurts as much as any physical blow possibly could.

Our *friend*, someone we welcomed into our lives, nearly destroyed their marriage. "I almost do" is now synonymous all over the world with "malicious compliance." The unfounded rumor that James married her for her money and actually despised her so much that he wouldn't even kiss her at the altar deeply hurt them both.

I wish I'd punched Louis in the balls.

From the hallway, Dad says, "Louis, you're not a smart man, are you? A little spoiled? Never faced any real consequences for your actions?"

Gabriel snorts.

Franki, wearing pink pajamas with cartoon wiener dogs all over them, crawls through Henry's legs, across my colorful braided farmhouse rug, then stands to pull me into a sweet-smelling hug.

Dad continues talking. "We're going to have a little chat about the consequences you can expect. I don't think you're going to like them. But, as they say, 'the truth hurts.'"

Then the doorway clears of its spectators as Dean, my father, and both of my brothers frog-march Louis out of my bedroom and, presumably, my life.

Dean turns his head toward me at the last moment. "B, if Phee wakes up before we're done here, can you—"

"I'll take care of her. No problem."

Then the guys are gone.

Mom watches them go, then turns back to me, her blue eyes, so much like mine, filled with concern. "Are you okay?"

"Yes."

The truth is, I have no idea.

I'm full of fragile hope because Dean trusted me with Phee, even if she is asleep.

But also, Louis betrayed me. My adrenaline is up. My knuckles, my head, and my shoulder hurt. I'm embarrassed. I'm angry. I need to wash Louis's disgusting spit off my hand.

I wish Dean had stayed with me. My dad and brothers would have taken care of Louis on their own.

But from the look on Dean's face, that was never going to happen.

I've never seen him lose his temper. I've seen him angry on very rare occasions, but never in a state where I wasn't sure he was in control of himself.

When he hauled Louis out of my bedroom, he didn't look in control at all. And I'm not sure my father and brothers are any better.

When I pictured Dean bonding with them this weekend, I thought they might toss around a football. Discuss various smoked meats. It was definitely not over whether to murder my ex or just kneecap him.

36

Kryptonite

DEAN

Henry and Gabriel McRae are hugging me.

That's what I'll call it later. Right now, it feels a hell of a lot like I'm being restrained.

I'm bloody, but none of it is mine.

"Let." I lunge forward and drag the two men with me. "Me. Go."

Henry shakes his head. "We're not letting you kill him like this. You're going back to my sister tonight, and when she asks you what happened, you can honestly say you let him go. Otherwise, you have two choices: lie to her for the rest of her life or let her blame herself for it. Because she will, even though none of it is her fault," Henry says.

"We'll make sure he's learned his lesson," Arden adds.

I stop fighting and glare at Louis. The pathetic piece of shit.

He's alive, and he'll make a full recovery. Eventually. That's the best I can say for him. He's even conscious. Sort of.

He whined for a remarkably long time about his family's lawyers before reality penetrated that the McRae family would not, in fact, see him in court.

It was almost funny considering Arden is a lawyer—among other things. I thought Louis had to be bluffing that he didn't know about Bronwyn's family connections.

But if he didn't know then, he does now.

Before we took Louis out to B's gardening shed, he'd continued to posture. Threats, lies, begging, insults—none of it was beneath him.

He was fine to attack someone he assumed was weaker than he was but not nearly so brave when the tables were turned.

He assaulted her. He hurt her. Emotionally and physically.

When we arrived in the shed, Gabriel had pulled a patio chair from the small porch in with us.

Arden pushed Louis down onto it. "Your cousin had some photographs, Louis. Someone shoved his camera phone under my daughter's skirt. It occurs to me that you might know something about that."

"I didn't give those to him. He stole them from my phone," he said defensively.

That's when I lost it *again*.

When I was back under control, shaking off my brothers-in-law with a jerk of my head and an "I'm cool," Arden quietly picked up a pair of pliers and broke one of the bones in Louis's pinkie.

When the screaming finally stopped, Arden simply asked, "Have you been in contact with Kevin?"

Louis shook his head. "I told him I couldn't help him."

Arden broke another bone. "Do you know where he is?"

Louis screamed. Gagged. Cried. "No."

"We have to be sure you haven't forgotten anything you might want to tell us," Henry said, rolling up his sleeves. "Go ahead and stop me if you remember anything important."

• • • ● • ● • • •

I scowl at Henry as I haul Louis in a fireman's carry to his pretentious tricked-out Hummer. "You invited this prick here."

Henry sighs. "I thought a little jealousy might be motivational for you. That was an error in judgment. You're familiar with those."

"Your 'error' ended up with Bronwyn hurt."

Henry shakes his head. "My sister can handle herself. If you hadn't ridden to the rescue so quickly, she'd have had Mr. Larrabie here in the fetal position and begging for mercy."

I growl, "She shouldn't have to."

Louis is still conscious. Not, I might add, by my choice.

He whines against my back through his snot and tears. "Henry, how can you be on his side? He's a con artist."

Gabriel nudges me with his elbow. "Do you hear that? Someone thinks you're smooth enough to be a con artist."

Henry laughs. "How would that work? Wouldn't he have to, I don't know, *look friendly*?"

"Only our sister would go for such a mean-looking son of a bitch."

Yeah, my knuckles are dripping with blood. And I'd very much like to plant Louis in a shallow grave on the back forty.

But I almost crack a smile.

They're talking me down, distracting me from my rage. And it's working.

I don't have the luxury of losing control. Because Henry, as usual, is right. The secrets I've kept from Bronwyn are stacked up like a house of cards. I can't balance Louis's murder right there on top and imagine it won't bring the whole thing crashing down.

Henry opens the passenger door, and I dump Louis inside. Gabriel climbs in the driver's seat and starts the ignition.

"Where did you say you're taking him?" I ask.

Gabriel grins. "He's about to fall asleep at the wheel. But the good news is, it'll be a ten-minute drive from the hospital, and some nice anonymous person will call for help.

"That's the good news?"

Henry says, "I suppose it depends on whose perspective you're considering."

When Gabriel has pulled out with Henry following in his own vehicle, I meet my father-in-law in the shed with a gallon of bleach.

Pretty sure the gardeners wouldn't appreciate it if we didn't clean up after ourselves.

Finally, I'm headed back into the house. I grab an extra set of clothing from a go bag in my trunk and shower in one of the downstairs bathrooms. I'm not coming to B with Louis's blood all over me. I decide to shave while I'm at it since I noticed some red marks on her inner thighs earlier.

I pass Henry and Gabriel in the hall as I go upstairs.

But when I creep quietly into Bronwyn's bedroom, expecting to slide in next to her sleeping form, I freeze in alertness.

I nearly turn around and leave, thinking I've somehow wandered into the wrong bedroom. But no. In the light from the hallway, I can make out her colorful rug. There's my duffel still sitting on the chair in the corner.

I couldn't tell you if that's her comforter on the bed because I can't see it. Every inch of real estate on the king-sized space is covered in women.

Considering Phee is there, too, I take it back. They are humans of the female variety.

Charlotte is cuddled up with her arm around her daughter. Phee is starfished in the center of the bed in her yellow footie pajamas, no pillows or blankets anywhere near her, one hand outstretched holding Bronwyn's. Janessa is on the left clinging to my side of the bed. Sydney and Franki are squished across the bottom.

The only person who looks even mildly comfortable is my kid, but they're all sound asleep.

I note, with some guilt, a small pile of crumpled facial tissue on B's nightstand, as if she's been crying.

The sound of the door or maybe the light has woken my mother-in-law, because her eyelids bob before she focuses on me. "Are the boys home yet?"

I wonder if she has any idea what her boys were up to tonight. From the look in her eyes, I'd guess she does.

"Yes. Arden never left the property. And I saw the... uh... boys were back when I was coming upstairs."

She smiles a little at my awkwardness, then slips her arm from around B, disentangling herself from the pile. She stretches when she stands and grimaces a little, holding her lower back. "I might be getting a little old for the cuddle puddle. Next time I'll have to take some Advil first," she says quietly, humor lacing her words. "She was wanting some company, but now that you're here, I should track down my own bed."

I'm probably supposed to say something to that, but I'm thrown by the whole thing. Bronwyn wanted her mother. And her mother was there.

I have a feeling that if she'd been halfway across the world, she'd have hopped straight onto a plane if any of her children called.

Bronwyn's friends are here, too, looking less than comfortable but undeniably present.

Charlotte must notice me looking at them in confusion. "Bronwyn FaceTimed Clarissa for about fifteen minutes tonight too. Then we watched a movie. Phee woke up a little fussy, but she liked the cuddle puddle. Then we all just conked out while we waited," she says, as if any of this scene makes sense.

She reaches out and lightly pats my bicep. "We'll get out of your hair."

She wakes Sydney first, and between the two of them they slowly rouse everyone but Phee and B, both of whom are sleeping like a rock.

I gather Phee and gently deposit her back into her crib in her own room.

Then I crawl in next to my wife and pull her close. I smile a little when I realize she smells weird. There's her mother's perfume and some of Franki's, as well as the vague scent of strawberry cereal puffs and possibly a small milk spill.

She smells different, but this time, I don't resent it. I love that I know what all of it means. That I'm here to know it.

• • • • ● • ● • • •

I blink the stinging sweat from my eyes. The hard-packed grainy sand crunches beneath my boots, then beneath my knees. I don't feel the impact. "Vasquez, get down. Get the fuck down!"

Jordan is dead, a film of dust already forming over his open eyes.

Jacob screams, "Get it together, man!"

I snap back online, scanning for the enemy. This is not the time to mourn. It was less than a second of distraction.

I can't see through the motherfucking sweat in my eyes.

Impact. A screaming, burning pain in my shoulder.

Keep going. Fire back.

Shouted orders.

Where are the rest of them?

Take cover.

Sweat in my eyes, but I'm cold. Losing too much blood.

Vasquez. Shit. Vasquez.

So fucking much blood. Warm and sticky. Slippery. Soaking into the sand.

Maddie's hit. She's going down. She's missing half her face. I need to get to my sister. Maybe it's not too late. Maybe—

"Brady, get the baby."

"Let me up. I need to save them. Let me up!"

A toddler screaming. Phee. She's standing there in yellow footie pajamas. Her face is red, tears leaving clean tracks through dust-covered cheeks. No cover.

Artillery strikes the wall behind her, a chunk of concrete hitting her cheek. Blood runs from a wound in her temple.

Can't move. Brady's applying pressure to my shoulder.

"Not me. Save the baby. Save Phee! Goddammit, Brady, get my kid!"

My left arm is useless. I've lost so much blood. They're pulling me away. Laying down cover fire.

Why don't they see Phee? Why are they saving me?

"No. Get the fuck off me."

"Shhh. Dean, it's okay."

"What the fuck is wrong with you? Get Phee."

"Phee isn't there. She's safe." Bronwyn is here.

I turn my head toward her voice, but I can't see her, not through the sweat and blood in my eyes.

"Phee is safe," she repeats.

I shake my head. "She isn't. She's going to die. Like Jordan and Vasquez and my sister. Like you are."

"She's in her crib. In our house in Pennsylvania. Can you see that? Phee in her bedroom?"

I turn my head again, looking the other way for Bronwyn. Where is she?

Her beautiful face finally comes into focus. She's there, covering her eyes while lying on a sofa.

"You can't be here," I say desperately.

"I'm safe. Phee and I are safe."

"Nobody will save my kid."

"I'll keep her safe. You're in my bedroom. The comforter smells like Downy fabric softener."

I can smell it.

Bronwyn runs out to Phee and scoops her up.

"No. You'll die too. You always die."

This is the part where they both go down. I wait for it.

"It's a dream."

It isn't real. But I can never change it.

Bronwyn's voice is firm. "You see what you expect to see, but I didn't take classes to learn how to dance."

Henry's leaning against the wall wearing a suit and a baseball cap. "My sister can handle herself. She doesn't need you to ride to her rescue."

Bronwyn smiles at me. "I have Phee." She carries Phee back to me.

"She's hurt. She's dying."

"She's not hurt, just a little dirty. What makes her happy, Dean?"

I practiced this. I think. Yes, I did. "She likes Blippi."

Bronwyn laughs. "Think that's why she likes Henry? Is it the glasses?"

That's new. I picture Henry dressed as Blippi and huff a little with a trace of humor.

Bronwyn asks, "What's her favorite thing to do?"

"She likes to swing."

I push Phee on the toddler swing back and forth, on and on. The weather is warm. There are sounds of children playing. Traffic. Phee giggles.

Bronwyn laughs. There's that dimple of hers. The breeze dances through the yellow fabric of her dress, rippling around her legs.

• • • ● • ● • ● • •

I open my eyes.

The room is dim, but Bronwyn has turned on her lamp, the setting low. It's not much more than a nightlight, but it's enough.

She's watching me with those piercing blue eyes. So pale with the dark ring around the outside. They see everything.

For long seconds we're there, caught in the breathless moment between sleeping and awake. Dreaming each other.

Then awareness creeps in and heat floods through me, from my chest, up my neck, and into my face.

I fell asleep.

Did I pull myself out of the dream, or was that her? I don't even know. I try to wipe my face on the pillow without being obvious about it.

"Are you okay?" she asks.

"Yes. I didn't... sometimes I... move. Did I hurt you or—"

"No. Dad told me not to touch you. That you might not know it was me."

"Who did you let see me when I was asleep?" I want to shove my fist through the drywall. As if it would do anything except prove how fucking unhinged I am.

"No one. I talked to Dad in the hall."

Some experts estimate up to 97 percent of veterans who've seen combat have nightmares a couple of times a week. There's nothing unique happening here.

If I weren't one of those assholes who talks in his sleep, no one would even know.

I run a hand through my hair and throw the comforter off, rising on legs that still feel shaky. "Did I wake the whole house up?"

She sits. "Not the whole house."

I dig through my bag and pull out a pair of sweatpants and a long-sleeved T-shirt. "Where's Phee?"

"She's asleep. Her room was far enough away that—"

"Great. Good to hear."

"Are you going somewhere?" She clutches the quilt, then smooths it under her fingers.

"I'm getting some fresh air. I can't breathe in here."

"Oh. Okay. Do you want me to come with you?"

"Do you think I need a babysitter?" I snarl.

"Excuse me?"

"I'm not weak." I yank the shirt over my head.

She crosses her arms tightly over her chest, her chin wobbling. "How can you think I could ever believe you're weak? You're too strong. You never accept help from anybody."

I remember that chin wobble. Then the determined smile. So many times I've done that to her. Hurt her, then watched her pretend she was fine afterward.

The realization makes me nauseous.

Why does even a hint of gentleness toward me feel like proof of my failure?

I stop. Just close my eyes and pull my shit together.

When I open them, I say, "Forgive me. I'm embarrassed that you saw me like that."

"I puked on you before, if we want to talk embarrassing. Nobody here is going to judge you for having nightmares."

That seems unlikely. I swallow thickly. "Did you talk to me? In the middle of it? I heard you, and then...."

"Just a little. I reminded you that Phee was safe and where you were. I remembered the things you said to me in the hospital. I wasn't trying to wake you up."

"You didn't. You were...." I want to sound eloquent and in control. I want to explain to her how she—just her voice, the reminder of her—pulled me out of the hell my subconscious tries to live in. And how sorry I am that I let my pride and fear of her rejection get in the way of just rolling over and dragging her into my arms.

My own fragile ego is a shock to me. But once I've peeled off the blinders, I'm seeing evidence of it everywhere. I don't like it.

"You were perfect. You helped me," I admit. "Thank you."

First, she looks startled. Then a gentle sort of joy fills her face. It's humbling as fuck.

Right. Ask for what you want. Don't push her away.

"I'd like it if you came with me. If you're actually willing to go outside. If you want to go back to sleep, that's fine."

"I want to go with you."

I pull the quilt from her bed and wrap her in it like a burrito.

She squirms a little, unable to even move her arms. Then I grab a small bottle from my bag and the baby monitor, shove them into my pockets, and pick her up bridal style.

"Dean, I can't hold on like this," she laughs.

I shrug as I head for the stairs. "You don't have to. I'm holding on for both of us."

37
Work Song

BRONWYN

We take a pit stop in the dimly lit kitchen for Dean to grab a glass of water. He sets me on the counter first, and I wiggle enough to free my arms from the quilt.

He eyes me warily for a moment before he seems to come to a decision and produces a prescription bottle from his pocket.

He sets the amber container on the counter and says, "Anxiety and depression. Meds help. I forgot to take it before I went to sleep. Didn't take my anti-inflammatory for the shoulder either."

He says the words casually, but I'm not even a little fooled. He looks tense enough to shatter under the slightest impact. It's a kind of hard shell that has no give.

There are only two potential results when going up against it: the shell shatters... or the person battering themselves against it does.

But I'm not interested in cracking his defenses.

Let him keep that stoic shell if he needs it. I'll climb under it with him.

The fact that he's willing to share this part of himself with me is more than I could have believed possible.

He takes the pill with calm, calculated motions. But he's watching me and waiting for my reaction.

I could give him a speech about men's mental health. It was a point of study in several of my college classes, so I know the statistics and how few men will overcome some perceived stigma to get the help they need.

I could tell him I'm proud of him for doing the work to take care of himself.

But that's not what he needs right now.

Under the shell, not through it.

So I raid the ceramic jar on the counter for cookies and say, "I hear you. I'm on something for ADHD and anxiety. It helps."

There. I just admitted to it. He's not alone in his vulnerability. And wow, yes, my adrenaline is popping from my admission.

I switch gears. "How do you feel about Oreos at 4:00 a.m.?"

He lifts his brows. "I think if you don't share, we can't be friends anymore."

"You do realize I would share without the need for duress? You could say, 'I'd love a cookie,' and I'd just miraculously give you a cookie. It's wild!"

Dean's lips twitch. "I'm hedging my bets. Cookie insurance."

I wrinkle my nose.

He unwraps the blanket from my bottom half and inserts his bulky body between my thighs. I love the way he's so big that I have to work to make space for him.

Dropping his face just to the place where my shoulder meets my neck, he clutches me so tightly it almost hurts. I run my fingers through his hair, and he rocks us slightly.

"I love you." The words are like my heartbeat—strong and ever-present, living inside me. They are part of who I am: Bronwyn has a pulse, and Bronwyn loves Dean.

He nods against my neck and says roughly, "I'm holding you to that."

He straightens and clears his throat. "I can't go back to sleep for a while after one of those."

I nod. "What do you normally do? Read?"

"I play the guitar." He gives a self-deprecating laugh. "It's about the only time I do. I kind of suck, but it takes concentration, so it helps."

So many callouses on his fingers, and yet he only plays when he dreams.

"Will you play for me?"

"Not sure there's anywhere it won't keep people awake."

I waggle my eyebrows. "I know where."

At my urging, he puts together a thermos of hot apple cider. Then he grabs his guitar from where he's currently stashed it in the family room.

When I ask for shoes, he frowns. "No."

He pulls the blanket over and around me instead, then puts the guitar and thermos in my hands.

"What are you doing?"

He picks me back up. "You just tell me where I'm headed."

"I can walk." Probably. Honestly, it is a slight hike for me given where I'm at in my recovery.

"I need to hold you right now."

I nod. "Okay."

When I lean away and stretch back toward the counter, he pauses. I snag the stack of cookies and bundle everything against my chest like the precious treasure it is, then wave a lofty hand. "Proceed."

He narrows his eyes at me in an absolutely fake show of annoyance.

I stuff a cookie into his mouth, purely on impulse. He freezes for a moment, then accepts it with a "Mmmm." I snicker.

We flick on the lights to illuminate the patio and terraces, and Dean takes me down to the gas firepit area. The whole thing is sunken and surrounded by built-in cushioned benches. He fires it and the surrounding heaters up.

I sit on the orange upholstery, picking up a single brown oak leaf that's drifted to land on the fabric and twirling it between my fingers as I pull my knees against my chest, the blanket wrapped around me. Our breath fogs in the cool night air, the delicious scent of October in Pennsylvania filling my senses.

When he settles on the edge of the bench, I remember what he said about holding me, so I keep the blanket wrapped around me and climb behind him, straddling him.

He turns to look at me with a crooked smile. Then he picks his way through a bunch of songs, occasionally stopping to warm his fingers back up when they get too cold. I lean against his back and wrap my arms around his middle, shoving my hands under his shirt to absorb his heat. The music vibrates through us both.

After a time, the tension leaves him the chords flow more smoothly, and he even sings a little. If my brothers were here, they'd join him. But I have a terrible voice. Normally I don't care—I'll howl along to the music because it's fun—but tonight... tonight I just listen.

When he's done, he sets aside his guitar and holds my hands against him. I crawl around and climb into his lap.

His big palm cradles the back of my head. He leans in but doesn't close the last two inches between us. He *likes* to wait for me. Dean *enjoys* it when I chase him. It makes him feel wanted.

The realization lifts a weight from my heart.

I sift my fingers through his short hair, and he lifts his head to catch my gaze and hold it tight. I close the distance between us.

One of my favorite things in gymnastics was the trampoline. I'd start out with short little jumps. But each successive bounce had more lift, more power, until it felt like I was soaring to touch the sky. There's a moment at the top when you hover, just before you begin the downward descent.

That's where I am right now.

He's smiling, and I'm falling. There's no patience left inside me, but he seems to have none either.

We collide, crashing together.

Inside, down low, a firestorm of need ignites.

He lifts the soft blue cotton of my pajama top, his hand clenched tight at my waist and his thumb sliding down below my belly button. He plumps my breast with the other hand, tweaking the nipple.

"I need a taste of these," he says.

I smile. "Are you a boob guy, Dean?"

He gives the tiniest shake of his head. "I'm a Bronwyn guy. Whatever you have, that's what I want." Then his hot mouth is on my breast, sucking, flicking, then sucking again.

He looks up at me as his cheeks hollow out and his mouth works, and I shudder from the tremor of lust that stabs me.

He pulls the knot free on my cotton drawstring pajama bottoms and sends exploring fingers under my panties and into the wet haven of my sex.

When he makes contact, he drags his open mouth from my breast, across my collarbone, and up to suck on my earlobe. "You are always so wet for me." His voice is a rumble.

"I'm ready."

His erection is a solid weight just there. But there are too many layers of clothing between us. I yank at the waistband of his sweats.

He guides my wrist away and moves it behind my back. "Not yet," he chides gently.

"We haven't made love in more than two months. I need you now."

His words come on a combination of a laugh and a groan. "Believe me, I feel the same way."

He enters me with two fingers, scissoring and stretching me as he works my clit with his thumb, and I gasp at the delicious intrusion. "But you have to give me an orgasm first, B. You know the rules."

I do know the rules. I don't care, though. Not tonight. If the initial stretch aches a little, so be it.

But I don't fight it. I can be Dean's angel. Just for now, I can try.

I drop my head back and let him work me higher and higher.

"That's it. Almost there. You like my fingers," he coaxes.

I growl, just a little. "I like your *dick*!"

Amusement glints in his eyes. "So impatient." He gives my clit a light slap.

It doesn't hurt, but it ignites something inside me.

I yank him into a kiss and speak against his mouth. "Again."

"Yes, ma'am." He gives me another slap, then more of those firm, tight circles under my panties.

I don't even realize I'm getting really loud—louder even than the guitar was—until Dean plants his palm over my mouth with a small laugh. "I love to hear you scream, woman. But if we draw another crowd before I get inside you, I might actually cry this time."

My own laughter cuts off in a choked gasp when the orgasm hits. Hot, electric spasms thrill through me, all the way to my toes.

He coaxes me through it, his breath hot against my neck, one hand muffling the sounds I can't stop myself from making. "That's it, B."

When I've stopped shaking, I reach for his sweats, but he pulls the blanket over and around me instead.

He stands up with me in his arms, then strides across the lit stone pathways and patio, heading for the wooden bench swing hung beneath the big oak. I'd been surprised to see it here the first time I looked out across the backyard when Henry brought me back to Blackwater. I'd immediately realized that Dean had to have hung it when he'd overseen installation of the security systems.

This swing had boosted my confidence in a way I hadn't even realized I needed. It was Dean staking a claim here before he'd even packed his bags.

He heads straight for it but jerks a little when I manage to work a hand down inside his boxer briefs and wrap my fingers around his thick length. He grunts in approval.

I huff in annoyance, however, when he sets me on the swing and starts to back away. "I'm going to murder you," I seethe. "Get your butt back here."

"Well, now I'm spanking your clit *and* your ass, you bossy little thing."

I smirk. "Promise?"

His lips twitch, and then he gives me a little test swing to evaluate the height.

"This feels premeditated, sir."

Sitting beside me, he reaches out and draws me to sit sideways on his lap. His hands creep beneath my pajama top and skim over the skin of my stomach and back. "If you're asking me if I've been evaluating every surface I see to determine how I'd fuck you on it, then you'd be correct."

I smile and shiver in the cold. He wraps me entirely in his arms, surrounding me with heat and affection. His mouth lands on mine, and we taste of the apple cider we shared.

I lean back as a thought occurs. "There aren't security cameras out here, are there?"

"They're closed circuit. I'll delete the footage immediately," he says.

I grin. "Can we watch it first?"

His eyes widen, and then he breathes, "Fuck yes."

I shimmy my pajama bottoms and panties down and toss them to the side, then straddle him. I lift my body away enough that I can tug at the waistband of his sweats.

When I wrap my hand around him again, he shudders. "Holy shit, your hands are cold."

But cold or not, it hasn't done a thing to calm his erection. He's hot steel in my palm. If we weren't freezing out here, and if it hadn't been months since he's been inside me, I'd tease him a bit more.

But it's been way too long.

He snakes a hand between us, checking that I'm still ready for him. God, his hands are cold too. And the contrast against those extra-sensitive nerve endings feels amazing.

He taps my clit with the head of his cock and then slides through my wetness. I could come again like this. But I want him inside me now.

I position myself. A hard shiver racks me, and Dean grabs the blanket from the swing where I'd laid it. He envelops me in the quilt, then pulls me forward so I'm plastered against his chest. When my freezing nose touches his neck, he shudders and flexes beneath me as I squirm, seeking friction.

He sucks on my bottom lip while I lift and shift enough to catch him at just the right angle.

I can't just fill myself with him in one go. My body accepts him slowly, one small thrust at a time.

When he finally bottoms out, we both groan. The feel of him is delicious, like we were both made for this. Made for each other.

An ache of lust coils inside me and urges me to move.

He cups my butt under the blanket and helps me with that, using his hands to lift me, then pull me back down onto his length. Hard. Perfect.

"Goddammit," he growls, and I wait for his usual torrent of dirty talk. Instead, he drops his forehead to my shoulder, shudders, and says so quietly that I almost don't hear him, "I missed you."

And there it is. That deep, wild craving inside me to protect this big, strong man.

I don't fight it, just wrap him in my arms and love him.

The chains rattle as we move, but I don't care. If someone hears, they can just take it as a warning to stay away.

Abruptly, Dean stands, taking me with him. Then I'm back on the swing, on my knees and facing the opposite direction.

I hold on to the backrest when Dean places my hands there.

I shudder when he slams back into me from behind. He fills me up. I'm practically losing my mind with it when he uses the swing to pull me in hard, then push me away.

He bends over me, caging me, his hands swallowing mine as he works me over. I can't be quiet, no matter how hard I try.

His hips snap against mine as he lets go of my right hand to reach around and play with my clit.

He makes me crazy. Oblivious to anything outside of him. Is it still cold? I wouldn't know. There's only Dean. The size of him. The strength. The hard thrust of his cock that's almost, but not quite, too much for me to take. The fresh woodsy scent of him and the smell of his laundry detergent. His hair-roughened thighs against me. The weight of him. Physical, yes. But mostly the emotional gravity that is Dean Priester.

I'm lost.

He pulls his hands away from me, and I feel untethered for two whole seconds. Then he's got them on my ass, spreading me.

I should be embarrassed. I know what he's looking at in the shadowy glow of the landscape lighting. But it's impossible to ever be embarrassed with him when he makes his admiration so clear.

"You're so pretty, B."

I thought I'd been as turned on as it was possible for a person to be. I was wrong.

I thrust back toward him with a moan, his cock filling me with mindless pleasure.

He makes a low sound of satisfaction. "Do you want me to touch you there, angel?"

I make a noise, not a yes or a no but an incoherent babble that feels like the only thing I'm capable of.

"Use your words." He sounds stern, though his voice is quiet and his grip is gentle. "Only what you want. We only go that far."

I would trust this man with anything. "Yes. I want to try... a little."

He swats my ass, the sting absolute perfection. Then he—

My thoughts stutter. I can't think. I can't—

But *holy shit*. He's touching me there, gentle with that virgin territory. And then he carefully sinks his thumb inside me. My nerve endings explode with pleasure. My thoughts go off-line entirely.

My knees are weak, and I sag against the back of the swing. He uses an arm around my middle to haul me back into position.

"You like that," he says with a smile in his voice.

He leans into me and nuzzles my cheek, and I turn my head and give him my mouth. And I come.

Every cell inside me ignites in an electric spasm that clenches every muscle in pleasure. For once, I don't make a sound, for all that I've probably resembled the audio for a low-budget porn video for the last twenty minutes.

How can I make a sound if I can't breathe?

He grunts into my mouth, then loses his rhythm, his last thrusts jerky and rough.

He collapses onto the seat beside me, and I climb back onto his lap, leaning up and whispering in his ear, "I like your swing, Dean."

38

Skinny Love

DEAN

Henry is annoyed at breakfast. He refuses anything but coffee and mumbles about sleeping with noise-canceling headphones the next time he's in this house.

So I guess I did wake pretty much everyone but Phee with my nightmare. I don't know what I say in my sleep, but whatever it is, it isn't good.

I don't respond to his words at all.

I set down the half-finished mug of hot cocoa that I've managed to choke down. Bronwyn presented it to me this morning, whipped cream and all. I'd smiled at her and said something stupid like "Mmmm. My favorite."

I started that lie about chocolate way back on the night we decided to get married. I didn't want to admit I only had the ingredients in my house because I was obsessed with her.

Now I smile as she stuffs Oreos into my mouth and gives me liquid sugar for breakfast because I don't want to admit that I lied.

Phee is shoveling Cheerios into her maw as fast as she can manage it, and I start combing her little blonde curls out with apple-scented detangler to put them into two pigtails that look like round puffballs on the sides of her head.

When the clatter and hum of voices around us abruptly crashes into silence, I glance back in curiosity. I'm met by the sight of my wife, still in her pajamas, not a speck of makeup on her, and a floppy bun thing on her head that's in danger of falling out completely. She's brandishing a spatula at her brother with righteous flames of fury in her eyes.

Instead of raising her voice, she speaks with quiet intensity. "You will respect my husband or you will leave."

Henry's eyes go wide behind his wire frames. Then in an annoyed huff, he says, "This has nothing to do with your husband. He's not the one who makes me want to wash my eardrums with bleach. My bedroom faces west. My windows were *open*."

The spatula clatters to the floor, and she scrambles to pick it up. Standing back up, she walks over without her cane to drop it into the sink, sputtering, "Why would you have your windows open in October?"

He mumbles, "I was overheated."

Franki puts an arm around Bronwyn. "He was fine. We closed his windows and fell right to sleep."

And just like that, silence descends once more.

Bronwyn stares at Franki, clearly trying to make sense of those words. Then her attention snaps back to Henry. At his stony face, her gaze shoots straight to mine. I lift my eyebrows slightly in a microexpression I know she'll understand. Her face says, "What the fuck?" And mine says, "How should I know?"

Charlotte beams. "Are you two seeing each other? Arden, did you know this?"

Henry pushes to stand, his chair scraping loudly over the hardwood floor. "We are not in a relationship. No." He laughs. "That would be absurd."

And then he walks his ass right out of the kitchen and leaves Franki standing there with her mouth tight and fists clenched.

Bronwyn's jaw drops. "Franki, are you—"

Franki waves a hand. "None of that was what you think it was. I just… ran into him in the hall. When we both got up. For a… glass of water."

No lie detector necessary for this one. She's so bad at it that it almost comes across as a comedy sketch. But, as I look at the faces around me, I realize they all believe her.

To them, the idea of her coincidentally running into Henry in the hall seems more believable than the rigid, fussy man fucking around with someone as seemingly sweet and silly as Franki.

It reminds me a little of the way Bronwyn's friends had dismissed the idea of a relationship between the two of us. Simply because, from the outside, we look like we don't "fit."

I know Bronwyn sees something on my face, though my expression hasn't changed, because she hobbles over to me and wraps her arms around my waist. I give her a squeeze and kiss her forehead.

Phee fusses and tries to climb from her highchair, reaching for me. Bronwyn pulls back a little to allow me to get to her. But when I pull Phee from her little seat, it isn't me she wants.

She's practically throwing herself out of my arms to get to Bronwyn.

Bronwyn sends me a wary glance, and I know she's remembering the way I snatched Phee away from her in the past.

My expression is more serious than a family breakfast warrants as I turn to hand my child to Bronwyn. But I need her to know what I'm saying.

I trust you not to hurt her.

She nods, then puts out her arms. Phee goes with a happy squeal. Then the little stinker wraps her arms around Bronwyn's neck, gives me a belligerent pout, and says, "Mine."

Arden laughs, as does one of the women who's working here this morning doing most of the cooking and cleaning up.

I put my arms around Phee and Bronwyn both and smile. "She's ours," I say. "We share."

I don't have a clue if that was the right approach. Maybe I just traumatized her. Maybe I should let her claim Bronwyn all for herself. She's never had a woman she called hers. And to be honest, I'm not sure why she's decided on Bronwyn in this moment over, say, Franki, who has given her plenty of attention.

It may be that she senses how much Bronwyn wants to be part of her life. Or maybe it's because she sees the way Bronwyn and I are interacting. She's never seen me show affection to anyone but her.

I'm grateful she didn't claim me and try to push Bronwyn away.

Phee's lower lip juts out, and she holds on tighter.

Bronwyn shakes her head at me just the tiniest bit. She lifts Phee high into her arms and blows a raspberry against her belly. Then she pulls her into a rocking bear hug.

I pretend to be offended, then fake wrestle her out of Bronwyn's arms. "Hey, give me back my baby."

Phee squeals with laughter as Bronwyn and I pass her back and forth several times, claiming her as ours.

Each time, she reaches for the adult "claiming" her. And when the other steals her back, she goes willingly until, finally, she pats my face and says, "Share, Daddy. Share."

"Share, is it? Fine. I'll share you with Bronwyn."

Phee smiles back at me like it was all her idea in the first place. "Good Daddy."

Bronwyn has a tiny dent between her eyebrows now, despite her smile. I keep Phee in my arms for the moment. "Your head is hurting."

She scowls at me. "I'm fine."

"Don't lie to me. The doctor said to listen to your body."

"I don't want to have a headache right now."

"That's not how it works. You do have a headache. Phee's too much for you to handle at the moment."

Her back goes straight, and once more, the room goes silent.

Then Arden whistles something from an old Western TV show.

My expression doesn't change, but inside I'm grasping for something to say that'll take that look off her face. The one that, in about two seconds, is going to be followed by her dazzling smile. Then she's going to get up and walk out. Or tell me to.

"Bronwyn," I say quietly enough that it's for her ears only. "If I wasn't an unreasonable idiot in the past, would you be reacting this way? Or would you be willing to take a painkiller and lie down for an hour until you feel a little better?"

She clenches her jaw.

"You don't have to prove anything to me."

This is why I don't talk. The more words that come out of my mouth, the grimmer Bronwyn looks.

"Why are you upset?"

"Did I say I was upset?" she asks. "Do I look upset?" My words have been quiet, but hers are not. They ring through the kitchen.

Gabriel has dragged himself in for some coffee, bleary-eyed but recently showered. He bops Phee on the nose and smirks at me. "Don't borrow trouble, brother. If she says she's not upset, leave her alone."

Phee throws her arms out to him, and I let her go to "Uncle Gabel." He takes her with a chuckle and says, "What's good for breakfast today, princess?"

I don't like Gabriel's advice to ignore that Bronwyn is upset. I've learned better than to do that. If we can't be honest with each other, how can I give her what she needs?

I flinch internally at my own hypocrisy. I sit here on my high horse judging her for not wanting to share every thought in her head when I haven't even considered telling her the truth about so many things, including the way I manipulated her into signing that prenup.

She asked for honesty. I haven't given that to her. If I could have avoided sharing my dreams with her, I would have.

I'm glad she knows now. But the dreams are different from admitting to the things I've done.

And that list of lies and secrets is growing. This morning when she asked what happened with Louis, I'd pretended I was distracted looking for socks for Phee and had mumbled, "We let him go."

Technically true. But not at all what she wanted to know.

I've justified my behavior the way an addict justifies taking a hit. At first, I decided that since my goal was to protect her, the stalker shit was harmless. Almost innocent. Then I justified it because I had to do it. She wasn't with me, and I needed to know she was okay. She never had to know what I'd done.

But the secrets have stacked up under me so that our foundation is practically built on top of them.

"Dean?" Bronwyn's voice is sharp and concerned, and I realize I'm standing here in the middle of her kitchen with my eyes closed. There's a certain humiliating sort of poetry to it all.

I lift my lids and there she is: mussed up and wearing pajamas, concern on her face.

"You okay?"

"Yes. You are so beautiful."

She looks a little bemused by my words. Then she pushes me toward a chair. I sit, and when she presses her palm into my left shoulder, I realize I've been rotating the arm out of habit. She leaves me there, then returns with a bottle of lotion. She doesn't ask me to take my shirt off in front of her family, and I'm grateful for that.

Instead, she reaches under the collar to massage my shoulder. Her warm hands offer instant relief. She's gentler than my physical therapist was, but her technique is surprisingly good.

"Where'd you learn to do that?" I ask.

She shrugs. "After I realized part of your PT used massage, I asked my own to teach me a little. And then I paid someone to come to the house to show me what to do. I'm not good with anything except the most basic stuff. More relaxation than medical. I'd never pass any tests or anything...."

She says it like it's nothing. It had to have been hours of her time. And in the middle of her own recovery when her primary job was supposed to be resting and building her strength back up. She did it just to be able to offer me some relief. Because she loves me.

She was mine all along. And I pushed her away. I hid myself behind half-truths and manipulation.

I was so busy trying to control every variable that I forgot the most important one.

No one can truly be happy with someone they can't trust. Over time, it will tear any relationship apart.

39

Enemy

BRONWYN

It's the first time since Dean and Phee moved in a month ago that I don't know where he is.

I can't explain why, but I have this weird sense that I'm watching a horror movie, just waiting for something awful to happen. It's the same feeling I had before I got sick.

It's because our routine is disrupted, I'm sure. But I hate it.

Dean texted around four o'clock that he'd be working late.

It's eight now. I check his tracker dot only to find that he's turned it off.

He used to disable it when he worked for James. I understand it can be a security issue with his job, but since he no longer works directly in protection, he doesn't do that anymore.

I want to text him, but I could be interrupting something important. Besides, it would be clingy to call him while he's working just because I'm freaking out.

I've got this feeling up my spine about Dean. It's paranoia, pure and simple. But I'm worried sick about him. I'm picturing an accident. Or some job he took on that has him in danger.

Phee is in her pajamas and sorting through her little shelf full of board books looking for the one she wants me to read to her before bed. I'm sitting on the floor in her bedroom, waiting for her to crawl into my lap, when my phone buzzes with an incoming call.

I'd never normally pick up an unknown caller, but it could have something to do with Dean, so I answer.

"Hello?"

"Bronwyn."

I don't immediately recognize the voice. "Yes?"

"Call off your dog."

I freeze, my heartbeat pounding in my ears. "Kevin."

"Call off your *fucking dog*!"

At Phee's wide-eyed squeal, I realize I have Kevin on speaker. I click over and bring the phone to my ear. A tremor nearly has me fumbling the thing even as I give Phee a reassuring smile. "What are you talking about?"

"He's not taking anything else from me. I will die before I go to prison. And I'll take you both with me."

"I think your guilty conscience is getting to you. Nobody's chasing you," I say, working hard to keep my voice strong and steady.

"I warned you. I could have picked you off with a rifle, instead. I gave you a chance. I was being *nice*. But you're too stupid to listen. Call him off or I'm coming for you both. Priester can learn what it feels like to be hunted."

He ends the call.

Shaking and nauseous, I block his number and dial our head of security here in Blackwater. He's quick to assure me that there hasn't been a hint of trouble on our property.

I want to call Dean, but what if it distracts him at a dangerous moment?

I lift Phee when she pulls at my pajama pants and says, "Up."

I hug her against me.

Where the hell is my husband, and what is he up to?

40

You & Me

DEAN

It's 2:00 a.m. before I drag myself home, tired and frustrated as hell. The lead on Hallman took me to Wheeling, West Virginia, only to discover that I was forty-eight hours behind him.

He started out with a lot of cash, but he's blowing through it fast. Initially, I'd expected him to stay in Mexico. His attack on Bronwyn was a shock, but his obsession has him making riskier and riskier choices. Most recently, he tried to lie low at a home owned by his aunt. She claims she didn't give him money, but the withdrawals from her accounts amounting to fifty thousand dollars say otherwise.

He'll surface again. He's getting sloppier every time. But I'm getting tired of this shit. It's not my job to chase the man down—Arden has people on it, notwithstanding the authorities—but it's personal for me. I won't pretend it isn't.

I try to be quiet as I enter our bedroom, undressing quickly before heading into the bathroom to shower.

Bronwyn is sprawled near the edge of the bed when I return. She must have drifted to sleep reading on her phone because it's fallen from her hand and is lying on the bed beside her.

I retrieve it and plug it in for her. I also place a tumbler of ice water on her nightstand in case she wakes up thirsty.

I told her I'd be working, but this is the first time I've come home so late. She teases me that I don't like to leave her, but she doesn't know how true that is. I spent too much time away from her the first year and a half of our marriage. Now I work from home whenever I can just so I can be wherever she is. I follow her around the house like a fucking golden retriever.

There was a time when I thought I understood women. What I "understood" was a whole lot of fucked-up bullshit based on stereotypes and my own toxic mother. Bronwyn challenged my perceptions from the very beginning, and she hasn't stopped yet.

She says she doesn't care that I need to be near her or know where she is all the time. But I can't help wondering if she looked at tonight as a break from my constant hovering.

I won't know until tomorrow when she wakes up and tells me. I'm learning it's better to ask than guess—I get things wrong all the time.

I climb in beside her and put one arm between her legs and one under her shoulders. Then I pull her up and over me in one smooth motion. It's our "thing," and her normal reaction is to snuggle against me, even in her sleep.

Tonight, she flinches away with a sound of distress and punches out with a solid fist to my gut.

I tense before she makes contact, and her blow doesn't do any real damage. But I jerk away from her in shock.

Bronwyn is a cuddler. She says she sleeps better when some part of her is touching some part of me. But she scrambles to the edge of the bed like I'm contaminated with something.

She wraps her arms around her midsection and mutters, "Shit. Shit. *Shit.*"

Then she punches the mattress.

I back off with my hands up.

She presses a palm to her chest, her breaths hard and fast.

When she says nothing, I drop my hands and wait for the accusations. I don't have any defense against the lies I've told her, but I'm mentally scrambling to figure out which ones she's uncovered, trying to work out damage control. My voice is hoarse when I say, "Bronwyn…."

"Are you safe?" she asks.

The question confuses me. "Am I *safe*?"

She wheels on me. "Yes," she hisses. "That's what I asked you. Do you have any injuries I should know about?"

I shake my head slowly. "No."

"Were you in danger tonight?"

I frown. "No."

"No broken fingers?" she demands angrily. "Perfectly capable of using a phone?"

"What the *hell* are you talking about?"

She says nothing, just turns her back to me and sits stiff and unyielding on the edge of the bed.

I throw off the covers. It's obvious she doesn't want to see or speak to me, but she hasn't thrown any accusations yet. Maybe she's angry that I left her alone to watch Phee all evening. But the more I talk, the angrier she seems to be getting.

"I'll sleep somewhere else." I sound as though I couldn't care less where I sleep.

Before my feet hit the floor, she's flying from the bed. She gathers a pillow and drags our blanket with her. "Don't bother. If you don't want to sleep next to me, then I'll sleep in the living room."

As far from me as possible without leaving the house.

And just like that, she's gone.

She *left* me.

"*If you don't want to sleep next to me...*" Is that what she said? As if any of this was my idea.

I know exactly what comes next. We lived out a pattern over and over during our first eighteen months of marriage.

I'd see her for a weekend, or even one stolen night, and the closer we got to the moment I had to come home to Phee, the more distant she got. Until she was pretty much ignoring me as I packed my bag, and I was defensively saying some stupid shit about seeing her in a couple months.

I can't go back to the way we used to be.

And I'll be damned if I'm going to lie in here while my wife sleeps on a sofa.

Grabbing one of my pillows, I stalk down the stairs and straight into the living room. One of the security lights outside the window lends a shadowy glow to the room. Bronwyn is huddled, curled up around herself, on the sofa.

She goes still at the sight of me, then quips, "Come to smother me in my sleep?"

I look down at the pillow in my hand, then toss it onto the floor, right next to her. "I would never hurt you."

She rolls her eyes. "It was a joke. Why are you here?"

"Because you said if I didn't want to sleep beside you, you'd sleep down here. But I do want to sleep beside you."

I lower myself to the floor next to her, lie on my side, and reach my hand up to place it on her abdomen.

"You can't sleep on the floor."

"The way I see it, I have three choices. I can sleep on the floor next to you. I can sleep with you on that sofa. Or I can sleep in our bed with you in it. The only way I'm leaving is if you tell me you don't want me here."

Her hand inches forward and eventually comes to rest on top of my own.

"Why are you angry at me?" I ask.

It takes so long for her to answer that I start to wonder if she's fallen asleep.

Then she says, "I was freaked out tonight because Hallman called me. I answered before I realized who it was. And then you didn't come home. And I didn't know what you were doing or how long you'd be. And I just…. Sorry I punched you. I didn't mean to fall asleep. I was strung so tightly and didn't realize it was you at first."

"*Hallman* called you?" I lurch to stand.

She shudders. "Yes. He wasn't making any sense. He said you were hunting him and that if you didn't stop, he was going to kill us both."

"*Son of a bitch.* Don't listen to him, angel. He's never getting to you again."

"*Have* you been hunting him?" she asks.

"You should have called me right away."

"I was afraid to call you. I didn't know if my ringtone could give your position away or distract you."

I run a hand through my hair. "Angel, if I'm going in somewhere that I need to be silent, I don't leave my phone on, and I take backup. Your brothers were with me. There was no danger tonight for me. Hallman was long gone. I spent most of my hours driving there and back."

"What if you forgot to turn off your phone?" she asks belligerently.

I dig my palm into my eye. "Trust me to know what I'm doing when it comes to this."

"I reported it to the security team. I figured I'd tell you when you got home. It wasn't like he was here. He could have been calling me from anywhere."

"What exactly did he say?"

"Not much more than what I already told you. He said, 'Call off your dog,' and that if you didn't stop hunting him, you'd learn what it was like to be hunted."

She shudders. "He's so creepy."

I rub my eyes. "That's an understatement."

"Dean, have you and my brothers been hunting him the entire time?"

I flex my jaw. "Yes."

Her eyes narrow, and she glares at me hard. "Good."

I turn out the lamp and return to my pillow on the floor. I'm not pushing my way into her space. "I'm getting you and Phee something you can wear so that if you lose your phone, you can still call for help."

She nods and lets out a long breath before she says, "Okay. But you have to get one for yourself too."

Her response surprises me, but I don't argue. "All right. Me too."

She lies back down on the sofa, and I lie beside her on the floor. I put my hand back on her abdomen.

She sits up abruptly and huffs. "And don't pull this crap on me again. I expected you home at four o'clock. I didn't hear from you again until you climbed into our bed at two in the morning."

I sit. "I texted you that I was going to be late," I say, confused.

"You said something came up. Then not another word. You're *ten hours* late. I made myself sick worrying about you. If the situation were reversed, and you didn't even have GPS coordinates, you'd have been freaking out too."

I get my ass off that floor and sit beside her on the sofa, then haul her onto my lap to straddle me. Smoothing her hair out of the way, I press my forehead to hers.

"You're right. It never even occurred to me that you might be concerned or worrying about me."

She shudders. "However much you think you worry about me? Next time, just realize that I feel the same way about you."

That's not possible.

I run a hand under her shirt to trail a path up her spine. "If I have to be away from you like I was tonight, I'll try to check in regularly and keep you posted on my ETA."

"I'm sorry if that comes across as clingy."

I push her hair back from her face and hold her head between my hands. "You hang on to me as tightly as you need to. If our relationship is different from other people's, then so the fuck what? I have issues. You have issues. We'll figure out what works for us together."

She huffs. "Yeah we do."

"And?"

"Yeah we will," she says.

She wraps her arms around my middle and holds on tight. "Thank you for not leaving me alone down here, even though it would have been my own fault if you did."

"Bronwyn," I tease, "the last thing you need to worry about is me *leaving you alone.*"

She sighs and pushes her face into my neck.

Tonight sucked, but I do have some news that may make her happy. I run my fingers up her spine. "I spoke with my lawyer today. She wants to know if you'd like to initiate adoption proceedings for Phee."

"The lawyer wants to know?" she repeats cautiously.

I shake my head. "*I* want to know. I'd love it if you did. I think my sister would too. Aside from the fact that Phee already sees you as her mother, adopting her would give you legal protection if anything ever happened to me. I was trying not to pressure you. I want you to think about it and decide if you think it's best for you and Phee both after you've had time to weigh the pros and cons."

She shakes her head, then smiles at me in exasperation. "I've been thinking about it for weeks. Months. The answer is yes. A great big, honking yes."

I let out a breath. "Good. This is...."

"You're sad," she says. Because she can read me like a book.

"Maddie wanted to be her mother. She loved her before she was even born. And Phee...."

"Phee will wonder about her. She'll probably miss her sometimes, even though they never met. Or... maybe not. I don't know for sure. I just know how I feel about my own dad."

She takes my hand in hers and kisses my knuckles, right there next to my wedding ring. "We're going to give her the best life we know how to give. We'll screw up sometimes, I'm sure. But one thing is for certain: she'll know what it is to be loved."

"And safe," I say.

She agrees. "*And safe.*"

41

Secrets

DEAN

Early May

Bronwyn and I are the kind of happy that feels almost terrifying.

We spent Christmas in the Hamptons, and we'll be there for a month this summer.

But today? We're throwing a party. Bronwyn is calling it a "Welcome Spring" celebration.

The hiking trails have been cleared and will be open to the public starting next weekend, and the renovations to the old barn theater here are now complete. Teenagers and staff from the youth center will be the first to put the space to use in the community. Swarms of kids have been running around here for the last week, filing in and checking out the lighting, stage, and sound systems.

There is security that separates the public areas from our private home, but given that half the town has been invited to the party today, some of those protocols are relaxed. I've attempted to compensate by having more staff working. Most of them are trying damned hard, for Bronwyn's sake, to blend in. Flannel and denim galore.

It's an interesting blend of people. Business tycoons in designer labels and farmers in John Deere hats. Senior citizens and babies. And everybody in between.

Bronwyn named the theater after my sister. When the huge sign went up on the side of the building proclaiming it the Madison Priester Community Theater, we'd stood with Phee, and I'd shown her pictures of her mama onstage.

A local artist created a mural in the lobby with scenes from all sorts of different shows. And Maddie is there peeking out in a painting created from a photo of her when she'd played the role of Puck in *A Midsummer Night's Dream* at sixteen.

My sister would have loved every bit of this.

I stand in the corner of the kitchen, nurse my beer, and watch my extroverted wife enthrall everyone she greets.

She's dressed like she's straight out of the 1950s with her hair curled, red lipstick, and an ice-blue dress that matches her eyes. It nips in at her waist and puffs out around her knees. She has a jaunty blue silk scarf tied in bow around her neck.

Phee wanted a dress like it, too, and somehow, Bronwyn found one for her. Phee is in pink, and the two of them together are cute as hell.

She's two years old already. I can hardly wrap my brain around how fast she grows. And damn, she's a spitfire. She likes banana oatmeal and despises broccoli. She hates naps but loves to cuddle with her Mom-win or me until she accidentally falls asleep. She likes playing in mud and wearing princess dresses. She's my own personal miracle.

Clarissa and James are here. Bronwyn threw herself at Clarissa when she arrived, exclaiming over the remarkable fact that the woman has a tan.

My former employer is standing beside his wife with an expression I'd call "neutral annoyed." Which means he looks the way he always does unless he's actively observing or thinking about his wife.

When he looks at Clarissa, his expression relaxes into adoration. It's a kind of vulnerability that's almost hard to look at. No one has to guess at what James Mellinger's weakness is. She's standing right beside him.

That's not to say Clarissa always makes him smile. In the course of my former job, I've also seen the man drunk and despondent while fighting with his wife, as well as half dressed and horny, also while fighting with his wife.

Clarissa humanizes him. Otherwise, the man looks cold as ice.

Bronwyn finishes hugging Clarissa. Phee is on her hip, and she keeps watching Bronwyn's interactions and imitating them, right down to the twinkle in her smile and pushing her hair behind her ear.

Their matching silver bracelets sparkle in the sunlight pouring through the massive windows in the morning room. Those bracelets may look like normal jewelry, but they're far more precious. They contain a GPS locator, an alarm system, and a direct line to the leather and silver device strapped around my own wrist. In order to teach Phee how to use hers, we made a game of it. Some day, she'll understand its real purpose. For now, she tends to send me an alert if her sippy cup is out of juice, and I don't mind at all.

Bronwyn leans forward as though she's going to hug James, and he takes a subtle step backward, putting his arm around Clarissa and using her as a shield between them.

To the casual observer, it probably looks like an accident of timing. But I've seen him dodge friendly overtures enough times to know avoidance when I see it.

The man does not like to be touched.

Phee reaches grasping hands toward him, and I nearly choke on my beer when Bronwyn pushes Phee right at him.

He holds her for an awkward moment, his arms straight out. Clarissa tips her auburn head toward his ear and says something. He gives her a sheepish grin and pulls Phee against his chest.

And then James Mellinger melts for my kid like a snow cone spilled on a summer sidewalk. His smile lights his whole face, and he says something to Phee that has her giggling.

Arden sidles up beside me. "She's something else, isn't she?"

I nod. "She is."

"You two are making things work." There's a tinge of skepticism in his tone that I don't like.

"Yes, sir. We are."

It's a miracle this conversation hasn't happened before now. I manipulated his daughter into a secret ceremony on the Strip in Las Vegas. I railroaded her further into a prenup that was only slightly better than a deal with the devil. I abandoned her the same weekend I married her. He's seen me ready to commit murder. And he's heard me cussing up a storm in the middle of the night during a nightmare.

Those are just the things he *knows* I've done.

"I loved that girl from the moment I met her. I was friends with her father, Steve. Did you know that?"

I shake my head.

"He was a freshman at Colombia on a scholarship, and I was there as a guest lecturer. But sometimes you meet someone and you know you're meant to be friends. He needed a part-time job to send money home while he was in school. So I gave him one."

Arden clears his throat. "Good guy. We were from different backgrounds, but he was easy to talk to. He'd just found out his high school girlfriend was pregnant. I knew a little something about what that was like."

Bronwyn has Steve's picture in a frame. A kid with a wide grin and a dimple, posing for a prom picture with an equally young Charlotte. Bronwyn has a box full of someone else's memories. His CDs, a baseball, and photos. The letter he wrote back to Charlotte when she'd sent her own telling him she was pregnant.

He'd told Charlotte he loved her and was excited to be a dad. He couldn't wait to meet his kid. And he'd asked her to marry him. He never got the chance to do either of those things.

I picture Maddie, terrified but excited to be a mother.

I remember Jordan. Vasquez. So many others. Their families waiting at home, dreading that knock at the door, praying it never came. And then it did.

My throat is tight. "A lot of bad things happen to a lot of good people."

Arden's gaze is tender as it lands on his wife. "That's the truth. That's why when you find happiness, you hold on to it with both hands."

He shakes his head and huffs a laugh, like he's embarrassed to be caught acting sentimental. "I wrote to Charlotte for years. Just checking in on her for Steve's sake, making sure she had enough. That kind of thing."

I'd always wondered how someone like Charlotte met someone like Arden McRae III.

His smile is devilish. "Then one day, I got an email. It said, 'I need a lawyer.' Then she proceeded to tell me how this big, bad real estate company that owned half the town was about to tear down a local landmark, and that she'd tried everything she could think of, but the project managers wouldn't put her through to anyone with authority."

He chuckles under his breath. "Then she said that if the company tried to go through with their plans, she and a bunch of her friends were going to sabotage the equipment and chain themselves to the building. And she'd like to retain my services in case that happened because she had Bronwyn and couldn't risk going to prison. So exactly *how much criminal activity* was too much for me to get her out of?"

I laugh hard enough to make my eyes water. Every time I look back at Arden, I laugh again. "What did she do when you told her your family owned that big, bad real estate company?"

His face loses the humor. "She wasn't happy about it."

"I'm sure she wasn't."

"She was especially angry because I married her first."

I blink.

"Don't look at me like that. I know it was asinine. Believe me, she made me suffer for it."

That makes me laugh again, even though I know he isn't kidding. "At least tell me you didn't tear down the landmark."

He just gives me a peevish look. Then his attention swings back to Bronwyn. "You don't show it, but I can guess that you wonder if we think you married her for her money. Especially after you had her sign that prenup, which was a damn stupid thing to do."

"Yes, sir, it was."

"I suspect you've done some other things you aren't proud of in an attempt to win my daughter."

The ever-present lead weight of guilt in my gut lurches into my chest.

He indicates Bronwyn with his bottle. "I've never seen her so happy. And that's saying a lot because, in general, she's already a happy girl. You light her up inside. Even more importantly, you have her back. Don't think we haven't noticed."

When I stay silent, he says, "You've made some mistakes, son. The important thing is to learn from them. Deal with them and face them head-on."

I clench my fist around the sweating beer bottle in my hand. "What if she doesn't forgive me?"

"What if she does?"

I look back to the other side of the room, expecting to see Bronwyn still standing there with Clarissa and James. But she's nowhere in sight.

Phee is still in James's arms, but he and Clarissa both look concerned.

Unease climbs up my spine like ivy, rooting and digging in. I move in their general direction even as they both head toward me.

When I get close, James says, "We have Phee. Bronwyn took off for the theater with one of your security team. Louis—"

I'm already running when Bronwyn's alarm vibrates an SOS silently against my wrist.

42

In The Air Tonight

BRONWYN

It's a beautiful day. The sun is shining. Crocuses are peeking their little purple heads up in the flower beds. I finished Phee's new "toddler" bedroom more than a week ago. Now I'm trying to turn Dean's and my bedroom into something that's reflective of both of us.

The party is a total smash. My husband is laughing with my dad like they're old friends.

And I got to watch James have a mini freak-out at the idea of holding a baby. Even better, I got to watch him turn into a giant pile of mush for Phee.

We had a delightful moment when his eyes grew wide with panic. Then Clarissa softly told him that Phee doesn't bite.

Under the circumstances, I didn't think saying, "We're hoping it's a phase," would hit the right note. So I'd simply smiled encouragingly and said, "Phee knows how to be gentle."

She'd laid her head on James's shoulder and patted his face. The look of shocked delight he'd given Clarissa almost had me falling in love with him too.

Yeah, no. But still, it was adorable.

And while I was standing there, basking in the pure success of the day, one of the security guards approached me with news custom-designed to tick me off.

"He's insisting that you'll want to speak with him. I just need to confirm that you want us to turn him away."

That asshole.

And there he stands, center stage. Louis looks... terrified.

He clears his throat. "Hi, Bronwyn. Long time no see."

I shake my head. "You shouldn't be here."

Louis's eyes are wide. He nods subtly, as if he's agreeing with me. "I'm so sorry. Leave. *Go!*"

I turn for the door, but before I make it a single step, I'm yanked hard by my hair back against a male body, his arm tightening painfully in a chokehold. The smell of his cologne nauseates me.

"Nice place," he says, using the big-ass gun in his hand to indicate the theater, like he's some kind of action hero.

I press and hold the concealed button on my bracelet. The security guard who came with me has drawn his weapon. Kevin lifts his arm straight out in front of the two of us. "Should I shoot him, Bronwyn? Is that what you want? Tell him to drop his weapon or I'm killing him."

It's the gun that's preventing me from fighting. Kevin's holding a Model 500 S&W revolver. The longer barrel brings the weight on the thing close to five pounds. It's a beast. Lotta power, but he obviously doesn't have a clue how to use it. His hand is already shaking as he holds his arm straight out.

It's just getting heavier the longer your arm is extended, asshole.

Hallman clearly asked someone to provide him with the biggest, scariest handgun they had. He's overcompensating. But he can't shoot that thing one-handed and expect to actually hit his target. The recoil alone will knock it out of his hand. If I'm lucky, the way he's holding it, he may even break his wrist.

Under the circumstances, it doesn't make him less dangerous. A stray bullet can kill just as dead as one that's been aimed. There are people here. Stage crew were scheduled to arrive ten minutes ago. Eight teenagers and their director, Gayle.

"Tell him to drop his weapon!" Hallman shrieks.

"Lower it to the floor, Austin."

Austin shakes his head with a jerk. When he doesn't do it, Kevin shoves the barrel against my temple. "I'll kill her right now. Drop your weapon and step away from it."

Austin slowly lowers his gun to the floor, even as Kevin drags me back up through the bleacher seating. He's got his finger on the trigger. One slip. That's all it'll take.

Not even when I was sick did I feel so close to death. I can't die. Phee needs me. Dean wouldn't survive it.

"Finger off the trigger, Kevin. Unless you want to kill me by accident."

He scoffs. But in my periphery, I can see that he moves his finger away.

"What do you want from me?" I ask.

Kevin hisses, "I'm not the only person who's made mistakes. But I didn't destroy lives, Bronwyn."

Spittle rains down on me as he rants. "Maybe I skimmed a little off the top. Who did it hurt? Not you. You have more than you could ever need. That's no reason to destroy someone's life. You have no idea of the degradation I've suffered. Your fucking bodyguard is obsessed. If he'd just let me go.... But I've had to watch my back every second. I've had to change my name over and over. I've lived in squalor. No more. He should have heeded my warnings. I showed him I could get to you. I proved it, and he still didn't stop. This is his fault."

A flash of activity in the mezzanine. My panicked eyes land on Jesse. Seventeen years old. He runs track. Lives with his grandmother. He writes poetry and wants to be a dog trainer. The whites of his eyes gleam in his dark face. He has the determined expression of someone with no training about to do something very heroic and very stupid.

"Don't!" My words are addressed to Jesse, but Kevin hasn't seen the boy. He thinks I'm talking to him.

"You're the ones who pushed me to this. You made this choice, not me," Kevin says.

A hand comes around Jesse's mouth, cutting off sound as Dean draws him back out of sight. I don't collapse in relief, but there's some small measure of it.

Then Dean is there with his Glock braced in both hands as he aims for Kevin's head.

It has to be his head because Kevin is using me as a shield. Dean can't shoot him, though. Not with that barrel against my temple.

Kevin directs his words back to Austin. "Call her dog. Get him here. I don't want *you*."

He sounds like a pouting three-year-old.

Austin nods placatingly. "Sure, man. Sure. You want her husband? Mr. McRae?"

"Call him," Kevin says.

I'm trying not to look at Dean. I don't want Kevin to notice and try to see what's caught my attention up there. But I'm loose and ready. If he swings the revolver toward Dean, I'll move.

Austin drags his phone from his pocket.

"I said call him," Kevin shrieks.

I flare my eyes at Austin and mouth, "Don't."

Maybe Dean has his phone shut off. But I don't want Austin taking the risk of dialing his number.

"I'll kill her. Put it on speakerphone. I want to hear his voice."

Austin swallows. His honey-blond hair is dark with sweat. He looks me in the eye and pushes one of his contacts.

It goes straight to Dean's voice mail.

Kevin jerks his head at Austin. "Hang up and go get him."

Austin pushes End Call.

"Now."

The guard slowly backs toward the exit.

Kevin makes a sound of disgust. "And you still think *I'm* the bad guy here. You let Priester steal everything from you. He even took your last name, for fuck's sake." He stomps his foot like a child. "He's never been on your side. He *trapped* you. He took advantage of a gullible girl. Whisked you away, then pressured you into signing something that would make him millions. He wins either way. If you leave him or violate any of his ridiculous stipulations, then he walks away with most of your assets."

"Maybe we don't have a prenup at all," I stall, unsure if the kids have all gotten out of the building.

"I've not only seen your prenup, I have a copy of it. My cousin spent some time here. By invitation. It's not his fault you left the thing in an unlocked drawer. He was looking for a pen and paper."

"Of course." I'm trying to sound placating. At this point he could tell me trained hedgehogs infiltrated my filing cabinet, and I'd calmly agree. My mind is barely on his words. All I can think about is the pain of the hard press of the muzzle against my temple, and the heat and weight and disgusting smell of his body against mine.

"He took photos and sent them to me on a burner phone. He was concerned you'd done something stupid that you couldn't get out of. He knew I had reason to hate Dean Priester and thought I might be able to do something about it."

"The prenup is equally as strict with him as it is with me."

I look back up with only my eyes, trying to get a glimpse of Dean.

"Right. You can take his pickup truck and three-quarters of a $500,000 house. He can take millions in personal assets from you."

"But he wouldn't," I say.

Dean indicates the area near the south exit, and I give him one slow blink in acceptance.

"He would," Kevin snaps. "He *tortured* Louis because he was in love with you. He was in Priester's way. Your 'husband' told him he'd kill him if he ever spoke to you again."

Louis whimpers, and Kevin screams, "*Shut up!*"

Speaking to me once more, he continues. "Priester took all the evidence I'd collected on you for a competency hearing. I can't prove it, but every single piece, whether it was in paper form or digital that showed you were erratic and emotionally unstable, was gone from the internet within forty-eight hours of your wedding. What do you think he wants with it? He's been hiring staff because you can't handle things on your own. Taking care of everything. Telling you not to worry your silly little head. He's been collecting evidence that you can't manage your own life so he can go forward with that competency hearing. And who's in charge of your money if you're declared incompetent? Your husband." He tightens his arm, cutting off my air supply until white spots dance in my vision.

"He wouldn't do that," I gasp, reaching up and pushing against his arm. "I can't breathe. What kind of hostage will I be if I pass out? Dean will think you killed me. He won't hesitate. He'll shoot first."

He loosens his grip slightly, enough, ostensibly, for me to breathe. Taking the opportunity to slide my arms up farther, I pull the silk scarf off my neck, hiding it in my hands. If he looks, he'll see it, but I'm counting on keeping him distracted enough that he doesn't.

"You have a lot of confidence in a man who stands to gain from your death. If he doesn't show, I *will* kill you. Then I'll go for the kid. None of this had to happen. All you had to do was cooperate. All he had to do was let me go."

So casually, he threatens to murder my child. Hallman is dying today. Whatever it takes.

I reach a placating hand up to rest on his forearm. "I understand that you're angry. But this isn't going to make anything better. We'll give you lots and lots of money. And when you disappear this time, I'll tell Dean to let you go."

"He's not going to listen to you! He has to die. You spent eighteen months of this marriage separated. People didn't even know you *were* married. You did it to get ahold of your trust fund. That's fraud, Bronwyn," he accuses, completely unironically.

I close my eyes on one slow blink and dip my chin a fraction of an inch. *I'm ready.*

Then I say, "My family has a motto, Kevin."

He scoffs.

"Love hard…," I say. Kevin doesn't even notice the blue scarf billowing out into a flag at my hip.

Dean steps onstage from the right, straight into the light, deliberately drawing Kevin's attention. His Glock is braced in both hands and aiming for Kevin's head. Voice pure gravel, he says, "Remain loyal."

Kevin swings his revolver toward Dean, the arm around my neck loosening automatically in his distraction.

I toss the silk scarf to billow in front of his face and yank on his forearm, using every single pound of my body weight to drop as hard and fast as I can.

Two shots, so close together as to be nearly simultaneous. The revolver kicks straight out of Kevin's hand as the bullet fires into the empty bleachers below us, tearing a hole through splintered wood.

The other bullet is a direct hit to the man behind and above me. Something warm and wet splatters the top of my head and my back. Dead weight collapses against me. The report from the S&W rings so loudly in my ears as I shove Kevin off me and roll down the stairs that for a moment I can't hear anything else at all.

Henry lowers his smoking weapon, stepping out onto stage left. Though I can't hear his words, I see his mouth move to finish our familly motto. "Fight dirty."

Louis wails and curls into a ball, covering his head.

I don't look at the carnage behind me. I drag myself to stand and stomp down those steps and right up to my former friend.

"Louis. Look at me," I demand.

He tentatively lifts his head and flinches in horror at the picture I present.

I lift my right arm. And I flip Louis the bird with my whole fucking chest.

43

Something Real

DEAN

I'm beside Bronwyn before she lifts her finger.

I need to get her in my arms. But as I reach for her, she throws up a defensive hand and snaps, "Don't touch me."

I drop my arms and try not to hyperventilate. I *have* to touch her. I have to feel her breathing against me. "I can explain about the things Hallman said."

Voice low and angry, she says, "I don't give a shit about the things Hallman said."

I nod, holding my hands up like she's a skittish animal. "Okay. Are you hurt?"

She stands there, covered in gore, looking pissed as fuck. "I'll have some bruises. Mostly, I'm just—" She gags, and it's then that the shaking starts.

She was solid as a rock in the middle of the crisis. Now, tremors take her hard enough to make her teeth clatter.

I reach out slowly, watching to make sure she doesn't flinch from me.

"I'll get brains on you," she whispers.

"Don't care."

The moment I make contact, she shoves herself at me, pressing against me so hard, it feels like she wants to crawl inside and hide there. I'm almost definitely holding her too tightly—some of the bruises that show up on her may be from me—but I can't let go, and she doesn't want me to.

Henry pockets his phone and watches his sister with concern. "Bronwyn, do you need a hospital?"

She shakes her head against me, my chest now as wet as her hair. "I'm not hurt."

"Do you need someone to give you a sedative? Or a therapist? A counselor?"

God love Henry. My mind hadn't even gone there yet.

"I'll be okay. Thank you, Henry. I love you," she says.

He puts his arms around both of us in the most weird-ass awkward hug of my life. "I love you too."

He steps back and nods. His voice is just a little too gruff when says, "Good job not dying. Both of you."

Her breathing picks back up, and she pushes away from me, her voice on the verge of panic. "I need a shower. I need a shower, Dean. I need a show—"

"Yes. There's one here, remember?"

Arden runs toward us, and I look at him in helpless entreaty.

He tries to pull her into his arms, but Bronwyn flinches away. "No, Daddy. I need a shower."

I've never heard her call him that. It's as much an indication of how vulnerable she's feeling as anything else I've seen.

Arden's eyes fill, but he gives me a tight nod. "Okay, baby. Dean will take you."

I guide her there, my arm tight around her as we walk.

Gabriel stands guard duty just outside the door so none of the first responders barge in on us until she's ready. Arden and Henry handle the rest.

When we're in the dressing room showers, I turn on the water. My plan is to warm it while I help her remove her clothing. But she kicks off her shoes and steps under the freezing spray as she is, fully dressed, so I do the same.

Her lips are blue, and we both shiver under the icy blast. She sobs quietly, but the worst of the panic seems to subside under the torrent of clean water.

As the shower heats, I peel the layers of stained clothing from her body, careful to slide each piece down her hips and not over her head.

When I've removed the last of it and tossed it with a wet plop to the tile floor outside the stall, I shove my own clothing off and toss it to cover hers, pants last and on top of the pile because they aren't showing blood.

She stands perfectly still as I wash her. The water runs red, then sudsy pink, and finally, clear.

She turns, pushing into me. I press my back against the coolness of the tile wall, spreading my legs and dropping low so I can bring myself closer to her height. I pull her into the V of my thighs.

Usually, I lift her up or lay her down. I make her come to me.

This time, I go to her.

I hold her, and we both cry. The water turns frigid and my thighs burn from holding my position, yet still we hold on. Until we've given enough of ourselves to each other that we're strong enough to face the world.

Then she straightens her spine and asks, "Did you get all of the Hallman out of my hair?"

When we finally leave the shower, I dry her carefully and retrieve the fresh clothing and toiletries I'd asked Gabriel to sort out for us.

We emerge from the dressing room to find that the first responders and FBI have been and gone. Louis was taken away in handcuffs and Hallman in a body bag.

Bronwyn and I will be making our statements tomorrow at the station with Arden acting as our legal counsel.

The Youth Center director has made arrangements for the drama club kids to have access to a counselor. And Clarissa and James remain on babysitting duty at the house while Bronwyn's mother has taken over as hostess.

Charlotte ushered most of our guests out in the ensuing hours, though a few remain.

Somehow, Bronwyn's beloved Louboutins survived the carnage without a speck of blood on them. Now she's marching up the paved drive like a soldier in a black silk dress, those red-soled high heels clicking with every step. Her grip on my hand is tight enough to cut off circulation.

I slow, attempting to pull away so I can put my arm around her shoulder. "I can cover you," I say.

She hangs on to my hand like she's dangling from a cliff. As if I'm the only thing keeping her from plunging to the rocky shore below. But she paints on a serene expression and says, "Public image. Keep walking."

She's right, of course. There's no avoiding the paparazzi at the gate as we move from the theater to the house. And she would never cower beneath my shoulder when there are others who could see it. She is a McRae.

I slide into my role as bodyguard and block the paparazzi from getting a clear shot of her, even as we both walk with our backs straight and our strides purposeful.

"Do you have any injuries, Ms. McRae?"

"Did you know you had a stalker?"

"Is it true that your marriage isn't real?"

"Was your husband working with Hallman?"

"Were you having an affair, Bronwyn?"

"Is it true that your husband conned you into marrying him?"

I grit my teeth, and we pretend we can't hear the questions being fired at us by the sharks at our gate.

Clarissa is walking toward us. She gives Bronwyn an encouraging look and mouths, "Keep going."

Bronwyn nods, then says to me, "Smile and kiss my forehead."

I show my teeth. Then I kiss her forehead.

As Clarissa passes us, she reaches out to give Bronwyn's free hand a squeeze.

Then she heads toward the paparazzi with a gentle expression on her face. She's always reminded me of a freckled, curly-haired Audrey Hepburn.

She's barely behind us when the paps start shouting questions at her. I can't hear her answers, but she's using her own notoriety to deflect attention long enough for us to get into the house.

James will go ballistic when he realizes what she's done. But Clarissa only *looks* like a strong wind would blow her away. She's a far cry from that insecure girl I once guarded. Her spine is pure steel.

She says something I can't hear, and the tone of the questions changes.

We're almost there.

I tug on Bronwyn's hand and try to lead her around to the back of the house, my heart racing and my palms sweating. "We have to talk about the things Hallman said to you. The things those kids heard and are telling reporters."

She balks. "We aren't doing anything right now except going back inside until every single one of our friends and family has gone home."

"Bronwyn, he twisted everything."

"Not now."

I blow out a hard breath.

Not now. But soon.

44

Please Keep Loving Me

DEAN

Three Hours Later

My father-in-law gives Phee a gentle smile as he buckles her into the car seat. "You're going to have so much fun at Poppa's house. You can stay in Mom-win's old room. And in the morning, we'll have pancakes."

Phee claps.

Bronwyn turns to her mother. "If you need anything at all, call right away. No matter what time it is."

Charlotte smiles. "I will. But we won't have any problems." She winks at Phee. "It's our first grandma sleepover trip."

Phee yells, "Yes! Sweepovuh!"

Charlotte wraps her arms around Bronwyn and asks quietly, "Are you sure? We can stay here with you."

Bronwyn hugs her back fiercely but says, "I'm sure, Mom. Thank you for taking her for a couple of days until the worst of the media storm settles down."

Arden wraps his daughter in a warm embrace. "I'll be back here with you before you make your statements tomorrow."

Phee motions to Bronwyn with both of her hands. "Bing it in, Mom-win."

The first time I'd heard Bronwyn use the phrase was when Clarissa was grieving her father. Bronwyn had said, "Bring it in, Harcourt," then held her friend until Clarissa's tension had eased.

Bronwyn says, "Bring it in, Phee Bee," a lot. When Phee's tired. When she's frustrated. When she's excited.

Hearing the way Phee has absorbed that kindness and is now giving it back into the world... it's fucking beautiful.

Bronwyn laughs and hugs and kisses her. "I love you, Phee Bee."

When Bronwyn climbs out of the back seat, I lean in myself and kiss Phee's forehead, then say, "You're going to have so much fun. What do you do if you ever need Daddy or Mom-win?"

She holds up her arm with the toddler-sized bracelet on it. "I poos the button."

"That's right, baby girl. I love you."

"Love you, Daddy."

• • • ● • ● • • •

When the gates close behind her parents, I thread Bronwyn's fingers between mine and look down at the single fist our hands form. There's a metaphor somewhere in that. Or maybe it's symbolism. I don't know. Clarissa is the writer, not me.

All I know is I don't want to fight my wife. I want to fight *for* her. *With* her against the world.

My confessions are long overdue.

I take her hand and lead her upstairs to our bedroom.

This room muffles sound too. Unlike the other house, sound dampening is built inside the walls, not layered on top of them. It looks like a normal bedroom that simply has a lot of drapery and upholstered furniture as a decor decision rather than a practical one. The dreams aren't as frequent, but they still happen.

When the door closes behind us, I begin to speak. "You don't know how much I regret—"

She slaps her hand in the air. "Not yet."

She kicks off the stilettos that have been torturing her poor feet all day. With jerky movements, she removes her earrings, tossing them onto a small crystal tray on her nightstand, then starts piling her hair on top of her head.

Once finished, she sits on the dark blue upholstered bench at the end of our bed. "Lay it on me."

"Today is going to give us both nightmares for a long time."

She nods seriously. "Yes. I'm sorry you had to see any of that."

Only Bronwyn would be more concerned with how seeing her like that impacted me than what the experience did to her.

She never looked back at Hallman. And she avoided looking in the mirrors in the dressing room bathroom. At the very least, she won't have that visual in her head.

God knows I do. But I don't care about Hallman's corpse. The part that will haunt me is that gun to her head. That forearm choking her. The way she shook afterward.

When the shock wears off, today is going to hit both of us hard. The trauma is real. A fifteen-minute cry in the shower is just the beginning.

I shake my head. "You're okay. That's what matters. It ended the way it needed to end."

I run a hand through my hair. "So... okay, yeah... I need to talk to you about the things Hallman said."

She waves a hand at me. "I don't believe his lies."

"The thing is... not all of it was a lie. But...."

I turn to my nightstand and pull out the envelope I'd stashed there weeks ago.

I try to pass it to her, but as soon as she sees that I've written her a letter, she shoves it back at my chest. "I'm not reading that when you're standing right here. You do it."

I clear my throat and remove the letter from the envelope, then begin reading. "My sweet B."

I shoot her a look, and Bronwyn rolls her hand in a "get on with it" gesture.

"You are the love of my life. Please know that I never, ever meant to hurt you."

I give her another worried-looking glance. At my words, she's brought her hand to her chest, her eyes wide.

I clear my throat, blow out a hard breath, and turn back to the paper.

I don't want to read this letter. Don't want her to know the things I've done. But I can't let what Hallman said about me be the last word on the subject.

"I told you once that I was obsessed with you, and you thought I was kidding. I should have told you the truth right then and there. I have loved you for nearly as long as I've known you, and I did things I never should have. To be near you, to keep you safe, and to trick you into loving me back."

My voice drops in register as I continue. "You'd be within your rights to request a restraining order for me."

I look up and go off script, my eyes wild and my voice pure gravel. "This is where I was supposed to say I'd respect your wishes if you want me to leave. But that would be a lie. I won't. You're *mine*."

"You're not going *anywhere*." She nods at the letter. "Keep reading."

I clear my throat and go on. "Enclosed, you will find a list of my transgressions."

I switch the paper to the second page. "In no particular order, they are as follows: I spied on you when you told your friend what jewelry you liked. And I bought your engagement ring months before we got married. I didn't have to propose with a bread tie. I already had your ring. But I didn't want you to think I was a weirdo."

She frowns, confusion knitting her brow.

"I requested that I follow Clarissa to Blackwater so I could be near you, despite the conflict of interest. I went behind the bar every single week and looked at the work schedule at Jack's so I knew exactly when you were working and could be there. After you left your shift, I followed you to make sure you made it back to your dorm safely. I installed the tracker on your phone before that day in my kitchen. I know you didn't believe me when I told you I did it. I let you think I was kidding. I wasn't.

"I installed cameras at the back entry to the bar so I could make sure nobody jumped you back there. Jack thinks I told him he needed cameras for everyone's safety, but I didn't care about anyone else. I only cared about you. And when I installed the permanent cameras, even after I came back to New York, I kept them linked to my phone so I could watch you at work."

I rub my forehead and push out a harsh breath. "I'd planned to buy the youth center you used to volunteer at in New York and then act helpless with it, as if I'd ruin everything if you didn't step in, thus taking advantage of your generous nature."

"My bossy nature," she corrects, one eye squinted at me in what I think is annoyance.

I swallow. "I had a five-year plan for that because it was going to be expensive. When a certain asshole showed up in Blackwater, I decided that I didn't need to wait. So I didn't try to talk you out of marrying me at all, even though I knew you were only doing it on impulse. Worse, I made sure no one else had the chance to talk you out of it either.

"I tricked you into signing the prenup from hell by pretending I was a really good guy and that it would protect us against fraud accusations. That was a lie. It actually made us look like we didn't trust each other. I thought if I could guarantee four years with you,

you'd be more likely to fall for me. And I'm a jealous bastard who can't bear the idea of anyone else putting their hands on you. Ever.

"I hate chocolate. I only had it at my house in case you ever came over. I broke into homes and businesses to find and destroy every personal record I could find on you. I beat the hell out of a certain person after he assaulted you. And I would have killed him if other certain people didn't calm me down and remind me that you wouldn't like it if I did."

She frowns. "I have to admire the way you're deliberately leaving out names. It's the lawyer's daughter in me. But we'll be burning this confession when you're done."

I nod jerkily, then continue to read. "I installed the security system here for you, and even before I lived with you, I used it to watch you."

I look up at her again. Once more, I go off script. "When you got sick, I'd have been there right away if I'd known. I couldn't... I had to know you were all right. And you had construction crews in here and movers, and I—"

"I'm waiting for the part where you break my heart," she says with a frown.

Flustered, I go back to the letter. "I only went to the diner so I'd have an excuse for knowing where you were. You hadn't really removed your dot from my phone. You just deleted the icon from your home screen."

I heave a deep breath. "I steal your hair ties so whenever you need one, I can miraculously produce it just to look like a hair tie hero. Also, I deliberately keep my shirt untucked and lift my arms over my head so you can see my biceps flex and that I have abs." My ears go hot at my last admission.

"Wait a minute." She stands abruptly and steals the paper from my hands, skimming my list. "These are your confessions?"

I nod brusquely.

"I already know this stuff. Well, not the ring—that was a lovely surprise. But Clarissa told me you requested a transfer to Blackwater. I was the only one convinced it was because you liked me, but I had a good feeling about it. I knew about the bar. And the cameras. Dean, how the hell would you have texted me that day about a bear rooting around in the dumpster if you didn't still have access to those cameras and weren't still checking them?"

I lift my brows, startled by her reaction.

She appears strangely... *guilty*.

She eyes my list with a hopeful expression. "Is there more?"

I look down at the letter as if more words might magically sprout on it. "I don't think so—oh, wait. I really didn't like Henry the first couple of times we met. I do now. I'd trust him with my life. More importantly, I trust him with yours and Phee's. But your brother can be manipulative—"

I cut off as I realize that I just confessed to being manipulative, then accused my brother-in-law of... being manipulative.

I stand helplessly as Bronwyn rises from the bench and begins to stomp around our bedroom.

She removes her dress and throws it onto a chair, then retreats into the bathroom. I follow her, watching warily as she scrubs every bit of makeup off her face, revealing a lurid purple bruise on her temple that sends a fresh rush of tension and nausea to my gut.

She brushes her teeth, then angrily slathers her face with the stuff from the jar with the French words on it, muttering under her breath, "You had to say it. Now I have to say it. And dammit, I don't want to say it."

I wait because she's not really talking to me. Not yet.

Of every scenario I pictured—and I imagined many, from her angrily telling me to get out to her gentle offer of forgiveness—this one never made the list.

"You think the sun shines out of my behind. And dammit, I liked having a shiny ass," she says, throwing a hand into the air. She stomps past me, through the bedroom, and into the walk-in closet. Then she retrieves one of my T-shirts she uses for a nightgown, yanking it over her head.

Finally, she begins pulling clothes from their hangers, dropping the items haphazardly into clear plastic crates at her feet.

I follow her, filling the doorway, and shove my hands in my pockets. I aim for the expression she calls "adorable" and give her my "Aww, shucks, ma'am" look.

Not a single other person on the planet, besides my kid, thinks I'm anything but a scary-looking bastard. But Bronwyn says I'm "cute" when I do it. So I'm fucking doing it.

She squints at my posture and expression. Then she growls and throws a balled-up sweater into a crate with far more force than necessary. When that doesn't appear to be enough violence for her, she kicks the crate for good measure.

This is bad.

I straighten and take my hands out of my pockets, my troubled gaze meeting hers. "I'm sorry, B. I never meant to hurt you."

"You didn't hurt me." She's giving me her fake smile. It's the same one she wore when she said she was going to Europe. The same one she gave me when she handed back her rings and said we'd keep our marriage just between us. "It's fine, Dean. I'm not upset with you. I forgive you. Absolutely. Totally. Forgiveness isn't even necessary."

I'm not comforted whatsoever. "You don't have any questions for me? You don't want to yell at me? You seem... agitated."

She nods. "I do have a question. How long has this been bothering you?"

"Always? I tried to tell you, but...."

"Why didn't you?"

I don't answer.

She moves into my space and takes my hand, her expression earnest. "Tell me the truth. Is it because you don't trust me? That when I say I love you—"

"I trust you—"

"I don't think you do." She takes a deep breath. Then she tries again, her voice trembling. "You have never trusted me—"

I shake my head, eyes pained. "Bronwyn, no."

I pull her against my chest. She doesn't fight me, though she's stiff in my arms.

I admit, "I don't trust *me*."

I tighten my arms around her rigid figure. I'm hunched over, our height difference awkward.

Then I drop to my knees before her.

I gather her to me, my forehead resting on her collarbone, my lips just over her heart. "I don't trust me, B. It's so hard to believe I could be enough for someone as perfect as you. It didn't make sense. And I was going insane without you. I would do anything for you. I know now that all I've ever needed to do was be honest with you. I was so stupid every step of the way. If I'd just told you how I felt... if I'd told you I needed to know where you were, you'd have understood and handed me your phone."

If possible, she becomes even more stiff in my arms. "You called me perfect."

"Because you are."

"Dean, I'm not."

She runs her fingers through my hair. "And you weren't stupid. You had shitty parents who traumatized you. And I was the worst possible person for you to be in a relationship with."

I scoff and shake my head. "That's bullshit."

"I'm a runner when my feelings get hurt. I scurry off somewhere to hide under my covers. For someone with abandonment issues, I had to be triggering you. I'm getting better about that, though. And so are you. I won't run from you. And you won't push me away. Never again."

I rock my forehead back and forth against her.

"I have my own confession." Her voice is barely above a whisper.

I lift my head to look in her eyes.

"Gah." Her hands convulse in my hair. And then she spits it out in one long stream, barely pausing to take a breath. "*I* tricked *you* into marrying me, Dean. Hallman freaked me out, but all I had to do was tell Dad. I'd have never asked anyone else to marry me. That was a bluff to pressure you, which is a truly terrible thing to do. And I'm supposed to be sorry. But you married me, so I *wasn't* sorry."

"And I wanted that prenup. I knew exactly what it was. Actually, I wanted the original one where we were never allowed to sleep away from each other. But I was afraid it would look suspicious if I didn't let my lawyer make some changes."

"That prenup is patently unfair to you."

"No more unfair than it is to you. If I had to give away over 70 percent of my assets, I would still have more than the average person. I'd have a home, vehicles, and some remaining sources of passive income. If you lost the same percentage—which I would never have accepted, by the way—you would be scrambling to make do in a tiny apartment somewhere. It's not me that prenup is unfair to."

I frown.

"I didn't really leave you." Tears are streaming down her face, and I gently wipe them away, even as her words sink in.

"I knew you could still see my dot. I sat exactly where I did and talked out loud because I knew you'd be watching on the security camera. It was a bluff. You were the lion. I was the zebra. I knew if I ran, you'd chase me. And I didn't know how else to make you think it was your idea."

She moans. "Oh my *God*, that sounds absolutely horrible."

I freeze. "Wait. You didn't leave me?"

"Technically I did. But it was a bluff. So you'd see it was time to fish."

"What?"

"Fish or cut bait. I was counting on you fishing. Clarissa recommended couples therapy instead. We can still do that, if you want," she says, her voice an octave too high.

I drop my head against her, and my shoulders quake.

"I am so sorry. I'll never do anything like that ever again. I didn't realize about your mother before then or how it would hurt you. I thought you'd threaten to sexy-spank me. Please forgive me. Don't cry."

I shake harder, and she keeps talking. "I love that you show me your abs. I don't want you to ever stop. I don't even want you to stop when we're old and your six-pack is a keg. And I love that you always have my hair ties in your pocket."

I lift my head, and I'm not crying, though I have to wipe tears from my eyes. "Woman," I say, laughing, "there's not another couple on this planet more perfect for each other than we are."

She flinches, and then she spits out her final confession. "I know you hate chocolate."

I still, then rear my head back. We speak at the same time.

"You were torturing me."

"I was teasing you."

I nod, my lips pressed tight. "I deserved it."

"I was trying to get you to admit you were lying to me. You were just so bad at pretending to like it. You're a horrible liar. Your ears turn red every single time. And it was funny, and... well, now it feels mean-spirited. But chocolate is delicious, and it was your own fault for pretending you loved it."

"It wasn't that bad. It was just chocolate." Though I say "chocolate" like I'd say "dumpster juice."

"It was your just desserts." She smiles weakly at her own pun.

"Hilarious," I say dryly. But I know she can see the smile behind my eyes. "And the thing with Louis and breaking into Hallman's office?"

"Don't pretend it wasn't you and my dad and Henry in that shed with Louis."

I clear my throat. "And Gabriel."

She huffs. "Right. My point is, nobody fucks with family. If Louis had done half of what he did to me to you, I'd have been out in that shed too."

That night on the lawn at the Blackwater Inn was nothing. She is constantly knocking me on my ass.

"As far as retrieving that garbage from Hallman's office? That's the sweetest criminal activity anyone has ever performed on my behalf. Especially knowing what a bad place you were in at the time and the way I left you there alone."

I falter. "You're welcome?"

"I wish you knew how much I love you."

I put my hands on her face and indicate her packing with a dip of my chin. "Six months ago, if I had walked in on this scene, I'd have thought you were packing to leave me."

I give a small shake of my head. "I was afraid my confession would hurt your feelings. But I knew you wouldn't leave. You weren't happy, but there was no way. I don't know what you're doing in here besides stubbing your toes, but you aren't leaving."

"I'm making more closet space for you. I started working on it a couple of days ago."

"I don't know how to believe that I have this life. That it's real and I'm not going to open my eyes and discover it was a dream. That you won't be stolen right out of my arms. This much love and happiness feels like I'm daring fate to destroy me."

She grips my shirt with both hands. "Maybe you can't always believe in a perfect future. Bad things happen sometimes. But if you can't believe in anything else, believe in me. Because I'm going to love you so hard. Till the day I die, I'm going to do that. And if I go first, I'll be waiting right there when it's time for you to join me. And I'll *still* be loving you."

"You are so sweet, B."

"I'm not sweet. I'm terrifying. Even James says so."

I stand and hike her into my arms. She wraps her legs around my waist, her arms circling my neck.

I press a gentle kiss to her lips before pulling away and brushing her hair behind her ear. "You're a fighter. You're strong and loyal. And brave. And kind."

She lowers her eyes, and I tip her chin back up, holding her gaze. "I'm not done," I scold gently. "This is my big, romantic declaration. I've been working up to it, and you have to listen."

She nods. "Okay."

"You like to top from the bottom," I say. "You want me to take the lead, but you like knowing I'm really your slave. You feel insecure when you can't always be the person you think others want you to be. You feel torn between two worlds."

She sucks in a hard breath, her eyes wet.

"You wear a mask, and it's beautiful, B." I wipe the tears from her face. "But underneath it, you're even more beautiful. You're a marshmallow. You're hurt so much more easily than anyone ever realizes. Not even your family knows. You're messy and sweet on the inside, and you're fucking perfect."

The smile she gives me is wobbly, caught between laughter and tears.

"I love your messy. I love your loud and sweet and bossy. I adore every single part of you."

Her breaths hiccup in her chest.

My palm anchors her head, fingers wrapping around the back of her skull as I hold her steady, my scowl fierce. "You worry that I don't know your love?"

I choke out my next words. "Your love is the reason I can breathe. You think you don't belong anywhere, but, Bronwyn? You. Belong. With me."

She laughs, and she cries. And I hold on to my wife.

When I can speak again, I say, "I'll never lie to you or manipulate you again. I swear it."

"Please keep stealing my hair ties."

I nod. "Okay."

"And flashing me. I really like it when you flash me."

My expression is earnest. "I can do that."

Then I carry her into the bedroom and toss her onto the center of our bed. She lands in a laughing heap, then immediately scrambles onto her knees.

I reach behind my head and pull my shirt off one slow inch at a time, just the way she likes.

She lifts her chin. "Now the belt."

Smirking, I unbuckle it. Then I slide it through the loops of my black trousers with a *ffft* that makes her shiver.

I stalk her across the bed and pull her under me, caging her from every direction.

She gives me a watery, joyful grin, and I smile without smiling back.

"You always loved me," I say in satisfaction.

"I always did."

Epilogue

DEAN

Dance with Me Tonight

A Little Over One Year Later

Jack's is bustling this afternoon, packed end to end with Millers, Hunsics, and McRaes.

The sign on the front door says Closed for Private Party, and the banner on the back wall says Happy Anniversary, Bronwyn and Dean!

It was a hell of a thing to plan a surprise for the woman. No one gets anything past her.

But she put on a good show when we pulled up to the back of the bar and came in through the employees' entrance.

I made some lame excuse about checking on a security camera in the back lot, and my ears went hot as hell when I did it.

Because I meant it when I said I'd never lie to her again. But I've also learned the difference between a surprise and a lie. And my girl loves surprises.

Everyone watched us arrive on the camera feed and lay in wait to jump up and yell, "Happy anniversary!"

That's when I knew she had my number. Because instead of shrieking loud enough to break my eardrums, then laughing, she'd laid a delicate hand on her pearls and said, "Oh my goodness! You guys! This is so sweet!"

Clarissa and James are sitting in one of the corner booths, and Bronwyn's attention goes straight to her friend. I can guess exactly who spilled the beans.

Clarissa and Franki handled the decorations and the menu for today, including the fancy chocolate wedding cake. I'm going to let Bronwyn feed me a piece of that thing later, purely so I can watch her eyes dance with laughter when she does it.

Franki is looking a little sheepish. The giant diamond ring on her left hand flashes as she pushes her hair behind her ear and gives us a finger wave. So maybe they *both* ratted out the surprise.

Bronwyn shoots me a sly look. "Did you really need to check on those cameras, Dean? Or did you tell me a fib?"

I stare at her for a moment, stunned a little stupid by that sexy grin of hers. Then I jerk back online, nodding. "Yes, ma'am. I scheduled a maintenance check last week so I didn't have to lie."

She fans herself with her hand. "Keep sweet-talking me like that, Dean, and I'm going to want to get started on that plan to give Phee a brother or sister early."

God. Damn. I love this woman.

I wasn't sure I was going to be able to reconcile myself to the idea of a pregnancy, but Bronwyn had asked me two simple questions. "Do you not want more children? Or are you afraid to have more children?"

She wasn't pressuring me, just asking me to be self-aware.

I wanted more kids if we could have them. What I didn't want was to risk my wife. So I went with her to the ob-gyn and asked a list of questions as long as my arm. And in the end, I left that office excited... but still a little terrified. I won't stop feeling that way until we're on the other side of it.

Gabriel lifts a hand to us across the bar, then makes his way over, first hugging Bronwyn, then clapping me on the back.

Phee sees Henry standing near the jukebox and immediately squirms for me to put her down. She runs straight to him and tugs on his pant leg until he picks her up.

He pretends to stagger under her weight, and she giggles and pats his shoulder.

She'll be starting preschool in the next six months. She doesn't imitate Bronwyn all the time anymore, though it's easy to see she's absorbed some of her mannerisms.

I miss my sister. I always will. I think about her every day. How crazy she'd be for Phee. And how, even though Phee never knew Maddie, she's still so much like her mother. Her "terrible twos" weren't really terrible at all. But she is fiercely independent, just like Maddie. She's also inherited some of her theatrical talent.

I hope Maddie knows that Phee will never have a moment in her life where she doesn't have family who love her.

Phee's outfit today is purple rain boots, a green princess dress, and sparkly leopard print pants. I fought her on her outfit choice at first, afraid someone would look at her and think I wasn't a good parent for letting her go out mismatched like that.

But Bronwyn had smiled and said, "Let her be herself. If people don't like it, fudge 'em."

Phee had yelled, "Yeah, Daddy. Fudge 'em."

Right now, Phee appears to be telling Henry something incredibly important. And he keeps nodding seriously in response.

Henry's raptor gaze lands first on me, then goes straight to his sister's midsection.

No wonder he knows everything. He's got informants everywhere. My own kid is a mole.

Henry reaches into his jacket pocket and pulls out a pair of preschooler-sized black-framed sunglasses. Phee puts them on, and he sets her to stand on a barstool beside him, keeping an arm around her waist to prevent her from falling.

She stands beside him, hair in two curly puffballs on the sides of her head, and folds her hands in front of herself, stance wide as she surveys the crowd with a stoic expression on her sweet round face. She bops her head a little to the music playing in the background.

I turn to point out how cute she looks to Bronwyn. And to warn her that her brother knows we're trying to get pregnant.

But the crowd of friends and family has pulled Bronwyn away from me. I step farther into the room, scanning for the gleam of her blonde head, but I don't see her anywhere.

The DJ is playing a slow song, and I turn to survey the tiny dance floor. Her parents are slow dancing with each other.

And there's Bronwyn.

Her cousin Deirdre and Tommy, Deirdre's husband, both have their arms around her, swaying and laughing.

She's so gorgeous. So full of life and energy. So *interesting*. I could watch her for hours. And let's be honest. I have.

The song changes, and the beat picks up.

Her attention lands on me, and she grins when she realizes I was looking for her. She pulls away from her cousins, giving them a nod in my direction. Then she stops dancing.

The crowd parts, laughing at whatever they see on my face as I stalk straight toward her. I catch her around the waist and spin her in my arms.

She reaches up to cup my face and smiles. Not the big one she always gives the world but the quiet one that's just for me. "Heyyy, Dean."

I rub my thumb over her dimple. "Hey, Bronwyn."

I kiss her right there on the dance floor, in front of God and everyone. And then we move.

I'm a terrible dancer. I lumber around like a bear, and that's the truth. But Bronwyn's face is so full of joy and love that it almost hurts to look at her.

Phee runs out to join us with a happy squeal, so I pick her up and tuck her in tight.

My girls hold on, and I hold on right back. And we dance.

What's Next?

Say You Will

Sneak Peek

Say You Will

Henry has already unzipped my bag and reached inside for Oliver's blue dog bed. I cringe as stretchy lace in a variety of colors clings to the fleece.

I'd had everything neatly organized. But after arriving on Park Avenue, I'd haphazardly shoved the car bed back into my bag rather than stand on a New York City street with open luggage.

Now that fleece and lace have created a staticky combination.

Henry's face is utterly blank as he takes in the sight of Oliver's lingerie-covered bed.

Heat starts somewhere around my belly button and shoots all the way up and out the top of my head.

I reach for it, but before I manage to make contact, Henry attempts to pull a scrap of lace off the fleece. A zap of visible electricity sparks as he lifts it between two fingers and his thumb.

I see the exact second Henry realizes what he's holding in his hand. His face goes so red that between his white shirt and blue eyes, he looks positively patriotic.

He blinks. "Panties."

I hiss, "Don't say 'panties.' I don't like that word."

His eyebrows lift. "What word do you prefer?"

I snatch the other two off the dog bed. "Just call them underwear," I mutter under my breath.

Face still red, his fist clenched around the fabric in his hand, he says. "These are not underwear. If you want to see underwear, I'll show you underwear. They're made out of cotton. And they are white. Sometimes they are black or navy. They are not... not...."

He waves the scrap of red lace in the damn street, and I shoot a concerned glance around to be sure no one has a camera out.

"These are panties, Franki," he whispers.

"Call them what you want, then. But stop waving them around. Put them away and let's go."

He nods brusquely. "Put them away," he repeats. Then he *shoves my underwear in his pocket*.

"Henry?"

He runs a hand through his mop of hair. "What?"

I planned to tell him to take my *panties* out of his pocket and put them in the suitcase where they belong. But he's so embarrassed, and so am I.

And if I tell him what he did, it'll just prolong it. And, oh my God, he's cute.

And he's my Henry. Even after all this time, this flustered man is *my Henry*.

So I don't tell him he put my underwear in his pocket. He'll figure it out sooner or later.

Instead, I say, "Let me strap Oliver's car bed in, and we can get on our way."

Afterword

Thank you for reading *I Always Did*. I hope you loved Bronwyn, Dean, & little Phee. Franki and Henry's story is coming next, and I can't tell you how excited I am to share them with you. There's so much sweetness beneath the surface with these two.

Sign up for my newsletter hereto receive sneak peeks of upcoming releases, access to freebies when they're available, and even occasional bonus content and deleted scenes.

Can't get enough Trust & Tequila? Visit my website at www.evangelinewilliams.com and apply to join my Street Team. Street team members are the first to see everything from sneak peeks at future books as they're being written, to ARC copies of every new release, freebies & fun swag.

www.evangelinewilliams.com

Acknowledgements

It really does take an entire team to bring a novel to life, and I am eternally grateful for everyone who had a hand in the creation of *I Always Did*. I absolutely could not have done it without each and every one of you:

To all of you in our little Romance, Spice, and Laughs Writer's Group! Thank you! You (arguably) kept me sane throughout the process. Ivy Fairbanks, Robbie Shaw, Karen, PHW Love, Caroline Edmonston, and more! Alpha readers, Trish Alexander, Annalisa S, and Juliet Brandywine. Thank you for your endless patience and feedback as I bounced ideas off of you. Annalisa S., thank you for both your emotional support and for sharing your professional expertise and experience in wealth management. Any mistakes are mine. My editors at Hot Tree, Kristin Scearce, Kim Deister, and Keeley Catarineau. Thank you to the designers at GetCovers for a beautiful cover. Kurt, Megan, and Ben, thank you for tolerating both my distraction and my incessant need to bounce ideas off of you and "read just one more scene" to you. My beta readers: William C., Megan S., Kurt S., Juliet Brandywine, Kimberly Rose, PHW Love, CeeCee (Caroline) Edmonston, Kimberly Rose, and Annie S. Thank you. This book is better because of your contributions and support.

Printed in Great Britain
by Amazon